EVEN THE FAITHFUL

Even the Faithful
A Novel

Sara Thomas

Fox and the Dove Press

Published in the United States by Fox and the Dove Press.

For more information, please write to:

Fox and the Dove Press
2800 East Third Street 1026
Dayton, Ohio 45403
hello@foxandthedovepress.com
www.foxandthedovepress.com

eBook ISBN: 979-8-9937723-1-8
Paperback ISBN: 979-8-9937723-0-1

Even the Faithful Book Team
Proofreader: Roxana Coumans
Cover Design: Sarah Kil
Author Photography: Sheldon James

First printing 2026
Printed in the United States of America

For David and Margaret

My good young friend, love is natural; but you must love within bounds.

-Johann Wolfgang von Goethe, The Sorrows of Young Werther

CHAPTER ONE

Cincinnati, 1941

Outside, the world was beautiful and blooming, but the baptistery was dark and cloudy with incense. A stifling heat, the only sign of July in that marble tomb of an antechamber, rose in shimmering waves and cut off the breath of all assembled.

The shifting of bodies and a steady child's wail drowned out the voice of the lecturer and the ceaseless drip of water. Henry wondered if he dared run his finger along the inside of his collar, but everyone else was standing stock still and flush-faced, so he decided against it. His hair was damp and fluffing into tendrils. Dripping salt from his brow stung and burned his eyes, but even John Markwell wasn't moving, and if he wasn't fidgeting, neither would Henry.

The baby changed pitches, and the resulting shriek was like diamonds on glass, only endless. Dulled by heat and irritation, Henry didn't even bother to wonder who the child was or why they were allowed to practice upon him. He imagined that if he could master the writings of Ambrose and Aquinas, he could probably pour water on a baby's head with no trouble, but the choice to be present today wasn't his to make.

"Mr. Werther, why don't you go first?"

Henry started and noted the smirk on their professor's face.

"Yes, Father." Jostling the sweaty bodies before him, he trudged to the front of the room and regarded the baby in their

1

teacher's stiff, outstretched arms. The older man's expression was just as awkward as everyone else's, and he thrust the baby at Henry like a sack of flour.

His hands involuntarily slackened, and he nearly dropped the child out of shock. Warm, elastic flesh and the ridges of ribs beneath the cotton baby gown met his hands, and the child quieted. Henry realized that his grip was now cold and clammy. With tender caution and care to avoid the eyes of his classmates, he brought him to his breast.

He knew he was supposed to be meditating on the innocence of childhood, saving young souls from limbo, and reminding himself that he did not intend to baptize in truth, but the alien creature made him think instead of hearing his brothers read *The War of the Worlds* aloud to the rest of them. "The coming of the Martians," he thought and almost laughed aloud. "I baptize thee, Martian Child…"

"We're waiting, Mr. Werther." The professor glowered at him and rubbed a handkerchief across his brow for emphasis.

Henry found the Latin tucked behind his tongue and duly performed the false ceremony.

"Very good. Mr. Markwell?" The professor nodded to his next victim, who approached and took the baby out of Henry's icy hands. After the sixteen-tentacled octopus was secure in John Markwell's incapable grasp, the professor nodded to Henry, then toward the door, and Henry fled.

Down the concrete path, through the main house, and out the back door to the rolling hillside beyond, Henry did not stop until his legs were flailing beneath him. He skidded to a halt near the top of the rise and looked out over the terraced lawn below at brothers tending the gardens, vegetables ripening, roses climbing, wisteria vines spilling over a pergola, and beyond them, the river, peppered with steamboats and barges.

The sun dazzled his eyes, warmed his hands, and burned his awkwardness away. He was the youngest of seven; what did he know about all that? His brothers would have manfully scooped the shrieking thing up and doused him, but they were fifty miles away, and he was here.

Dayton, 1942

The rich violet and indigo swirled together and bloomed in widening patterns intricate enough to make him think of tiled patterns or tapestries, a cope or an altar cloth. A vine here, a mosaic there, deep and sharp against an ivory background.

"The scarring should fade within a few weeks." A doctor—another one—tapped a more sensitive blossom, and Albert shrank from his touch. "But you should notice improvement right away." He dropped Albert's arm without ceremony and scrawled the orders, which he gave to one of the nurses. "Mr. Walheim is to be discharged today. Mrs. Koppelman needs another insulin shock. We'll do it this afternoon."

The nurse nodded, tucked Albert's papers under her arm, and went out.

"If you don't notice a change," the doctor said before Albert could follow her. "There are other therapies we can offer. We've had some early success with lobotomy—"

"No." Albert's throat convulsed before he realized he'd said the word. He coughed. "Er, no. I don't feel the urges at all now. I think you've really cured me, doc."

"Excellent." The doctor clapped him on the shoulder, and Albert felt it all the way to his weary bones. "But if anything should change."

Albert nodded and scurried out the door. Outside, the lawn, usually barren, was full of patients, nurses, orderlies, and families. A blast of early springtime air and the scent of magnolias assaulted his nose, and a stiff breeze made the tail of his jacket fly up. Rather than wading through the throngs, he hurried past the guards and took the sidewalk down Wilmington Avenue to the trolley stop. When the trolley rumbled up, he ignored it, although it was the one that passed

3

by St. Paul, and his parents knew he was coming back today. Instead, he crossed the street and continued up Wayne Avenue. Weaving and varying his steps and route, Albert was at last assured of not being followed and plunged straight toward Illinois Avenue and a ramshackle blue house.

"You're out."

The door swung open, and Albert darted inside.

"I'm out. Thank God." He met James's gaze, dropped to his knees, and began to weep.

"Albert." James joined him on the scuffed floor. "What the hell did they do to you in there?"

Albert shook his head, but pulled back the sleeves of his jacket and shirt.

"Goddammit." James glowered into the middle distance, picked himself up from the floor, and drove his fist into the wall.

"Don't snap your cap, James. I'm out now, remember?" Albert dragged a fist across his eyes and started to feel a little foolish for breaking down boohooing. "And I'm never going back. If I do, the doc as good as said I'll get the knife."

"Then what's the plan?"

"Marry a dame. That'll fool them." Plenty of guys like him had done it before, and plenty more would keep on doing so. Albert didn't like the idea, but he would like getting his brain hacked up even less. "There's plenty of girls around here who wouldn't even know the difference. And you know they're all gunning to get hitched. Even if I'm not some big war hero."

"Sure." James grimaced. "The old lady introduces at least six of them to me every Sunday. What're you going to do? Play Romeo or give it to them straight?"

Albert shrugged. "Don't know. Depends on the girl."

CHAPTER TWO

Dayton, 1946

It was Friday, and Lotte was sad. Of course, one was supposed to be sad on Fridays, especially in late March, but her eyes were heavy and her tiredness something more than the abstract sorrow everyone else proclaimed. And they proclaimed it readily enough. Barbara Morris was announcing the Mysteries—as hostess, she always got to announce the Mysteries—with a special kind of smug anguish. She also tacked on every concluding prayer she could think of, plus a few she was making up on the spot.

Beside her, Albert stifled a yawn, and the beads drooped in his hand. Lotte caught them, slick with sweat and hamburger grease, before they could slide to the floor.

"When is she going to stop?" Albert asked in a mutter, on the pretext of thanking her for the slimy rosary. "It's late."

Lotte shuddered and wiped her hand on the sofa. Her own beads chattered across her lap, and the ridges of the crystal-cut glass dug into her tightening fingers. Sadness, irritation, disgust, if she could name an unpleasant emotion, it was swirling around inside her somewhere.

Albert really did fall asleep then and only started awake when the Morris children, supposed to be in bed, but giddy at the sound of guests, started rattling the floor above them. Dick went upstairs with a paddle, and Barbara deemed that reason enough to stop with the prayers.

"Please stay as long as you like," Barbara said. "The girls and I made some Jell-O."

The last foodstuff Lotte wanted was lime Jell-O crafted by Barbara Morris and the three blonde Morris girls.

"Looks like you and the young ladies worked awfully hard on this," Albert said. "But I'm feeling a little under the weather tonight, and we'd better be going."

Lotte could see the others wondering and smirking, but was grateful for the excuse. To be with them to pray wasn't much different from daily Mass, but socializing was too dreadful. Back when Lotte had first arrived in Walnut Hills, Barbara had spent weeks calling her 'Lot' until Albert finally corrected her: Lottie, not Lot. Barbara still managed to make *Lottie* sound like an affectation. No one corrected Barbara Morris.

"Sorry to see you go, Lotte. Albert," Barbara said, and Lotte could tell she smelled the hamburger on Albert's breath. She raised an eyebrow. "We'll see you two tomorrow morning, then?"

"Hope I'm better by then, sure." Albert gave her a jaunty grin while Lotte accepted their jackets from Dick. God and everyone knew they'd only be seeing Lotte.

Outside, they walked down Heaton in silence, the air still cool, the world quiet and peaceful. Neat lawns shone like brushed nickel in the moonlight, and streetlamps cast eerie shadows across sturdy, comfortable houses. Albert sometimes wanted a bigger house in Dayton View, but Lotte liked Walnut Hills, and for once, he listened.

When they rounded the corner and started up Edgar, Albert said,

"Why do you keep insisting on that boring old crowd?"

"They're our neighbors," Lotte said. "You ask me that every Friday. Why shouldn't you come with me? You're my husband. You ought to care more about appearances than I do, but you hardly even come to Sunday Mass with me."

"I do plenty." Albert sighed. "Look, just forget it, okay?"

"Fine. Are you going over to James?" The name sat heavily on her tongue, but she forced herself to sound light. "It's been a while since you've been to see him. Trouble in paradise?"

"The brass."

Lotte nodded. "Well, be careful."

"Yeah, thanks. I'll see you tomorrow." With a slight wave, he cut down a side street and hurried toward Illinois. As eager as he seemed, his shoulders were tight with anxiety, and he stole through the shadows as though someone could read his thoughts.

Lotte quickened her own pace for the last few yards home. Not that she worried for her safety, but it would be nice if Albert were at least gentleman enough to see her through the front door before tearing off to meet his... To meet James. James was nice enough— he'd been to the house for supper more than a few times—but her needling jealousy toward him always troubled her. She didn't pine for Albert, not really, but James and his presence bothered her all the same.

In the house, she clicked the radio, found "Casta Diva," and reminded herself to listen to *Norma* on Sunday afternoon if Albert was out. The singer's voice was velvety and rich as cream, and something about the chorus made the hairs on the back of Lotte's neck rise as if to greet each note. Undulating, lulling, the sound soothed her enough to splash water and Pond's on her face before slipping into a nightie and kneeling before her narrow single bed.

Without much thought, Lotte knelt there until Callas warbled her last notes. It wasn't so much the words she could think of at times like these, but the silent thanks and the reminder that something in the world was truly divine. When the radio announcer's baritone burst into her thoughts, she added petitions for Albert, Father Kestner, their neighbors, and even her parents. Lotte crossed herself, turned off the radio, and flopped onto the bed.

When she woke in the morning, Albert's bedroom door was still open and his bed unrumpled. Of course. Friday nights were mostly spent with James, and Saturday mornings, they went to the pictures. The pictures, she could handle. The less said about what happened on Friday nights, the better. She warmed a pan of hot cross buns in the oven, set one aside for later, and wrapped up the rest for poor,

7

overworked Father Kestner. At least, that's what Barbara Morris had called him when she'd organized the rotation.

With her hat and a tea towel full of food, Lotte set off and hastened up the street toward the spire that drew, like a lightning rod, all its energy from the rolling hills and carefully kept houses of the neighborhood. Some of her bitterness ebbed away in the nip of early spring air. She was as much drawn to St. Jerome's as anybody else; the place was familiar, the smell of incense comforting.

The trolley rumbled past, and when she looked again, there were the three church doors, flung wide and filled with streams of people. She dashed across the street and clattered up the stairs.

"Good morning, Mrs. Walheim," said one of the hundreds of Morris children. "Where's Mr. Walheim?"

Did Barbara slip the child a penny? No, she must be imagining things. Not even Barbara cared so much that she'd bribe a child to ask a question like that.

"Is that your baby?" The littlest girl pointed at the tea towel, and when Lotte turned to look at her, she was definitely cradling a new penny.

"Good morning," Lotte said. "Frances, would you like to take this to Father for me?" Penny or not, she could ignore the children when they asked where her husband was and ignore their parents when they made pointed offers to pray to St. Anne and St. Rita on her behalf. Besides, Father Kestner made her unaccountably ill at ease, as though he had enough time and interest to care about her boring, venial sins. She counted among those sins the way she avoided his steely gaze and jowly face at all costs.

"Okay," the little girl said and grabbed for the towel.

"Don't use slang; it's vulgar," Lotte said. "Now run along with these."

A prickle of awareness slithered down Lotte's spine, and she craned her neck toward the far left of the vestibule. The man standing in the doorway was young—he might have been a year or two above her thirty years—with a flop of ringlets and dark eyes that had the bobby soxers swooning. He held her gaze, smiled, and she felt herself blush. When she noticed his collar and cassock, she blushed even further.

The man shook off his coterie of Julienne High girls, but the bells tolled and called them into the sanctuary. Was Father Kestner to no longer be poor and overworked? Lotte willed her cheeks to cool and nearly rolled her eyes at her own stupidity.

"Dreamboat, ain't he?" Dorothy Dailey winked at her as they found their seats. "Waste of a perfectly good one, if you ask me. Bet he's left broken hearts to Cincinnati and back."

Lotte nodded once, unwilling to gossip where the tabernacle was present. Dot was kind, if a little coarse. And she was probably right about the broken hearts. What business did that man have smiling at her anyway? He was probably smug and cocky and… And she shook her head. For heaven's sake, he'd only smiled. She'd been around Father Kestner so long, she'd forgotten priests could smile. Besides, she might have turned thirty, but she certainly didn't feel old enough for the priests to be her own age.

He sat in the front row and kept his head bowed.

"He's Father's new curate," Dot whispered during the Sanctus.

Lotte stared straight ahead at the altar and Father Kestner's violet-clad back. The schola was chanting, but all she could hear was Maria Callas singing "Casta Diva" on the radio. She wasn't as respectable as she'd thought. Evidently, she couldn't be in a room, in a church, with an attractive man without imagining romantic music and neglecting her prayers. In the silence that followed the raising of the Host, she offered her contrition. Coming back from the rail, she edged away from Dot.

CHAPTER THREE

Here's my handsome boy." Henry's mother ruffled his hair and smoothed the front of his black cassock. "Father Henry Werther. I knew I saved the best for last."

"Mom." He glanced at Clara, but she didn't seem offended in the slightest.

"Oh, don't worry your pretty head." Clara grinned at him. "We all know you're Mom's favorite."

Henry rolled his eyes and shoved her, although she was two years older and a married mother of three.

"Now, now, Father," she said, and her tone was dust dry. "Honor thy sister."

"That's not a real commandment."

"It should be."

"Children, please," Mom said. "Henry Michael, didn't they teach you any better at that seminary? It's about time they sent you back to us. Come on, darling, everyone's in the kitchen. Are you hungry?"

"Yes, darling." Clara smirked. "You are hungry, aren't you?"

"Maybe I am," he said.

"Of course you are." Mom turned away to fuss with a Mason jar full of beet juice. "We made red eggs, and Mary's brought icebox pie. Her Annie is quite the little cook. Clara, fix Henry a plate."

Clara snorted, but she took a plate from the cabinet.

"There's the runt of the litter." John thumped him on the back and handed him a can of Schlitz.

10

Henry took the beer from John and the plate from Clara and gave his brother an awkward smile. John was ten years older, and his oldest kid had been born while Henry was still in grade school.

"Happy birthday, Dad." Henry turned to his father, who was draped with kids, ages two to fifteen years.

"Hello there, son," Dad said. "Or is that 'hello there, Father'?"

"Son's fine." Henry gulped his beer. It was still unsettling to hear strangers using that deferential tone. He wasn't about to let his own family get all awed and respectful. "I think 'hello there, Father,' is my line for you."

Shrieks, thudding footsteps, crockery, silverware, everything added to the comforting din. As the last of seven, Henry was born into chaos. He was pretty sure he had twenty nieces and nephews, but since most of them were born while he was in seminary, he'd lost count.

"Uncle Father Henry," said Anna's youngest boy. "Are you allowed to listen to the radio? Because my brothers and me, we all like *The Shadow*, he's real scary."

"My brothers and I," Henry said. "All like *The Shadow*. He's very scary." He thought about that woman on his first morning, correcting the little girl with the tea towel.

"Yeah, so d'you listen to him or what?"

"Sometimes," Henry said. "But I'd rather listen to the opera. I'm old and boring, remember?"

The boy made a face, jumped into Henry's lap, and began to recite the most recent episode word for word.

"And there's gonna be a movie about him, and Kane Richmond's gonna be in it, and my old man says I can go all by myself."

"Tommy, you leave Uncle Henry alone." Anna chased the little boy off, lit a cigarette, and joined her brother in one fluid motion. "Sorry, honey, he's a big talker. So, tell us, how're things at St. Jerome's?"

"It's not all that different than Immaculate." His family lived in Belmont, one neighborhood over from Walnut Hills, and acted as though the people five streets away were a complete mystery. Closing his eyes, he fell into a reverie, although Anna was still watching him and sucking smoke from a Virginia Slim. Saying his first Mass there, the morning sun splintering on the gilt columns, his mentor's inscrutable gaze, the schola chanting, the sad, beautiful woman with the tea towel. "I can do some good there, I think."

Anna tapped her cigarette against their father's ashtray and ruffled Henry's hair. "Well, that's good, sweetie."

"Sweetie yourself. Honey yourself." Henry polished off the last of his beer. "You're thirty-five, not seventy-five."

Anna grabbed the hair she was fluffing and pulled a good chunk until he yelped. Clara laughed, the children laughed, and their mother came in with the birthday cake.

"I do wish you wouldn't let them call you 'Father Henry.'" William Kestner's jowls shook, and the dim light made him more forbidding than usual. "I've always found a respectful distance appropriate."

"I can't shepherd them if they're too busy being in awe of me," Henry said. "Besides, doesn't 'Father Werther' sound like the start of a nursery rhyme to you?"

"Excuse me?" William's short, pudgy form trembled with outrage.

"Nothing, Father, I apologize. I'll think about that." Henry bit down on a corner of his cheek. Let's see, he thought. *Father Werther could… What rhymed with 'Werther'? Father Werther could go no further when eating his curds and whey.* No, that was taken. *Father Werther went to—*

"Henry." William's sharp bark broke into his thoughts. "Have you caught a single word?"

"Yes, Father." Henry furrowed his brow. He'd learned early on that a furrowed brow was the key to a serious, priestly mien.

"Good. So what do you think?"

"Well, I think… I think it's interesting, certainly."

"I think that lying is far more serious a sin than inattention," William said. "You may go." But he clapped Henry on the shoulder as he ambled away.

William's heavy footsteps faded, but Henry soon realized that he was not alone. The shadows of twilight were falling, his favorite time of day to watch the sun filtering through the stained glass. It was suppertime, and the trolley was buzzing past, the men marching home from National Cash Register and the banks downtown.

One bent head, rusty auburn with a sweep of birdcage lace, dotted the empty rows of pews. He saw a chaplet, a pale oval of a face, and knew that he should leave her alone, but it was the woman from his first day. Her eyes were closed, but her expression was as sad as before, the beads listless in her gloved fingers.

Her eyes fluttered open, landed on him, and her cheeks turned pink. He almost smiled—he couldn't help liking it—but she smiled first.

"It does," she said.

"I beg your pardon?" Emboldened, he took the twenty steps toward her, but wasn't forward enough to sit down. "What does?"

"Your name." Her grin was mechanical, as rusty as her hair, but she stood to greet him. "It does sound like the start of a nursery rhyme."

His laugh was so abrupt that they both jumped. Why had he been so pensive?

"Would you mind explaining that to Father Kestner for me, Mrs…?"

"Walheim," she said. Her face shuttered and closed again. "Mrs. Walheim. I'm sorry to bother you, Father. I should go, I—"

"You're no bother," he said. "I was bothering you. Besides, you've made more progress in my namesake rhyme than I have. I was busy trying to rhyme with 'Werther,' but you're quite right. 'Bother' and 'Father' go much better together."

Of course, he'd heard certain rumors about Mrs. Albert Walheim. Putting her face to her name now, the listless beads and the rusty smile made sense. Childless, almost always attended alone, husband handsome and indifferent. One never wanted to listen to gossip, but in Cincinnati, even while in school, he'd found that parishes thrived on rumors more than he'd ever realized.

"I really should go," she said. "I have to get supper together."
"Of course," he said. "I won't keep you. But if you find... If something is troubling you..." So much for his grand visions of shepherding his flock through their trials and suffering. He could barely mention his office hours without stuttering.

She nodded, slammed her prayer book without apparently meaning to, and clicked away, her low heels tapping a telegraph beat into the marble.

Outside the church, Lotte caught herself on the railing. Her legs were trembling, and she wanted to sit down, but she wanted to be seen sitting on the curb even less than she wanted to stand. The trees rushed overhead, flowery branches buffeted by the wind, and the sky was fading from ultramarine to cornflower wash. The breeze caught the veil of Lotte's fascinator; it stirred against her forehead, but she didn't notice. The railing was at once alien to her and a part of her hand. Her neck snapped back, but the doors were closed, and the wide, stone steps empty of people.

On her rubbery legs, she wandered off in a velvety haze until the shrieks of children running home for supper snapped her out of the reverie. Her limbs straightened; her breath returned; she remembered that Albert was probably home by now, with or without James, sipping a Dewar's and soda and dancing to Hoagy Carmichael on the radio.

Lotte scurried down Wyoming and thought about how stupid she was. What an idiot Father Henry must think her. Every woman in the parish fawned over him daily. Even Barbara Morris slicked on extra lipstick and added a touch of Shalimar on Sundays, simply because he was young and he wasn't Father Kestner. She wondered whether he was patronizing her and decided he probably was. Why had she decided to talk? A frosty look, a clipped 'good afternoon, Father' would have been just fine. That's all she had for Father Kestner, so why should this new one get any different?

Inside the house, Albert and James were locked in Albert's room, and the radio was playing "Skylark" loudly enough to fill the house. She changed the station, got *Tristan und Isolde*, kicked off her shoes, and poured a sidecar into a blue glass. Trying not to think, she sipped, eyes closed, and tried to get swept up in Isolde's beautiful death.

Of course, her mind ran away with the spoon, and she thought about her father's big house on Grafton Hill, the way she would find cats and dogs outside, and mice in the attic. She kissed and pet them—even the mice—fed them, named them, and kept them until her father found out. A whole family of animals lived in the attic by the time they were sent away to God only knew where. Lotte certainly didn't want to know.

"Hey, what gives?" Albert and James came tumbling down the stairs in shirtsleeves, and Albert glowered at the radio.

"Would either of you like some supper?" Lotte polished off her drink and rose with a beatific smile. "There's chicken left over."

"Gee, thanks, Mrs. Walheim." Sometimes, James reminded her of an overeager child getting his nickel for mowing their lawn. She suspected he cultivated this to get under her skin, but Albert never noticed.

"You're very welcome, James." She glanced at the bar cart, hesitated, then poured herself another. Surely it wasn't gluttony if she rendered herself senseless tonight. She rarely drank to excess, but never bothered to confess it when she did. God, Lotte figured, understood.

James and Albert were already seated at the table, and she realized she was expected to serve them, like Albert's foreman at the factory had come to visit or the Morrises were there for supper or, well. Like they weren't abnormal.

"You know where everything is," she said to Albert. "There's iced tea made, too."

Albert raised a blond brow, but wasn't dumb enough to argue. His pursed lips softened, and he gave her a slight nod.

"Thanks, doll."

She turned away, but not quickly enough to miss his squeeze to James's hand.

CHAPTER FOUR

C at got your tongue?"

"Hm? Oh, no." Henry winced. "Just most of my right thumb." He displayed a bloody scratch, and Clara's cat scampered away, leaving tufts of beige fur on the black of his clothes.

Clara chased it off with a broom, and its striped tail disappeared around a corner.

"Here, try some iodine."

"No, thanks." Henry shuddered and wrapped the wound in his handkerchief. "And sorry if I've been rude. I'm just tired."

"Tired my ass." Clara didn't bother to apologize. He appreciated that. "Who is she?"

"Clara." That, he did not appreciate. "I'm— That isn't—"

She shrugged. "Just because you don't have a penny doesn't mean you can't visit the candy store."

His indignant yelp broke her into chuckles so loud they drew her oldest into the room.

"Uncle Father Henry," she said. "Come sign my autograph album."

"Leave Uncle Henry alone," Clara said. "And stop calling him that ridiculous name."

"Some people are more respectful than others," Henry said and hit his sister with a cushion. When the child had gone, he added,

"You shouldn't make jokes about the sacred promises, Clara. It isn't right."

"I took a sacred vow to keep you from getting uptight," she said. "But listen, how are they treating you over there?"

"Well enough," he said. "William is stern, but he's a good man. I've learned a great deal from him already, but I think it irritates him that people come to me first. He likes to be remote, and it's true, they should respect him. But I don't think he's, well, he can be intimidating."

"Does he intimidate you?"

"No." Henry paused for a moment. "Not anymore. It's more that I want him to…"

"Respect you?" Clara tilted her head.

"I suppose. I know it sounds silly." William's praise wasn't unlike what Henry felt when he'd told his parents he was entering the seminary or when he'd smacked a ball his father had pitched straight through the backyard and over the alley.

"Nah. He is your boss, right?" She eyed him. "Is that really what has you so quiet?"

"What is this, psychotherapy? Are you going to shock me if I don't spill my guts to you?"

"Maybe," Clara said. "So you'd better tell."

He bit the corner of his mouth hard enough to draw blood. Undoubtedly, Clara was going to hound him until he told her something, but he didn't even know what there was to tell. Perhaps there wasn't anything at all.

"There is a woman," he said.

For all her teasing, Clara looked a little horrified. He smirked.

"No, no, she's a married woman. She comes to Mass every day, never misses it." Not that he was sinful enough to think about the tendrils of hair on the nape of her white neck, but he was grateful his back was to her most of the time. "She knows everyone, but hardly speaks. Her husband's only there on Sundays, if that. She's sad. I wonder if I can help her; that's partly why I got into this game. The community."

"Oh." Clara blinked and tugged on a strand of her long, dark hair. "Have you spoken to her at all? What does Father Kestner say? Has she spoken to either of you?"

"A little." Henry didn't want to admit that he felt drawn to her, that he was called to help her, that there was something off about the husband that he couldn't name. "I think she's shy."

"A lot of women are sad, Henry." Clara took both his hands and gave him a piercing stare. "Our mother and sisters and me, we're different than a lot of people. Plenty of housewives are unhappy."

Henry felt more idiotic than he had in a long time. It was an occupational hazard to know nothing about women, but given his background, he'd been a little prideful about the inside scoop. Why had he even opened his mouth about Mrs. Walheim?

"I should probably get home," he said. "Thanks for the chat."

"Anytime," Clara said. "See you next weekend, right?"

The night was balmy, especially for mid-April, so Henry bypassed the trolley and set off toward Watervliet on foot. He was grateful for the little crackerbox house near St. Jerome's. In Cincinnati, he'd shared the rectory with four others, and the thought of rooming with William was just about too much for him. William had his own house, and Henry gave thanks daily for the rare luxury.

Content to take his time, he strolled by Angie's Tavern and the movie house and savored the smell of early lilacs and dewy earth. Tomorrow, the Triduum began, and he'd have no time to think for four whole days. He wondered whether he'd see Mr. Walheim and wondered why he cared. Of course, he should care. Mr. Walheim was a parishioner; he should be encouraging him, too. Henry shook his head in irritation. Perhaps William was right to keep out of people's troubles until they came to him. The Walheims likely didn't want him meddling, but he pondered whether it wasn't his job to meddle. They were both his parishioners, after all.

Henry took a deep breath and sighed. *The Shadow* crackled from someone's window, "Caro mio ben" from the house next door. He stopped to listen to the latter and hoped he wouldn't be seen, dressed in black and standing behind a tall hedge. His eyes slid closed for a moment, but he realized how strange he must seem and hurried away down the street. He'd seen in the registry that the Walheims lived on Edgar Avenue and even thought about taking a detour, but decided he'd done enough creeping through the darkness for one evening.

At home, he recited Compline alone, rather than joining William. As wicked as it was to cut an office short, he was tired, and William liked to linger over every line, especially when he could tell Henry was tired. Whether it was those words or the ones he'd spoken with Clara, he began to relax, and the worry over his flock ebbed away. He always kept silent between now and morning, not that there was anyone to speak to anyhow, and that soothed him. Sometimes he had dreams that were full of color and empty of sound, bright suns on places he'd never been: *Carnevale* in Venice, cages of parrots in Rio, the sullen tropic isles he'd seen in newsreels during the war. The water was aquamarine, the palm fronds green, the sand sugar-white, but the parrots never squawked, the waves didn't rush, no one shouted or laughed or spoke. His mind kept the Great Silence even in slumber.

When he woke in the morning, it was Holy Thursday, and he joined William for Tenebrae. William chanted slowly and methodically, although it wasn't yet five o'clock in the morning and they had a full day ahead of them. Henry clamped his jaws on a yawn and tried to concern himself with the solemnity of the hour and the day rather than with a morning spent surrounded by bare feet. William was the only priest he'd ever met who included the rite of foot washing, and, of course, Henry was sent to him. He couldn't suppress a shudder and earned his first glower of the day.

"Is something the matter, Henry?" William mopped his brow with a crisp white handkerchief.

"No, Father." Henry glanced toward the dark corridor. The smell of coffee was filtering through the entire building, and the sun had yet to pierce the red, blue, and gold of the windows.

"I don't need to tell you what an important day this is for you." William paused. "But I find myself doing exactly that. You're a curate, yes, but someday, God willing, this will be your church."

The fog in Henry's head dissipated in an instant. "I'm sure I'm not worthy, Father."

"Well, no. You're not." William's lips twisted, not unkindly. "But you will be. You're a bright young man, Henry, but you have a young man's irreverence."

Henry bristled. Here he was, bound to holy orders while men like Albert Walheim dozed through Mass, and he was the one accused of irreverence.

"I don't mean to suggest that you're not devout," William said. Henry's irritation seemed to delight him. "Merely that you require training. And that is why I think that you should celebrate the ceremonies this morning."

"I don't think—" The thought of all those sweaty feet—long gangly toes, callused heels, and yellow nails—made his skin crawl. Of course, he knew what a sacred thing it symbolized, but the feet of twelve men made twenty-four feet. He was happy, honored to say Mass, but afterwards... "Perhaps you could— It might be best if you..."

"It might be best if I did what, Henry?" William pushed aside his glasses and pinched the bridge of his nose. "This is precisely what I mean. You are mindful of the holiness of things, but you think too much of yourself: your tiredness, your needs, your inexplicable disgust of feet. You told me when you arrived that you wanted to serve, so learn to serve."

Henry nodded and sank to the wooden bench beside him. William gave his shoulder a brief pat and walked off toward the sacristy. All thoughts of coffee and breakfast and slimy toes were gone, and in their place, a deep contrition.

While Lotte fasted, Albert busied himself with the only meal he knew how to cook: bacon and eggs.

"You sure you don't want any?" he asked. "There's a little more on the stove."

Lotte rolled her eyes and raised an eyebrow at the clock in the corner. Albert would probably think she was trying to hurry him—and she was—but really, she wasn't sure how much more of the wafting scent of perfectly crisp bacon she could bear.

"You look hungry," Albert said. He nudged a bite of fried egg toward her. "I don't think you'll burn for this."

"How would you know?" Lotte glowered, hunger and irritation making her hands tremble.

"I know a thing or two about sinning," Albert said. "A forkful of eggs isn't the end of the world."

"Then what is the end of the world?"

Albert began to laugh and polished off the bite he'd been using to tempt her. "You didn't have to sit here with me, you know."

With a slight shrug, she said, "We're going to be late. I don't want to have to sit in the back again." Everyone had always sat in more or less the same places, creatures of habit and all that, but since Father Henry's arrival, most people had crept up a row or two. Lotte liked hearing him speak as much as anyone. On his tongue, the Latin had a smooth, ancient fluidity that made her skin prickle, while Father Kestner pronounced everything correctly, but in a flat, nasal monotone.

"All the better to see the new one, eh?" Albert grinned.

"What?"

"What? Even St. Barbara Morris gussies herself up for him. I can't help but look, and you know, he's not too—"

"Please," she said. "Help but not finish what I'm sure is going to be the most disgusting sentence I'll ever hear."

"Fair enough." Albert's grin sank. He stood, cleared away the plate, and took Lotte's hand when he emerged from the kitchen. "Do I do anything that doesn't disgust you?"

"In the last fifteen minutes, you've gorged yourself on bacon right before we're supposed to receive the Blessed Sacrament; you've made... Made...? You shouldn't talk about Father Henry that way."

"Don't snap your cap." Albert gave her a strange look. "I didn't mean anything by it. He's a decent fellow. Even I can stay awake when it's him up there."

"I'm sorry," she said. "I don't mean to give you grief."

Albert pulled at her hand until she was in his arms. His body was lean, tall, smelled of fresh aftershave and Marlboros, and was utterly foreign to her. He hugged her occasionally, mostly in public, and then, as now, her body never stirred. It was as though her entire self, mind and body, knew that he belonged to James.

"I'm sorry, too," he said. "I'll get the coats. Maybe I won't worry about the sacrament today."

He was trying to help, but he still managed to set her teeth on edge. A thousand retorts leapt onto the point of her tongue, but she kept them back and nodded.

The streets were empty when they ventured out, their neighbors already well on their way toward the tolling bells. With a smooth, practiced hand, Albert unlocked the gleaming, black Ford parked along the curb and swung Lotte's door open. He'd bought the car last year after a raise, drove it less than once a week, and Lotte couldn't drive at all.

After Albert maneuvered the car into place, they clattered up the stairs just as the bells ceased to sound. Incense rose up around them and curled around the corners of the sanctuary; neighbors crossed themselves. Only a small space toward the very back was wide enough for both of them, and they crept toward it. Lotte's stomach quivered when she finally looked up and saw the back of Father Henry's head.

She hated the feeling. It was the same one she felt in groups of strangers or when she was called upon to speak publicly. Her cheeks flushed, her hands trembled, her heartbeat sped, all because he'd exchanged eight sentences with her. He hadn't spoken to her since. Granted, she'd made avoiding him part of her daily routine, but there was no reason she should react with terror upon seeing him. For heaven's sake, he wasn't even facing her. Even if he were, he'd never see her, wedged in the back row between Albert and Martin Anderson. His Confiteor snapped her back to the present. He struck his chest so hard, his back jumped, even through the heavy brocade of his vestments, and Lotte wondered what he was feeling guilty about. Even Albert raised both of his eyebrows.

Father Henry sounded a little winded when he continued, and Lotte smirked. Served him right for getting theatrical. The breathless Latin affected her strangely, though. His overzealousness amused her, but the slight pant raised the hair on her arms despite the stuffy room.

She frowned. Surely, she wasn't the only one who noticed it. Out of the corner of her eye, she glanced at Albert, but he was slumped on the kneeler, bored as ever, no matter what he'd said about Father Henry and his decency.

Sudden tears pricked her eyelids. Why shouldn't she have someone to ask things, even banal things? Tears started all the time, but today, she couldn't keep them back and had to flee like a child. She thought about the powder room, but didn't want Barbara or Dot or someone coming in and seeing her. A dark corridor loomed before her; she turned and flung herself into the first room she saw. Padded leather met her backside, and she dropped her head to the desk to sob. For someone so often sad, she rarely cried. Shudders rippled through her as Albert's embrace, his squeeze to James's hand, and the smell of bacon passed across her thoughts. *I am sad because no one loves me*, she thought, but that didn't tighten her throat the way recalling the heavy, panting voice did.

When she finished, she felt empty and clean, like grass and pavement after heavy rainfall. The schola's chanting wove a ribbon of sound that snaked beneath the door of whatever office she'd stumbled upon, and she knew she should go back. A silver salver reflected her blotchy, red face back to her, however, and she thought the better of it. No one would want this room anytime soon, so she searched for a sink or a pitcher of water and, finding one, scrubbed the worst of the tearstains from her face. She smoothed her hair, straightened her hat, and snuck back down the hallway to Albert, who was snoring just lightly enough not to be detected. The quick fist that squeezed around her heart, she dismissed as leftover sobs.

Albert woke when she knelt beside him and looked over at her. Although she tried to avoid his gaze, he saw the bloody red in her eyes and winced. He patted her thin, white hand, straightened up, and actually paid some attention to the Angus Dei. Father Henry was much less dramatic this time, and even Albert grinned at that.

Afterwards, when the feet were washed and Lotte was fairly weak with hunger, she sped toward the door in advance of Father Henry, who was washing his hands with unnecessary vigor in a nearby font. People were scattered here and there, chattering or dashing away to forage for breakfast, and Albert was off to the side with Martin Anderson. If her husband could do one thing well at Mass, it was socialize, no matter how much he professed to hate the neighbors.

"Excuse me, Mrs. Walheim?"

The voice stopped her cold, halfway through the vestibule.

"Could you hand me one of those towels?"

She gathered her bearings, which was ridiculous given that she was about to hand someone a towel, but gather them she did, turned around, and pulled a linen cloth from an open cabinet.

"Thank you." Father Henry rubbed his hands nearly raw and set the towel aside.

She gave one sharp nod and began to turn away.

"Is something the matter?" she asked instead.

He hung his curly head, and his cheeks reddened slightly. With a sheepish smile, he drew her in closer and whispered, "I can't abide feet."

"Feet?" Lotte felt herself smile. The very idea of Father Henry's trying to wash off the taint of everyone's collective toes was enough to drive the last of the red from her eyes. Surely, he hadn't expected Father Kestner to insist upon the rite. She'd never seen it herself until coming to St. Jerome's.

"I know," he said. "It's a sinful thought. You should have heard the set down Father gave me today."

He was trying to draw her into a conversation, and she hated that it was working. She ought to go. Albert was probably bored with the Andersons. She hadn't taken the fried egg.

"Was that why you…? You seemed…?" The question was too personal. His private confession was none of her business. "Tongues don't bother you?" she asked instead.

"Tongues?" He chuckled. "No, I'm not bothered by those. If I were, I'd likely be teaching philosophy at the university instead of talking to you now. Tongues are every day. Feet are only once a year, if that."

"Touché, Father." She began to chuckle, too. "And now you're done for the year."

"*Deo gratias*," he said. "What were you going to ask?"

"Nothing." There was no way on earth she'd ever ask him what it was that had him knocking the wind out of himself. "It wasn't important, Father, I'm sorry. I think my husband is ready to leave. I should go."

Father Henry glanced over at Albert and the Andersons, who were still deep in conversation. "I'm afraid you're stuck with me for the moment."

"Shouldn't you be out among the parishioners?" Trepidation made her rude, but he didn't seem offended.

"They've seen enough of me today, I think." His tone changed, and he stooped to look into her eyes. "Why are you always in such a hurry to get away from me? We're having a pleasant enough conversation, aren't we? Am I really so terrifying?"

"Well, right now I'm hungry," she said. Did he honestly think she was going to answer him? "Aren't you?"

"The Socratic Method." He chuckled again. "Very sneaky. And yes, as it happens, I am. It's easy to tell who keeps the fast and who doesn't just by how quickly everyone leaves."

"Albert had bacon," Lotte said. "And eggs." Apparently, so had the Andersons.

Father Henry scowled, and Lotte bit her lip. She hadn't meant to rat Albert out.

"Is that so? Did you try to discourage him? I noticed you both at the rail earlier."

"I— Yes, of course, I tried, but—" Her hands began to shake again, and she looked up. "He doesn't listen to me."

"I apologize, Mrs. Walheim." Father Henry sighed. "It's not your fault. No wonder you think I'm terrifying. We're chatting away, and I haul off and scold you."

"Well, perhaps I might have tried harder," she said and ventured, "You sounded quite a bit like Father Kestner just now."

He snickered and crossed himself. "Heaven forbid. I think that's my cue to leave you alone for the moment. Go enjoy your breakfast, Mrs. Walheim. Will I see you tomorrow?"

"Of course." She found herself beaming as she walked toward Albert, who was finally finished with the Andersons. "Are you ready to leave?"

"Past ready." Albert followed her down the stone stairs. "Those Andersons are a gas, though. We should have them for supper one night."

"That would be nice." She blinked, but didn't comment.

"Is Father recovering from his wounds okay?" He started the car and gunned the engine across Wyoming. "Looked like you had a nice chat."

"I suppose." Albert's words barely registered. Lotte mulled over Henry's words instead, both serious and friendly, his eyes intent upon hers. "I told him about your eggs."

"What gives?" Albert nearly drove into a lamppost. "What'd he say?"

"You're going to hell."

"Ha, ha, very funny."

"He already knew. He said he can tell when people aren't running for the door." She paused, hunger needling her. "I wonder if he can tell which other sacraments you don't take seriously."

Albert flung the car against the curb, slammed the brakes, and stormed toward the house without bothering to open her door. Rather than going after him, she sat for a moment before tapping the lock on his door and climbing out. The morning air was just barely chilly, and no breeze tickled at her arms. She looked at the tulips in their beds, the magnolias in bud, and thought of Father Henry's boyish chagrin, his 'I can't abide feet.' Lotte chuckled, even after Albert brushed past her and headed off toward Illinois Avenue.

CHAPTER FIVE

W
hen Good Friday dawned, the sky was slate grey and the
pavement slick with drizzle. The walnut tree on Henry's
postage stamp lawn drooped, branches hunched, and the
grass was matted with rain and dewdrops.

Henry popped his umbrella and sauntered the half block to St.
Jerome's with light feet, his cassock flapping around him in the wind.
He knew he was much more cheerful than he had a right to be during
a rainy Good Friday, but there was no dampening his mood. His eyes
had even fluttered open for Tenebrae, and he'd fallen back into one of
his sunny dreams afterward. He had done well yesterday, he knew he
had, and the feet were gone for another year. And Mrs. Walheim had
laughed, even though the sacristan had seen her crying. He imagined
she was responsible for the blistering on his sheaf of papers and the
crumpled washcloth on his desk.

"Good morning, Henry."

"Good morning, Father." Henry shook out the umbrella and
stepped inside. Small puddles stood on the red and white tiles, and the
sound of rain pinging against the windows filled the space with weird
echoes. "How are you this morning?"

"Well enough." William shrugged, stretched his shoulders, and
led Henry toward his office. "I was pleased with the way things went
yesterday."

"Thank you. So was I."

"I wouldn't be prideful just yet," William said.

"Of course." Henry felt his mood begin to deflate a little. Absurdly, he wondered whether Mrs. Walheim had been impressed and why it mattered.

"You did well." William's voice was gentle. "It's obvious you were contrite about your irreverence. You nearly rendered yourself unconscious."

Henry's good cheer evaporated almost completely. He stared into his reflection in the desk, at the wall hangings, anywhere besides meeting William's eyes. Everyone would be talking about that today. He hadn't been thinking of everyone, and maybe that was his problem. When it was just him and the altar, sometimes it was easy to forget everything else. No one was likely to say anything to him directly, but that didn't help somehow.

"I wouldn't worry over it too much," William said. "When I was just out of seminary, younger than you, of course, I nearly drowned the first child I ever baptized. Most people had forgotten about it by the next morning."

"Not his parents, I would imagine."

"No, not his parents." William offered a wry grin and stood. "I'll leave you to it, then."

Henry rubbed the rippled surface of the paper in front of him. He'd been told that Mrs. Walheim had run off early on, and one of the servers had seen her slip back in just before the Agnus Dei. His office was the first on the corridor—the draftiest, of course—so it made sense that she would have happened upon it and ducked inside. What might have happened if he'd been here when she stumbled in? He thought about putting his arms around her and was unsettled to discover a quick flash of heat. Comforting her, that's all, he would have comforted Mrs. Walheim. He tried to find something to purify his thoughts, but words and objects all blurred into rusty hair. Even the saints' pale faces were the perfect oval shape.

After a few moments, he opened his eyes and managed to shake away the thoughts. Of course, he was going to notice her. He wasn't disinterested in women; he was as imperfect as anyone else. With a shake of his head, he laughed and paged through the book

28

before him. With no time to do anything but work and eventually eat, he was worrying about a fleeting awareness of a woman who would barely speak to him. Surely, he hadn't grown so discontented in celibacy that the idea of hugging Mrs. Walheim, married and unable to exchange pleasantries without bolting for the door, was what passed as sinful fantasy in his mind.

It wasn't even eight in the morning when Albert came back, and in Lotte's mind, it wasn't nearly late enough. After a sleepless night of worrying about her waspish tongue and her bizarre laughter in the garden, the last person she wanted to face was Albert. Even Father Henry would have been preferable.

"How was your evening?" She stood to greet him while "Rusalka" warbled from the radio. "How's James?"

Albert's clothes were rumpled, his hat askew. His chin was covered with blond stubble, although Lotte knew he kept razors and things at James's place.

"I wasn't with James."

"Then where were you?"

"One of the rooms above the Wayne Tavern." Albert rubbed his eyes with grubby-looking fists. "James didn't know I was coming. He had company."

The Wayne Tavern was one of those places where men like James and Albert could go for drinks and for other things Lotte couldn't even name.

"What company? Another man?"

Albert closed his eyes, sank into a chair, and began to snicker. The sound wasn't mirthful at all. "No, Lotte, not another man. His parents."

"Oh. So, what did you say to them?"

"I said, 'Good evening, Mr. and Mrs. Mills, would you mind terribly if I screwed your son for a few hours?'" Lotte knew he was trying to bait her, but couldn't help starting. He regarded her with relish. "What do you think I said? I got the hell out of there. His parents are the ones who told mine it might be wise to send me to Dayton State. They're still plenty keen on James heading to the nuthouse, too." Albert's sigh was almost a growl. "Will you turn that nonsense off?" He slapped at the radio, and Dvorak faded into silence. "James is smart. He passed it off real quick."

"Really quickly," Lotte said just to bait him in return.

"He said I was coming around to get a dish he'd borrowed from you, that you cooked for him all the time, that he wanted to find a girl just like you. That kind of stuff."

"A girl just like me." Lotte shuddered at the thought of some other woman sharing her fate. But maybe if James did marry, she and his wife could be friends. "Do you think he might?"

"Nah, not James. It'd be safer, but he says he just can't. He won't have a wife dragging him to church and nagging him for things he couldn't change."

"Please don't be angry," Lotte said. "I'm sorry about yesterday."

"Do you know why I don't want to go with you?" Albert asked. "Why I don't bother taking things seriously?"

"Because... No, I don't know."

"I'm an atheist, Lotte." He glanced over at her and shook his head. "What the hell did you think? I've been in the can. I've been in the loony bin. I married a dame. There's nothing that can turn me away from James and all of that." For once in his slangy, lethargic life, Albert sounded eager and intelligent. "It's nothing that can be fixed, doll. So, what am I supposed to think? James and I were made this way, but we're still going to hell? And this isn't some deep thought. Half the guys down at the Wayne will ask you the same thing. And the other half are ready to off themselves or take a knife through the nose and forget all about it."

"Perhaps you're not looking for help in the right place." Lotte's throat convulsed around a lump, and she tried not to cry for the second time in as many days. "Everyone has the inclination to sin. You could perform a penance, and—"

"Who am I going to tell this to? Father Kestner? That Father Henry?" Albert snorted. "I hardly think that's going to help when every doctor at Dayton State tried to shock it out of me."

Lotte blanched and grabbed both her forearms, which were tingling from the very thought. Her stomach felt queasy, and she wasn't even sure if she was right, if Albert could be contrite, be absolved, and somehow abandon James. And that's what she should want, but it wasn't.

"Do you really want me to be like the other husbands?"

"Well, I don't want you to be an atheist," Lotte said. "But I don't love you like a wife should, no."

"Fair enough." Albert shrugged out of his coat. "I do feel bad sometimes, you know."

"I agreed to this."

"Still. Why shouldn't you be able to talk about all that catechism nonsense with someone who gives a damn?" He squeezed her arm and turned toward the stairs. "I'll be in the shower. If James comes by, send him upstairs, would you?"

When he was gone, Lotte didn't move to turn the radio back on or even to breathe. She'd agreed to all of this. She had. She'd stood before everyone, her parents, their society friends, Albert, and his family, and before Father Goetz himself and given her consent. And why?

The wind ruffled over the back gardens and made the tree branches tickle the brick walls around them. Lemonade trickled through the lace fingers of Lotte's gloves and stained the tips. She knew she'd be washing them herself that night, but for now, she flicked away the droplets. Turned earth and lilacs mingled their scents, and she thought how joyful the Easter season might be if she weren't sitting here right now.

Her father puffed away on his pipe. Her mother ordered the housekeeper to bring another tray of petit fours. The duet from *Lakmé* trilled from the Victrola, which was comfort enough, Lotte supposed. She knew she should be speaking to the slight, blond man beside her, but she always hated speaking to strangers. Perhaps he wasn't yet another of her mother's friends' sons, who were forever suave and sophisticated and expected the same from her, but he was a stranger all the same. He looked like he might own one evening coat at most instead of five. It was a wonder her parents had let him past the threshold.

"Excuse me for a moment, Mr. and Mrs. Klopstock." The man, Mr. Walheim, rose and darted for the French glass doors.

"Could you be any surlier toward our guest?" Lotte's mother asked as soon as—Lotte hoped—Mr. Walheim was out of earshot. "We certainly don't have young men here every day, do we?"

"We don't." At least, not for a few years. Lotte couldn't even blame the war. Men were scarcer now, but her woes had begun well before Pearl Harbor. Slowly but surely, Chas and Bobby and Dougie and Frankie had all found better wifely prospects elsewhere. Lotte set down her cut-crystal glass and stared at the brick walls, 'prison yard walls,' she always called them. There was a gate at the bottom of the hill, but it was padlocked. All the houses and yards along Belmonte Park had stone or brick walls around sweeping gardens, but these bricks seemed the coldest and this chain the thickest.

"Precisely," her mother said. "We don't. You'd do well to encourage this one. Your father says he's one of the brightest young men at the factory. A plant manager in the making. Isn't that right, Carl?"

Her father ignored her mother completely, but the set of his shoulders told Lotte he'd better be rid of her sooner rather than later. She was almost twenty-six, and this was probably her last hope. And her father's. Never mind that she looked at Mr. Walheim's tall, rangy form, the blue eyes that girls probably dished over, and felt less than nothing. That aside, it was probably time for her to bite the bullet, and the best hope she had now of pleasing her parents was to disappear entirely.

She wiped her sodden glove on the watered silk of her dress and abandoned the sweating lemonade. Lotte had almost completely composed herself when Mr. Walheim came back and said,

"Miss Klopstock? May I speak with you privately for a minute?"

"Father?"

Despite his resolution to do nothing but eat and work, Henry had made almost no progress with his tearstained sheaf of paperwork. He looked up and nearly dropped his pen from the jolt of it.

"Mrs. Walheim." The bottom of her skirt was damp, and droplets crisscrossed her arms. "Good morning. A lovely day for a walk, isn't it?"

"Father Henry—" She twisted her hands and began to edge backward. "You must be terribly busy today. I'm so sorry to intrude."

It was Good Friday. At least seventeen thousand other things required his undivided attention. 'Terribly busy' didn't even begin to describe his schedule. Mrs. Walheim rose to the balls of her feet, Vergil's fleeing stag.

"I didn't mean to interrupt." She spun on one sodden foot.

Henry closed the gap and actually grabbed her wrist to keep her from bolting down the corridor.

"Mrs. Walheim," he said. "You came to me. Kindly refrain from fleeing in terror."

"But—"

"I'm not busy," he said and closed the carved wooden door. "Is something wrong?"

"No." She frowned and stared off into space, intent on either the middle distance or a leather-bound *Summa Theologica*.

"Just in the neighborhood, then?" In Cincinnati, he had always been with parishioners, talking and advising. He'd thought he was pretty good at it by now. "Mrs. Walheim?"

The wisp of lace on her head fluttered when she jumped. "Yes?"

"What was it you needed?" Again, he abandoned his desk and this time, slouched in the chair beside hers.

"*Madama Butterfly*," she said, glancing at the radio. "I forgot they were playing that today."

"You enjoy the opera?"

Someone tapped at the door, and the sacristan's head appeared from behind the corner. Henry shook his head, and the door clicked shut.

"I want to talk to you," she said. Her eyes were bleak for a moment, anxiety etched over her entire face, and her voice was husky, sandpaper over velvet. Although he had counseled dozens of people through their troubles, something in her tone made him unaccountably alarmed. His skin bristled, and he began to perspire beneath the heavy black fabric.

"Of course," he said. "What's troubling you?"

"I'm worried about someone," she said. "An atheist."

"Oh." Whatever he'd thought she was going to confide, it certainly wasn't that. "I see."

"He's destined for hell, isn't he?" she asked and bit her lip before continuing. "He makes a mockery of the sacraments. He receives them and pretends they mean nothing. He doesn't want people to know he's an atheist; he lies to everyone."

Not that it was his business to know, but Henry guessed it was the bacon-eating Mr. Walheim's soul that was in question. He'd thought them indifferent to one another, but if she was so worried about his soul, maybe he was wrong. A quick jab of irritation zinged the very center of his chest. Before he could contemplate it, the zinging ebbed.

"Those are very serious sins," he said and tried to ignore her wince. "Have you tried to talk to this person?"

"He laughed at me." Her entire bearing drooped. "What did you expect? But that's not the worst part."

Henry passed her the same linen cloth she had presumably used the night before and waited.

"His reasons were really quite good."

"His reasons for being an atheist?" His shoulders relaxed. "Most reasons for atheism are quite good."

"Father." Her head snapped up, and she lost her droop and her awkwardness for a tiny, zinging second.

34

"Well, they are." He smiled at her. "Especially now, in modern times. Atomic weapons, the science of the universe. It's enough to make anyone waver. Humans are prideful. We think we're done with needing all of this." A wave of his hand took in the holy books and statues scattered around his office. He could breathe now. How many of the doubtful had he seen before?

"Yes," she said. "I've heard of the humanists. But this isn't about atomic bombs. It's, well, I can't say the reason, but it's worse than any of that."

"Worse than atomic bombs?" He couldn't hold back a teasing grin, a quirked brow. "That is serious."

"Well." She actually chuckled. "Maybe not worse than that. I think it feels worse to him. But what am I going to do? I told him to come talk to you, but he acted like I'd asked him to boil himself in oil."

"A flattering thought."

"Have you known many atheists?" she asked. "Do any of them ever come back to the Church?"

"Yes," he said, glad to have a ready answer. "I knew one in Cincinnati, the year after I was ordained. He stopped believing after his father died. It's fairly common."

"Really?" She twisted the towel in her hands. "Don't they get any comfort knowing that their family was given eternal life?"

"Not everyone is so strong in the faith," he said, but smiled. "I'm glad you are. But anyhow, he said that his secular views were supposedly based on facts and logic, but he spent more time trying to disprove the faith than following his logic, and that disproving our way of life wasn't so easy after all. Atheism was supposed to set him free, but he was constantly at the ready, full of militant anger. Anyhow, Mrs. Walheim, we're given the ability to doubt right along with our free will. If this friend of yours finds himself truly repentant, even at the hour of death, he could be redeemed." Henry was proud of his long speech and of the relief in her stark gaze. "He might spend more than a little time in purgatory, but who among us won't? And really, who among us knows how anyone will be judged?"

"That's true," she said. "You don't think I'm sinful for saying his reasons were good?"

"Not at all," he said. "I think you're kind and wise to try and help."

She beamed for half a minute, and her cheeks grew as red as the leather on his chairs. Henry beamed, too, and decided that making someone so joyful was worth being late to None.

A half-hour late. He tried to keep from groaning when the clock on his desk chimed the quarter hour.

"I'm sorry to have taken up so much of your time," she said. "Especially today."

"You don't need to be sorry," he said. "I wouldn't really have much of a vocation without people needing counsel, would I?"

"No." Her lips twisted, and her eyes—hazel, he noticed—gleamed. "You're fine with Barbara Morris needing to confess twice a day, then?"

"That I can't discuss," he said, but rolled his eyes to the coffered ceiling. "Will you come to prayers with me?"

"Yes," she said. "Yes, of course."

"Good." Henry rose and swung the door open. "I need someone to keep Father from jumping down my throat."

"Oh." Mrs. Walheim laughed as though she hadn't been expecting to. "So, I'm not the only person he frightens."

"Not by a long shot." When he swept his arm to lead her out the door, his fingertips nudged the base of her spine. His hand jerked back in shock, both from its own presumptuousness and from the warmth that zinged through it.

CHAPTER SIX

Were heard you were very impressive last week, dear." Henry's mother hovered over him with a platter of oatmeal cookies. He took one; she looked hurt; he took another. "Perhaps your father and I should go to St. Jerome's one morning. We'd love to hear you say Mass again, wouldn't we, John?"

"Sure." His father was focused on a can of Schlitz and the Reds game on the radio, but he looked up and nodded.

"Well... That'd be... Sure." To be honest, Henry was a little surprised they hadn't already come, but he didn't entirely mind that they hadn't, either. It had been a good two years since they'd been to hear him say Mass. Cincinnati was a fair trek on a Sunday morning. "Anytime you want. I'll telephone with the schedule." He figured Clara would keep them at bay when the time came. "What's the score, Dad?"

"Three to nothing, Cubs." Dad took one of the uneaten cookies from Henry's plate. "Elizabeth, would you get your son a beer?"

"I can get it." Henry started to stand, but his mother shoved him into his seat.

"Nonsense, darling, you've had a long week. We missed seeing you at Easter, of course." She disappeared and returned with the beer. "We always miss you, but it almost seems worse when you're a few streets away."

"I did try to come," he said. "But I was needed there."

37

"Well, I would expect no less," his mother said and started to smooth the curls on his head.

"Don't baby the boy. He's a priest for Chrissakes." His father's tone was gruff, but Henry saw him squeeze his mother's hand before she swatted him on the head and meandered toward the kitchen.

When his mother was gone, Henry raked his fingers through his hair, leaned back on the sofa, and let the sound of the radio wash over him. He closed his eyes to savor the comfort of being back home, rather than rattling around alone in his little house. True, he was glad of his separate quarters, of being away from William, but he was happiest among people, and the best people he knew were his family. His parents, his brothers and their wives, his sisters and their husbands, Clara's youngest—the godson he ought to spend more time with, the twenty nieces and nephews. A man could do a lot worse.

With all that joy and riot and beautiful chaos, he wondered why Mrs. Walheim hadn't had children. She'd been married a while—nearly four years, William had said—and was a devout enough woman. Maybe the possibly atheist Mr. Walheim was opposed to it. She'd said her atheist made a mockery of the sacraments, and he couldn't think of a bigger mockery of matrimony than that. His heart twisted a bit for her then. He had used to worry, and still worried in his darkest moments, that he hadn't really been called to holy orders, that he was only pleasing his parents, but he was happy in his vocation. The idea of his fate being tied to someone who disdained his beliefs was unimaginable. His celibate state really did seem a gift when he thought about unhappy people like the Walheims.

"Uncle Father Henry." The godson in question placed a sticky palm on each of Henry's cheeks. "Come play with us."

"Leave Uncle Father Henry alone. He's listening to the game." Clara's husband, David, sank down beside Henry. "What's the score?"

"Five to nothing, Cubs," he said. "And 'Uncle Henry' is fine by me."

"Goddammit, the Reds are terrible," David said. "You and I and your old man could go down to Crosley Field and do a better job."

"Damn right." Dad swallowed the last of his beer and crushed the can in one fist. "Bunch of sad sons of bitches ever since the war.

Remember going to the fireworks when you were at seminary, Henry?"

"Yeah," he said. "That was about the only time they let me out. You wouldn't believe how jealous the other fellows were when Dad came down. They were practically paying him to take them along."

The game went to the ninth, and his father snapped the dial on the radio into silence. "No point finishing this out. Come on, boys, I think supper's on. Another night of leftover ham."

Everyone in the parish had thought Henry might need their leftover ham, so he suppressed a groan and trudged to the dining room behind David and Dad. The only thing he'd had to break up the monotony all week was a cabbage roll from Mrs. Walheim. He grinned; his mother noticed and plopped an extra-large slice of ham on his plate.

"Perhaps Henry would like to say the blessing?" she asked.

People were always doing this. Every time he dined in someone's home, in fact. It was humbling and honoring and irritating all at once. People wanted him to offer prayers in their homes, but acted as though he'd have some special insight into the blessing everyone had said since they could talk.

"Of course I would." Henry crossed himself, and his family followed suit. "Bless us, O Lord, in these thy gifts…"

The sidewalk outside Rike's was always crowded shoulder to shoulder, but Saturdays were the worst. Lotte hunched in upon herself and tried without success to avoid brushing and bumping against the dozens of people trying to swim upstream.

"Hurry up, will you?" Albert blazed ahead like a steam barge. "They're closing in an hour."

Lotte didn't care, nor was she certain why she had to help him choose a birthday present for James. It wasn't as though she knew what James liked, aside from her husband.

"I am hurrying," she said, tucked her chin to her chest, and stepped as quickly as she could through the wide entry doors. "It's crowded." Someone stepped sideways and knocked her hat askew. "Albert, could you—?" But he was miles ahead of her, almost halfway to the men's department. Lotte inhaled; the smell of chocolate and newness tickled her memory. Her mother always preferred to come in by special appointment, when the store was closed, and Lotte thought that was the best way. Surely it was worth whatever fortune her mother paid just to be able to see two steps ahead of her. She didn't think Albert had the money for that, though, and she certainly wasn't going to ask.

Plunging into the thick, she waded to the men's department, where Albert was already holding up two neckties for inspection.

"There you are. What'd you think of these?"

"The red one is very nice," she said. She didn't see why it wouldn't suit James. An image of Father Henry in the same wended its way into her thoughts. Without his vestments or his cassock or the white collar, how might he look? Would the grey suit on the headless mannequin flatter him? Or perhaps the navy. Definitely the navy.

"Lotte."

"Yes?"

"I said, you really like it better than the green?"

"Much better," she said. If Albert could be decisive, they'd be gone that much more quickly. A set of night robes caught the corner of her eye, and she turned the bright crimson of James's new tie. Just because Father Henry probably did wear a night robe was no reason to imagine it.

"You all right?" Albert glanced at her and nodded to the clerk, who boxed the tie up.

"Fine. Just overheated." She fanned herself with her pocketbook. "You know I hate crowds."

Albert took the bag from the clerk and offered her his arm. "Gee, I'm sorry, doll. I just want him to like his present, and you know all about the styles. Come on, I'll buy us an ice cream, or say—how about we have some supper in one of these restaurants down here?"

"I'd like that." She straightened her hat with her free hand and let herself be steered toward the exit. Albert hardly ever went to respectable places, and she hardly went out at all. "That's nice of you."

"You put up with all of this," he said.

She'd rather he behaved himself at Mass or on Friday nights with the neighbors than take her out for a steak, but she supposed she'd better take what she got. Maybe Albert would even take her to the opera at Memorial Hall one night, although he'd sleep through it anyhow. When she'd gone to Father Henry last week, he'd been listening to *Madama Butterfly*. He probably wouldn't sleep through an opera. No, he'd be attentive and courteous and everything else. The odd sensation of his sweeping fingertips still made Lotte's spine prickle.

"Are you doing anything special for James's birthday?" she asked when they were seated in a leather banquette in one of the shopfront steakhouses along Main Street.

"No." Albert's eyes darted from side to side, but no one was paying them any attention. "Too many raids on the bars this past month. The cops even raided the Wayne a few days ago."

"Why so many?" Lotte hated for him to look grim; it was too disconcerting.

"Lots of guys give it up for Lent," he said. "The bars and all that. Now they're back."

Not that she wanted Albert to do whatever it was he did, but he'd told her what a terrible place the hospital was, and if it worked as little as he said it did, she hated to think of anyone going there. Albert was in for plenty of sorrow in the next world. She didn't see why he had to be miserable in this one, too.

"I'm sorry you can't go out anymore," she said. "But isn't it easier that way?" She didn't ask what she sometimes wondered, whether Albert ever saw any of the neighbors at those bars and whether any of them knew about Albert.

"I guess," he said. "It's easier, yeah. But it's also worse. Sometimes I want to grab James's hand and march up Main Street, laws and knives and that baloney be damned."

His voice rose, and Lotte stiffened so quickly that beads of water missed her lip and soaked into her skirt.

"You hush. Do whatever you like in private, but you hush."

His butter knife slid into the pat on its own tiny plate. "Sorry."

"It's all right," Lotte said. "Listen, I wanted to ask you about

41

something."

"It'd better not be about me and atheism." He had the decency to keep his voice low. "I'm tired of talking about it."

She twisted the linen napkin in her lap. "But couldn't you just—?"

"Lotte." A deep swig from his wineglass. "No. I'm not going to Father Kestner. I'd cook my own skin before I went to Father Henry. I'm not confessing. I'm not contrite. Just leave it alone. Don't be a nag."

"Sorry." She turned to buttering her own roll. *Even at the hour of death*, Father Henry had said. Lotte hoped it wouldn't come to that.

In the morning, the air was warm, the sky bright and cloudless. Lotte loved the brilliant lapis blue, especially on Sundays, when she could wear her best dress. It was that exact color. She dressed with extra care for Mass now, even though it irritated her to be as shallow as Barbara Morris with her Shalimar. Adjusting the brim of her hat as she walked, she took her time to enjoy the white flowering trees against the sky, the birdsong, the bells, and the dewy smell of spring.

"Good morning, Mrs. Walheim."

"Good morning, Father." Lotte squinted up at him. "I brought you something."

"Not ham, I hope." They ascended the last step together.

"No, chocolate cake." When she pulled the foil-wrapped slice from her purse, her hand shook slightly. "They gave it to us at the restaurant last night, and I like chocolate about as well as you like feet."

"They tell us not to play favorites among the parishioners," Father Henry said and accepted the slice. "But you're making it difficult not to."

Lotte blushed, but couldn't help saying, "I should hope so. I feel badly that you get what everyone doesn't want, though."

"I'm always glad to take your unwanted chocolate," he said. "Never feel badly about that. I'll be right back."

She took that to mean she should wait for him as he scrambled down the corridor with his quarry, so she stood stock still beside the church entrance and willed the others not to see her. Despite her best efforts, her cheeks were still pink, and her heart was beating sixteenth notes no matter how long she held her breath.

"Where's Mr. Walheim today?" Lotte jumped, and he apologized. "He usually comes with you on Sundays, doesn't he?"

"He's not feeling well." He was hungover and had thrown a pillow in her general direction when she'd gone to rouse him. "Funny how that always seems to happen on Sundays. Well, and Saturdays. And weekdays."

Father Henry laughed. "You're welcome to sit with me today."

"With you?" The bell stopped tolling, and they had to go in, but she couldn't move.

"Yes, with me. No one should have to sit alone on a Sunday. Come on, we're late." With a patient look, he added, "Really. I don't bite."

Lotte followed—he was walking away and gave her no choice—but the image of him grazing the tips of her fingers with his teeth rose unbidden. She squelched the zip of awareness along with a less pleasant awareness of the stares of every other woman in the church. They slid onto a wooden bench at the very front and turned toward Father Kestner as he spoke the Introibo.

Afterwards, they were the last to leave. Father Henry led her again, not up the central aisle, but off to the side and down a short hallway to the suite of offices.

"I wanted to talk to you again," he said. "But as usual, you've been avoiding me."

"What do you mean, avoiding you? I brought you a cabbage roll. And cake." She couldn't help but scowl at him. "If that's evasion, I'd like to know how. I've been downright friendly." Or at least as friendly as she knew how to be. Even she knew she wasn't the most ebullient person in town.

"I didn't mean to hurt your feelings," he said. "It's true you haven't fled at the sight of me. I've just been wanting to ask you about your atheist. Have you seen him since we spoke?"

"Yes." Of course, she'd seen him; he lived with her. "I've tried to talk to him dozens of times, but he won't hear it."

"What did he say?"

"He said..." Oh, to hell with it. "He said, 'I'd cook my own skin before I went to Father Henry.'"

Gratifyingly, Father Henry looked taken aback, but he burst out laughing, and after a moment, Lotte joined him. How had she ever had the nerve to repeat that to him?

"I see," he said. "Well, I can't have someone cooking his own skin, so I suppose we should let the matter drop."

"Yes," she said. "Perhaps we should."

"Dare I ask what the gentleman in question would do if faced with William?"

"William? Oh, Father Kestner. No, he just said he wouldn't go to him. You were the one he really dreaded." A fizzing mirth bubbled up through her chest and dissolved in giggles. "Imagine that."

"Imagine it, indeed. I'm the friendly one." Father Henry shook his head in mock outrage. "Or so I thought."

"Perhaps you're not if women flee before you and people would rather cook their skin than confess to you." She smirked. "I do hope you enjoy your cake."

"Oh, I will," he said, but frowned. "Mrs. Walheim, you really are kind."

"Not as kind as you." Her voice sounded breathless even to her own ears. "It was good of you to ask me to join you for Mass. I do hate coming alone."

"It's not a time to be alone." A pause. "Are we friends yet, Mrs. Walheim?"

The question made him sound like a bashful schoolboy, but it sent a tremor through her heart. When was the last time she'd had a friend, a real one? High school? Grade school? Never?

"I'd rather cook my own skin," she said.

"You wound me, Mrs. Walheim." He winked at her, the sinful man. "I'll take that as a yes."

"My name is Lotte." The words tumbled out before she could stop them. "Please call me Lotte. 'Mrs. Walheim' is too…" Formal. Abnormal. Practically untrue. "Too cold."

"Certainly, Lotte." He hesitated and added, "I wouldn't be offended if you called me Henry. If we're to be friends. Hardly anyone calls me that. Even my nieces and nephews call me Uncle Father

Henry."

"Uncle Father Henry," she said. "I don't think I can do that, Father, but you may call me Lotte if you like."

"Understood," he said. "But really, it's fine with me."

"But not with me." She bowed her head and gave him a small smile. "I should go make sure Albert's feeling better. Enjoy the rest of your day, Father."

CHAPTER SEVEN

Tangerine sunlight poured through the transoms and warmed Henry as he stretched his legs beneath his desk and shoveled in the last forkful of cake. He swept chocolate crumbs from the notes for his sermon and rested his cheek on one curled fist. Friends with Mrs. Walheim. Perhaps he truly was called to friendship with her.

It was late in the day, and he thought he might go home or go to Clara's for supper. First, of course, he would celebrate Vespers with William and the handful of others who always turned out on Sundays. Perhaps because he was an evening person or perhaps simply because he liked walking home with the fragrance of incense close against him, Vespers was his favorite office.

In the sacristy, the prayer card taped to the wall was faded, and the ends curled no matter how much Henry bent them back. William refused to change it out because, of course, he didn't need the thing and had been reciting each devotion from memory since he was twenty-eight.

The man in question snuck a peek around the corner and tsked when he saw Henry squinting at the faded text. Henry finished and turned toward him.

"I'm glad you're so eager to celebrate Vespers," William said. "It's gratifying that you've taken my counsel seriously. Shall we?"

Henry nodded and followed him out, although William's

pompous words irked him. The man might have been his mentor, but Henry wasn't a mere sponge, there to leech up every last drop of chilly wisdom William had to impart. Henry had helped a woman, *ad majorem Dei gloriam*, and fostered a friendship when she had none. When had he seen William reach out to any of their people? He took a breath and began the Latin.

Afterward, when the vestments were laid aside once again, Henry found William, already in his office, and said,

"I'm going to my sister's for supper. I'll see you tomorrow."

William nodded, although Henry didn't think he'd heard, and waved a hand toward the door.

"Say," Henry said, knowing he would probably regret it. "Would you like to come?"

"Pardon?"

"Would you like to come with me to my sister's? It's Clara. She wouldn't mind." Repeating the offer only made it seem more ridiculous. Henry was very near to blushing.

"Oh." William set down his pen and shoved his glasses up the bridge of his nose. "That's kind of you, Henry, but Barbara Morris brought me something earlier. I have some things to finish up."

"Tuna casserole? Trust me, Father, you could make a better one yourself." Henry wrinkled his nose. "I convinced her I was absorbed in a certain and very particular yearlong fast, and the casseroles have stopped coming."

"It doesn't do to lie about such matters." William glowered, but it lost steam, and he said, "Perhaps I shall accompany you after all. Could you wait a moment?"

"Yes," Henry said. "I'll telephone her and have her send David with the car."

"I ought to kill you." Clara's apron was splotched with red sauce. Light and noise spilled out from behind her. "You telephone at seven o'clock wanting me to entertain not just you, but two priests. Where are your manners, Henry Michael?"

William looked stricken and ready to retreat.

"She doesn't mean it," Henry said.

"The hell I don't," Clara said and kissed his cheek. "Well, you may as well come in. Sorry about the mess."

"Father William Kestner, my sister, Clara Gerber." Henry held back a chuckle. "I don't believe you two have met."

"I'm pleased to meet you, Father," Clara said. "And Henry's right, I don't mean it. What can I get you?" She tossed a beer in Henry's general direction, but missed, and the oldest boy caught it.

"Finders keepers, Uncle Father Henry." He waggled the can before Henry, who snatched it away.

"Not 'til you're sixteen." Henry popped it open. "Which is how many years away?"

"I'm seven," he said to William. "And a half."

"So, what's sixteen take away seven?" Henry balanced the boy on his knee.

"I don't know; that's borrowing." He eyed the beer. "Can I at least try it?"

"Count it up, remember?" With some reluctance, Henry handed over the can. "One sip. Then count like I showed you."

He took a sip, wrinkled his nose, and proceeded to count to sixteen on his fingers. "Nine, right, Uncle Father Henry? Nine?"

"Very good." Henry ruffled his hair. "Now run along and help your mother."

"Uncle Father Henry?" William's pursed mouth relaxed a fraction, and he accepted a scotch rocks from David.

Henry shrugged. The sight of his mentor in Clara's house reminded him of the one stately rosebush in his mother's wild English garden. Delphinium and larkspur and unchecked lavender grew riotously around a single upright blossom. William did not seem uncomfortable, merely out of place, and Henry supposed a flower that didn't fit was nonetheless a flower.

"Did you have a nice Easter, Father Kestner?" Clara asked over the rattling of plates and silverware. "Will you three keep it quiet? You're setting the table, not carpet-bombing Munich."

"I did." William was hesitant, and it disconcerted Henry. "Of course it was busy. I enjoy the Triduum immensely, but I admit to hiding away for a few days following." Solitude energized William. Sometimes Henry wondered whether his mentor might not join an order when he retired from his duties. It was probably a mistake to have brought him out. William seemed so inextricably bound with his vocation that Henry had never even heard him speak of anything that was not the Church or related to the Church or chiding someone, usually him, for not being more attentive to the Church. Outside the stone walls and the brick house that shared a yard with them, William confused him.

"And then, Captain Midnight comes, and the Baron is there, and he snaps his cap good about that, and hey, Uncle Father Henry, hey." Frank swatted him on the knee, and Henry started. "You weren't listening."

"Your uncle is often inattentive," William said. "I scold him daily for it."

"You give Uncle Father Henry scoldings?" Frank's eyes bugged, and Henry thought he was going to genuflect. "No joke? D'you box his ears and all that?"

"No, no, nothing like that. I can't even send him to bed without dinner."

"Well, no wonder if he doesn't listen," Frank said. "Say, d'you want to sit next to me? The old lady's going to put you next to Uncle Father Henry, but you can sit between me and Helen. She's a girl, but she's all right."

"I suppose I could do that," William said.

Henry saw Clara smile slightly and switch the chairs out. He stood and went to her. "Sorry to spring an extra guest on you."

"Oh, that's all right. I was only giving you grief. I'm glad you asked him here. Seems like he needs a night off." She tugged at his sleeve. "You sure you're not getting too lonely over there?"

"I was lonely in Cincinnati, but not anymore, not when I can hop over here or to anyone's."

Clara nodded and poked her head into the sitting room. "Supper's on."

The night was warm, and William declined David's offer of a ride home. He and Henry ambled toward the trolley stop, at first in silence, until William said,

"You enjoy family life, don't you?"

"Well, sure." Of course, he enjoyed it. Who wouldn't enjoy it? "Sorry if you don't. I just thought—"

"I know what you thought." William paused for an endless second. "It was very good of you."

Henry let out a breath he didn't know he'd been holding.

"We've given up a good deal, you and I," William said. "In order to live more richly. I wonder if you realize this."

It was franks and beans at Clara's. Of course, William was going to argue moral transcendence. "Father, what are you trying to say?"

"Very well. I worry that that life might attract you. Hearth, home, children. A wife. The lure can be very strong for a man like yourself."

"It doesn't lure me," Henry said. 'A man like himself,' indeed. "I was just saying to Clara how nice it is that I can go to any of their houses to get my fill of that. And as for children, I'm an uncle of twenty. It's plenty. So many of us are from large families, and it makes this life easier, doesn't it?"

"I was an only child," William said. "So, I wouldn't know. My father had been a Jesuit brother. He and my mother were married five years before I was born; they'd almost given up hoping. It was nothing, I would imagine, like your sister's house, but I wouldn't say my life has been difficult. I've been more successful at it than my father, it seems."

Four sentences of personal information. Henry decided not to push his luck and simply nodded. However, the image of a musty house full of curios, a scholarly father, quiet, oppressively orderly, made him curious and sad.

Albert would never come out with her. Not to the park, where the great dome of Dayton State hunched golden above the tree line. He had stared, he said, over the treetops every day for the weeks he was imprisoned. No matter the image of her husband trapped in a tower, Lotte kept on returning to the park. It was a close walk for her. Bigger than the backyard with more trees and a better view. No neighbors poking their heads over the fence when she wanted solitude to focus on her untalented watercolors.

She dipped her brush in blue and added a strip of sky with downtown peeking just over the rise. A splash of indigo, the scrape of a steeple, a little yellow wash to the east.

"Painting *en plein air*. Very impressive." Father Henry's footsteps hissed across the manicured grass. "Let me guess. You've asked me here to wash out your brushes and fetch your paints."

"I didn't think you would come."

"So that's the reason." Father Henry dropped to the grass beside her. "You thought you could be friendly and avoid me all in one fell swoop."

"You wanted to be my friend," she said. "I thought this was what friends did."

"Cleaned each other's paintbrushes?" He rose to his knees and craned his neck to look at her ugly painting. She covered it, but not quickly enough. "Don't. I like it."

"I'm not very good." Embarrassment made her savage with the brushes when she packed them away in her tote. She'd been at the bottom of the class when her mother signed her up for lessons at the Art Institute, but she only cared when someone was watching.

"Say." A hand closed around hers before she could toss the cup of water across the grass. "I didn't mean to make you stop. Listen, I'm about the worst artist you'll ever meet. If I promise not to look at the works in progress, will you show me a thing or two?"

Surely the last thing Father Henry wanted to do was learn to watercolor, but he hadn't let go of her hand. A strong current flowed from the pulse of his fingers to hers. It tingled its warmth through her arm until at last, she had to jerk her hand free.

"I suppose," she said. Her tongue felt strangely heavy, although she kept her tone light and cool. "But I'm not cleaning your brushes for you."

She saw him rub his fingers against the base of his thumb, almost as though he had been shocked, too. But he laughed and said,

"First you'd cook your skin, and now you'd make me clean out all your paintbrushes. I'm beginning to wonder if being your friend isn't a little dangerous."

"I don't know," she said. He was a safe distance away, and she could relax. "I don't exactly have any others."

A flash of pity, which she hated, crossed his face, and she worried he might grab her hand again. When he opened the tote and fished through the mishmash of brushes and paints, paper and pencils, she felt half relieved and half hollow.

"What do I do first?"

"Don't you think you ought to decide what to paint?"

"Ah." His lips twisted. "I told you I wasn't any good at this."

"Why not start with something easy? Like that tree or the wall over there." Her heartbeat slowed, and she sketched her hands through the air. Just because she had as little aptitude as Father Henry didn't mean she didn't enjoy it. "First, you make a drawing, a simple drawing. Be light with the pencil, or it'll show through. The lightest colors come first, then the darks. It's easy to make a mistake, and it's not like acrylics, where you can go over it. Most people don't bother with the drawing, but since you're new at painting, you should make one."

"I can't draw." He shook his head and laid aside the pencil. "Perhaps you could start it off?"

He was trying to get her to keep painting, which was high-handed and irritating, but it touched her, too. No one else cared whether she painted or not, although she had all of her bad artwork tacked up Salon style in every room of the house. Was it better to enjoy the feeling of worthiness or not to be tricked?

"Father," she said. "I know you're trying to be kind, but I'm not an idiot or a child. If you do want to learn painting, which I doubt, then I'll show you, but otherwise, you don't need to pretend."

"I'm sorry," he said. "And I was trying to be kind. Of course you're not an idiot; I never thought that."

"Apology accepted." Unease rippled with the wind across the grass. She'd made too much of a fuss, but it was bound to happen. Embarrassment was always around the next corner for a person who loved the opera but couldn't sing, loved art but couldn't paint, and loved the very essence of life but wasn't loved. She sighed and brought out a jar of lemonade.

"I've hurt your feelings, haven't I?" Father Henry accepted a paper cup. "Lotte, I'm—"

"Why do you want to be friends with me?" she asked, which she hadn't expected to do. "Do you truly want a friend? Or are you simply fulfilling some kind of…? Do you have some idea that you need to minister to my troubled soul because…?" She dropped to the ground and sprang up again almost at once. "Because if it's only to make you feel better, I won't. Or if you're just nosy about my life. Heaven knows everyone else is." Her cheeks and even her neck grew hot, and she couldn't keep the tremble from her voice. "I won't be tricked and used, not by you."

Before he spoke, Father Henry glanced around, but the park was empty of people. Climbing to his knees, then to his feet, he grabbed both her hands, and his eyes were on hers. Dark and intense. The iris was barely lighter than the pupil, which flared and contracted in the sunlight. His chest rose and fell, and the wind flapped his hem against her ankles.

"Lotte," he said. Father Henry tilted her chin with his forefinger when she bowed her head. It sent a spasm that closed her throat. "I make no secret of the fact that I want to help you. From the beginning, I've felt…" He paused, and she realized he was as uncomfortable as she. He even started to blush. "This sounds simplistic. Or trite. But I do feel called to help you. Perhaps I've been too earnest because that really does sound stupid out loud. But I won't offer advice unless you seek it. And if I have it. Truly, I do want friendship."

"Mine, though?" She pulled her hands and chin out of his reach. Her throat didn't loosen.

"Yes, yours. Why not yours? We always laugh at the same things when you're not running from me or scolding me." He sank to the picnic blanket, and she followed. "Can I prove my honesty by confiding in you?"

"I can keep a secret." The golden dome above the tree line caught the corner of her eye. It loosened her throat, but her stomach tingled at the idea of knowing a secret from Father Henry. It had to be more palatable than the Wayne Tavern, and only they would know it.

"Good. So here goes—I don't have any friends either. I'm from a big family, but that's not the same thing, is it?"

"I was an only child," she said. "So, I wouldn't know."

Father Henry gave her a queer look, which she couldn't read. "I shouldn't be bellyaching to you about all this, then. Never mind."

"No," she said. "It's all right. But you must have some friends. Everybody has friends from school, don't they?"

"Do you?"

"Well, no." The in-crowd had sniffed around Lotte at first. The Klopstocks' daughter could have made a useful addition to the group, but as always, she'd been awkward with them. No point in elevating a square oddball to the popular squad. Lotte couldn't have shaken a pom-pom if her young life had depended on it. Not if the very maws of hell had opened to consume her whole. "But you're different. You were probably the top dog at Chaminade."

"I wouldn't say that, but yes, I had friends. We drifted apart from each other when I went off to seminary, and now none of them wants to be friends with a priest. Not real friends, anyhow. You're not the only one who worries about being used."

"Who would dare use you?" A twinge of anger sizzled across her thoughts. "They'd have to be the worst sort. You're such— Well, it wouldn't be right."

Father Henry shrugged. "Well, they try. My point is, I do want to be friends with you. You forget to be in awe of me sometimes. I'm tired of awe. I don't really think we should be remote from our people, at least, not as remote as William wants."

"Well." Lotte sensed that he was spent and awkward. "Now that all that's out of the way, would you like a chocolate cookie? I bought them on the way. They had sugar ones, too, for me."

"That's the best idea I've heard all day," he said. Underneath the black fabric, the tension melted from his shoulders, and his entire manner relaxed. He grabbed one of the cookies and bit. "Of course, this hasn't been a good day for ideas. You'll never guess what William tried to plan."

It was strange to hear Father Kestner referred to as 'William,' but she supposed she should get used to it. At least he wasn't calling him 'Billy' or some other such thing.

"What?"

"Well, you know we keep office hours, right? He thinks we should get rid of that and replace it with extra hours in the confessional. According to him, if people are going to be going on about their sins to us anyway, we might as well be able to absolve them. So, I said, I never thought you'd go that far to keep from seeing people, and he got huffy, which meant I was right."

"Did he really mean it?" The thought of them arguing like any coworkers was amusing to her. Albert had the same kinds of stories about his line supervisors.

"I doubt it. There's a certain parishioner who likes to hog his office hours, but he rightly figured that they'd probably just spend all afternoon confessing to him if it came to that. Half the time they do anyhow."

"I can't imagine doing enough sinful things in one day to warrant coming back each and every morning. Or afternoon," Lotte said.

"No," Father Henry said. He reached for another cookie. "Most people don't, but every once in a while, someone is overly scrupulous and comes in with a daily record of their most venial thoughts. I shouldn't complain because I don't think they know better, but it does take time away from more pressing things."

"Do you ever try to tell them they're being selfish?" she asked. Above her, the clouds drifted along the sky toward downtown. "It seems if they're coming every day, whether to confess or just to talk to you, they're not really accepting your advice or your absolution. It's a sin in itself, isn't it, not to accept the grace given by the sacrament?"

"Theoretically," Father Henry said. "But, as I said, I don't think they know better. Most of them go from me to William to other parishes and back again. It's sad, more than anything else. When we studied the condition, for it is a condition, in seminary, the book they gave us said, 'the scrupulous person makes shipwreck of salvation either on the Scylla of despair or the Charybdis of unheeding indulgence in vice.'"

"Oh."

"Yes. Oh." He smirked, reached for the final cookie. "Imagine reading that kind of thing for eight years."

"It's a wonder you've turned out so well," Lotte said, and her hand froze on the paper cup. Liquid sloshed over her wrist.

"You think I've turned out well?" The cookie, halfway to his mouth, was lowered and set aside. The low, studied tone pooled around them.

Lotte realized she could say one thing, and it would change something, be sinful, make being friends with her truly dangerous. Or she could say another thing and spoil the sudden stillness entirely. Sin was damning, but the alternative was heartbreaking.

"Father, I—" Three breaths bounced along her throat.

The trolley bus clanged past, fresh from its stop at Wayne and Wilmington. People shouted and clattered up the street in a surging crowd. The bell nattered against the back of Lotte's skull. The swaying trees, the smell of cars, everything came back to her in a rush, and she realized there was lemonade dripping down her forearm. Chocolate crumbs scattered across the faded quilt like accidental stars, and Father Henry was rising to his feet.

"Lotte," he said, and tossed her a handkerchief. "This was the nicest afternoon I've had in a long time. Thank you."

"Thank you for coming," she said. "You're right, you know."

"Am I? What about?"

"You are about the worst artist I've ever met." Lotte smiled over her shoulder, tossed the blanket across her arm, and cut north through the grass.

CHAPTER EIGHT

Alone after Vespers, Henry toyed with a piece of Clara's cold fried chicken. It was Anna's oldest son's name day—or maybe his birthday?—but it was always someone's name day or birthday, and Henry wanted solitude for once. He'd never be like William, energized by the lonely hours in his house, but even gregarious men needed to sort through their thoughts once in a while.

Henry stabbed at the chicken and wondered why he needed to justify his quiet night to his own mind. He knew why, of course. Every time a puff of incense had drifted past, he'd thought of clouds sailing over Walnut Hills Park, and the blue of his plate was the same pale wash as the interrupted streak of sky over downtown. Lotte—or should he be calling her Mrs. Walheim still?—was mistrustful and angry and sad and wistful, and he wondered whence all of those unhappy feelings had come. But what truly disturbed him was the fragile point of her chin against his forefinger, the soft collection of bones beneath the pale silk of her hands.

He wasn't blind, of course, nor insensate. Hell, even William probably noticed women as, well, women. They'd had a whole class on that at seminary, sort of. His thoughts weren't all lustful, and that was the problem. He knew all about expiating lust, but couldn't figure out where lustful thoughts began or stopped or diverged from the feeling when she'd traced her thoughts through the air like brushwork and he'd realized he felt more than just pity and misplaced desire.

Behind him, the radio warbled with "Casta Diva" of all unnecessary tortures. The sleepy opening eighths gave way to the long breaths of the hymn, the goddess's name elongated. One pleasure in solitude was absorption in this, rather than simply letting the music fill the silence as he worked. When Henry devoted his full attention to an aria or a canzonetta, it was absolute, as kinesthetic and mentally demanding as the ritual of Mass.

When the chorus swelled, Henry's eyes flew open. The chicken was still uneaten before him as the fat melted into a shiny oil slick. He got up. He threw it out. He picked up the breviary and set it down again. Sat on the sofa. Got up. Opened a beer. Set it aside.

How did William do this night after night? It was probably still early enough to beg a piece of cake from Anna or give Johnny a big birthday (name day?) hug from Uncle Father Henry. He was probably sore that Uncle Father Henry hadn't shown. Probably. That irritated him almost as much as the fact that he was calling himself Uncle Father Henry like the others. He ought to be with his family, or praying Compline early, or reading something edifying, or doing anything except thinking what he was thinking right now.

When he had tilted Lotte's chin and met her eyes, his first impulse had been to kiss her. Her mouth had parted, just a little. She hadn't even realized it, but it had, and her lips were soft and plump. They might have been his. The thought made him swell and ache, and so he stripped off his clothes and dove into the shower.

Cold water pounded his skin, but he slumped against the wall. Lotte wasn't trusting or warm or effusive, but she'd trusted him and cheered him and laughed with him. 'Not by you,' she'd said, which only meant she'd been tricked and used by others. By whom? She was probably married to an atheist, and she had a frank, sweet, innocent faith. Surely the atheist had used her. Everyone knew her father was Carl Klopstock, who owned the soap factory Mr. Walheim managed. Perhaps Mr. Walheim had wanted her money or wanted a promotion, and—

Henry knocked his head against the wall. Naked, numb with cold, the water squealing through the pipes, and he was thinking about parish gossip. None of it was any of his business, not even what they confessed to him. He could say absolutions or give counsel, but even then, his place wasn't to know every detail of every life. He was ordained Father Henry Werther, vested and indelibly changed, set apart from other men, yet still the same. Outwardly the same, inwardly transformed. This was his vocation, and he was in danger of taking it lightly. Perhaps William was right. Perhaps he was irreverent.

Realizing his thoughts were too deep for the cheery yellow of his bathroom tiles, Henry began to shiver, saw his toes turn paper white and twitch. He wrinkled his nose and turned the hot tap. The bar of Ivory finally lathered, the room filled with steam, and Henry let his eyes slide closed.

Sirens wailed in the distance, off toward Wayne Avenue, but grew fainter and fainter while Albert and James sat in silence, shrouded by darkness, and with their right hands clasped.

"At least come away from the window," Lotte said. "Let me get you a drink." Enough moonlight beamed through the treetops to cast both men into smooth bas-relief. Anyone passing could have seen them entwined as though plighting their troth.

"James." Albert's voice was gentle. "Best do as she says." With a firm tug, he pulled James to his feet and steered him to the sofa.

Lotte poured three strong whiskeys and added a few splashes of coffee left over from dessert.

"Thanks, Mrs. Walheim."

She used to think James was like an overeager child, but now wondered who he was trying to wound by calling her Mrs. Walheim, himself or her. The whiskey burned her already roiling stomach, but she didn't care. When Albert and James had shown up, winded and sweaty and wild-eyed with sirens blaring somewhere nearby, she had been grateful for the distraction. She'd gone out on a precipice with Father Henry today and had very nearly leapt.

"You told me the bars were dangerous during Eastertide," Lotte said. "Why did you go?"

"It's close to June," Albert said. "Hasn't been a raid in a couple of weeks. Just figured it was safe."

"Safe, indeed," Lotte said, mostly to herself. What was safety, anyway? Surely the bars where Albert and James went were never safe. Lotte wasn't safe anywhere now, not even nestled in the stone walls of St. Jerome's. Father Henry would always be there, and although he was warm-hearted and kind and wouldn't hurt her, he was not safe.

"Say, why're you jumping down his throat about it?"

Startled, she looked up. James had leapt to his feet and was scowling at her.

"You leave her alone," Albert said. "She's damn well right."

Shoving his hands in his pockets, James stared at the carpet. Albert rose from the sofa and joined him again in the patch of moonlight. With one tender finger, Albert tilted James's chin before bending to kiss him. Their lips merged soundlessly, and their shoulders relaxed. James's hand cupped the base of Albert's head with fingers splayed.

Someone's footsteps pounded up the staircase, and when Lotte regained her breath, she found herself on the landing. Albert had always been careful not to do anything like that in front of her. She knew they did that and more behind closed doors, but seeing their lips meet wasn't as disgusting in actual practice as she'd feared. It wasn't disgusting at all, and that frightened her, too.

Father Henry's low tone was as intimate and soothing as Albert's with James. He'd tilted her face to him the exact same way. What if he'd closed the small gap between them, bowed his head, and touched his lips against hers? What might she have done? She was Albert's wife, and although he had James, she was not an atheist and could not mock the sacrament as her husband did. Could she? No. Not even for the low pull in her stomach and current up through her chest. Especially not for that.

"Lotte?" Albert appeared before her and perched on the top step. "Sorry you had to see that; we— It's been a tough night." It wasn't until he pressed a handkerchief to one cheek, then the other, that she realized she was weeping again. "I do try to keep all that away from you, doll."

"I know," she said. "I appreciate that, and I'm sorry. It wasn't you. It was a shock, is all." He wouldn't care if she'd had an oddly charged picnic with Father Henry. He wouldn't even care if she seduced all the husbands and every priest in town, but she wasn't in the habit of confiding in Albert. She didn't even know what had really happened at the park today. "Are the two of you okay? I should get back to sleep."

"We'll be fine," Albert said. "Tired. I think we'll stay here tonight."

"Of course," she said, although he wasn't asking permission. "Good night, then."

From her bed, behind the closed door, she heard them climbing the stairs, water running, footsteps in the hallway, low murmurs. All she knew of James was that he loved her husband, was a typesetter for the newspaper, and had lived in Walnut Hills for years. And that his parents had had Albert locked up. Lotte didn't know how the two of them had met, but could imagine it. Sultry low lighting, dirty floors, oyster shells, another kiss in the sparsely furnished rooms above the Wayne Tavern. Maybe the bells of St. Jerome's were what drove the hours of her day, but she knew, could envisage, things that would send Barbara Morris running for her rosary and Father Kestner running for the storm cellar.

Would they send Father Henry running? She doubted it and hoped they wouldn't, although she should want him to leave her alone. Vocations had been chosen long before now, both his and hers. She had consented to be married, and she prayed for Albert's conversion. Henry had prostrated himself before the altar and received the chalice. Yes, their vocations were sealed, but the sweetness of his friendship, even for one afternoon, sent a pang of sadness so deep she bit down on the blanket to keep from crying out. In the space of a few hours, she had felt more cherished, more alive, and yes, safer, than in the rest of all her thirty years combined.

In the morning, Lotte woke for Mass, and the others slumbered on, spent and exhausted by the shriek of sirens and frightened men. The tiny prayer book from childhood, her name on the flyleaf in tipsy capitals, had recommended a course of prayer upon waking, rising, washing, and dressing that even she hadn't the energy to follow. It floated into her mind today, but the half-remembered, youthful prayers couldn't quell her very grown-up anxiety nor the fizzing excitement she wanted to ignore. Even the sententious morning office in her Lasance *Prayer-Book* couldn't dispel the urgent whisper that today was an important day and not a normal Saturday at all. Would she sit with Father Henry? Would Father Henry say Mass? She blushed with shame when she realized her thoughts were all for him and not for the sacrifice, but nevertheless, she added another swipe of lipstick, wiped it off, added it again, and left the house in silence.

A brilliant sun, too brilliant for quarter after eight in late May, beat down on her arms and white hat. The heat wilted her linen dress and flushed her cheeks. The men ahead of her sported damp collars, and their wives fanned themselves with missals and gloves. Everything and everyone looked so utterly banal that Lotte wondered if everything she'd fretted over wasn't all in her head. Father Henry wanted to be her friend. He'd eaten cookies and had a chat with her. His tone might have been teasing—heaven knew she had little enough experience with tones—and those dark eyes gazing into hers might have been simply to reassure. Among the neighbors, on the stone steps, with the schola warming up, she felt like the biggest idiot in the world. This was what came of having a husband whose embrace felt like an alien body and who loved a man named James.

"Hello, Mrs. Walheim." Father Kestner still wore his cassock and was floating among the crowd, which meant his curate would lead.

"Good morning, Father." Lotte fought, as she always did, the absurd urge to curtsey. His stern, jowly face and steel-rimmed glasses belonged in the portrait galleries of black-clad aristocrats that lined the Art Institute.

"Where is Mr. Walheim today?"

There was a raid on the Wayne Tavern last night, so he and his male lover decided to sleep late this morning. Lotte wanted very much to say it. Instead, she assumed her usual apologetic shrug and said,

"Feeling a touch under the weather, I'm afraid. He'll be here tomorrow for sure."

"I do hope so." Father Kestner offered one sharp nod and turned on his heel like he had more troops to inspect.

Father Henry began the Mass, and Lotte forgot to think of him as the man from the park. How could she, when he was intent on leading them eastward and the candles burned above him? Although he had been in his vocation for nearly four years, he was still young enough that even daily Mass had not yet become rote or routine for him. He invested each phrase, even each word, with a youthful, joyful zeal that connected them all to something that was often remote. His sermons, bashful and incredulous, uplifted them anyhow and made her smile with recognition. It was strange to think that someone set specifically apart to perform such sacred tasks was the same man who had lain back on her faded patchwork quilt to watch the clouds pass overhead. It seemed impossible to her just then that a human being could be both.

But yet, when Father Henry loped toward her after setting aside the white brocade for his customary black and grinned without a trace of her own anguish, she couldn't help but smile back.

"Hello," she said. Something had changed between them, almost imperceptibly and certainly unnamable, but the air was thick with it.

"Lotte." Too much cheer boomed off the marble and probably caught the ears of anyone nearby. He cleared his throat. "Lotte, how are you?"

"Tired," she said. "I didn't sleep very well. Albert had some trouble with a friend, and I was worried and such."

"Sorry to hear it," he said. "I suppose that explains his absence this morning?"

"His troubles always do seem to start on Friday evenings," she said. "When he's lucky, they take him out of commission until Sunday night. Well, never mind him. How are you, Father? I enjoyed your sermon."

"Thank you," he said. "And I had a long night, too. I was still awake when it came time for Matins."

"It must be hard never to have an unbroken sleep," she said. "No matter the reason."

"It's not easy, that's true," he said. "But not even William always prays them strictly at nine and midnight and three and so forth. There's really no exact prescribed hour for the offices. We can anticipate them, too. That does help. Anyhow. Do you have a busy Saturday ahead of you?"

"No," she said. "Albert has plans with a friend, and I was going to listen to the radio and paint. I'm not terribly exciting. What about you?"

"I might go to my sister's later on. Her son's birthday was yesterday." He frowned. "Although it might have been his name day. I forget which John he's named for. I'm a terrible uncle."

"No, of course not," Lotte said. "You said there were twenty of them. Goodness, all those birthdays and name days, plus baptisms, first communions, confirmations, you're lucky you took a vow of poverty."

"I didn't, actually," he said. "Although I may as well have. You're right, those gifts do add up, even the boring Uncle Father Henry gifts like leftover candles from Candlemas."

"Perhaps you are a terrible uncle," she said.

"Now." Father Henry gave his head a half-shake. "You said yesterday I'm the worst artist, and today I'm a terrible uncle. I was going to see if you wanted to take a walk down the hill, but now I think I'll go alone."

"You don't want to go alone," she said. "You can't stand to be alone."

"Well." His smile was self-satisfied, almost smug. "You have me there. How did you know?"

"It's obvious; you'll even talk to me." Lotte smiled up at him.

Her worries and the thought that she was crazy disappeared, and she was as light as yesterday. "It's awfully hot, though. You'll roast once we start back up the hill."

"I'm more used to wearing black than I am to waking up at all hours," he said. "Come on."

Before Wyoming Street dipped, a person could stand and look out at the maze of streets, all of downtown, even the spread of distant fields. Houses and a smattering of shop fronts slid along the sidewalk in a neat terrace, the lawns hemmed in by brick and stepping one after the other. Cars and the trolley rumbled by, and all around them, Saturdays began.

A group of kids was playing Kick the Can, and a couple of men were mowing their lawns, but no one paid Lotte or Father Henry any mind. At least, she hoped they didn't. It was as though the entire world could read her thoughts or sensations or whatever caused the unfailing awareness of his hand swinging beside hers. She wanted to talk to him, but wasn't quite sure what about. Friends or not, she'd never shared anything intimate with anyone, ever. And really, what could be more humiliating than Father Henry knowing that a lonely housewife was unfailingly aware of him?

"Lotte." His voice startled her. He appeared to be contemplating something. "May I ask you something very personal?"

Her heartbeat sped, and she didn't trust herself to speak. She chose to blame the sudden heat in her cheeks on the sun and nodded.

"Is—?" He paused. Looked pained. "Lotte, is—?"

"Yes?" What was he going to ask? Why were they in full view of everyone?

"Is your husband an atheist?"

"Oh." Confusion and a slight, strange disappointment settled in.

"I'm sorry. Please don't answer. I shouldn't have…"

"No, he is an atheist," she said. Was it a secret? Too late now, and she doubted Father Henry was going to spill the beans to anyone. "That's just not what I thought you'd ask. Was I really that transparent?"

"Well, he hardly comes to Mass, sleeps when he does, and eats bacon and eggs before receiving the Blessed Sacrament. It wasn't a particularly difficult puzzle to solve." Father Henry shrugged and drew a handkerchief across his brow. "Perhaps we should turn around?"

"I told you it was too hot."

"And clearly, you're the sensible one." He gave her a sly smile. "I have four sisters. I know when to give credit where it's due. And that would be to the female party, of course."

She chuckled. "You've been well trained, Father."

Although they had only gone halfway, the sidewalk uphill gleamed white in the sun, and Lotte groaned to herself at the trek.

"I'm sorry to have pried, though," he said. "It's just that you're very attentive to your faith, and to have married an atheist seems— But I suppose you have other things— Oh, never mind. I shouldn't be asking."

Was Father Henry trying to gauge how happy she and Albert were? Why should he? Perhaps that's what friends did. Surely it was. She didn't answer and focused on the last quarter of the hillside. The final steps were agony, and Lotte dreaded the rest of the summer.

"Anyhow," he said, and again it startled her to hear him discomfited. "I shouldn't have dragged you outside in the heat, but I enjoyed yesterday and all."

"I enjoyed this," she said, although her dress and hair were sodden with sweat. "Really, I did. And yesterday, too." They stopped beside the steps of St. Jerome's, and she jumped when a police car wailed past. Wide-eyed, she watched it speed down the hill, but it didn't turn into the neighborhood, thank God.

"Would you like to rest for a moment?" he asked. "You have to walk home yet, don't you?" He started up the first step, but glanced at the three rows of doors arching into the stone façade. "I live just down the block. If we go inside, William will want me to pray an office, or someone will want me to see them for something. Do you mind? It's only a bit further."

"I don't mind," she said. "I'd rather avoid— That is…"

"It's all right; I don't fault you for wanting to avoid William." He nodded down the leafy street. "I'm doing the same thing after all."

"Do you call him William?"

"Not to his face. He is one of the few who calls me Henry, though."

"That hardly seems fair." She eyed the white cracker box house trimmed in deep green. "This is yours?" Lotte had only seen one bachelor's house before. Of course, she had walked past James's one day when she'd known he and Albert were elsewhere.

"Yes," he said. "William hoards the rectory. He can't abide people in his lodgings, so I live here. I certainly don't complain." Father Henry unlocked the door and led her into the sparse living room.

She had never thought of being in a clergyman's home, and had pictured something else: candles, maybe, or monastic stone floors. Certainly not an ordinary blue sofa and chair, a pine table, a Frigidaire, and an electric fan.

Father Henry flipped on the fan and filled two glasses at the sink. "Most people don't believe I drink out of glasses. They think I keep cupboards full of silver chalices."

The corner of her mouth jerked upward. "They do not."

"My nephews do. The younger ones." He gestured toward the sofa and flopped down. "You can sit, really."

She sat beside him on the sofa, although she should have chosen the chair opposite. Artificial breezes ruffled her skirt, but the water and the fan did nothing to cool her. Again, she thought of Albert tilting James's chin, their mouths moving against each other, of Father Henry's hand on her face.

"Yesterday," he said, and his voice sounded odd. "You said you wouldn't be used and tricked by me. I wondered, does that mean someone else has tricked you?"

The air and the conversation were too heavy. She shifted, upsetting the water. Its coolness flowed over her lap, which eased her overheated skin, but the water was also seeping into his couch.

"I didn't mean to— Here." He leapt up and grabbed a tea towel. "I really don't mean to pry. I really don't." Instead of simply handing her the towel, which he ought to have done, he sat beside her and blotted the water himself. His knuckles brushed her thigh as he pressed the towel against the couch. Deep concentration furrowed his brow. The bowed head was so close to her, she could see the ripples and twists of each individual curl and wondered whether it would be silky under her hands.

Her breaths grew shallow, which she couldn't control. He looked up and handed her the towel.

"Perhaps you ought to finish up."

She took it, stood, and followed the tip of his chin to a short corridor. The bathroom tiles were canary, and the towels bright white. His mother or his sisters or someone from St. Jerome's had their laundering cut out for them. Lotte patted her skirt dry and left the tea towel over the shower rod.

Without really thinking, she checked the lock on the door, stood in the center of the yellow room, and popped the buttons on her dress. Linen swished past her ankles and pooled on the floor. The rest followed, and she stood there for a minute with the air cooled by tile and marble dancing against her skin, stark naked in the middle of Father Henry's bathroom. There was a mirror above the sink, and she forced herself to meet her own eyes. Of course, she was blushing, but when she smiled, the woman in the mirror smiled back. Calmly, quietly, Lotte scooped the things from the floor, put them back on with a rustle of silk and linen, and stepped back into the corridor. When she glanced back at the yellow bathroom, the tiles winked their secret at her. Lotte's stomach swooped with her own daring.

He was still on the couch when she returned, and his head was sunk deep in his hands. As she walked toward him, her thighs felt sticky and damp where they met.

"Is something wrong?"

He tugged a fistful of hair, but shook his head.

"I ought to start home. Thank you for this."

"You never answered me," he said.

"I can't," she said. She'd half-hoped he'd forgotten asking who'd used and tricked her. "But I will. Soon." Something inside her shimmered at the thought that she had been completely undressed just two minutes before, and he had no idea. Why did everything with him have to be at once thrilling and disheartening? Why had she even done it?

"After you compose a response suitable for my ears?" His eyes crinkled at the corners. "You don't need to censor things from me, you know. I've heard things in the confessional that would curl your hair."

"So that explains it," she said in a murmur and thrilled at his slight blush. It was doubtful that he could shock her, but she was fairly certain she could shock him. "No, I'm not censoring it. I just want to think."

Outside, the bells tolled eleven. Father Henry walked her the few feet to the doorway, but when his hand reached for the latch, it grabbed Lotte's hand instead. She curled her fingers around it and looked down at the melding of them, hers pale and tapered, his just beginning to tan. With each pulse of the hour, she felt the vein in the base of his thumb jump. Perhaps cars and people were bustling on the street, or perhaps it was silent. Blood rushing, bells, and quiet breath were the only sounds that mattered to her. Even the arias that played in her head ceased their trills and cadenzas.

The eleventh bell struck. Time had passed, but Lotte could do nothing but stare at their twined fingers and not think.

"Lotte." Father Henry's voice was strained, but he made no move to separate. "This is a dangerous path."

Her head inched upward as though he were guiding it once again with a finger, and she met his eyes. His gaze was steady, troubled, the entire struggle clearly etched. She thought of him both with the maniple and sitting on the ground in the park. And what of herself? Marriage was just as indelible as any other sacrament, even marriage to one like Albert. He and James had grasped hands just like this.

"You're right," she said, but held his gaze the way she'd held her own just moments ago. "I know you're right. I just can't—"

He nodded, appeared to want to say something, but instead bent his head and touched her lips with his. They were firm and warm. She fell against him, but was aware of nothing, not even the sensation of being kissed. If her arms moved or if he cradled the back of her head, she didn't know it. Everything dissolved, and she only became aware of him when the very edge of his tongue caught her bottom lip. The deliciousness popped her gauzy bubble into deep longing, but she stepped back, mouth still agape, and regarded him in a daze.

With the pad of her finger, she traced a salty path over her bottom lip and licked it away. Kissing him had made her feel no better. A low, steady throb had started someplace she didn't want to name. Up on her tiptoes, she kissed him again, and this time she kept enough of her senses to feel the wetness of teeth—they were both clumsy at it—and the way his hand trembled against her shoulder. She kissed his cheek, the edge of his mouth, the soft place where his jawline met his throat.

For once in her life, Lotte wasn't startled. She had understood to some degree that this had begun as soon as they'd met eyes that first day. But this could be all. Predestined or not, it would never do to forget that they were both promised to others.

"Henry," she said. "I had better go."

He nodded, opened the door, and clasped his hands behind his back as though he distrusted them.

CHAPTER NINE

The bright whirlpool of noise that usually comforted him was today for Henry a great, sucking Charybdis. Everything, all sounds, all touches, all scents, were like stepping into sudden sunlight. His mother squeezed his arm as he walked past, and for the first time in his life, he wanted to slap her hand away. Johnny—turned out it was his birthday—bellowed to the others that there was cake and punch, and Henry winced. His field of vision flashed as though he was suffering a migraine.

"You look rough." Clara plopped down beside him. "Not hungover, are you? You priests are the worst. Why, Father Daniels over here at Immaculate practically keeled over the other day when we went to have the new rosaries blessed. Could have smelled the whiskey on him from a mile away."

"I'm not hungover." He speared the tines of his fork into the slab of cake.

"Then you wouldn't mind if I switch on the radio?" She turned the dial and got Al Bowlly singing "Guilty." Really. Who the hell was up there mocking him?

"I mind." His voice was too brusque, and he got up too abruptly. "Just leave me alone already."

He stalked into one of the bedrooms, and Clara followed. Why wouldn't she? It was Clara.

"What's got your collar in a twist?" His sister was slight, pale,

and dark-haired as Snow White, but she drew herself up and planted a
fist on each hip. "You sit out there grumbling and pummeling your
cake like a spoiled little boy. No one's done anything to you. Have they?
For Christ's sake, Henry, all I did was turn on the radio."

He might have cut her off here—letting Clara gather steam
was always risky—but decided he deserved a scolding.

"The damn radio. So maybe it wasn't *Tosca* or whatever high-
and-mighty thing you like, but you don't have to blow a fuse and storm
off and make me dog you all over the damn house."

"You didn't have to follow me," he said, knowing it would
make her angry. Clara's wrath was doing wonders for his mood.

"What? I should just let you grouse around and ditch me? You
have some nerve, Henry Werther. This is just like that time Anna and
I caught you trying to ditch school for the opera of all things, and you
went wandering off down Smithville. I have half a mind to tell the old
man and let him sort you out." She appeared to run out of gas, and her
ire sputtered to a halt. With a curious look, she tipped her head to the
left and regarded him with something like alarm.

"Say, why're you letting me grill you like this? Any other time,
you'd be slinging it right back. What's eating you, Henry?"

If anyone could be told, it was Clara, but he wasn't going to
spill. Maybe he was still her kid brother first and Father Henry second,
but she'd be plenty horrified. In a way, it would be worse than enduring
William's disappointment. Not that he would confess it to William. He
had to confess it before long, but when he examined his conscience,
he didn't entirely regret what had happened. Yes, he had led Lotte into
adultery and himself into practically the same. It was unpardonable, but
he didn't feel entirely guilty and felt guilty about not feeling entirely
guilty, and—

"Henry. I asked you a question."

He looked up. She had inched closer. "What?"

"What's wrong?" The bed sank beneath her. "Did something
happen? Is it that woman you told me about?"

"I can't talk about the things people tell me, Clara," he said,
which was true enough. It was a little surprising she hadn't figured the
whole thing out; he felt like it was stamped across his face. "I'm sorry

I was a jerk." His mood began to shift. "And I'm sorry about that time I tried to ditch school. That was the only time, I promise."

"I worry about you, is all," she said. "You have to do so much living up to things. I could never do any of what you do."

An image of Clara crouching in the confessional booth and scolding penitents in her colorful tongue made him grin.

"No, you couldn't."

He was ready for the pillow that came bashing down toward his head, parried it with a forearm, and tugged her hair just hard enough to make her yelp.

"I really am telling Dad now," she said. "Come on, Father, let's finish our cake."

"Sure," he said. They both rose, but he grabbed her arm halfway to the door. "Say, Clara?"

"What is it?"

"What exactly…? When you and David…?" God, why was he about to ask his sister this nonsense? "Before you got married, what did you have in common?"

"Oh." She frowned. "Well, I guess the usual. We both went to the same grade school and the same parish. He liked jazz dancing and swimming at the parks. Nothing terribly interesting. It was more…" A deep breath and a sigh. "More that we laughed at the same things and wanted the same kind of family someday. We haven't gone dancing in years, but we still laugh at the same things." Her expression softened, and he could tell she was elsewhere. "It's not easy to explain. Why, Henry?"

"I just— There's this couple who I'm trying to help, and I couldn't think how."

"People ought to have better sense than to ask you about being married," she said.

"You'd think. But I get asked about everything, including plenty of stuff I'd never ask you about."

Clara squealed with laughter and led him back into the living room.

"What's so funny?" David came around the corner and grabbed her around the waist. "Where did you two run off to?"

"Oh, somebody up at St. Jerome's was asking Henry for bedroom advice."

"Told you those people in Walnut Hills don't have any sense." David chuckled and kissed her just behind the ear, the same place Lotte had caressed him only hours ago. He whispered something in her ear, and Henry gathered he was telling her they ought to be the ones doling out advice in that quarter. Good Lord. His sister. Time for a beer.

When he cracked the can of Schlitz open and returned to the sofa, he was suddenly aware of Clara and David, John and Peggy, Cathy and Paul. His smug sense of pride at being better than the Walheims was long gone, and in its place, a dull, steady ache began to throb.

Only once had he regretted his life. Four years before, one of the first couples he'd ever married had been to see him to arrange the date. Their names were fuzzy now, but he remembered the woman's elegant nose and the man's warm brown eyes. They were a couple of years younger than he was but older than most, and they'd swept him up in their cheer. The woman touched the man's hand to reinforce a point; the man helped her shrug into her long fur coat as though she might shatter in the cold. Afterward, he'd sent them out laughing into the frosty night and watched from the rectory door as they threw their arms around each other's shoulders to brace against the wind. The Nuptial Mass had been like any other. He rejoiced with them, but didn't envy. One bright laugh, shattering the night sky like a handful of stars, was what had sent him reeling toward his confessor.

"Sorry, Henry." Clara gave him a cheeky look. "Didn't mean to offend your superior moral sensitivity."

"Offend my eyes is more like it." He took a swig of beer to mask his discomfort. "You've driven me to drink."

"Oh, ha ha. Mom, Henry's being a nuisance."

"Be polite to your sister, Henry." His mother looked up from her playing cards. "And, Clara, for heaven's sake, be a little more ladylike."

Henry stuck his tongue out at Clara, counted it as a victory, and finished his beer in silence.

It had rained after Clara castigated him and before he started home from Mom and Dad's. Air so clean it was almost sweet tickled against the shadow on his jaw, and the soft chirrup of crickets followed him from one block to the next. As a child, he had read about night lilies in a German fairy tale. Their white blossoms shone forth only at midnight, when no one could see, and perfumed the moonlight with their heavy fragrance, languorous enough to lull unwary princes and sailors to sleep. Tonight was a night for night lilies. He could almost see the raindrops trembling on their perfect, creamy petals before they shushed out of sight at Lauds.

While he walked, Henry thought about things that were both outrageous and tender to him. Pretty women abounded almost anywhere he went, but he had learned to simply acknowledge their beauty in the abstract, like a connoisseur of Italian Masters or French wines, and move on. Lotte was pretty, yes, but worse than that, she was like the lilies and bloomed only when she thought no one would see. With her, he was aware of witnessing something precious and perhaps holy all its own.

'Henry,' she had said in that winded voice. The memory made him curl his fingers in upon his palms. How good it was to hear his name spoken without embellishment by someone other than his sister and his mentor. He could probably bottle those two syllables and live on them for days, the way fasting saints lived solely on the Host.

Henry winced. Of all the blasphemous thoughts he'd had that day alone, that was probably the worst. He should make his confession tonight: go tap on William's door, tell him everything, and speak to Lotte. Or rather, he'd speak to Mrs. Walheim, tell her what a grievous sin they'd committed, and encourage her to seek a confessor herself.

He wouldn't do any of that, of course. Blasphemous thoughts about the Blessed Sacrament were one thing. What had happened with Lotte was quite another. The nagging thought remained that he was called to her somehow. And as ridiculous as that was, why should he not see it through? They could control their concupiscence. They were faithful people, after all. Henry would speak to her tomorrow and set it all straight, and if that sounded dreadful to him, well, then that was one more wrong he'd committed today.

This time, he did walk down Edgar Avenue and stopped in front of Lotte's house. It was dark, save for one upstairs window, and he imagined the two of them, the Walheims, reading and chatting and possibly... Perhaps... He thought about Mr. Walheim reaching for Lotte's hand, kissing her the same way, although he was probably suave at it. The idea made Henry hot with envy, but he found he couldn't picture the reality. As sweet as Lotte had been, she was as clumsy as he was. Whatever was happening upstairs at the Walheims', he didn't think it was the two of them making love.

The light switched off, and Henry realized what a fool he was, not to mention unsavory, standing here on the sidewalk and staring up at their house. Half the people in Walnut Hills could recognize him at a single glance, and he was outside Lotte's house pining like Abelard. Not to mention that the thought of her husband touching her made him as jealous as a child at someone else's birthday party. Mr. Walheim half ignored her, and he was an atheist. It stood to reason that he could have disregarded common morals enough to trick her into marriage. Maybe he'd married her for her money and kept a mistress?

A lamp flicked on in the downstairs window, and he heard the doorknob begin to turn. Henry hastened away, but looked back and saw Mr. Walheim slip into the shadows.

"Henry?" William's glower was flecked with impatience, and Henry gathered this wasn't the first time he'd said his name.

"I'm sorry. Yes, Father?" Henry brushed past the servers and followed his mentor from the sacristy.

"You've been distracted." Of course, he had. And naturally, William didn't seem to notice the irony of calling him out while he was in the middle of proving the point. "Is something the matter?"

"Well." It was tempting both to say no and to confess the entire thing. "Not exactly. I discovered something rather shocking about one of our parishioners, and I've thought over it a lot these past few days."

"They confessed it to you?"

"No, that I can forget. At least they're contrite then. I saw…
I found out one of the men has something on the side."

William, stodgy, rule-minded William, was unimpressed. "This
can hardly be a revelation for you. He's certainly not the only one
among them. He'll confess it or he won't. It's admirable that you're so
concerned for one of the souls entrusted to us, but meddling won't
serve you well here."

He was plenty worried about quite a few souls, his own
included, but that wasn't the point. When he thought about it, William
was right. It wasn't shocking in the least that someone from St.
Jerome's or anywhere might have a mistress. How naïve he was to even
bring it up.

"How exactly did you find this out, Henry?" William's eyes
were keen, his attention rapt now.

"I was walking home from my folks' the other night and saw
him sneak out of his house."

"And meet a woman?"

"Well, I didn't see her, but—"

"Surely nothing good can come of skulking in the shadows,"
William said, and Henry wondered whom he was chastising. "But all
you saw was a man leaving his house? How has that managed to rattle
you when both of us have heard parishioners confess hours' worth of
theft and carnality and vice?"

Henry shrugged. 'A man leaving his house' made him feel well
beyond naïve and something more akin to dumb.

"The shock of seeing it, I suppose. You're probably right,
Father. Maybe he was sneaking out for a drink or a poker game." Not
that he could betray a confidence, but he wondered whether the news
that Mr. Walheim was an atheist would make William take notice.

"Whatever it is, he'll likely be running to us about it before
long," William said. "God willing. I'm not jaded, Henry," he added.
"I've simply learned that it's best to keep one's own counsel and help
only those who ask for it. I do care for this congregation."

"I know you do." Henry bit his lower lip. "I'm sorry for my
inattention."

William nodded and began to walk up the corridor toward his

office.

"Henry," he said over his shoulder. "Were you concerned for the man's soul or for his wife's feelings?"

The door clicked shut, and Henry stood like an imbecile, mouth agape and trembling. Footsteps echoed behind him, and he turned, hoping to find Lotte, but instead saw the new sacristan scurrying into an antechamber. Lotte had avoided him these past days, much as she had done in the beginning. Some friend. He had half a mind to give her a real set down, and the fact that she was right to stay away only irritated him. For she was right, especially now that William knew or suspected or simply wanted to frighten him. But how could William know that he had kissed someone? Although he felt branded with it, he knew he wasn't.

William's office door cracked open. "Was there something you needed, Henry?"

"No," he said. "Just thinking."

"You will want to be careful," William said and beckoned him forward to catch his whisper. "With Mrs. Walheim."

Clawing bile rose in his throat, and he felt his cheeks pale. "Mrs. Walheim?"

"You're on some misguided quest to help her, are you not?"

"I wouldn't call it misguided." Henry struggled for normal breath. "She has a lot of sadness. And she did ask for help with her husband."

"Not the most attentive man in the world," William said. "Very well. Counsel her when she comes to you, but stay well out of their troubles, Henry. I should hope you don't have any grand ideas about telling her what you witnessed. Chances are, she knows about it already. Why else would she be so sad and beleaguered?"

Henry nodded. Why else, indeed? Only that Mr. Walheim was an atheist, and a priest was leading her into adultery.

"I do understand, Henry," William said, his voice softening. "But you must be mindful of your place." He tugged at Henry's sleeve, pulled him into his office, and locked the door behind them. "Not that I think you would do too grievous a wrong, but I'm reminded of a story my father told me about his days with the Jesuits. There was a woman who came to him one day. She was unmarried, but she'd lost a child before its birth."

"And he gave her counsel?"

"He did. Even had things out with her lover, if I'm not mistaken."

Henry winced. "He became overly involved, then?"

"She was my mother." A sardonic look, a twist of the lips. "So I suppose you could say that, yes." William noted his expression. "Not that I think you're in any more danger of such things than anyone else. I simply wanted to let you know what a dangerous path that sort of thing can be."

"You would never have been born." The words fell out before Henry could stop them.

William raised his eyebrows so high his glasses slipped down the bridge of his nose. "Very true. And my father never took holy orders, of course. He was a brother, as I said. I don't think that justifies his decision; however, I am entirely grateful to have been born." A fleeting smile escaped before he could stop it. "You may go, Henry."

Henry didn't hesitate or stand in the hallway or even speak. For all he loved to talk, he had no idea what to say to William's story. *For heaven's sake*, he thought. He had only kissed Lotte. William's father had married the woman. Perhaps it had led to William's existence and all, but Henry suddenly felt a great deal lighter about his own trifling faults.

"Dear Editor: The idea that the government might employ degenerates and perverts is nothing short of un-American. Harsher penalties for deviance and sodomy are the only way to protect this nation from depravity." The newspaper rustled, and ice clinked in Albert's glass. He lit another Marlboro and inhaled. "Last week's story about the place called the Wayne Tavern made my wife and me downright sick. Our city's policemen need to be tougher in dealing with these criminals, no doubt about it."

"Just stop." Lotte closed her eyes and reached for her drink. Not again with this.

"Here's another one. Dear Editor: Dayton's policemen are wasting their time by locking up homosexuals. It is widely known to be a mental disorder, caused by castrating mothers, according to the theories of Sigmund Freud. These men and women should be hospitalized and treated, not jailed." Albert tipped back his glass and finished the Rusty Nail in one swallow. "Jesus Christ. Sigmund Freud. That's not even what he said."

"Freud? Or Jesus Christ?"

Albert actually laughed. "Freud. According to him, I can't be changed. Too bad the doctors at Dayton State aren't as well-read as me."

"I don't want to talk about this anymore," Lotte said. "Why do you read that nonsense? The paper, I mean. All it does is make you angry."

"Put it this way." Albert stood and went to the liquor cabinet. "Another? Let's say Barbara Morris was gossiping about you, and you knew it wasn't true. You'd still want to know what everyone was saying, right? Just to know?"

Lotte wanted to say gossip didn't matter and that she'd take the high road, but the fact remained.

"Yes. I'd want to know."

"Plus, if any of the crowd's in the can or the nuthouse, I want to know that, too." He sighed and handed her a drink. "You'd want to know if, say, Father Kestner was in the can, right?"

This time, Lotte was the one to laugh. "I'm not sure I could live through the shock, actually." She was grateful he hadn't mentioned Henry. Father Henry.

"The shock, indeed," he said. "That's what I worry about."

"Is the hospital...?" The drink twisted around in her hands. "Is it very awful?"

The lighter clicked, and another flame bloomed. Albert's eyes fixed on the curtains, but were oceans away or perhaps only blocks away in reality. It was the same faraway, drawn, hollow stare most men got when asked about their months or years of bombing Japan or liberating French villages where there was no one alive to liberate. This had been Albert's war, Lotte supposed. Much like the war heroes, he hadn't talked about the details.

"Depends on what you mean by awful, I suppose," Albert said. "You've had a shock from a bare wire, right? Think about touching the bare wire over and over, twice in a day. Your arms, your privates, your head. It's worse than touching a wire, though, really. You touch it yourself, you pull your hand back. When it's doctors shocking you, you've got no say."

Her teeth clenched, and she upset her drink for the second time in a week. Albert made no move to get a towel or touch her hand or even notice. He was still off in the middle distance. Back on the front lines of Dayton State.

"I was lucky," he said with perverse relish. "Next time, they said, they have other treatments. Do you want to know?"

She shook her head. He ignored her as he always did. Her stomach was already clenching.

"You've heard of lobotomies, right? Who hasn't? When I was in the nuthouse, they drilled holes in people's heads and got at their brains that way. But a couple of months back, this guy Freeman decided he had a better way. Now what they do—" Albert settled back into his chair as though he was relating some light little story to the Andersons. No more war stories. His gaze shifted from her curtains to her face. "—is use an icepick. This is after they shock you unconscious, of course. And they stick it in above one of your eyes."

"Stop it." Lotte forgot the sticky sidecar soaking into the sofa and her dress. Her throat burned with bile, but the tiniest part of her was curious, too. Nearly four years of marriage, and Albert had only hinted at the horrors he'd endured. How many months ago had this icepick thing been invented? He'd held onto it all this time, although she supposed he had James to discuss it with.

"Takes ten minutes for both sides. So they ram the pick up there and squish it back and forth."

"Albert." Mostly, he was lazy with his grammar and peppered their conversations with vulgar slang. Of all the times to have missed his calling as a novelist.

"Of course, they tap it with a hammer to really get it in there." Her interruption hadn't registered. "In ten minutes, the front of your brain looks like a bloody, mashed-up beet, and you're either dead or worse than."

Stomach roiling, Lotte took the stairs by twos, but hardly made it to the toilet before heaving up her guts and most of the first sidecar. 'A mashed-up beet.' Who knew Albert had such a way with words? To think she'd never heard of this Dr. Freeman, whose invention was making her husband's life into such a hell.

"Come on, doll." A long-fingered hand rough with factory work appeared before her, but she shook her head. "I'm sorry. It's not your fault, is it?"

Lotte clenched her back teeth. Any idiot knew it wasn't her fault. It wasn't as though she thought he could be cured or wanted him to be. This was happening daily within walking distance and had happened to the person beside her. It was widespread. A decent person ought to be sickened.

"At least try some water." Still clutching his third or fourth cigarette, Albert slumped beside her on the floor. He had filled the glass she used for brushing her teeth. The water was tepid and minty, but she sipped it.

"Why do you hate me so much?" she asked him.

"I don't." He sounded genuinely horrified. He even put the cigarette out. "For Christ's sake, doll. I've never hated you. You're my wife. Just because I don't think it's some kind of mystical sacrament doesn't mean I don't care. I provide for you, don't I? Are you wanting for anything?" She didn't look at him, but could picture the wry grin. "Anything I can give, that is."

"No." Even if he could love her, she wouldn't want it from him. "I'm not. You're right. You're a good provider."

'A dangerous path,' indeed. She wondered what it was she'd done to deserve a husband who talked about icepicks and brains and electric shocks until she lost her dinner, and a priest who could make her as live and hot as any bare wire. She prayed when she ought, fasted when she should, and was kind to people. If she were as flighty as

Albert, she might become an atheist for that reason alone.

Her head ached. Whether it was from sickness or the power of suggestion, she didn't know. Finally, she knew how caged Albert must feel in their shared home. The thought of one of them leaving was the only thing that brought her up from the floor.

"Go away," she whispered. "Go to James. I don't care. Just go away."

"I was going to go later anyhow," he said. "You're probably right." He refilled the water glass, wet a washcloth, and gave the top of her hand a dry pat before he turned to leave.

Lotte waited until he was out the door and halfway down the block. Although she'd been drained by everything Albert had told her, she felt strangely awake, too. She'd wanted to be alone for three days, ever since Henry and she had been together. Thousands of thoughts whipped across her mind daily, but now that she had space to think, she hardly bothered with them. The pulse of his thumb, the brush of his tongue, the slight salt of his jawbone under her lips, lips which she now licked at the memory. He wanted to talk to her so badly after Mass now; she could tell.

Her clothes dropped to the floor, and when she closed her eyes, she saw bright yellow and white, her own scarlet cheeks, a swish of green linen against black and white flooring, and a mysterious deep pink. She wanted to take her brush, dip it in every one of those colors, and swirl it against the canvas until the bristles broke.

Pulling the pins from her already mussed hair, she turned the tap on the shower as hot as it would go and stepped inside. The pain was more than she expected. Its shrieks zapped like the shocks on every single place Albert had mentioned. When she could stand it no more, she tempered the water with cold and picked up the washcloth. Lotte exhaled and leaned back against the tile wall. Her body had taken the shower's unbearable wet heat and drawn it all inwards.

Lotte's breath trembled from between her lips. She wasn't quite sure if this was panic or desire or some unholy combination of both. Her mind played the kiss again like a newsreel. Henry's scent, the incense and the tiniest bit of aftershave and the sweaty musk from their walk up the hill. His fingers slipping against her cheek. Their bodies pressing together.

What if she had gone out of his bathroom without getting dressed first? He'd have marched her back in to get her clothes before tossing her out of the house, but suppose he'd still kissed her. Put his hands on her bare flesh. Slowly, her skin cerise from the heat, Lotte wound the washcloth downward and across all the sensitive points that still ached three days after Henry had kissed her.

After Mass, Henry didn't even bother watching for Lotte. She would have disappeared again, which made him morose and too sour for a bright Thursday as June opened. Ignoring William, he stormed toward his office and threw himself into a chair.

"Henry?" A soft knock, and his heart lifted despite itself.

"Ah." He opened the door, closed it, and turned the lock. "The prodigal friend returns."

"I've wanted to talk to you," Lotte said. "But I didn't think it would be wise."

"It's not wise," he said and regretted her wince. She was trying to do right, and he was too harsh. "I'm sorry. This hasn't been an easy couple of days."

"No, it hasn't." A shade of a smile flicked on, then off. "My life was difficult before you— Before we kissed."

Dammit, the word 'kissed' from her mouth made him blush and tremble like some idiot obsessed with romance magazines and Hollywood stars.

"I know it was," he said and finally offered her a chair. Because he couldn't bear to sit across the desk from her, he sat beside her as usual. "And if you've experienced anything like I have in the past four and a half days, I imagine it's far more difficult now."

"Well, yes," she said. "But it's also better. That's what I wanted to tell you. I can tell it's not the same for you. I should go."

"Don't leave." He was kneeling in front of her, blocking the exit before he even knew what was happening. "Lotte, I want your life to be better. You're one I think is truly deserving of it. I want nothing more than to keep on being friends. We can control ourselves, we—"

Her fingers twisted into his hair and stroked a light, timid path down his cheeks. She was going to kill him.

"I do want to be your friend, Henry," she said. "And I know that we've done wrong. I just can't bring myself to…"

"To regret it?" He sprang up and clutched her shoulders. "Neither can I, and I've tried everything."

"Everything?" She half-laughed. "What all have you tried?"

"The usual round of priestly penances." Something in her look and tone comforted him enough to sit down. "Rosaries, chaplets, more rosaries."

"More chaplets?" She reached across the gap and squeezed his hand. "I've tried everything, too."

Their chairs were close enough together that when they both leaned forward, their lips met with ease. Henry traced the line of her hair at the base of her head, cupped it in one hand, and moved a hand down to her back, where the outline of a brassiere rested just out of sight. The taste of her was familiar now, and he grew bolder, drew her onto his lap, and felt her soft, plump thighs shifting against him.

When she pulled away, her eyes were hazy and her mouth swollen. He was swollen, too, and impatient with need, but she rested her cheek on his shoulder, buried her face in his neck, and he found another sort of bliss just in that. He wondered at her shyness—she was the one who was married, after all—but thought maybe all women were modest. His mother had lectured his sisters about modesty often enough. He'd been stunted in all this by his celibate years, and now felt no more confident than a seventeen-year-old behind the movie house.

"Henry?" She raised her head. Her eyes, when they met his, were no longer dazed, but dark and penetrative, as though she could read every thought he'd ever had. "Have you ever?"

"Once," he said. "Well, twice. Before… Before."

"I haven't." Her gaze remained steady, even as her eyes filled.

"What? What do you mean?" Maybe the atheist had a mistress, but how could he not at least consummate his marriage? A tiny shivering thrill shot through Henry, which disturbed him.

"Albert," Lotte said. "He's—"

"He's got a mistress." Well, perhaps William was more worldly than he looked. Lotte did know.

"I suppose you could say that." She seemed almost amused for a moment before her expression became utterly chilling. "He's not able to do anything like that with me, and I wouldn't want him to. We don't desire each other. Albert needs me for other things."

Money, of course. Using and tricking. Henry wasn't so naïve after all.

"Albert's not what you think," she said. "He's— He's a homosexual."

A...? What the hell? Fine, Henry was naïve. "He—? Really?"

Lotte nodded. "He's an atheist because he claims he was created a homosexual, and yet sodomy is a sin. It doesn't make sense to him. Nor to me, honestly. And he does have a mistress, but his name is James."

"Did you know?"

"That he was a homosexual before we married?" The corner of her lip tipped upward. "After Julienne, I practically lived in my parents' attic, painting and keeping animals in secret. They opened the College for Women, but my parents thought it would be a waste. I imagine the attic was a bit like being in the cloister. I had no idea that men could even love each other that way. All he said was it wouldn't be a normal marriage. That I shouldn't expect to have a baby—and even I knew how that worked—and I was doing him the greatest favor in the world."

"You do realize that you're not validly married," he said.

"Of course I realize it." She jumped off his lap and left him cold. "What kind of moron do you think I am? It wasn't consummated, and we knew beforehand we wouldn't have a child. But do you have any idea what would happen to him if I left?" Her pale skin went green around the gills, and she clenched her jaw. "It's unspeakable."

"Do you care for him, then?"

"No. Yes, I do. I care, but not in the way I—" She looked at her feet. "I care for you. But he saved me from my parents' house."

"Were they cruel to you?" His voice was lower and more menacing than he intended, as though he could leap aboard the trolley to Belmonte Park and confront the dastardly Mr. Klopstock.

"Not cruel," she said. "Cold. I suppose coldness is cruel for a child to endure. They wanted me gone, and I wanted to be gone. I was twenty-six, and none of their friends' dreadful sons had taken the bait. At least with Albert, I don't have to hide in the attic. He lets me do as I please."

"You care for me?" He rose to his feet, too, and took both her hands.

Still not meeting his eyes, she nodded, and this time, the tears did spill over. "I know it's the most wicked thing in the world to love you, but it doesn't feel wicked at all. It feels natural, and nothing I've ever known is natural. Parents should love their daughters. Men should desire their wives. It's the way of things, right?"

Henry shrugged. He found he didn't care if Albert Walheim desired fruitful union with men or with sheep or with trolley cars, as long as he didn't desire Lotte. He passed her a handkerchief, but didn't wait for her to use it before flinging his arms around her neck and kissing the dewy salt cheeks. He was a priest. He was probably going to hell. But Lotte cared for him. He supposed he'd deal with hell once he got there.

CHAPTER TEN

Y ou know what? I grew up a mile away, and I've never been here once," Lotte said. She licked her tongue around the edge of an ice cream cone and wiped away the drips with a paper napkin.

"Not once?" Henry swung his legs into the space between the water and the pier. "My folks started bringing the kids up here once they built the band shell."

"I think James and Albert come here sometimes," she said. How freeing to speak openly about them. "But I can't stand any of those Victorian marches and brass bands. And the place was considered vulgar when I was young, especially by my parents. Remember the headlines about shimmy dancing and drinking while it was still illegal?"

"Not really," he said. "I wasn't keen enough to read the news as a child. I do agree with you about the Sousa bands. My brothers and sisters and even their children give me grief, but I've been pretty fixed on the opera since I was a kid."

"So have I," Lotte said. "I used to attend before I was married, but my parents won't let me use their box now, and Albert won't take me. He likes his Hit Parade and that's about it."

"That's a shame," Henry said before he polished off the rest of a chocolate cone. "A damn shame. He ought to be considerate, considering."

Henry's ire on her behalf made her insides warm and melting as the rest of her ice cream. She tossed the cone off the pier and turned to look at him. "Considerate, considering? You have quite the eloquent tongue, don't you?"

He grabbed her hand and yanked her toward him, but seemed to reconsider, given his cassock and the broad daylight. Wearing a cassock to Island Park was ill-advised, but so was going out without one under Father Kestner's eye. "I've given you no reason to be dissatisfied with my tongue."

Lord, but he was terrible. Lotte stood.

"I'll be party to no more of this," she said. "Henry Werther behaving like Caliban in the middle of Island Park."

"You're right." Henry ambled to his feet. "I ought to get back. We've been gone for three hours. William will wonder. Not that I regret this." He reached for her hand and kissed it. "It was very sensible of you to stop avoiding me."

"You are an ass," Lotte said, and was thrilled when he didn't take offense. Teasing Henry in fun was much more satisfying than needling Albert in spite. "Perhaps I was right the first time."

"I have half a mind to dunk you in the river," he said. "But you're far too pretty."

"Stop," she said. As flattering as his words were, she wasn't strong enough to take them as mere words. And she shouldn't. After all, they weren't mere lovers. Between seeing Henry and denying herself, or not seeing Henry and denying herself, it was better to see him. Both their hearts were continually slapped and churned up, like water under the oars of those famous Island Park canoes. Tiring, bruising, it was all of that, but she'd rather keep her heart bobbing in the current than entombed at the bottom. Lotte didn't enjoy the hurt, but it was undeniably better than being frozen and suffocated.

"I'm sorry," Henry said. "I don't know what to do. Your friendship has been..." He bit his lip and started across the island toward Helena Street. "A blessing. Yes. A blessing. And to think of losing it..."

"I know," she said. "It is a blessing. It feels as though you were put in my path and not simply to test me. I don't know what to do either, but I don't think it's this."

Because it was the middle of the afternoon on a Monday, the band shell was empty, and everyone who'd bothered with the park that day was busy along the riverfront. They ducked into one of the concrete alcoves where the air was cool and dark.

Henry bent to kiss her, but she pushed him away. "You taste like chocolate." There were some things she couldn't abide, even for him.

He didn't sigh or groan or protest. He simply moved to the tender skin at the base of her neck and attended to that instead. Her skin prickled with gooseflesh, and her cheeks grew hot.

"Henry," she said in a low tone, and he stopped to look at her.

"Never again," he said. "Will I take hearing my name spoken for granted."

Her eyes were level with the bump in his throat. She could lean forward with ease and kiss the spot where she imagined his collarbone came together. How wrong, but how delicious would it be to see it for herself, the collar gone, the high buttons undone. Or all of them undone. Lotte shivered, and it wasn't from the shady shelter of the band shell.

"What's the matter?" he asked.

"You don't want to know." The look she gave him was coy, lazy, told him without telling him that she'd undressed in his bathroom without his knowledge, had done the same in her own, and had held herself in thrall to a terry washcloth. "I was wondering something, though."

He kissed her almost apologetically, sticky, chocolaty lips and all. "What is it?"

"You said that you'd been with a woman before. What—? That is, why? When?"

Henry laughed, which she hadn't expected, and eased away from her until she could breathe and think like a regular person.

"Her name was Evelyn," he said. "She was a couple of years older than me. A friend of my sister Clara. I was seventeen, about to go off to seminary. She found that…" He narrowed his gaze into the middle distance and plucked a word from the breeze. "Attractive. And

I wanted to see what I was giving up. It wasn't some great romance. To this day, I'm not sure if I was able to— Well, if we… Anyhow, it was short-lived."

Lotte raised an eyebrow. How nice of him to be circumspect around her when her husband kissed his lover in the middle of their living room and described the rape of a man's brain with brutal poetry. "So it wasn't the stuff of Shakespeare?"

"Well, I gave it up."

"Yes." Her conscience prickled. "Yes, you did."

A deep sigh. He took her hand and led her back into the sunlight, down the street to where the trolley stopped. "That's what I gave up. That kind of thing. Not this. I was stupid, a teenager, dumb enough to think that's what lovemaking looked like. If it had been with you…"

The unfinished sentence wove a tapestry with the heat, the smell of wild clover, and the breeze from the river. The trolley screeched to a halt. They paid their fares and found it almost empty.

"What? You regret your vocation?" It ought to have thrilled her, but Lotte was oddly uncomfortable with inciting such a thing. Priests gave up marriage, first and foremost. Giving up lovemaking and movie house fumbling was implied. "That's an awful thing to say."

"I don't," he said. "Honestly. From the time I was, good Lord, eleven probably, it's been all I've wanted. I don't know what I mean; probably only that I wish it were possible to have both."

Some people thought it was. She thought about Protestantism and heresy and the strange talk about 'the parson's wife' she'd heard among the Lutherans in her art class years ago. Henry was an ordained priest, not a heretic, but Lotte found herself wishing the same thing.

"Nice time at the park, Father?" The trolley driver glanced back at Henry and gave Lotte a dubious look.

"Yes, thank you for asking." Before her eyes, Henry dissolved, and Father Henry, equal parts warm and earnest, appeared on the bench beside her. He didn't move, but his shoulders seemed straighter, and he was no more the man she'd kissed and bantered with than he was on Sunday mornings. Father Henry and the trolley driver fell into chatting, and Lotte edged away. Perhaps she fled from him often enough, but he could flee from her without moving so much as a hair.

When the trolley, now mercifully full of people, dropped Henry near St. Jerome's, she didn't move to depart with him. The next stop was closer to her house. The driver was suspicious, and she could do without the awkward goodbye.

Cars honked and swerved at the intersection. The hospital's dome loomed above them all. A couple of the houses along Wayne Avenue had flowers blooming in their terraced gardens, but the flowers were starting to wilt. The air was stiller and hotter here than it had been along the river, and the humidity pressed close to Lotte even as she rounded the corner to Edgar's quieter sidewalk. After the trolley ride, the disappointment, the subtle change, and the river breeze, Lotte remained taut and aware. Little things like her dress shifting against her or the jounce of concrete beneath her low-heeled shoes made her more tense and more miserable than she'd been when he'd pressed her into the rough band shell and teased the skin she was cradling now. Facing Henry in the morning would be terrible. Not only was she more aware of him than ever, but she also had the sense that they'd argued during the trolley ride without even speaking.

"Albert?" The house reeked of stale Marlboro smoke and too many male bodies. "Hello?" Lotte closed the door and heard the radio sputtering with what she assumed was Sammy Kaye's newest.

"...another place we can go?" A voice she didn't recognize filtered through the smoke and staticky trumpets. "What're we supposed to do?"

"Get the hell out, that's what." James's voice. "What'd'you think this whole thing in the papers is about? They've even started naming fellas they think are queer."

"Naming?" Another strange voice, higher-pitched than the first. "Naming who?"

"No one we know," James said. "No one anyone knows. Some jerk must not know how to set the type, 'cause the names printed up all wrong."

Lotte recognized Albert's laugh and walked through the living room to find a bunch of men all clustered around her dining room table. A huge ashtray—one of her urns, actually—sat smack in the middle of some sweaty cheese, a jar of pinky-sized pickles, some empty cans of Schlitz, and a bottle of Old Mr. Boston.

"Back already?" Albert flushed and blew out a puff of smoke. "Some of the guys and me, we were just talking."

James regarded her as he always did, but the other three had glints in their eyes she didn't like. Maybe they had wives, maybe they didn't, but to them, she wasn't just the dumbest girl they'd ever seen. She was an intruder in her own house.

"So this is the beard, eh, Albert?" If someone addressed her or if Albert introduced her as Mrs. Walheim, she was going to die.

"How was shopping?" Albert shifted in his chair and flicked the ash from his cigarette one too many times. "Guys, this is my—"

By the time he would have said 'wife,' Lotte was halfway across the yard. Her pocketbook smacked against her thigh, so she tossed it into the shrubbery. Her shoes slipped and clacked on the sidewalk, so she slid them off. If Barbara Morris and her daughters were out for a stroll, they'd see lonely, childless Lotte Walheim running barefoot through Walnut Hills in the middle of the afternoon. She couldn't have cared less. Her throat burned after the haze in her house, but she sucked in air and exhaled shame all the way up Wyoming Street and past St. Jerome's.

Henry's block was quiet, and this time she did take care to avoid being noticed. She could run wild as though she'd escaped Dayton State, but she wasn't about to compromise him. Too winded and wounded to feel anxious, she rapped on the door. Then again. No answer.

Likely, he was in his office or in the confessional, but she didn't want to see him in the church. Going to him in the confessional would be more than tawdry, and she had been oppressed by enough close walls, enough dim light, and enough shame today. Possessed by some demon, Lotte tried the doorknob and wasn't entirely surprised when it turned in her hand.

When she stepped onto the carpet just beyond the patch of tiles that served as a foyer, she dropped to her knees. Pain clawed and jabbed at her insteps. The white tiles bore drips of blood. Lotte crawled into the bathroom, turned the tap on the tub, and tugged off her shredded nylons while the water burbled away. She let it half fill. She wasn't bold enough to undress here a second time, especially when she had broken into his house. The bath was warm and soothed away the pebbles and tiny shards of bottle-green glass. She reached up to splash her face, too.

God, she was an idiot. Friends, friends who kissed each other, or whatever else they were, Henry wasn't going to like her barging in, not after their lack of words on the trolley. She could leave before he got home, but what was she going to do without shoes? Borrow Henry's? He was a head taller, and besides, she'd have to return them, and how would she explain that? And even at a sedate pace, clerical shoes were bound to attract more attention than stockinged bare feet.

When she felt capable of standing, Lotte pulled the plug on the tub and watched the water whirl down the drain. The bright white towels looked too nice to mar, so she dabbed at her feet with toilet tissue and found an evil-looking bottle of iodine to dab on the last bloody cut. It zinged worse than the carpet had, but it slowed the bleeding and would keep her from getting lockjaw.

Listen to her being practical. If that wasn't closing the barn door after the proverbial horse had run down the street barefoot, she didn't know what was. Since breaking into Henry's home, she'd used his bathtub, raided his medicine cabinet, and gotten blood on his tile floor. Damn. The blood. She wet another tissue and padded across the living room.

Cold and unyielding beneath her fingers, the tile gave away the blood easily, even to the flimsy paper. Lotte's fingers trembled and crushed the sodden bit of tissue. It was unconscionable, really. She wanted Henry not just to come home, but to come home to her. Come home to her, kiss her, take her into his lap again, and make her forget about 'my wife,' 'the beard,' and those smirks that had flayed her open.

Of course, Henry wasn't going to react with tenderness. He would be furious, fuming, livid, outraged, and she had nowhere to go. Perhaps if she nabbed just his socks or carpet slippers or just walked back barefoot over the gritty concrete or the tickling lawns. Her stomach swooped and fluttered a cadenza, and her pulse beat in cut time.

Once, shortly after she'd married, she'd seen the trolley tip on the Wilmington hill, people flung out all over the road. Everyone had stopped to stare, even she, and the wail of sirens was as haunting as the evening bell clanging away after Vespers. Transfixed, she'd floated outside herself, up and over the park, the hospital, and the sprawling trolley, until someone had grabbed her by the elbow and shoved her aside. That was when she'd realized she was staring and that she couldn't move.

She was so stupid. What if Father Kestner came back with him or one of his sisters or the woman who cleaned the clergymen's homes? The wreckage of her humiliation would be bad enough to bear with only Henry as a witness, and she would humiliate him, too.

When the doorknob began to turn, her back teeth clenched, and her eyes didn't blink, even when the tips of his shoes appeared around the door.

"Lotte," he said. "What on earth are you doing here?"

She kept her focus on his shoes and hem and found her throat too tight for speech.

"Look at me." And again, "What are you doing here?"

"I don't know." Lotte doubted he could hear her.

Henry stuck his hands under her armpits and hauled her to her feet. The bitter spice of smoked out myrrh floated about them. He was angry, but his hands stayed curled around her ribcage, wrists brushing the sides of her breasts.

"Lotte," he said. "If you want to see me, this is not the appropriate—"

"I know, damn it." Her sharpness and the curse made Henry leap back. "Don't scold me like some naughty child. I've been dreading you coming home for over an hour."

"An hour? How long have you been here?"

"What is it you want? I avoid you, and you come and find me. I come to you, and you tell me it's inappropriate." Lotte reached out both hands, shoved the broad chest aside, and scrabbled for the door, the devil take her bare feet. "I told you, I don't understand all this any better than you do." All this suffering between extremes was too much like purgatory. Perhaps she'd had enough for today.

95

"Where are your shoes?"

"What?"

"Your shoes." He was trying to suppress a shudder at the sight of her naked toes. "Did you walk here without them?" His temper subsided, and he asked, "What happened, Lotte?"

She produced the crumpled, bloody tissue, which rested on her palm like a snowball.

"Has Albert been cruel to you?" His figure seemed to double in size, but his words were soft.

"Yes," she said. For heaven's sake, what did Henry think he was going to do? Barrel through the neighborhood himself and challenge Albert to a fistfight? "But he hasn't touched me. I don't think he ever would. And I don't think he was cruel on purpose."

Henry mussed his hair with both hands, tugged the collar from around his throat, and nodded to the sofa. "But you're hurt."

"I lost my shoes running here," she said. "I couldn't leave without shoes. I didn't mean to come in. I knocked. There was glass on the sidewalk. A bunch of Albert's friends were at our house. I think they're closing the Wayne Tavern. His friends aren't terribly kind. Not to me, anyhow."

"His friends are unkind to you," Henry said. "Despite the fact that you're protecting him at your own expense?"

Lotte shrugged. Who could explain the Wayne Tavern set to a priest who believed he was called to help people?

"You could have come to my office," he said. "I've been there all afternoon."

"I wanted to see you here," she said. "I'm sorry. I know things ended badly today."

"Badly?" He blinked. "What are you talking about? We rode the trolley home."

Despite everything, a giggle burst forth at his or her or their mutual cluelessness.

"Now that the shock has worn off," he said and bit his lip. "It is nice having someone here in the evening."

"When we're not together," Lotte said. "I miss you." More than that, she found herself storing up things she wanted to tell him, practicing looks she might give him, and pressing the soft parts of two fingers to her lips and pretending it was he.

"You ran straight here?" He took her hands in his and kissed her fingertips.

"I wasn't thinking clearly, but yes." She freed her hands, but kept her fingers against his jawline, where rough stubble had started. "I should go. Albert might be worried."

"You think so?"

"Maybe," she said. "He's not a bad man, Henry." The drawn, battle-weary look and the stories about electric shocks weren't hers to tell, not even to Henry. Lotte was willing to put up with James and the Wayne Tavern set if it meant keeping a person's brain from looking like a mashed-up beet.

"What if he could be cured? You'd be his true wife then?"

"He can't be cured," she said. "I don't think it's a disease. Nothing as simple as that. He's as sane as anyone else."

"Hm. Well, don't go yet. Aren't you hungry?"

Lotte laughed. "Yes, I'm hungry. You're going to cook me supper?"

"My sisters leave things for me," he said. "And my mom. They never got around to teaching us cooking amid the Scylla of despair and the Charybdis of unheeding indulgence in vice."

"Oh, not that again." He really ought to start reading novels or magazines or the like. "It's not hard. I learned after I married Albert."

"Do your parents do nothing for you?" he asked.

"Not really," she said. "They fed and sheltered me for twenty-six years, which was eight more years than they'd intended. They're through. But never mind. What did your sister leave you?"

"Some ham or something. I don't know. Lotte." He closed his eyes. "I'm no good at all this. I'm not supposed to be good at all this. I told you about Evelyn, but that was fifteen years ago."

"What do you mean?" Lotte asked. When Henry's eyes opened, the look was intent, the pupils wide and dark. The bare rectangle of throat thrummed and convulsed when he swallowed.

"I think about you, too, when we're not together," he said. His face edged closer, but he didn't kiss her, not even with his parted lips. Lotte could see every detail of his iris, the coffee-dark ridges, and the melting of them into hers. They very nearly filled for a second. The closest a person could come to almost crying without risking it. "I love you, Lotte. That's what this is. It has to be. I want you to love me just as much. And I know I've fallen into—"

"But I do love you," she said before he could say something like 'depravity.' How could love be depraved? Simple lust might be depraved, but she felt her soul opening and expanding when she was with Henry. He felt it, too. He had just told her so. Lotte wasn't going to cry either, but she couldn't help but blush. "Of course, this is love. And I think you're very good at 'all this.' If anyone's bad at it, it's me, and I'm supposed to be a wife." Henry's gaze didn't waver, aside from a small wince on the word 'wife.' Lotte felt safer and more comforted than she had in the rest of her thirty years, but she was still as hot as she'd been against her washcloth in her scalding shower. Where did love and lust begin or end or converge? Ordinarily and by the laws of God, with marriage, but nothing about this was ordinary.

When Henry kissed her, it was different than before. She leaned into him and thought of a dozen different things all at the same time. The places that had rasped against her washcloth in the shower pulsed and spread shivering waves in every direction. Would he know to touch there? Were they even going to do that? If she could read his kiss and the pressure of his hands, then yes, they were. Lotte drew back and pulled the pins from her hair, which licked down her shoulders in fiery points.

Her dress buttoned up the front, and he reached for the modest top button. His fingers against it made her skin snap to attention. Lotte nodded her assent, and the line of buttons fell open to her navel. Henry sketched the outline of her breasts with his fingertips and buried his face in the hollow of her collarbone. Coriander, myrrh, and balsam smoke tickled her nose along with his hair, which was soft and springy. His hands were heavy on her breasts now, kneading them, and she squeezed his fingers.

"Wait."

He raised his head, and the expression was guilty and pained.

"It hurts that way," she said. Lotte took his hand and traced the same path she had with the washcloth, grazing just the tips until he caught on.

"I'm sorry," he said. "I don't really know…"

"You will," she said. They were both whispering despite being alone in the house. His heavy grip aside, she was on fire for him. None of this was a challenge to solve. Her body knew where it wanted him to touch. "We will." Apparently the bolder of the two, she reached over and unbuttoned until they were equal. His chest wasn't bare beneath his cassock as she'd imagined, and she saw the snap of a waistband. "Oh."

He smirked in the middle of it all. "Sorry to disappoint." He stood and shrugged out of it, and pulled her up before she could admire him in shirtsleeves. Lotte's dress fell to the floor as she stood. His embrace while standing was more intimate somehow, running the length of each other, and barely clad. She moved as close to him as she could, their kisses more practiced now, but their hands still unsure. Henry desired her as much as she desired him. He felt hard against her when she pressed close, and she'd overheard enough to know what that pressure against his zipper meant.

"Henry?" she asked. "Will you touch me? I've thought about— I mean, that's what I want."

"You've thought about it?" He began to struggle with the rest of her clothes. The brassiere hooks. The panties. She reached up and unhooked, reached down and peeled off. His fingers found the spot that was embarrassingly plump and wet, and she lost control of her senses. His fingers were even more electric than her washcloth. This was Henry touching her, and not the mere idea of Henry touching her. Lotte moaned. "So have I."

Before she'd married, before she knew Albert wouldn't be bothering with it, the idea of being naked before her husband was part of the reason she'd resisted her mother's efforts to find her one. Being bared to Henry while he figured out what to do with her was the least humiliating thing she'd ever done. She was even plumper and wetter now, but it embarrassed her less with each slide of his fingers. Lotte wanted to know exactly what he'd thought about doing with her, but couldn't ask. And she shouldn't be the only one undressed.

Henry slipped out of his shirtsleeves to his chest, brushed with black curls. He eased his trousers over the swollen zipper, and she began to touch him, too. Living as she did, she ought to know more about pleasing men, but Albert had never so much as hinted at the specifics. Henry moaned, too, and every muscle in his body jumped before trembling.

"Lotte, wait," he said and lowered them back to the sofa. His weight cut off her breath, but she was maddeningly close to that bright burst she'd had in the shower.

"No waiting." She gasped it. If he understood her, it was a miracle. She moved his fingers back where they belonged until the world flashed pink around the edges. Well beyond the washcloth. A tiny shriek ripped from her throat, and she bucked against Henry's fingers and the full weight of him. Her legs flung around his waist as she arced off the sofa.

Henry closed the tiny gap between them, and they were as one flesh. Lotte had worried about the pain of it or the shock of it, but it wasn't altogether painful. How could it be, as slippery and as boneless as she was now? Her body adjusted to his as though he'd been fashioned for her alone. A tiny hum sounded from the back of her throat. She arced again. Henry was going out of his mind with desire, and she wanted to satisfy him, too. Make him shriek and lose his senses just like her.

He moved with unsteady and uneven pulses, breath rough in her ear. His muscles were still trembling. Lotte felt something primal in him take over, move him faster and faster until he groaned and went as limp as she. He didn't move away from her, and she noticed now that they were both wet and sticky, the lamps too bright, and that he still wore his socks. Unromantic facts aside, Lotte had the sense that Henry was now truly hers and she his, that feedeth among the lilies.

CHAPTER ELEVEN

I was especially prideful the other day. And gluttonous, of course. I took seconds on dessert two nights in a row, and…"

Henry felt his eyes begin to slide closed. Dessert seconds? Really? Worse than dessert seconds was the fact that he could recognize Barbara Morris's voice a mile away. He cringed with dread when he heard that nasal 'bless me, Father' and smelled her strange camphor scent in the close, stale air. Lotte smelled of lemon and lavender, and her voice was pleasing, especially when she'd cried out in his arms and gasped his name without realizing she had. With half an ear on Barbara Morris as she took him through the seven deadly sins—all of which she had somehow committed in forty-eight hours—Henry sank into a reverie wherein he was joined to Lotte, he knew what the hell he was doing with her, and he wasn't so damn terrified that he couldn't move them to the bed or damn well ask if he'd hurt her.

"Father?"

"Yes." Henry cleared his throat. Because this was Barbara Morris, he asked, "Was there anything else on your conscience?" Surely there couldn't be, but she mumbled something about coveting this or that. He assigned her some penance that would keep her at bay, absolved her, and sent her on her merry way.

No one else came in after her. Henry hung his head in the close darkness of his perch in the confessional and pinched the bridge of his nose. A pain though Mrs. Morris was, he had just celebrated a sacrament with the bulk of his thoughts elsewhere and on his own sins besides. He ought to be in her place on the other side of the confessional. It didn't escape him, of course, that all his aims to help and shepherd the people had fixed squarely on Lotte.

Henry emerged from the booth and stumbled into William.

"Could we have a word, Henry?" he asked, expression grave. Without waiting for an answer, he gestured toward his office. William didn't look back. Henry would follow him without question, of course.

Follow William, he did, on shaking legs, watery and wobbly as Barbara Morris's Jell-O seconds. If Lotte had gone to his house in broad daylight, it stood to reason some nosy parishioner had seen her, but his blinds had been drawn all day. Had someone seen her running barefoot down the street? That wasn't necessarily to do with him.

William's door thudded closed. The lock clicked, and William peered at his protégé over the rims of his glasses.

"It has come to my attention," he said. "That Mrs. Walheim was here in the church last night. Apparently without her shoes."

"Yes, she was." This he could explain. "She and Mr. Walheim argued, and she ran out of the house."

"To your office?" William crossed his arms over his chest, his ill-fitting cassock puffing over his plump form. "When you had already retired to your lodgings for the night?"

"She did knock on my door," he said. "But I informed her it was inappropriate." He had, hadn't he? Or at least, he'd tried before she'd snapped at him. Then he'd told her he'd fallen in love with her, and their clothes had started melting away. But never mind it for now. The only bare things William had asked about were her feet. "I did allow her to borrow my shoes under the circumstances." Borrow, keep. Even from Lotte, he didn't want a pair of shoes blemished by another's feet. "I took her to my office and let her telephone him. He came for her, they made up, and he took her home."

Whatever snitch had seen shoeless Lotte or Lotte in his clerical shoes had to have seen Mr. Walheim's shiny black Ford pull up out front. No sacristan would have known that Mr. Walheim's contrite expression had been on behalf of the Wayne Tavern set. Credit where it was due, Mr. Walheim had put an arm over his wife's shoulders and murmured something to her that had made her nod and her expression turn sympathetic. If Henry hadn't entirely liked seeing that, he had to admit, it would put people off the truth of the matter. People would suppose it was like Lotte Walheim to seek priestly counsel. It was like a woman to go dashing out without sense or shoes. And it was like any ordinary couple to have a little tiff.

William appeared relieved. "So I figured. But, Henry, you're a young man. You must notice the attention you get from the ladies of our parish. The majority are worthy women. Mrs. Walheim, I think, is no exception, but temptation can take the form of even the noblest of things."

"I am not," Henry said. "Tempted by Mrs. Walheim." For he did not consider it thus, not now. He could not be both called to her and tempted by her, for God would not tempt, and he refused to believe that honest love was anything but divine.

"I don't call your morals into question," he said, his tone softer now. "Only to suggest that if Mrs. Walheim is unhappy enough at home to dash outside barefoot, perhaps she might be tempted by you. I know I told you to counsel her, but if that leads to lustfulness on her part, it would not be right. She is bound by vocation as much as you are bound."

"Well, naturally." Lotte was right. It was irritating to be talked down to. He wondered what William would say if he told him that Lotte wasn't quite exactly bound by matrimony, and that Mr. Walheim was a homosexual atheist. "Father, I can handle my own affairs."

William shoved his glasses back into place and took a seat behind his desk. "Well, if the need arises, you could always send her to me. I doubt my face will be comely enough to rouse her interest."

"Was that a joke, Father?"

"I suppose it was," he said. "Henry, my father was a cautionary tale. I've learned to live a life contrary to his example. Therefore, I won't be a father in any literal sense. If I were, though." William turned his apparent attention to a leather-bound volume. "I should hope my son would have your conviction."

Henry bowed his head, but William was frowning into the

book. His head was bent, his face hidden, and the shock of grey on his pate falling forward. If Henry's love for Lotte were known, his true father, his entire family, would be sad and disappointed, but they'd come around in the end. His family would accept Lotte and pet her, and Clara would regale her with stories of Henry as a schoolboy. William would blame himself.

Walking away from William's office, Henry heard the one o'clock bell, sonorous and soothing above them. What was it William wanted from his life, anyhow? He didn't care to help anyone, or love anyone, or even befriend anyone. Helping, loving, and befriending, these things were all Henry wanted, and he had three in one person with Lotte. Initial flash of fear aside, given that William had almost followed him home yesterday, coming home to Lotte had settled the loneliness that had started with living closer to Clara and the rest, or had started years ago with that winter couple and lain dormant.

High giggles broke into his thoughts. Today was Tuesday, and the Legion of Mary meeting was just wrapping up. The so-called worthy women paid him plenty of attention. William was nothing if not observant. Henry, muttering an act of contrition even as he did so, ducked behind a pillar. He was in love, and he was hiding from eleven women. Whether that was comedy or tragedy, Henry wasn't sure.

"...another baby." Mrs. Morris again, sounding as though she had a carrot shoved up each nostril. "Already. And you know Bill was away for a month."

"Well, if that doesn't beat all." Muriel Anderson? Yes, that's who it was. "And you know what I heard about Bill's boss? It's been in the *Dayton Daily* and everything. He's a queer. They found it in his old army records."

It was funny, really. For all the confessing she did, Barbara Morris had never once brought up gossiping.

"And you know, they closed down that Wayne Tavern and arrested almost ten guys. Paper says it's closed for good now. It attracts too much of that kind. Makes you wonder, doesn't it?"

"Yeah," Mrs. Anderson said. "Bill's boss got fired and everything. Heard he was moving out to Chicago."

"Hang on." The women passed directly before him and

sauntered toward the door. Mrs. Morris flicked her lighter. "I thought Bill's boss was married?"

"Oh, I wouldn't know. Never met the woman, if there was one. You know what I did hear, though—?" The heavy door opened, slammed, and the women disappeared.

He had struggled since the early days in Cincinnati not to feel disdain for women like this, but today, he didn't bother to quench it. Not just because he knew those ladies gave Lotte the brush off every other day, but because they used St. Jerome's as a place to cool their heels, smoke Virginia Slims, and chatter. He was in danger of idealizing Lotte, he realized, but couldn't deny that she didn't and wouldn't indulge in any of that. With a wife like Lotte, a man could rest easy.

Was that what he wanted then? A wife? After nearly a decade of study and four years in the priesthood? On the other hand, he had lain with Lotte as a husband did. However ineptly. He grimaced. Perhaps he wouldn't need to worry about deciding upon a vocation. She very well might never speak to him again. He recalled her jerky fingers as she dressed, her wide eyes, and the way she'd walked five steps ahead of him the entire half block to the church.

"Did you hear old Mr. Braun bought the farm?" Albert's sister stubbed out another cigarette. "Last week. Heard it from Mrs. Hilgeman at St. Mary's. The old lady went to his Mass, but Pop didn't even bother. Baby, can I bum another smoke?" Without waiting for a reply, she grabbed for Albert's shiny, red-and-white Marlboro pack. "Thanks."

"Hyacinth." Albert snatched them away and lit one himself. "Get your own, why don't you?"

"Don't be a boor," she said. "Lotte, honey, d'you hear how he talks to his sister?"

"Albert, give her a cigarette," Lotte said. She snuck a peek at Cynthie's silent husband. Lou was twisting a dripping glass of iced tea that spattered across his linen trousers in a fine mist. They saw Albert's sister only occasionally and saw even less of his parents. Lotte wondered if she looked any different to any of them—Cynthie, Lou, or Albert.

"Thank you, hon," Cynthie said and patted the slight swell of her belly. "Gotta keep my strength up, don't I?" Ash drifted into Lotte's favorite candy dish. Albert grabbed for it and shoved his rank ashtray toward her.

"Thank you," Lotte said quietly. "Can I get anyone anything else?"

"No, no, you girls take it easy," Albert said. "Lou, you ready to tackle that fuse box?"

The men clumped toward the basement. Cynthie's sighing breath crackled through the Marlboro. A glossy band of pink lipstick around the yellow paper made Lotte cringe. She'd stood up with Cynthie last year at her wedding, but the younger woman wasn't what she'd call a friend.

"Does me good to see the two of you so happy," Cynthie said to Lotte as though she were a wise, old aunt and not flighty and twenty-four. She cut her eyes left, then right, and leaned in. "Truth is, we never thought we'd see Albert cured. I think Pop still doesn't believe it. You know what the two've you need to do, hon?"

Stop inviting Cynthie for dessert, Lotte thought. *That's what we need to do.* She knew for a fact Albert's mother had whined at him to call his sister until he couldn't take it anymore, and that he'd purposely muddled the fuses to give him and Lou something to talk about.

"Well, what'd you think?" Cynthie tutted and waved her cigarette toward Lotte. "Get started on some little ones already. Never thought I'd be a mom before I was an aunt. Jesus, Albert's thirty-two, and you're what? Thirty? People'll talk."

People were already talking. Lotte thanked heaven Cynthie didn't go to St. Jerome's.

"But no matter. Think about how excited Albert'd be to be a daddy."

Lotte barely kept from blanching, but her hand slid to her stomach. A baby was entirely possible now, wasn't it? Now that she'd

106

been with Henry and led him into adultery against the Church, which was, in Lotte's opinion, far worse than adultery against Albert. She didn't think there was any baby, which saddened her a little. Albert couldn't care less about being a daddy, but Henry would be the best of them.

"Maybe, Cynthie," she said. "If we're blessed with children, of course, we'd be happy. But not everyone is. You and Lou have been lucky."

"We have." She beamed. "Say, honey, do you have any more iced tea?"

Before Lotte could reply, Albert and Lou clattered upstairs, apparently having fixed whatever it was Albert had concocted for them. Lou dragged Cynthie away, but not before she could sneak Albert's cigarettes and Lotte's best candy dish into her purse.

"Your sister took our things," Lotte said.

"I'll call Mom and get 'em back," Albert said. "She doesn't mean anything by it. Say, listen. I'm sorry again about the other day. Those guys are like James. They won't hide. They think I'm a little yellow."

"Because you don't want—?" Thoughts of mashed-up beets and bare wires against her skin made her stomach turn. "I mean, do they want to go to jail? Or worse?"

"They've never been in Dayton State, so they're pretty well fearless," he said. "Maybe it did cure me a little because it made me want to marry you at least."

"But you didn't really marry me," she said. Neither of them had ever acknowledged it out loud. "You're married to James more than you're married to me." By that logic, she was more Henry's wife, but she didn't let that settle in.

"What's eating you today?" he asked. "Did Cynthie say something? Is she on you to get knocked up? She was after me the other day when I phoned. Just ignore her. She thinks she's helping."

"Sorry. I know she does." It wasn't the first time some well-wisher had told Lotte a baby might solve all her woes. She'd just never had to listen to that talk while she was in love before. She wondered how Albert had put up with it all this time. "She thinks we're happy.

Albert?"

"Yeah?" He picked up their stray glasses and carried them toward the kitchen.

"You love James, don't you?" Lotte asked as she rounded the corner with their dessert plates.

Glass shards and iced tea went off like firework sparks and bit into Lotte's bare ankles. Beads of blood clung to her skin as though they were unwilling to stain her shoes, and in the next minute, tea splashed against her, the lemon abrasive.

"Shit. Sorry." Albert hoisted her over his shoulder and dropped her on the kitchen counter. "You surprised me, doll. Here's a towel. I'll sweep the glass. Why do you want to know? Sure, I love him. But you already know all that."

"I know," Lotte said. "Did you always know you would love…?"

"A man? Not always, but it's been since I was sixteen. At Stivers, beginning of junior year." He didn't look at her as he spoke and worked at the glass with the broom and mopped up the liquid with a tea towel. "Remember it plain as yesterday."

"How did you know?"

"Lotte, really?" The floor was dry, and the shards were gone. Albert dabbed at her punctures with a clean washcloth. He looked up, saw her unrelenting face, and sighed. "Fine. I always had little girlfriends in grade school. Saw a couple girls at Stivers, too. You know how kids do. Never thought much of it. Every guy in my class had one girlfriend or another. Well, I get to junior year, and there's this guy in half my classes. We don't talk much, but one day, we're both late. We're in the stairwell, and he hauls off and kisses me. Just like that."

"And?"

"And what? We were in the middle of school." He dabbed at the blood and glanced at her eyes again. "Where's this filthy mind coming from? Afterward, I realized I should have punched him in the jaw, but when it was happening, I couldn't damn well think straight."

"Did you see him again?"

"Sure." Albert reached into the top cupboard for their bottle of iodine, and she cringed. When he moved back to her foot, he picked it up by the ankle and frowned at the jagged cut on her instep that had just begun to knit and scar. "Is this from the other day?"

"Yes. It's fine now. So, what was his name? Do you remember?"

"Of course, I do." A quick twinge on each ankle and a crooked grin. "His name was James."

"James?"

"Yep." Unable to suppress a fond smile, he darted his gaze away from hers before letting her foot fall. "All done."

"All done," Lotte said softly and slid from the counter. "Thank you."

"It's nothing, doll," he said. "Second time in a week I've gotten your foot sliced open. Least I could do."

During the lazy hour after None, when the sun was fullest and hottest and the sky hazy, the curtains in Henry's room filtered the strong light and fluttered in the wisp of breeze. Dust motes danced and settled in the broken column of pale yellow; heat slithered in and rubbed its back upon the carpet. Everything, mundane and sacred, wove a tapestry above them. Lotte stirred from her light doze in the bend of his elbow, kissed his cheek, and yawned. Her mouth opened wide and unladylike, and when she stretched, her breasts pressed against his side.

"You're not going, are you?" Henry clasped her and turned over to hold her fast. "We still have time."

"I'm not going," she said.

"Say, Lotte." Easing away from her, he sat up against the pillows and stifled a yawn of his own. "I'm sorry again about the other time."

"Stop saying that." Irritation threaded through her tone, and she glowered up at him. "If you regret it so much, why are we here now?"

"I don't regret it." He grabbed for her hand and shook his head. "That's not it at all. No, what I regret is taking you on the sofa and not knowing... Not asking... I hurt you, didn't I?"

"Henry," she said. "We have quite enough to feel ashamed of without worrying over that kind of thing. As it happens, you didn't hurt me at all. It was the best thing I've ever felt. This all takes practice. Why don't we just keep on practicing?" She buried her pink face in the sheet.

A punch of heat struck just between his ribs. All that worry over nothing. Lotte wanted him and loved him and had probably been just as frightened as he. Although now he wasn't frightened at all. All his other experience was borne of curiosity, tainted by fear of getting caught, of being seen, of how he would confess it. Lotte's words seemed to fit. And yet, she was still hiding. He peeled away the sheet, tilted her chin, and touched a lock of her hair to his lips.

"I don't need to practice loving you," he said at last. "But I want you to be happy."

"Well, I am happy." With a small smirk, she sat up, too. "My, but you're a quick study."

"Do you feel ashamed, then?"

"What?"

"You just said it."

"Well." Her glance took in Henry's entire room—the statues, the wooden cross, the breviary, the *prie-dieux*. "I don't know. Do you?"

"I end each day," he said. "As I suspect you do. By examining my conscience. I do plenty wrong throughout the day. Who doesn't? I'm prideful, selfish, irreverent, sometimes all three at once."

"I'm sure that's not—"

"But." He held up a hand. "I never find you among my sins. Lusting after you, yes, but not loving you."

"But how do you reconcile it?" she asked. "Not that I'd complain about your lack of shame, but, Henry, you can't have both."

"Neither can you." Her pragmatism nettled him. He was happy with his logic as conceived during Barbara Morris's endless confession. "What about that? Perhaps you're not validly married, but you do have a husband and a life outside of this. So, what? Are you sorry we've done this?"

"No." Her voice was almost a wail, and then he was ashamed. "It's confusing to me, is all. Why are you trying to be hurtful?"

"I'm sorry," he said and embraced her. "It's confusing to me, too. A couple of months ago, this was unthinkable. Come on, don't look so sad. A minute ago, you said I made you happy. Do you really want to be caught lying to a priest?"

"Henry." Lotte smacked him with a pillow, laughed, and he knew all was forgiven. She stood, her bare back to him, and wandered into the bathroom. The toilet flushed, the shower pipes groaned, and he got up, too.

Although he wanted to see her skin slippery pink and wet and bare, Henry wasn't quite bold enough to open the door. He padded across the carpet to the kitchen, fetched a glass of water from the sink, and leaned against the counter in his Jockeys. The room was quiet, aside from a couple of cars outside and the rush of running water. Henry sipped with his eyes closed, waiting for guilt and feeling only peace. Was he so lonely that the faint trickle of the shower was enough to restore his calm? He paused there, trying to discern something, anything, when he heard the cupboard open and the clinking of a glass.

When he opened his eyes, Lotte stood beside him, and her expression was faintly curious.

"Are you all right?" Her hair was pinned up, but she was wrapped in one of his white towels. "Busy day today?"

"No more than usual," he said. "You'll love William's latest scheme. Remember how I told you he wanted to do away with office hours and encourage more penance? Well, that didn't work out so well."

"What a surprise." Lotte reached up and brushed something from his face. "What happened?"

"The same three people every time. I could've told him that. Well, I did, actually. Anyhow. That's not the point." The peace in Henry's chest ballooned as he sipped his water. "So, you know how I sometimes come out of the sacristy afterwards and talk to people? He doesn't want me doing that at all. Says I should have one of the servers keep watch until everyone leaves and spend the time in silent prayer."

"How very hospitable of him."

"I see his reasoning," he said. "He thinks if I befriend all of you, you won't be able to confess to me. Makes sense, really."

"It does. Not that I would ever confess to you now, but before, the idea was scary, caring what you'd think." She pursed her lips. "But on the other hand, I've never liked confessing to Father Kestner because he's almost too remote."

"So what do you do?"

"Oh, I mostly go to Immaculate," she said. "You know half of us do, right? And half of them come here. That's not to say I wouldn't go further. I'd go all the way to St. Rita's if it meant avoiding— Well, anyhow. I shouldn't say such things. And he has a point. Talking to people has gotten you into some trouble."

"Trouble indeed." Henry cupped one of her bare shoulders and kissed her. "Speaking of which, I ought to get back or I really will be in trouble."

"Will I see you tomorrow?" She followed him back to the bedroom, where he shrugged on his clothes and smoothed his hair into a semblance of order.

"Sure," he said. "Come around eight; I'm going to my parents' for supper."

"I'll try. If Albert goes to see James, I'll come." Lotte unwound the towel and bent to pick up her things. "Go on, we can't leave together."

She was right, of course. He wanted to kiss her, push her back to the bed, and stay for the next week, but instead, he nodded. Wicked though it was, he couldn't resist another peek at her bare skin before heading back into the incalescent sun. Perhaps, he thought, William did have a point. Between Evelyn and the Legion of Mary ladies, he knew some women's minds occasioned sin simply because of his vocation. He was a challenge, or his face was wasted on a priest, or some such nonsense. If talking to them created sin, he might as well listen to his mentor for once and avoid them.

For all the sweetness he found in their physical love, the simple act of getting Lotte's two cents' worth, while propped against the counter and entirely at ease, was just as satisfying. He wondered if Albert asked her opinion about things or if they talked about their days over a nightcap, and decided he'd rather not know. Although it was probably the last thing he should want, speaking of sinfulness, Henry certainly hoped Albert would decide to see the mysterious James the following evening. He wondered briefly why Lotte would bother to hide a lover from a husband like Albert, but decided he'd rather not know that, either.

CHAPTER TWELVE

T hey're not going to let me do this without you." The night air was cool, damp, and wrapped them in a shimmering mist. A plume of Marlboro smoke shone blue in the streetlights, and Lotte bobbed along behind it.

"You shouldn't be doing it at all. It's too dangerous," she said, mostly because she felt she should. Quickening her step, she fell in beside Albert and tucked her hand in his. "Do you have the money?"

"Yeah, it's all here." Albert squeezed her hand and squashed his hat onto his head. "Now c'mon, doll, I need you to snap your cap good."

"I think I can do that," she said. "What did they catch him doing, anyhow? Why was he out without you?"

"For a drink. They caught him getting a drink." A low growl rumbled in his throat. "Told him not to, but he's good friends with Marv, who owned the Wayne, and he wanted a last drink."

Albert held the door open, and Lotte paused at the threshold. She'd never been in a police station, of course. Why would she have? Everything was loud and abrasive, even at eleven o'clock at night. A couple of officers lounged around the small lobby, one sat behind a desk, and beyond him, Lotte caught iron bars and darkness, drunken laughter, and the screech of metal on metal.

The officers moved off, and the man behind the desk eyed her in a way she didn't entirely like.

"What can I do for you, ma'am?"

Her insides were trembling. Albert draped an arm across her shoulders for show. Thank God Henry couldn't see her here. She was supposed to be furious right now. Lotte drew herself up and took a deep breath.

"I understand you've arrested one of mine and my husband's friends, Officer."

"And who would that be?" He kicked his feet onto the desk and gave her another insolent stare.

"That would be James Mills," she said, and narrowed her eyes. Did she really know how to 'snap her cap good'? She pictured her mother when one of the maids had laid the wrong table linens for her summer jubilee. Lotte could handle that much. "If you would be so good as to sit up straight and address us properly. I'm Charlotte Klopstock Walheim."

The officer's eyes widened just a touch. His feet swept off the desk. He straightened in his chair.

"Apologies, Mrs. Walheim."

The only useful thing Lotte had from her father was his name. Who had to know the truth? Let this unfriendly policeman think her doting father, Carl Klopstock, was going to exit his friendly dinner with the police commissioner and barrel into the station next.

"So you have arrested him?"

He rifled through some papers and actually blushed before looking up. "Well, yes, Mrs. Walheim, we have."

"Do you hear that, Albert?" She spun to him as though in a rage. "They have."

"So, was he soused?" With a confidential chuckle, Albert reached for his wallet. "Poor guy, just got the cold shoulder from his girl. I'd drink, too."

"Well, come on, bail him out," Lotte said. "We haven't got all night."

"Listen," the officer said, "it's not that easy. Mr. Mills wasn't a drunk. We found him at the Wayne Tavern."

"The which?"

"Oh, honey, you've seen it in the papers," Lotte said. "That awful bar they're closing down. But James would never go there," she addressed the officer. "There's been a mistake, I'm sure."

"I'm afraid not, Mrs. Walheim." The officer tugged at his tie. "That's what this here form says."

With some strange daring, Lotte grabbed the form, crumpled it, and shook her head. "I can't believe something so silly. Albert, pay the man already. I'm tired." She frowned at the policeman. "Really, Officer. James has been a friend of the family for years. He's a real ladies' man. He'd never have a thing to do with that Wayne Tavern place."

Yawning—Lotte didn't know how he managed it—Albert tossed a fistful of crumpled bills at the man, and said,

"Go on already. We're telling you, he's not one of that kind." To make matters clearer, Albert nuzzled Lotte's cheek with his nose, kissed her temple, and glared at the officer until he rose and disappeared.

An unpleasant tickle in her belly made Lotte almost shudder. How unlike Henry he felt and how sinful. Miasma pooled just below her navel at the thought that her husband's caresses should seem dirtier and reek of shame more so than those of a parish priest.

The officer returned with James, and, although she felt the tension slide from Albert's shoulders, Lotte had to be the one to run over to him, flutter, pinch his cheeks, and exclaim.

"I know you took Linda leaving hard, but for heaven's sake." She slipped a hand into his and led him to the door. "Were you so sauced you didn't even know it?"

"Huh?"

"That you were at that horrible Wayne Tavern," she said. "Come on, silly, let's get you home." It all sounded false and stilted to her ears, but the officer looked bored enough to satisfy her and presumably Albert, who trailed after them.

Once inside the house, Albert grabbed James by the upper arms and rattled him until he shoved away.

"What the hell were you thinking?" Acrid smoke twisted around them in a serpentine arc. Albert wove and paced and flicked ash right onto the floor. "Jesus, Mary, and Joseph, James. Of all the meatball things to do. D'you think they weren't going to watch the place? Why take the risk?"

"Why chicken out?" James grabbed the cigarette from Albert's mouth and ground it out on Lotte's new carpet. "I didn't ask you to come bail me out of the can, so don't snap your damn cap. Just because you're all dandy hiding behind a beard doesn't mean I'm going to."

"Are you kidding me? Your parents are the ones who got rid of me to begin with, and as far as they can see, it worked. If they think you're still a fruit, they'll cart you off faster than you can say 'Wayne Tavern.' You remember sitting on your damn floor, right? Looking at these?" Albert tore off his jacket, peeled back the sleeves of his shirt so fast the fabric ripped, and brandished his wounds. Faint weals still crisscrossed his forearms, and Lotte imagined that James had grown used to ignoring them. "You want a set of your own?"

"I'm sorry," James said and wound a finger over the scars in a tender tracing. He kissed both arms. "Of course, I remember when you were hauled off. Look, they didn't catch me at anything besides having a Rusty Nail and singing along to that damn green carnation song Marv made up when he was drunk."

"Which is bad enough," Albert said. "You think they're not going to make something up? They're going to hang back until you make a pass at another fella?"

"That." James laid a hand on Albert's shoulder and leaned in until their foreheads were just touching. "I'm not going to do."

Lotte had the sense that they'd forgotten her. They began to kiss with a special sort of fervor. If something happened to Henry, she imagined she'd react the same way. He was so dear to her already. What if she'd known him from high school on? Tears glistened in Albert's eyes and turned them the deep blue of the Madonna's gown. She wondered how far they would go in front of her and whether they realized they were in front of her.

Albert splayed his fingers at the base of James's skull. "Don't go out without me," he said. "Not at night."

James nodded and glanced over at her. "Mrs. Walheim, thank you."

117

"Don't call me that anymore," she said. "It's not fair for either of us. Just call me Lotte. And you're welcome." He wasn't welcome, but she wouldn't lose her composure in front of the two of them. Now that it was all over, she finally began to shake and wanted very much to cry.

"Yes," Albert said. "Thank you, doll. I'm sorry, we're both sorry, you had to do all that."

"I didn't have to," she said. "Now, if you'll excuse me, I'm going out."

"What the hell are you talking about?" Diverted from James, Albert glowered at her. "You're not going anywhere. It's practically midnight. It's not safe."

"It's safer for me than it is for the two of you, apparently," Lotte said. "Albert, you asked me to lie and help occasion sodomy. The least you could do is let me clear my head." Like her husband had so many times, she slipped out the door and into the shadows. For all his glowering and bluster, Albert didn't follow her. Down Edgar, up Wyoming, she kept her head low, but no one was out, and no lights flickered behind anyone's shades. At the stroke of midnight, a lamp brightened Father Kestner's window. She could see it just over Henry's fence.

Henry's house was dark, and she stole across the carpet, undressed, and crawled beneath the blankets before worrying that perhaps Father Kestner meant to come over here. Or that she should shower. She'd been at the jail, after all, and coming to Henry this way was probably wrong of her.

The bed shifted; the room was plunged into light. Henry swung his feet over the side of the mattress, yawned, and rubbed his eyes. Through narrow slits in her eyes, she watched him stagger to the *prie-dieux* and open the breviary. Like Albert and James in one another, Henry was so absorbed in the Latin that he didn't see her curled beneath the quilt before he began to speak.

At first, she closed her eyes and listened the way she did to Puccini or Donizetti or Mozart. About halfway through, she thought about kneeling beside him, but the last thing she wanted to do was startle him. She sank to her knees beside the bed. The words were unfamiliar to her, but she found something beautiful in herself, Henry, Father Kestner, people all over Dayton and Ohio and the entire world rising from bed and using these same words at this same moment. Everyone who spoke every language and dressed every which way and held entire world wars, could at least, in the middle of the night, agree upon Latin.

Henry finished the last *Pater noster*, cleared his throat, and said, "Lotte, how long have you been here?"

She opened her eyes. He didn't look particularly angry or upset. "Not long. I'm sorry."

"You shouldn't be sorry." Henry rose to his feet, helped her to hers, and drew back the blankets. "Come on, it's late."

"That was Matins, wasn't it?" she asked, sliding in beside him. "I saw Father Kestner's light on when I passed. It's strange to think how many people are waking up just now."

"And for the same reason," he said. "Latin echoing across the world. Our own version of the *Weltgeist*, in a way."

"The *Weltgeist*." Lotte raised an eyebrow.

"A man concentrated on a single point, yet striding over the world and ruling it," Henry said. "But never mind. I assume you're not here to discuss Hegel with me."

"Not tonight," she said, hiding a smile. "No. I didn't even come here to pray Matins with you, as nice as it was."

"What did you come here to do?" He passed a hand over her cheek and kissed her. When she didn't respond, he moved away and tilted his head. "What's the matter?"

"Oh, Henry." Now that Albert and James and the jail were blocks behind her, her shuddering laugh became one long sob. "I'm in mortal sin, that's what."

"Oh?" He didn't sound all that concerned, but he drew her close. "How so?"

"It's serious," she said and gave him the rundown.

"That is serious." But he didn't let loose of her. "You do what you do out of kindness, but you're right. It is mortal sin."

She'd said exactly the same herself, but his words still stung. "James is in danger of a fate worse than death," she said. "Albert was in Dayton State, you know. That's why he married me. The doctors do…" She thought about describing the mashed-up beet and the shocks, but couldn't get the words out. "…terrible things."

"Dayton State," Henry said. "I've been there a few times for anointings. I would lie to escape it, too, honestly." His eyes closed for a brief moment. "Would you do it again?"

"Probably." No one who had seen Albert's soft expression, his fear, or the way James wiped away the one, trickling tear would say otherwise. "I don't want to. I didn't want to tonight, but I probably would. It's funny, but seeing them love each other makes me kinder toward them now. Even though their love is sinful."

"In all honesty," Henry said. "I don't know what to think about all that anymore. It's one-thirty in the morning. Hegel and mortal sin can wait until the sun comes up. You'll go to see William before Mass tomorrow?"

"Of course." She curved against him and kissed the tips of his fingers before lapsing into sleep.

Although his mind and his eyes stirred, Henry didn't wake again at three. Nor did he wake at six. It was after seven when he finally acknowledged the orange glow of the sun on his eyelids, shook Lotte awake, and nestled her in the hollow of his collarbone. His dream had been of bright foreign shores, crystal sands, all the usual things, but filled with the rush of waves, the cry of sailors coming into port, squawking macaws, laughter, and Lotte, out of sight but beside him all the same.

"It's late," he said, more to himself than to her. The room was stifling, and William would be looking for him soon.

Her murmur buzzed against him, but she didn't move to dress or even to sit up. Time was, he had noticed, more of a suggestion than a system for Lotte.

"William might come." Might indeed. They'd be lucky if he

didn't come crashing in and discover them. "Lotte, I'm sorry, but—"

"Oh, no." She sat up. "I don't want to keep you from your responsibilities. I didn't realize— I was so tired after last night. I'm sorry. You shouldn't be sorry." Without waiting for him to speak, she pulled on her dress, stockings, and shoes with quick jerks. "I'll be late for penance, and I can't miss that."

"Now," he said, guilt prickling. "Ease up, there's no reason to panic. It's barely seven-fifteen; you have plenty of time." He caught her by the arm as she whipped past. "Come on, now. You can't just go barreling out of here in the morning. What about my neighbors?"

"Yes," she said. "So what am I supposed to do? Before you say anything, I wasn't planning to be here so late."

"I wasn't going to say anything," he said and led her to the kitchen. "Take this." A bread pan, still crusted with dough. Clara wouldn't remember it. He wrapped it in a tea towel. "It was good of you to bring it to me."

Lotte rolled her eyes, but cheerfully. She rose to kiss him and smoothed her skirt. "Don't you sit with me today. You make the other ladies jealous."

"Far be it from me to occasion envy," he said. "You'll come back tonight, won't you?"

"Of course." Just before she opened the door, she turned back with a devilish look. "Should I tell Father Kestner you're on your way?"

"Behave yourself." Henry stretched his arms toward the ceiling. "I'll see you soon." As he shrugged on his things and splashed his face with water, he marveled at how rested he felt, and not just because he'd skipped over two offices. That he'd done before on occasion, and he anticipated them often enough. What he'd never done, of course, was sleep beside Lotte. Henry recalled his buoyant mood on Good Friday, felt this was it a thousandfold, and positively bounced out of the house and into the church.

By the time he made it inside, the bells were ringing, and a crush of people was coming up the steps alongside him. Lotte was nowhere to be seen. He imagined William was frothing at the mouth, pacing the sacristy, and no doubt suspecting the worst. People stepped aside for Henry, who zigzagged to the small antechamber where

William would likely be.

When he saw his mentor, he breathed a sigh of relief. Henry was in mortal sin just as much as Lotte. Foregoing the Divine Office for no other reason than the comfort of his bed was as dangerous as what Lotte had done.

"Father," he said. "Do you have a minute?"

"You know very well that I don't," William said. "Where on earth have you been?"

"Asleep," Henry said, expecting the glare and cringing all the same. "I know. That's why I came to find you."

William peered at the clock opposite them, sighed, and said, "I hardly think oversleeping is enough to keep you from the sacrament this morning. The bells have stopped."

It wouldn't do to delay the entire Mass for his own personal woes. Henry nodded, let William pass, and slipped into the last pew unseen. When it came time to go to the rail, he slumped down and stayed where he was, face burning, but was happy to see Lotte go. On her way back, she noticed him and frowned in confusion. He hoped she didn't think his sins had anything to do with her.

Afterward, Henry ducked out while everyone else offered their thanksgivings. When William found him not much later, he was slouching in his office chair with a cup of coffee and a sheaf of unread papers.

"I enjoyed some notoriety in seminary," William said. "For having memorized not only a great portion of the catechism, but all of the relevant Scriptural passages as well. Unless the Athenaeum has changed its teaching considerably, sleeping late appears nowhere in the list of mortal sins. Even for those who've taken holy orders." He settled into the chair across from Henry's desk. "Which begs the question: do you desire a confessor?"

Normally, Henry wasn't apt to confess to his own mentor, but desperate times and all that. "I do. I'm sorry to have held you up earlier." He began to wonder what all Lotte had said and whether William thought his confession had to do with hers. However, even if she had told William every last detail of their lovemaking, painted it as lust and something unholy, her confession fell under the sacramental seal. William could never breathe a word of it to anyone. He couldn't even tell him that Lotte had confessed. Henry took a breath, went through his sins, and accepted William's four chaplets without a murmur.

The soft, sweeping lull of strings and flutes spread into a haze of sound that filled the entire first floor. Notes swelled; Lotte turned up the volume; the sound filled the rest of the house. It had been ages since they'd played anything from *Norma*, let alone "Casta Diva," which made her think of Henry now. Despite the soothing music, she was restless and moved from room to room, criticizing her watercolors, rehanging them, smoothing the carpet in spots.

She'd grown so used to spending nights with Henry that now, when he was busy at his niece's birthday party, she could barely remember what she'd done before him. Painting was out of the question. Reading and even praying required too much thought.

While she brushed nonexistent dust from a table, firecrackers popped on and off throughout the neighborhood. Albert and James were off to watch them along the river, and she prayed they'd be smart about it. Maybe Henry and his family had gone, too, the parents, the seven children, the twenty little ones. Someday, perhaps, she'd meet them: Clara, the brash sister, the handsome older brothers, the little godson.

Lotte finally sank to the sofa and fell into a half-dozing reverie to the music's gentle hum. Her mind caught the whisper of a cello and sailed forth on it to Henry's parents' home. In her dreamy haze, the place was warm and cozy, and the furniture sturdy, but worn. Crammed with stray family members, like any other house in Belmont. Children, the horde of nieces and nephews, played around them, tugged at Uncle Father Henry's hem, and eyed her with curiosity.

Henry ignored them, but kindly, and balanced a can of Schlitz on one knee and a plate on the other. Lotte wished she knew how to play with children or talk to them or look at them, but she cradled her own curly-haired baby, and it was comfort enough. The milky smell, the damp head, and the pudgy little body were so real in that moment that they were almost present with her.

Lotte opened her eyes, and the scene disappeared, no more than a vague, pleasant daydream. Before her were sticky glasses half-full of brandy and lime, burned-out candles, a record out of its sleeve, and a sampler box of fine chocolates James had brought over. The smell of stale liquor and cloying candy made her slightly sick, but she reached over for the chocolates and ate them all, one by one.

CHAPTER THIRTEEN

I n the days and weeks that followed, Lotte only grew more certain. July rolled in along the river, a sultry, peevish, unrelenting heat that made a swamp of the valley. Dayton, Cincinnati, Ohio, the entire Midwest suffocated every year, yet each summer, it was as though they felt it for the first time.

The factory was wide and open, but the floor was full of boiling steel kettles. Albert left each morning in a linen jacket and returned home each evening with his sleeves rolled past the elbow and no jacket in sight. He saw less of James. When he did, they lay side by side near the fan and touched only to twine their fingers. The radio snagged and crackled with their songs, "I'll Be With You In Apple Blossom Time," but it didn't annoy her. Some days were too hot for opera.

In the dog days, Lotte wanted to avoid Henry and mostly did. People married and died and baptized their babies and told him their sins, which took him away from her many days. Not that she didn't love him, of course, but if it was too hot for Albert and James, it was too hot for her. Besides, she liked the idea of having a secret all to herself. Henry would notice as surely as anything. Besides, what were they going to do? If they had been in limbo these past months, now they would have to act. The idea was exhausting in all this heat.

For now, though, she had a secret. She rose mornings, went to Mass, where on Sundays the incense was sweeter and sharper than ever, the chapel more stifling. She came home and drank lemonade and ate vast quantities of chocolate she hid away under her mattress. At night, she peeled off her wilted clothes, looked herself over in the mirror, and caressed the lower part of her belly with a fleeting hand. She wondered, while they were alone together, whether the baby could feel her touch or hear the arias or the Latin or the spurts of low conversation that drifted in from Albert's room. Cynthie had complained early on about being sick and wretched, but Lotte wasn't tired or queasy or anything else.

"Mrs. Walheim." She'd lingered too long over her thanksgiving, and Henry was swooping around the vestibule. "May I have a word?"

Her fingers tightened against her missal, but it wasn't like before, when she was avoiding him out of whatever that had been. The sense they'd end up like this, probably. "Of course, Father." Without hesitation, she followed.

"Why is it," he said when they were safely cloistered in his office. "That I feel like we've gone all the way back to Lent?"

"Lent?"

"When I had to dog you all over the city to get a word in." He slumped in the seat beside her and pinched the bridge of his nose. "Are you angry? Did I do something to upset you? Are James and Albert giving you grief?"

"No." He looked so anxious that she couldn't help but grab his hand. "Henry, you haven't done anything wrong. I'm sorry."

"What then?"

She closed her eyes, put her arms around him, and leaned against him fully despite the stuffy heat. Soon, she would be too round to fit against him this way; he'd certainly have figured out her secret by then. The deliciousness of having something all to herself was starting to wear. Her lonely life had made secrets natural and necessary, even routine, but Henry had made her unaccustomed to loneliness, and she couldn't keep her counsel as easily now.

"It's nothing." She couldn't tell him here, of course, not in the church, and besides, she worried about what he might do. Henry could be delighted, or he could throw her out. Lotte hadn't told Albert yet either, but she suspected he'd be delighted.

"I've missed you," he said. Fine, he probably wouldn't throw her out. "Lotte, why are you avoiding me?"

"I had to think," she said. "But I'm done thinking now, and I want to see you. Can I see you tonight?"

"You're seeing me now," he said. "In fact, you can see me all day."

"Really? All day?"

"Even we're allowed to be free once in a while," he said. "I thought I might go to Clara's, but hoped I could persuade you to stay home with me."

"You absolutely can," she said. "Are you sure your sister won't mind?"

"Mind, ha. She'll be glad her kid brother is out of her hair. Come take a walk up the hill with me. No one will notice."

"I can't," she said. "It's too hot, and well. I just can't."

"You can't take a walk." Henry puffed out a breath of air. "You can't talk to me. What can you do, then?"

"Don't be petulant." Lotte thought she sounded very motherly just then. "I'm feeling a little under the weather and don't want to go out in the heat. Can we go to your house?"

"Sure." All the parishioners would be gone by now, and Father Kestner was busy with whatever it was he did during the day, so Henry led her around the church and through the yard it shared with his house and his mentor's. The grass was dry and brown. It crunched beneath their feet, but the trees still drooped with green leaves. Once inside, he said, "You're not feeling well? What's the matter?"

"I'm overheated, I think," she said. "It seems a little cruel in the summertime to wear a skirt to my ankles and keep my head and arms covered in a church with no fans."

"A little," he said. "Although, if we're complaining, I'm going to say brocade vestments are worse."

"Well, at least you don't have to wear a hat." Lotte groaned. "Or a chapel veil."

"Some of them are quilted."

"I suppose you win," she said. "Quilted, indeed. It's a wonder you haven't expired on the spot. I almost have. Today, I felt so faint, I…" His gaze was speculative, eager, and she broke off. "What?"

"What nothing. So today, you felt faint…?"

If she went on, he'd probably figure it out on his own. He had all those sisters with children, and she wanted to tell him herself. She brushed the tip of his chin and his cheeks with one fingertip.

"Henry, do you really love me?"

"For heaven's sake, Lotte." He sounded offended, which boded well. "How could you ask such a thing? Of course, I love you."

"I'm sorry," she said. "It's just that we sneak around as much as James and Albert. We have to. But what if something—? What if…?"

"Lotte." Gentler than before. "We both memorized the sacraments as children. By category, no less. And we both know which ones imprint the soul permanently with a new character. Not Matrimony, not Penance, not even the Holy Eucharist."

"Baptism, Confirmation, and Holy Orders," she said by rote, almost bored, but her eyes welled up and spilled over. "What do you want, then?"

"Oh," he said and kissed her so hard his teeth pressed into her lips. "No. Not this. You're trying to tell me something, and it's certainly not this."

"We're going to have a baby, Henry," she said. Her breath caught, and she realized her heart was beating too quickly. "I'm very sure of it. I can't stop eating chocolates."

"But you don't even like chocolate." Henry pulled at his hair rather than looking her in the eye. "You're sure? I never— Never thought… Well…"

"I didn't consider it either," she said. "A bit, back at the beginning, but it never seemed real or likely. I don't know why. It was as likely for us as it is for anyone else. Now it's happened. I think it's a good thing. I'll be a mother. You'll be a father."

"It is good." With eyes closed, he rested his cheek against her hair. "Another soul is always a blessing."

"Henry?" That wasn't what she wanted to hear, not quite. Why had she considered only the two extremes and not the purgatory she always seemed to get with everyone, everywhere? The middle ground between being delighted and throwing her out. She pulled away and looked at him until he opened his eyes. "I'm sorry. If you had wanted to be a father, you wouldn't have gotten ordained."

He raised a finger to her trembling lip, his eyes creased and dark with worry. "What on earth are you sorry about? All I said was it's a blessing."

"Yes, but—"

"I'm called Father all the time," he said. "By all but you, William, and a few of my family. But I never thought I'd be one in the less symbolic sense. I didn't not want to. It just came with the vocation. It hasn't sunk in yet, is all. You've had weeks to think it over; I haven't. But I'm happy."

"So am I." She reached up, kissed him, pressed herself against him, and curled her fingers into his shoulders. "Please."

"Can we? It won't hurt anything?"

"No." At least, not if Cynthie was any expert. Lotte chuckled. "You said I could see you all day."

Henry swept her up, carried her away, and she cried out his name just once.

"Uncle Father Henry, c'mon out and play jacks." One of Clara's and one of Anna's bounced in front of him. Each girl seized a hand and flapped it up and down. "Helen can get to ninesies, come watch."

"Girls, leave your uncle alone." Anna flicked her wrist toward the door. "Go on outside now."

"But, Aunt Anna—"

"Helen, don't sass," she said, not unkindly. "Your uncle doesn't want to sit on the ground and watch the two of you bounce a ball."

"I might want to," he said and shrugged at Anna's beetled

eyebrows. "So what? Everyone's always telling them to leave me alone. My own godson leaves me alone."

"Well, don't snap your cap. Go outside if you want to," Anna said. "We just figured you'd be too high and mighty."

"Helen, Maggie. Do I strike you as the high-and-mighty type?" Henry asked. From the girls' blank looks, he assumed not. "Sure, I'll come play jacks. On one condition."

Maggie cheered. Helen narrowed her eyes and asked, "What's the condition?"

"You can't call me 'Uncle Father Henry' anymore."

"What'd you want us to call you?" Helen asked. "Just Father?"

"Just Uncle Henry." He started walking toward the door, and they scrambled after him.

"We all sit down on the sidewalk," Helen said. "And I give everybody ten jacks."

"But we can get a chair for you, Uncle Fath— Uncle Henry," Maggie said. "Let's make Frank bring it."

"No, because they're playing Cops and Robbers, and they'll steal Uncle Henry for their boy games. You go get it."

"I don't need a chair." Henry slumped to the ground and tucked up his ankles. "Now are we playing or not?"

"We're playing." The girls' skirts fanned out around them; they drew their scuffed Mary Janes out of sight. Helen bounced the ball, scooped up a jack, and passed the ball to Maggie.

They didn't talk as the ball went around the circle. The girls were too intent on collecting jacks, and Henry was waxing philosophical like the high-and-mighty type. He hadn't meant to snap at Anna, but it was true. His brothers and sisters were always telling their kids to go away, leave him alone, be quiet around him. Had he gone along with it because William was right, and he was attracted to this life? What did Henry know, anyway? He'd been called to one vocation, and he was living another. The thing he'd thought he was giving up at age seventeen wasn't that at all. What seventeen-year-old boy could honestly appreciate the difference between furtive kisses at the Belmont Theatre and the lived vocation of marriage? As much as Henry loved the Church and Her people, it wasn't quite the same as loving Lotte and their baby. The latter was his and his only.

He might have a daughter and spend hours on the sidewalk just like this. He might have a son and teach him to hit a ball or serve Mass or both. And Lotte, she would be the best kind of mother. They might have other children one day, and—

"Uncle Henry, it's your turn. Can you get tensies?" Helen thrust the ball at him. "Maggie and me, we're both out."

"Maggie and I are both out," he said. "And here, let me try." He could scoop them easily in one hand, of course, but he picked them up one by one and barely made it to seven. "Nope. Guess you girls are the winners."

"You mean I'm the winner," Helen said. "Maggie only got eightsies."

"Be nice to your cousin," he said. "Nobody likes a braggart."

"Fine. Sorry." Helen glowered for about ten seconds. "Maybe the boys'll let us play now. D'you want to?"

"Sure," he said.

"They have to let us play now," Maggie said. "Uncle Henry is a boy. And a grown-up. And a Father."

"Yeah, we can say they'll go to hell if they don't let us." Helen rubbed her hands together. "C'mon, Uncle Henry."

"You watch that mouth, Helen Gerber," he said. "I have half a mind to tell your mother and get it washed out with Ivory."

"No, no, please." Helen seized two fistfuls of his cassock. "I'm sorry, Uncle Father Henry. Real sorry. Don't tell my old lady."

"Well," he said. He had no intention of telling Clara. She'd probably laugh. "If you're really sorry."

"I am."

"Your name has a bad word in it," Maggie said. "Hell-en. So, every time we say your name, we're saying hell."

Before he could blink, Helen had her cousin by the pigtails.

"You shut up," she said. "You're just mad 'cause I beat you at jacks every time."

"Girls, please," he said, irritated now. Maybe this was why everyone kept the kids away from him.

"Helen." Clara's unladylike bellows sounded from the front

131

door. Helen gulped and slunk away. Maggie wrapped herself around Henry's right leg. "There's tapioca pudding," Clara said. "For everyone but these two, it looks like."

Maggie burst into tears and let her nose run against the fine black cotton until Henry took her hand and let her into the house. He handed down a hankie, which she took, but squirreled away in her pocket. Instead, she wiped her eyes and nose on Henry's hem, grabbed his hand again, and stuck her thumb in her mouth, although he'd thought she was too old.

"You're quite the good shepherd today," Clara said. "Good old Uncle Father Henry."

"No." Helen shook her head and wagged her finger. "We're not s'posed to call him that anymore. He's Uncle Henry."

"About damn time," Clara said, but quietly enough—he hoped—that the children couldn't hear. "Go back outside, girls."

Maggie folded the hankie over her head like a chapel veil. "Helen, let's play Penance again. This time, Frank can be Uncle Henry, and we'll go tell him our sins. Boy, and if I didn't sin mortally last week."

"That's a pretty dreary-sounding game," he said when they were gone.

"He gives them outlandish penances to do," she said. "In exchange for whatever ridiculous sins they come up with. That's the fun part. David likes it because he thinks it means Frankie has a calling, so he lets them play. They're not mocking the sacrament," she said to his furrowed brow.

"Sure sounds like it." But what did he know about kids? "I guess if it makes them more likely to go, then it's harmless enough. Why're they pretending to be me?"

"Beats me. I'd pick somebody dignified like your Father Kestner or our Father Daniels over here. Maybe they wanted someone funny."

"Funny, indeed." He swatted her across the arm. "Dignified, indeed. I've heard your stories about the whiskey. You think I'm any good with them?"

"With the kids?" Clara blinked at him, and tapioca pudding

slid from her spoon. "Well, sure. They're out there pretending to be you, aren't they?"

"They pretend to be The Shadow, too, and he's not so good with kids," he said. "Come on, Clara."

"Come on, what? Why do you care so much all of a sudden?" He could see her mind spinning behind her eyes, and her head tilted just to the left.

"No reason." It cost him quite a bit to shrug away Lotte and their baby, but he did. "There are a lot of kids at St. Jerome's, and I'm teaching the new servers and all."

"Oh, well. I'm sure you're doing a fine job of it, too." Clara twisted the pudding back onto her spoon. "Those kids're probably down on their knees thanking everybody they can think of that it's you whipping them into shape this year and not your boss. Although, come to think of it, he's pretty good with kids himself. Frankie still talks about him."

He thought for a moment about William, who thought his own existence was a sin, and grinned. "Funny. I'll have to tell him. And actually, I should get back." He'd mishandled things with Lotte, as usual, and ought to set them right. No matter his true feelings, no matter how much he adored her, he was forever offending her simply because he'd never learned what to say. Couldn't she understand he'd never imagined what he might say to a woman carrying his child?

"Henry?" Clara tapped her spoon against her bowl. "You're acting a little funny today yourself."

"Sorry. A lot on my mind." He pressed an absent-minded kiss to her cheek. "Tell the kids I'll see them soon."

Cynthie set her wineglass on the table and leaned back to accommodate her girth. "I don't get it. If the two of you were going to take my advice anyway, why'd you go ratting me out to Mom?" She gave Albert an indulgent look. "She damn well read me the riot act, I'll have you know."

"And she should," Albert said. "All this is none of your beeswax, is it, Lotte?"

Lotte couldn't bring herself to be as blunt as Albert, but no, it wasn't Cynthie's business. It wasn't even Albert's business. Henry had shown up a few days after she'd told him her secret and had given her a fistful of daisies and a bashful grin. They warmed her, although she'd already decided to forgive him for his reaction. For God's sake, what had she expected? She was already thinking of calling the baby Daisy for short.

"...and such close cousins," Cynthie was saying. "We'll have to see more of you two after they're born. We can take them to the park together. It'll be fun. Maybe we'll both have little girls—sorry, Lou—and they'll play dress-up with our clothes and try on our heels."

"Maybe they will." Lotte smiled. It was a sweet enough picture, although the babies wouldn't be cousins in truth, and Cynthie wouldn't be a real aunt. Perhaps Lotte would meet Henry's sisters soon.

"I hear that old friend of yours was in jail," Cynthie said. "James Mills. Lou's old man's got a friend whose son works down at the precinct. Did the two of you really go down there and bail him out?"

"He's been a good friend to us," Lotte said. "I couldn't stand to think of him in that jail cell."

"Down at the old Wayne Tavern, of all things." Proper conversation and decorum were not high on Cynthie's list. Lotte's mother would have clutched her smelling salts if a guest, a lady no less, had brought up the Wayne Tavern in her dining room, but what was Lotte supposed to say? This was Albert's sister. "D'you think he's still a pervert? I thought you said he stopped after you got cured."

"Enough, Cynthie." Albert's napkin was soft linen, but it thudded when it hit the table. He eyed Lou, but there were no secrets in a family that included Cynthie. "That kind of talk's not ladylike. If you thought Mom let you have it before, you ain't seen nothing."

"Haven't seen anything," Lotte said in a murmur too low for Lou and Cynthie to catch. She moved to clear away the dishes before anyone else could speak. For the first time since it happened, she felt queasy and tired. The sudden need for Henry's embrace and the smoky myrrh scent of his curls was so sharp, she could cry.

"I didn't mean anything by it." Cynthie grabbed Lotte's hand. "Sure, James is a nice guy. I was curious, is all. Didn't think Albert talked to him much these days."

"Come on now, Cynthie," Lou said. "Let's leave them alone." He pulled his wife's chair back from the table. "Don't act like you haven't been crying over every damn thing, too."

"True." She gave them a cheeky smile. "Thanks for dinner, you two. I'll give you a ring this week, Lotte."

"Is it Dick Morris?" Albert asked after Cynthie and Lou were safely in the car.

"Stop trying to guess," Lotte said.

"Bob Mueller?"

"Enough." She wandered back to the kitchen. He followed, of course. "Some of us like to keep our private lives private. Just because you flaunt James in front of half the city and lock lips with him in the middle of the front room is no reason for me to spill my guts."

"How about I'm your husband? That reason enough?" Albert took a stack of plates to the sink and settled in beside her.

"You can't be jealous." She rolled her eyes again. "If we were the type of husband and wife who told each other everything, you'd know who the father was. It would be you. But we're not, and you're certainly not, so leave it alone."

"Fine," he said, and under his breath added, "It's probably just the milkman anyway. Or the Immaculate Conception."

"I heard that," Lotte said. "And I think you're thinking of the Incarnation."

Albert scowled. To think he'd shown more visible excitement than Henry had at first when she'd finally broken down and offered him a shamefaced half confession over dinner one night. *Listen, Albert, this is going to come as a shock, but I'm expecting a baby in the spring...*

"You were pretty well delighted when I first told you," she said. "Has James been giving you grief? Otherwise, I think it's pretty rotten that you can go carousing with him and ignore me, but I have to live shut up like a cloistered nun."

Albert eased the dish towel from her hand. "Look, I'm sorry. James has been giving me grief. And if your kid comes out looking like one of the neighbors, I'd like to know about it first."

"It won't look like one of the neighbors," she said.

"I always…" Albert turned and set aside the dish he was drying. "I mean, I know how much morals and everything mean to you, so I never said it plain out. But look, I always sort of hoped you'd figure it out on your own. How to get along without me, as they say."

"I haven't forgotten about morals," she said and hung her head.

"You love him, I guess? He's married, I take it." Without waiting for an answer, Albert drew a cigarette from his pack and lit it. "Fine pickle we're both in."

If only he knew. She wondered whether her baby might look enough like Henry to cause a stir. "Yes, a fine one."

"We're a couple of sad sacks, aren't we?" He shook his head and puffed away. "Cheer up, doll. At least this way, we can stop worrying about the gossip and Cynthie's advice."

"You're right," she said. "I did get tired of all that. Those stares, the pity, even Father Kestner was in on it. But I'm sad for you. You won't have to worry about getting arrested so much, but the doctors will think those awful treatments actually work."

"Not much we can do about them," he said and squeezed her hand. "Say, whatever you want me to do, I'll do. Just don't leave me for this fella."

"I hardly think it's likely," she said, but it was. How could she and Henry keep from it? What man would be a better father than he would? A better husband? Theirs was a love and now a family that demanded to be licit and whole.

"So, he's not looking to leave his wife anytime soon?" Albert shook his head. "Good for me, but a damn shame, in a way. He's a regular old jerk for taking advantage of you, doll."

Lotte raised an eyebrow.

"Now, wait. I never told you anything but how it was really going to be."

"Yes," she said. "But you did take advantage because I'd have done anything to get out of my parents' house. You must have known that."

"There were rumors at the factory, yeah," he said. "I wondered why you'd even look once at a guy from Twin Towers, never mind twice. At first, it was just about getting to see James without getting sent back to the nuthouse. But you've been a good... I think you're really... Well, you're all right. I'm happy to play the doting daddy; that'll keep me out of Dayton State for sure. If you want me to."

"Yes," she said. For now, at least, he'd have to, and it was kind of him to offer. Lotte's lips landed on his cheek for the tiniest peck. "I want you to."

CHAPTER FOURTEEN

S ome interesting news from Holy Trinity," William said and settled into the chair opposite Henry's desk without waiting to be asked. "If our parishioners' wagging tongues are to be believed."

"Oh?" Henry set aside his Aquinas. "What are their tongues wagging about today?"

"Someone you may know. Father John Markwell?"

"Yes." That oaf. Henry bit the inside of his cheek. When the archbishop had called Markwell to the priesthood, Henry and half his class had lost a dollar apiece in wagers. "What did he do now?"

What hadn't he done at one point or another? Half drowned their practice baby, tripped over his own foot and sent a paten full of consecrated Hosts flying across the sanctuary, stood at all the wrong places at every High Mass.

William pursed his lips. "What indeed. Well, Henry, I think this time our good congregation is right to chatter. It appears Father Markwell is leaving the priesthood."

"Four years longer than I thought he'd last, actually," Henry said, hesitated, and added: "He was always at the bottom of our class."

"So I've heard," William said. "I rejoiced when they sent you to St. Jerome's and Father Markwell to Holy Trinity. But actually, his sins are little to do with the intellect."

"His sins?" Markwell was never to do with the intellect.

"Father, what do you mean?"

"Apparently, he's leaving to marry," William said. "Much like my father, I suppose. It seems one of the parish ladies has caught Markwell's eye. It's all uproar over there. I spoke to Father Amberley just this morning; he's beside himself." He mopped his brow with a hankie. "As well he should be."

"Uproar," Henry said, beads of sweat beginning to form on his forehead now. How had Markwell managed to woo a woman? Henry could barely do so himself, and Markwell breathed through his mouth six months out of the year.

"Yes," William said. "It's a great embarrassment for their parish. For all holy vocations, really. If the laity cannot look to us as examples, how will they ever overcome their own concupiscence and lust? Why would they even bother trying?"

Henry assumed the questions were rhetorical.

"It brings to mind your situation," William said.

Only by pinching his thigh very hard beneath his desk did Henry manage not to blush. His stomach swam and curdled.

"My situation?"

"No, my boy." *My boy?* Henry sent up a silent thanksgiving that William mistook his horror for being likened to Markwell and not for being like him. "I don't think you'll embarrass our parish in any regard. It's your desire to mingle with them, even innocently, that continues to worry me."

This again. He would have rolled his eyes if he hadn't been so relieved.

"And I worry about Mrs. Walheim, of course. I've seen her leaving your house with dishes of every shape and size. I told you not to encourage her."

"Father." Briefly, he closed his eyes and touched a hand to his temple. Everything was uncertain with Lotte. The only surety he had was the slight swell of her middle beneath his hand. "She's a good and modest woman."

"Yes." William had heard her confession; he might even know Albert was queer as an August snowstorm. "And you are quick to leap to her defense."

Henry shrugged, but he was growing irritated. Knowing he was in the wrong had a way of raising his hackles.

"I'm not your father, you know."

"I beg your pardon?" William sprang from his chair and slammed both hands on the edge of Henry's desk. "You speak out of turn, Father Werther." With that, he turned on his heel and marched away, too cool and controlled even to slam the door.

"What's eating Father Kestner?" Too soon, Henry saw Lotte's pale face peering around the edge of the doorframe.

"Did he see you in the corridor?"

"No, I hid." Lotte grinned and closed the door. "I'm not an idiot. Have the two of you argued?"

Henry rose and kissed her, led her to a seat, and said, "I've been stupid, I think."

"Never," she said.

"He called me Father Werther."

Lotte's eyes widened. "I thought you'd decided to rhyme with Father."

He snorted. "Anyhow, I should probably apologize."

"Probably. Listen, Henry, Albert's sister, Cynthie, told me something this morning. She heard it from her friend over at Holy Trinity. It sounds like their curate—"

"I went to school with Father Markwell," he said. "It's true. That's what had William all up in arms. He never comes out and says it, but he harps on me all the time about being too friendly, and I think he thinks I occasion scandal. Especially with you."

"You're a gregarious man," she said. "People appreciate that. It's not as though you stand at the church door shaking their hands as they leave Mass or...? Or...?"

"Or?" Her indignation warmed him. His tone grew teasing, and he traced the curve of her belly with one hand. "I might have taken gregarious a shade too far."

"That's different." Her tone was even edgier than William's had been. "Completely different. And we're different from Father Markwell. What Cynthie said is awful, and I hate to repeat gossip. But she said the girl's eighteen, and they were carrying on during Penance, and they're getting married down at the courthouse because her father found out."

"I see." William had skimped on details, probably by design. What the hell had Markwell gotten mixed up in? Disapproval and relief swept over him. Say what anyone might about himself and Lotte, Henry hadn't excommunicated himself with a teenager in a sacred space. But would anyone care for the details if or when everything came to light? Perhaps Markwell loved his bobby soxer as Henry himself loved Lotte. "You're right. It doesn't do to repeat gossip. This was third-hand from your husband's sister's friend. Who knows what they really did?"

"I'm only repeating it to you," she said. "I said it was awful. What's really awful is everyone at Holy Trinity. I've heard they've been terribly cruel. Father Markwell and his wife will have to move; they'll never be able to go back. Everyone's furious and outraged and writing to the archbishop. Even Father Amberley's taking heat for not noticing what was going on. I don't like imagining that happening here."

"Neither do I," he said. The last thing he wanted was for William to get the blame. Given William's past, the scandal would be like stabbing him through the heart with a skewer. He would want his son to have Henry's conviction, he'd said. Of course, William's son had emerged, Pallas-like, as a fully formed adult from an oversized Cincinnati parish. He pressed a hand to each of Lotte's cheeks. "I love you."

"I love you, too, Henry," she said. Her eyes filled with tears. "I'm sorry. I can't help it. It's the baby. I cry over everything."

"Whatever might be true about Markwell, we are different." His tone stayed low and soothing. "I would never marry you outside the Church. You deserve more than an irregular marriage. We would do whatever might be required of us."

Lotte nodded and wiped away her tears as though they were pesky flies. "Don't worry about that right now. You should make things right with Father Kestner."

"I know, I know." His conduct with William had been entirely out of line. If Henry had said something along those lines to his actual father, he'd have gotten his hide tanned. Perhaps even as an ordained priest nearing thirty-three. He drew Lotte to her feet. "I'll see you tonight."

"Yes, you will," she said. "Although, are you certain it's wise? Perhaps we ought to be more cautious, considering Father Markwell and all. Won't people be watching you next?"

She was serious, so he tucked his smile in the corner of his cheek for later. "I'm not sure that's how it works."

"You did go to school with him. You're young, too, and much handsomer than he is, and—"

"Why, thank you."

"That's not the point, Henry. The whole town's talking about it. I don't want the whole town talking about us. What about Albert? His family's celebrating how he's really cured and all of this nonsense." She clenched both hands into fists, but it was clear she wanted to wave her arms and shout. "If they found out the truth, I hate to think."

"Perhaps I don't want your husband raising my child," he said. "But I agree, it's not the right time to act. We're prudent already, though. If we were any more cautious, I'd never see you, and that's hardly the idea here."

"Touché, Father Werther," she said. "Now go apologize to poor Father Kestner."

"Poor Father Kestner, indeed." He smirked, but she was right. "I'll go sort things out. We can talk about the rest later."

Lotte nodded, crept out, and darted down the hallway as though William himself were chasing her.

William wasn't in his office nor in the sacristy nor the chapel. Of course not. He'd have gone to what Henry had slowly realized was his favorite place.

Seeing that the light was out, Henry drew back the curtain and slid inside. "Father, I'm sorry about what I said."

"Henry." Behind the screen, William snorted through his nose. At least he'd called him Henry. "This is highly inappropriate."

"It is." Henry bit down on his tongue, but couldn't stop himself from adding: "Using this place to hide, that is."

"I wonder," he said. "What it is that's made you so prideful and so arrogant of late. You strut around here like a puffed-up tomcat, more irreverent than ever."

Thankful for the screen and the dim light, Henry could only imagine the glare. "You're right, Father. My attention has wandered lately. I've been impertinent. I spoke to you out of turn. Twice." He wanted to add that he was saddened by William's lack of trust, but, really, was his mentor wrong not to trust him?

"I may have taken you into my confidence as regards my father's unfortunate past," he said. "But that was solely to illustrate a point. Like the parables, in a way."

"Yes, Father."

"It's not to you nor to anyone to fling such sordid things back at me, nor to try some half-baked psychotherapy. If you're going to be concerned about someone, Henry, you ought to be concerned about yourself and the state of your own soul at present."

"Yes, Father."

"You've been a help to me, Henry," William said. "More so than you realize. But that doesn't give you leave to take liberties. You've been in your vocation four years; I for thirty. Instead of presuming you have some new, better way, it might behoove you to first respect the traditions of the Church. There is a reason She has thrived these past millennia."

"I'll try to do better, Father."

"Don't try," William said. "Do better."

Henry nearly laughed and hoped his eyes didn't shine with it in the low light. As amusing as it sounded, William had a point. To try was slothful—anyone could say he was trying to do anything. Although becoming a father was probably an adequate excuse for distraction, he owed a debt to more than just himself and Lotte, and even their baby. The best thing he could do for any of them was be exemplary in what he'd been called to do.

"I will, Father," he said.

William launched into the Act of Charity, a strange choice, perhaps, but Henry joined in, and both of them lingered over the closing lines. *I forgive all who have injured me and ask pardon of all whom I have injured.*

"I have long felt," William said after a silence. "That lack of charity is my ruling vice. You might do well to discern yours and work at it prayerfully."

"I'm not sure I could pick just one," Henry said, and a smile crept into his voice.

"Narrow it to the top three or four, then." William's tone was lighter, and Henry knew he was fully forgiven. "If you'll excuse me, Henry, I have a Nuptial Mass tomorrow I'd best prepare for."

"You never told me you were getting married," Henry said, simply because he wanted to play with fire. "That's bound to cause a scandal."

"That would set them talking." Much to his relief, William chuckled, and he heard a rustling from the other side. The curtain drew back, and William extended a hand. "Probably more so than they will be about seven months after this wedding, if I'm any judge."

"Lucy Dailey and Bobby Valley? Doesn't surprise me." Henry headed toward the door, and William turned. "Have a good evening, Father."

It wasn't long after Henry got home that he heard a rap at the door. Worried about finding him in company, Lotte had stopped barging in at all hours. Considerate of her, but he hated the formality. *Gianni Schicchi* was hissing behind him on the radio, and his heart was already full from his talk with William. Henry turned the doorknob, but the eager look melted from his face.

John Markwell, sheepish and still in his cassock, twisted his hands and said, "Henry Werther. Star of the seminary."

"John." Henry's voice cracked right down the middle. He cleared his throat. "Say, Markwell. We've been in the same city again for months, and you're just now getting around to saying hello?"

"I'm sure you've heard," John said. "It's all over town."

"Yeah." He rubbed the back of his head and finally said, "Come in. Sorry, I wasn't expecting anyone." No one ever came over besides Lotte and his family. In trousers and shirtsleeves, he felt awkward and exposed.

"Sorry to barge in." When John stumbled over the hem of his cassock, Henry noticed that his cuffs were frayed and his collar more grey than white. "Listen, Henry, thanks."

"What for?"

"I didn't think you'd let me past the door, honestly. Whole town's gone nuts. Betty and I are headed for McCartyville week after next. After the wedding. There was a farm up for sale, and I can't really do much else."

No argument there. "Well, that's good. Sure she's cut out for farm life?"

"Doesn't much matter at this point," John said. "She'll get used to it. You know I've gotten letters from people wanting to kill me?" He paused. "And that's just her parents."

Henry chuckled in spite of himself, but thought for a moment. "What about your parents?"

"They're in Cincinnati, remember? And they won't talk to me. It's a blessing considering what they said before they settled on not talking."

He didn't want to pry, but imagined the word disappointment had figured heavily. Or worse.

"What brings you here, John?"

"Don't know, really." He scuffed at the carpet with the tip of his shoe. "Needed a friend, I guess."

"Ah." They'd exchanged maybe ten sentences during all their years at the Athenaeum. "Well. Have a seat. Do you want a beer or something?"

"No. Thanks." John paced and tapped and finally seemed to remember that Henry was there and that the two of them weren't friends. "Couldn't do it."

"Do what?" The answer was probably going to make him cringe, so he parried with: "No, really, you can have a beer. There's plenty."

"I couldn't go without."

"Without beer?"

John half-laughed. "Without a woman, Henry. I'm convinced it's not natural. Not a gift. And besides, the Lutherans and Methodists and everybody else doesn't demand it."

"They're also heretics," Henry said.

"Well, yeah." With a scratch to his head, John stopped

roaming the living room.

"*He that is without a wife, is solicitous for the things that belong to the Lord, how he may please God. But he that is with a wife, is solicitous for the things of the world, how he may please his wife: and he is divided.*" Henry quoted the passage and wondered when he'd become not only William, but a hypocrite as well. Why on earth bother quoting it, anyhow? It had practically been nailed to the dormitory door. Every member of their class could have said the entire passage standing on his head.

"Never heard that one before," John said without a trace of irony. "Ephesians?"

"Corinthians." Was John, an utter moron, more or less culpable in the sin of lust than Henry was? Of course, the more deliberate and well-planned the sin was, the more it slid toward mortal. On the other hand, John and his 'natural urges' seemed far and away more lustful than Henry's tender, purer feelings for Lotte. 'A woman,' he'd said, implying any one of them would do, when Henry would never have entertained the thought had he not been called to Lotte. One had to feel a little sorry for Betty, exiled to a farm and fulfilling John's urges 'til the cows literally came home.

"Listen, Henry—"

"Sorry." That would be Lotte at the door, of course. "Wasn't expecting anyone," he said again. He pushed the door open slowly. Lotte would be preferable to William. If William thought Henry was a puffed-up, irreverent, liberty-taking tomcat, Henry hated to think of him in a room with John Markwell. "Oh my. Mrs. Walheim, what's the matter?"

Droplets clung to Lotte's eyelashes; she regarded John through them with distrust. "I don't mean to interrupt."

"Get in here." He hoped John either didn't see or couldn't interpret his low growl and the jerk on Lotte's arm. "Please. Mrs. Walheim, meet Father Markwell."

"How do you do, Father?" She kept her expression smooth and closed, save for a polite smile. "I'm sorry to bother you at this hour, Father Henry. Do you have a moment?"

"Certainly. John, will you excuse me?"

John nodded, kissed Lotte's hand, muttered something to her, and slouched toward the door. Another puffed-up tomcat off into the night.

"Is everything all right with the baby?" Henry asked as soon as the door was shut.

"So that was Father Markwell?" The rest of Lotte's tears dried up, and she peered out the front window. "What was he saying? Did he talk about his wife? Or did he confess to you?"

"Come on, nosy." He tugged her hand and pulled her away. "What's wrong?"

"The baby's fine," she said. Her momentary fit of nosiness resolved itself once again in tears and shuddering breath. "But Albert and James aren't. They've been arrested, and there's no bailing them out this time, and anyone could find out. What if they get sent to the hospital?"

A spark of delight rose within him, but he squelched it before it could be entertained. Delight was uncalled for. Lotte was crying, and one of his parishioners was in jail and had sinned mortally. The back of Henry's mind wasn't so charitable. If everyone found out, they'd be worse to Albert than they were to John Markwell, and Lotte would be free of him. The back of his mind conjured up a Solemn High Nuptial Mass with William celebrating, Clara and the others attending them, Lotte rounder than she should be, but radiant...

"Henry. What am I supposed to do?" She grabbed two fistfuls of his shirt and shook him out of the reverie. "Their brains are going to look like mashed-up beets."

"What? Beets?" So much for the Nuptial Mass. If lack of charity was William's ruling vice, it needn't become Henry's. "Lotte, if you're asking me to bail them out, you know I can't."

"I'm not. I wouldn't. If it's a mortal sin for me to get them out of jail, I can't imagine you going there. You don't belong in there. You're too..." She blushed. "I'm not sure what it is, but you don't belong in there."

"Visiting the imprisoned is a work of mercy, you know," he said. "Besides, if you're not too delicate for the place, I'm not either. I've been there before, as it happens. But it's not my place to bail my parishioners out of jail. I don't think they'll drag them off to the asylum without any proof." Fat lot Henry knew about all this. The police probably had all the proof they needed and then some, but this line of conversation seemed to calm Lotte's nerves. "Besides, I wouldn't worry about your husband. A pregnant wife at home isn't going to get his brain mashed into a beet. His friend, though. I don't know. Are you worried about both of them or just Albert?"

"Albert mostly," she said. "It's more for his sake I'm worrying over James. And really, no one deserves to have their brain mashed." She leaned into him and buried her face in his shoulder. "You're such a help to me. Without you and the baby, I thought my life would swallow me up."

"I thought mine would, too," he said. "Come on. It's late." By the time she was tucked into bed, content and drowsy on tea splashed with whiskey, it was after eleven-thirty. With a weary sigh, he picked up the telephone and began to dial. "Sergeant Crouse? Father Henry Werther over at St. Jerome's."

CHAPTER FIFTEEN

S ounds swell to me," Albert said, as though replying to the radio. It was hissing that old tune that went *let's have another piece of pie*. "How 'bout you?"

The baby burbled and waved an arm, and Albert tucked him under one arm like he was running for a touchdown.

"Aw, come on, you'll make him sick like that." James grabbed the child and held him across his chest. "I'll take some pie, Lotte, if you don't mind."

"I'll get the damn pie," Albert said. "Lotte, you want some?"

"Please." Although she wasn't as ungainly as she would be next month, Lotte didn't mind a chance to stay where she was. The baby kicked and rolled under her hand, and she thought of Jesus in His mother's womb, leaping to greet His cousin. The image always made her smile, aside from the fact that Charlie and the baby weren't really cousins. Her child danced to *I Puritani*, to bells at the consecration, and to Henry's voice when he got it into his head to sing Vespers. "And James is right; don't manhandle poor little Charlie that way. Cynthie would never forgive you."

"Told you so." James had decided to forgive Albert for having a pregnant wife. Why not, since Albert wasn't even the father? He chucked Charlie under the chin. "Your sister won't be happy when you send him back with a bumped noggin and a queasy gut. Now go get the pie already."

When Albert returned, he had a towel draped over his shoulder and a bottle. Gingerly, he took the baby from James and let him guzzle down the formula, cheeks working like a hydraulic pump, face pink and plump as a suckling pig's. Albert gazed upon his nephew—his godson—with something approaching awe. James drew close to Albert's side and ran a hand between his shoulder blades.

While she watched them, Lotte thought of course about Henry, but not in raptures like usual. *I didn't not want children; it just came with the vocation.* James and Albert's life certainly wasn't a vocation, but Lotte began to wonder whether the two of them ever wanted to be fathers for real. Albert had really taken to little Charlie. Despite Lotte's baby being the child of a man she wouldn't disclose, Albert was soft with her. He got his own pie and handled people's comments that it was about time with good grace. Could men like Albert and James raise a baby together? Would the baby turn out like them? Would hers, being near them so often? She doubted it without knowing why.

While the radio scratched out another vulgar melody, Lotte nibbled the last crust of her pie. With James and Albert wrapped up in little Charlie, she was free to stretch across the sofa, spread both hands over her belly, fingers making a diamond around her navel, and close her eyes. Henry had been peculiar lately—no less attentive, simply peculiar. He snapped out of bed for the offices with military precision. He never spoke ill of Father Kestner if he could possibly help it. He didn't sneak off with her during the afternoon. It was frightening, in a way.

What had Father Kestner said to make Henry act this way? If he knew, if anyone knew... Lotte shuddered and thought of cadaverous, wan John Markwell in his ratty cassock. Mr.—Father?—Markwell and his wife had moved far away up north to keep from gossip. Lotte couldn't bear to move away, if not for her own sake, then for Henry's and his family's. If he found out about them, Father Kestner could send Henry away, or at least try to.

And what about Albert? Her eyes swept to the two men, trying in turns to burp Cynthie's baby. She'd meant for Albert and Lotte to practice up, as she put it, but then, she didn't know about James. What a mess this all was for Lotte's baby to be born into.

"That's it," Albert said. "All done. Want to hold him, doll? Give us guys a break?"

"Sure." Lotte reached for him, and his cousin really did jump in her womb. "He takes after Lou already, poor thing."

"My family's luck, he'll end up with Lou's looks and Cynthie's brains," Albert said. "Damn shame, unless he ends up a tail gunner, too. Don't need looks for that, although he won't be shooting down the enemy with a brain like Cynthie's. Hope you've got yourself a looker or a brainy one."

"Or a war hero," James said. "You think he'll look like you or like your fella?"

"Really, James," Lotte said. "We shouldn't be discussing this."

She hefted herself from the sofa and carried the baby upstairs, away from the snickering men. Dvorak hummed through her bedroom, where Cynthie had set up Charlie's things. Even Albert's sister was fed the fiction that her brother and sister-in-law shared the big front bedroom that overlooked the street. 'Song to the Moon' was so sad and beautiful that it made Lotte ache, but she was too shy to hum it, even to herself and a barely sentient child. Instead, she rocked him and sang in soft counterpoint the Thursday Compline. Henry had improved her Latin tremendously. Lotte wondered whether she'd be here, in this cell of a bedroom, rocking her own child all alone.

She and Henry no longer spoke of the future, although she knew they both dreamed of it. How much would they have to do to make things right? Her marriage annulled, Henry laicized, everything confessed, the two of them finally wed. How long would it all take? The baby would probably be born before they could get it all sorted, if they even managed it. He'd said it was up to the Holy Father himself whether he was free to marry, and his pained look when he'd said it gave her pause. With a kiss to baby Charlie's cheek, Lotte laid him in the crib, turned off the radio, and tucked her arms around her middle.

When Henry recessed down the aisle, preceded by candles and servers, his eyes were usually half-open and his lips working in prayer. It was especially important now in Advent, when he had only four—really three—Sundays of penitence before Christmastime. Lately, however, he was even weak while vested and couldn't resist a quick glance at Lotte, round and glowing with new life. The line between his consecrated life and his life with her blurred more each day.

Today, she caught eyes with him, bowed her head, and blushed. Albert was beside her, but hadn't cottoned on to the idea that he shouldn't be skimming the bulletin and reaching for his hat. He would be charging into the vestibule before the last hymn was properly finished, and would chat it up with half the parish while Lotte made her lengthy thanksgiving. Perhaps someday, Henry might kneel beside her, but he supposed it was wishful thinking that they would continue at St. Jerome's.

After the vestments were laid aside and the prayers said, the vestibule was mostly empty, and Lotte was gone. The heavy wooden church door creaked, and in bustled Clara, bundled in David's greatcoat and a Kleenex pinned askew over her hair.

"Are you ready or what?" she asked. "I left the car running. Frankie'll probably drive off with it if we don't get a move on."

"Frankie's about as qualified to drive that thing as you are," he said. "Where's David?"

"Under the weather, but don't let that stop you. He said it's fine. Just the sniffles." Clara clattered down the stone steps and held up a hand to Frankie, who was nosing around the driver's seat. "How was Mass today? Father Daniels blathered on for forty minutes about the final judgment. I was hoping the end of times would just start already. It'd probably be over quicker than that sermon."

"Ours was fine. I only blathered for twenty minutes, tops."

"On what? Never mind, I don't care. I've heard enough moralizing to last 'til Christmas." She swung the door open and let him into the chilly noontide air. "I'm glad you're finally condescending to join us, Oh Venerable Father Henry. We don't see you half as much as we used to."

"Busy time." He crawled into the passenger's seat and watched

Frankie slide into the backseat. "It's Advent."

"Yes, and I suppose the 273rd Sunday After Pentecost is a busy time, too?" She rolled her eyes, merged onto the street without looking for traffic, and gunned the engine down Wyoming Street. She went the long way just to speed and free-fall down the hill, circled around, and climbed back up Wayne Avenue.

"Clara," Henry said as they shuddered down Watervliet. "I am sorry."

The car squealed into a spot on the street, and Clara said, "I'm just giving you grief. Why so glum?"

"Because you're not just giving me grief, and you're right. I even missed Annie's birthday last week." A weight settled into his stomach, and he rubbed the back of his head. No matter where he focused his attention, he was disappointing someone. William and the Church, Lotte and the baby, Clara and the family.

"Oh, come on, don't pout," she said. "Frankie, get in the house. I want to talk to your uncle. Listen, Henry, I'm worried about you. You're run off your feet up at St. Jerome's, and why not? There's only the two of you. Didn't your old parish have eight priests? And over here at Immaculate, we've got five."

"I like a smaller parish," he said. "I promise, it's fine."

"But." She ripped the tissue off her head and wrung it. Little bits of white fluff clung to the bobby pins and showed up ragged against her black hair. "I don't know. I'm just uneasy. You were asking all those questions about me and David and that woman you were counseling, and now I've heard from Teresa Ritter from Holy Trinity about this Father Markwell. You knew him at school. I remember him getting ordained with your class."

"Enough." Forgetting that he was her kid brother and was dead meat for interrupting her twice, he held up a hand and squared his shoulders. The weight in his stomach had turned to ice. Just like with William, his hackles were on full alert, and he was going to say something regrettable. "I don't want to hear any more about that scurrilous tripe, especially not from my own sister. I've heard plenty of claptrap about how I'm next or I'd better strengthen my convictions, as if I've done anything to call them into question." Being in the wrong, he'd found, made it even easier to whip up righteous fury than when he was right. "What are you worried about, Clara?" He spat her name with just the right amount of condescension and crossed his arms over the black buttons marching down his chest.

"Oh, Henry." Her own chest heaved and shuddered under her husband's overlarge coat. The wind stirred the bits of Kleenex in her hair, and she pressed the rest of the tissue to her eyes. "I never meant to hurt your feelings. I don't think you'd do anything wrong. I really don't. I'm worried, and I care, and you don't talk to me like you used to."

"Aw, come on, Clara." Although he was used to Lotte's messy sobs at everything from the baby kicking to the sunrise, Henry hadn't seen Clara cry since she was fifteen and she'd gotten ink all over her Christmas dance dress. "Listen, I'm sorry for jumping down your throat."

She wiped her eyes and tossed the tissue over her shoulder. "I forget sometimes that you're not just brainy little Henry wearing Mom's pillowcase as a chasuble."

"I thought I'd lived that one down."

"Well, you interrupted me twice." She brushed the cotton out of her hair and picked some fuzz off the front of his cassock. "And you didn't let me get to the point before you turned into Father Cap Snapper."

He suppressed a chuckle before she remembered him using Dad's best necktie as a maniple. "What was it, then?"

"I wouldn't care. I'm not saying you're a public disgrace and a mortal sinner like Father Markwell. Hell, I don't even know the guy. Heard he was a fathead, though. Anyway, when I heard about all that, it got me thinking, well, what if that was Henry? He's a priest, isn't he? And I decided it wouldn't much matter to me."

"Ah." He blinked. "Still, though, imagine everyone thinking you would run around on David just because some woman up the block turned out to be a tramp."

"I know," she said. "I am sorry. Knowing Father Kestner, I'm sure you've been getting an earful. But everyone's been saying how awful it's been for Father Markwell, and I wanted— Who knows. It was stupid, I guess."

"It wasn't stupid," he said. "It was kind of you. Listen, Clara." They were alone. Despite the gossip she was spewing about Markwell, he could trust her. Maybe she knew already. He was closer to her than he was to anyone, save for Lotte, and she'd always been able to read his mind. Underneath all the worry about sin and secrecy, he was proud as any other father. His brothers had told half the neighborhood when their wives were expecting.

"Listen what?"

"Thanks for saying that," he said. "But I'm not planning to follow in Markwell's footsteps any time soon."

She let out a long breath. "Didn't think so. You had me scared for a second there, though. Come on, they're probably wondering what the hell happened to us."

Half relieved and half hollow, Henry nodded and fell into step behind her with the sense that the moment, now flown, would never resurface, and that he was forever doomed to his heavy, silent burden. He'd never lied to her before, and now he'd lie to her for the rest of their days.

It was time for Compline by the time Clara dropped him off at home, and he recited it, Matins, and Lauds all at once in a bid for a long night's sleep. As burdened as his conscience was, the visit with his family had energized him, and by the time he reached *Divinium auxilium maneat*, his ears were craned to the door. Nothing, of course, happened, so he switched on the radio, cracked open a beer, and was halfway through *Don Giovanni* before Lotte showed up, more than a little winded from the trek.

"Did you have a good time at your sister's?" she asked, and then, "Henry, what's wrong?"

For a supposedly celibate cleric, he did more than his fair share of consoling crying women and getting psychoanalyzed by the fairer sex. He was almost certain Lotte was carrying a daughter just for that. "Nothing's wrong. Why?"

She rolled her eyes and filled a glass at the sink. "Nice try."

"Fine. I think Clara knows."

"What?" The water sloshed over the rim of the glass. "Does

she really?"

"I don't know for sure, but I get the sense. She knows something's not right. Doesn't matter, actually; she'd never say anything. It's more that I've started lying to her. I wanted very badly to come clean, but I've gotten pretty good at keeping people's secrets. Even mine."

"I wish I could meet her," Lotte said. "At the very least, you wouldn't be lying to her anymore." She shook her head. "I'm sorry, Henry. It must be... Well, everyone knows I'm expecting. And then they talk about Albert and how it's 'about time,' and it hurts me. As awful as that is, I imagine it's worse not being able to claim our baby at all. And you're a man."

"I was hoping you'd notice." He tugged her down beside him, and some of the tension melted away.

"Isn't it always the men wanting to shout it from the rooftops and the women getting embarrassed at the word 'baby'?" She propped her feet on the coffee table and nestled beneath his arm. "I've never known you to listen to much Mozart."

"It was on," he said. "And it's a good recording—two years ago at the Met. I hear they're going to do it again next year. Wish they'd come up with something else. Something I haven't heard a hundred times."

"Have you been to the Met? I used to beg my parents to take me to New York, and they never did, of course."

"The furthest I've been is Kentucky," Henry said. "Where I don't think they've ever performed *Don Giovanni*. It's funny, isn't it, with the war and all, we were thinking every day about Japan and Germany, boys getting shipped off their farms, when most ordinary people have never been outside Ohio. I used to think about going to Rome before all the madness in Italy started."

"Of course you did," Lotte said.

"And escaping for a day to go see La Scala in Milan." He plied his fingers over her belly, and the baby wriggled beneath his touch. "That would be a honeymoon spot, wouldn't it? After the dust settles."

"The dust in Italy or the dust here?" Her eyes closed; she lifted his hand to her lips and kissed it. "You know, I read the other day that priests in the Eastern religions and the Orthodox ones can have wives if they want them."

"But we are not them." Henry brushed a lock of hair from her forehead. "And from what I've heard, it's not so simple. Their bishops are still celibate, and the priests who remain so are more respected, I think. So they see the inherent value of it. It's as you said before: we can't have both. To suggest otherwise is heretical and Protestant."

"I'm not suggesting anything. Can't I point something out without being accused of heresy?"

"Sure, sure." He shushed her and soothed her and sawed at his tongue with his front teeth. What an idiot and a boor he was today. "That's not what I meant."

"I only meant—" She puffed out a sigh. "You talk about honeymoons, but you can't even tell your sister, who you already said would keep her mouth shut."

"Albert would keep his mouth shut. Have you told him?" He shook his head and closed his eyes against her broken look. "Forget it, Lotte. I don't want to argue. Difficult as it is, we have to leave it alone for now."

"You're right," she said. "I just worry. We have a little over three months until the baby's born, and it'll take longer than that to fix everything. And some of it can't ever be fixed."

"True enough," he said. He was tired now and drained, all the vitality he'd absorbed with his family gone, the weight of lying to Clara sinking like a mantle on his shoulders. Standing, he helped Lotte to her feet, kissed her, and led her to bed.

CHAPTER SIXTEEN

Easter, 1947

H appy Easter, Father."

"Happy Easter, Mrs. Morris." Henry nodded and moved through the bright whirl of noise, white hats, and several dozen unfamiliar faces. The front doors were flung wide, three arcs of lapis blue sky spilling into the vestibule. Lilies marched down the stairs at each rail. Parishioners burst forth, and their din carried all the way to the sidewalk. The Morrises, the Andersons, the Daileys, even William smiled and waved to him, but where on earth were Albert and Lotte? Surely, Lotte wouldn't miss the most important day of the year, but he couldn't find her. He hadn't even seen her during the recessional, and, heaven help him, he'd looked.

"Are you off to your parents' house?" William appeared beside him as the last of the crowd filtered onto the street. "Give them my best."

"Yes, of course," he said. "I'm sure they wouldn't mind an extra guest, Father. I wish you'd reconsider. My nephew Frankie would sure be glad to see you."

"I don't want to intrude," William said. "And besides, I'd rather spend the day alone. We have quite the fifty days ahead of us."

"Well, feel free to change your mind." Henry turned away, but the question shimmered in his mind. It burned him so badly he couldn't ignore it. With studied, deliberate nonchalance, he furrowed his brow and half turned back to his mentor. "Say, Father, you didn't happen to see the Walheims today, did you?"

"I didn't," William said. "Why?"

"Just curious. Not like her to miss a holy day." He started on his way again. "I'll see you tonight, Father."

"Yes." William sounded odd, and Henry regretted his impulse. But Lotte was so fragile around her heavy burden and so wistful, he couldn't help but worry. The Walheims could have gone to St. Mary's with Albert's parents and sister; Albert might have refused to come; any number of innocuous things might have kept her away. Still, he was anxious. She was so far gone that she couldn't even walk to his house nights anymore. Last Easter, he had joked with her on Holy Thursday, counseled her on Good Friday, and spent Saturday and Sunday recalling the spark of his fingers against the base of her spine. A year later—less than a year, really—and she was just as weary, if not more so, and he was still called to help her.

"There you are, sweetie." Mom pulled Henry's face down and kissed him twice on both cheeks. "Happy Easter. How was Mass this morning?"

"It went well, Mom. Happy Easter." Henry heard shrieking and footfalls behind her.

"Uncle Henry, Uncle Henry." Helen, who had Maggie manacled at the wrist, skidded to a halt before them. "Maggie and me were playing outside this morning before Mass, and Grandpa said the sun dances in the morning at Easter, and we saw it dance. No joke. That's real, right? The boys say we're lying, but if you say it's real, they can't say nothing."

"Can't say anything," he said. "Sure, it's real. Who wouldn't dance at Easter?"

Dad had told Henry and the rest the same thing growing up. Nice to see it passed on down the line.

"Ha. Told them," Helen said. "Now come on, let's show him our candy. I'll give you some special jellybeans, Uncle Henry."

"Well, thanks." He allowed himself to be seized just as Maggie was and led over to the sofa.

"I usually just give people the black ones, cause I don't like 'em, but you can have three red ones."

"Three?" Maggie looked impressed. "Uncle Henry, you can have four of my greens. And one pink."

The jellybeans, no matter the color, were gritty under his teeth and left a syrupy, medicinal sweetness on his tongue. The sugar dried out his palate, so the taste lingered, although he resisted the girls' efforts to feed him any more.

"Come on now," he said. "You'll ruin your dinner."

"You sound like my old man," Helen said.

"I am an old man." Insofar as a ten-year-old was concerned, thirty-three was ancient.

"What're you talking about, Uncle Henry? You're not allowed to have kids; everybody knows that."

He blushed, although it was lost on Helen, thank God. "I meant old as in old fogeys."

"Well, you're definitely old," she said. "But you're all right. Can you sit next to me?"

"Your uncle's not sitting at the kids' table," Anna said. "Now, shoo, you two, and go wash up. Sorry, honey. I can't believe you ate those awful jellybeans. I got a pound for a penny, and they sure do taste it."

"I could use a beer," he said. "Or anything that'll go down better than those jellybeans."

"I think Mom has a bar of Lifebuoy under the sink," Anna said. "That'd sure taste better. Come to think of it, Helen's tasted it more than once. Here's a Schlitz; now come on. You know they'll want you to say the blessing."

"What did you all do before I came back to Dayton?" he asked. "Seeing as how they think I'm the only one qualified to pray over a ham."

"Well, Annie helped with the glaze this year, so I think it'll need the prayers of a genuine, honest-to-goodness priest." She tweaked his nose, he swiped at her hand, and they hurried off toward the table.

Later, tired and empty, Henry sat staring in his office, although it was well after Compline. Moonlight and the glow of a single lamp bathed the room in silvery shadows. He missed Lotte's visits more than he'd realized. Daily Mass was now more walking than she could manage, but she would telephone him. Only today, she hadn't, and Lotte was the last person he'd expected to snub him on the holiest of holy days.

Footsteps clicked across the marble floor, but they were all wrong. Heavy and shuffling. William rapped twice before poking his head around the corner and peering at Henry.

"Burning the midnight oil, I see," he said. "How was dinner with your family?"

"Just fine." Henry made an effort to smile, and William took a few steps across the threshold. "They all send their best. You ought to have come."

"The Daileys brought me some ham. I read Lasance, God rest his soul. As you said, it was just fine." William's words were too casual for his grave tone, and Henry's spine stiffened with alarm. "A quiet day, I should say." He nodded at Henry and walked five paces out the door before turning back with studied nonchalance. "By the way, Henry, someone from the hospital telephoned this afternoon. Mrs. Walheim had her baby. She can be excused from Easter Mass for that, wouldn't you say?"

A punch of firework sparks shot off deep within him and trailed shimmering flecks against his heart. His eyes wanted to widen, his mouth to grin, his entire bearing to leap up, to shout, to cry, to embrace William, and most of all, to run down the street, scoop up Lotte and their child, and kiss them both. Under William's keen gaze, however, he kept his expression one of mild interest and said, for he still had to speak,

"Yes, suppose so." His voice didn't tremble or catch, and he was proud. "That's nice for them."

William's expression was half-relief and half-disappointment, Henry wagered, but before he moved out of sight, Henry called out to him with his own studied nonchalance.

"Say, Father, d'you know what she had? I might send them a card."

"A little girl," William said. "Sign my name to it, too, would you?"

Henry nodded, for speech was impossible now, and William drifted away. For the first time since everything had begun, Henry dropped his face into his hands and sobbed. The firework sparks became hot tears, and the bursts resolved as sharp gasps through his chest and the shaking of his shoulders. Although he had been a father in truth since the baby began to knit in Lotte's womb, his daughter was now safely born, was someone he could see and hold, which he ached to do. He adored his nieces, his nephews, his godson among them, but a scant few miles away was a child who was half his and half Lotte's.

He dried his tears, steadied his breath, and wondered whether Lotte had suffered badly giving birth to her. Surely William would have mentioned if Lotte wasn't well. Henry crossed himself, bowed his head, and offered up a prayer to St. Margaret for her safety. Albert had taken her to the hospital, he assumed, and he was blinded with envy that it hadn't been him. It was Henry's duty to soothe her and wait for her and pray for her. What did Albert care?

Enough with Albert. How could Henry visit Lotte without it being remarked upon? Was it so bad to pray that someone would require a sick call? She'd be there for at least a week, after all, and was lawfully excused from Mass for six more weeks. It was unthinkable that the first time he'd see his daughter might be at her baptism, if William even allowed him the honor. The pain of waiting, of knowing how far Lotte was from him, was raw and physical, a jagged bit of metal in his heart. Perhaps he had been weak in wanting to leave things alone and avoid scandal.

He couldn't think any more upon it now. If he stayed in his office another minute, he'd go out of his mind. With one jerky movement, he opened his desk drawer, pulled out the cigar David had sent him after his and Clara's youngest was born, sliced off the tip with a letter opener, and headed home. Alone on his couch, he lit the cigar and found something on the radio, which did nothing to ease his loneliness. He leaned back, closed his eyes, and let the acrid smoke curl into a haze.

"Mrs. Walheim?" The nurse's shoes squeaked against the linoleum, and Lotte stirred, her heartbeat rising in anticipation. When she saw the woman's empty arms, she melted back into the pillows and sighed.

"Yes?"

"I know it's after visiting hours, but I think we can bend the rules a little, if you're up to it."

Bend the rules? The nurses were more rigid than Father Kestner and twice as stodgy.

"Of course I'm up to it." She sat up again, curious. Even Albert wasn't allowed to visit a minute past seven.

"Good evening, Mrs. Walheim." Henry's voice was mild and modulated. "Father Kestner told me your good news. I was here anointing another parishioner, so I figured I'd stop in."

"How kind of you, Father." She nearly cried, but the nurse was still sidling out of the room. His eyes were bright, hungry, as full as her own. "Although I'm sorry to hear you had to celebrate the Last Rites."

He nodded and crossed himself. "May God have mercy. It's never an easy task, and we'll probably be saying a Requiem before long. But anyhow. I'm glad to see you're doing well. Have they let you see the baby much?"

The squeaks moved a safe distance down the hall, and Lotte found herself enveloped in a cloud of black and the scent of holy oil. The tears spilled over as Henry kissed and caressed her head and said in a choked voice,

"I wanted to come sooner. Don't be angry. I had to wait, but I wanted to come right away when I heard. Are you all right?"

"I know," she said, raising her lips to his and patting the bed, although visitors weren't allowed to sit with her. "I never doubted it. And I'm fine. The birth was easy; I don't even remember it." She ran the back of her hand across her eyes. "Have you seen her, Henry? She's beautiful. She looks so much like you that I'm almost worried." But she wasn't worried. She was happy and would have spent every waking second with her daughter if the nurses would only let her. "I was afraid you wouldn't be able to come, and I didn't want to have them fill out the birth certificate without asking you about her name. I want to call her Daisy, but not Margaret."

"Daisy," he said, and produced one from the folds of his cassock. "And why not Margaret? I prayed to her for you when William told me you'd delivered. My mother's name is Elizabeth, and none of the others named a child for her. I always felt a little bad about that. Or there's always Henrietta."

"We're not naming our baby Henrietta." She laughed and set the flower aside. "Elizabeth Margaret. Maybe she'll take your name at Confirmation, although that's probably enough saints for any one child. You should look in on her, Henry. I'm sure they'll let you. I wish you could hold her." Lotte wished she could hold her for more than a few minutes at a time. Getting permission to feed her without a bottle had been a struggle all its own.

"I will see her," he said, lifted her hand, and kissed it. "But I wanted to look in on you first. I've been going out of my mind. Has Albert been in much?"

The mention of Albert irritated her almost as much as his presence did. "Some. He's got to come to keep up appearances. Cynthie and Lou've been in and his parents. He even made James come once. I've missed you, Henry."

The squeaks sounded up the hallway, and Henry sprang up from the bed. Both fought to compose themselves.

"Thank you for coming to see me, Father," she said with a slight catch underlying each breath.

"Certainly," he said. "But I'll let you get your rest. Do let us know when you'd like the baptism scheduled." Henry nodded to the nurse, glanced back at Lotte, and disappeared.

"Mercy," the nurse said when he'd gone. "What a waste of a good-looking guy."

Lotte didn't trust herself to be glib, but settled back against the pillows and sighed. Another two days here felt like an eternity, tired as

164

she still was from a birth that was mostly a hazy blank. She was desperate to lose herself in Daisy. Perhaps she moved in narrow spheres already—the church, the park, Henry's house, the neighborhood market—but when she'd set eyes upon her daughter, the world had shrunk into the ridge of a tiny fingernail, a delicate, spidery eyelash. The loneliness she'd felt all her life, eased but not eliminated by Henry, had quite simply disappeared. Daisy was always swaddled, and she wasn't allowed to unwrap her. Maybe that was for the best because she could pray the Joyful Mysteries on those ten little toes for hours and hours. Her prayers to the Blessed Mother were more tender now that she was a mother herself. She closed her eyes and lapsed into a mix of sleep and Latin and sweet reverie.

When she finally went home, Lotte didn't even murmur when Albert wheeled her out of the hospital and helped her into the car. She squeezed Daisy against her breast and tried to keep from devouring the tiny hands and feet and cheeks that were finally hers. While she was expecting, she'd always been afraid of hurting the baby or not knowing what she wanted, but none of that bothered her now.

"Has her daddy seen her yet?" Albert asked.

"He stopped by." The question made Lotte's hands turn cold. "Pretended he was my brother. Couldn't stay long."

"Sorry I dragged James along. His parents are dogging him about going in the nuthouse. I thought it'd be good if he looked like a family friend. Like I was showing off my kid to him, you know." Albert was concentrating on the road ahead and not on her face. Perhaps she wished Henry had been the one to bring her to the hospital and take her home, but it was good of Albert to do so. Daisy wasn't his baby, and Lotte was barely his wife.

"Of course," she said. "That makes perfect sense. You don't need to apologize."

"Does his wife have any idea?"

"Albert," she said, an edge rising in her voice before she pursed her lips and thought the better of it. "No, I'd say she doesn't."

"Would she toss him out?"

"I don't think so," Lotte said. The Church wouldn't let Henry go easily. "She'd probably make him move away. What's this about

James's parents?"

"You were kind of right. They do think the cure works. Seeing as how I've got a kid now, they want him to get shocked into oblivion and fry all the queer out." Albert shook his head and steered the car onto Edgar Avenue. "They know he's still queer, but not that he got arrested a couple of times. They'd be after him lock, stock, and barrel if they knew that."

"Sure." Lotte yawned and used a fingertip to trace around Daisy's fine nose and chin—her own features transplanted to someone else, and the wide mouth that was just like Henry's. The car door opened, and out they climbed. "Are you going to see him?"

"I ought to," Albert said. "But we can't shake the feeling that his parents have somebody watching the place. His brother, maybe. The real dumb one."

"Isn't that a little paranoid?" She stepped ahead of him. "Open the door for me; the neighbors are watching."

He stretched his mouth into a grin, chucked Daisy on the cheek, and bowed them into the house.

"Better," she said. "Very caring."

"Aw, come on, doll, I do care. Maybe—" He patted the baby again, more gently. "D'you mind if I hold her for a little bit?"

"Wash your hands with carbolic," she said, and hugged Daisy a little tighter. Perhaps she ought to get used to Albert manhandling her baby, claiming her in public, but why did he have to bother them in private? It would be hard enough for the poor child one day, so why confuse her? The last thing Lotte wanted was for Daisy to think Albert was her father.

"Lotte," he said, a little less phlegmatic now. "Don't be ridiculous. I've held little Charlie plenty. I'll give her right back." He prized Daisy out of her hands, and Lotte nearly wept. "I'll give her right back," Albert said more gently. "She's a pretty little girl, doll. Got your nose, doesn't she?"

"Yes, she does." Lotte's voice trembled. "Thank you for being so kind to us."

"You don't have to thank me. I figure you've put up with James for long enough," he said. "You think maybe he could be the godfather? Otherwise, it'll have to be Lou, right?"

"Absolutely not. James is out of the question." Her voice was so sharp it made Daisy wail. She snatched her back from Albert, rocked and soothed her, and sank to the couch, where the baby rooted at her breast. Within a moment, Lotte forgot her anger and even Albert's presence while her daughter latched onto her, tangled a hand in her necklace, and steadied her breathing. "That's better," she said. "Mommy's sorry."

"So am I," he said. "Of course you don't want him as your kid's godfather."

"I didn't think," she said after a long pause. "That you particularly cared about God or godparents."

"Well." Albert rubbed the back of his neck and shifted his weight from his toes to his heels and back again. "It's just what you do with a baby. I knew you'd be wanting to do it, and you probably don't have anyone in mind. Lou and Cynthie'd like the job; we did it for them."

Come to think of it, they were her only choices. If only Henry's sister could sponsor Daisy. Lotte liked Clara sight unseen, and she was Henry's godson's mother besides. From what Lotte knew of her, Clara would probably be thrilled.

"You're probably right," she said. "Telephone them and ask them soon."

"Sure thing," Albert said. "Do you want me out of your hair? I could probably go to James's."

"I've only kicked you out of your own house once," Lotte said. "It's up to you. I'm going to take a nap with her. Did your mother bring any casserole? She said she would."

"Yeah," he said. "It's here. She dropped it before I left to bring you home. You're lucky she doesn't like you and has baby Charlie to fuss about."

Lotte couldn't help but grin. "You'd think she would, considering I cured you and all. I would forgive you for overreaching your station, personally."

"You'll never forgive me at all," he said.

She thought of Henry's frantic voice and the smell of oil

before she draped Daisy over her shoulder and patted her back. "No, I won't. But you're not likely to forgive me, either."

Albert shrugged. "Guess I'll go to James's after all. Give me a ring there if you need to."

CHAPTER SEVENTEEN

In choir dress, Henry paced the ten steps across his office, then back again. His stole flapped against him, slid partway down his right shoulder, and he jerked it back into place. He'd better compose himself before William saw him, but he couldn't help but be eaten alive with fury.

"Henry." William's voice filtered down the corridor. "I have a favor to ask of you."

"What is it, Father?" With a great deal of effort, he straightened, evened out his stole, and peered at William, who hadn't even vested yet.

"There's an urgent situation—another anointing, sadly. I need to see to it right away. Would you be so good as to step in for me at the Walheim child's baptism?"

Henry clenched his jaw around the burst of joy. "You're certain you wouldn't rather have me go to the hospital?"

"I'm certain." William clapped him on the upper arm. "Come on. They'll be here in a couple of minutes."

"Yes," Henry said. Pretending not to be overjoyed was growing wearisome. Half of him wanted to kiss William on both cheeks, and the other half was ready to sing show tunes.

"You've already vested?"

"In case you needed help." He shrugged it off, hoping William was too distracted to wonder why Henry thought he'd need help with a baptism. "Guess I'm a mind reader."

"Very sensible." His mentor sighed and stretched out his shoulders. "The parishioner in the hospital asked specifically for me, you see. They can't all be in thrall to you, I suppose."

"Who is it?"

"Mr. Holz. I've been his pastor for a long time."

"I'm sorry." Henry crossed himself. "May God bless him and keep him." Henry was sorry, particularly at the joy Mr. Holz's final agonies were causing him. He was ecstatic, of course, but this was worrisome, too. Although he'd been angry, it had been for the best when the baptism fell to William. He wondered whether any priest had ever baptized his own child and how he would keep from falling to his knees and weeping.

Then again, he thought as William went out, perhaps it wouldn't matter so much. Furious as he'd been just seconds before that it wasn't to be he, Henry and Lotte had agreed upon William before Daisy was even born. If Henry were overcome, everyone would know the truth. If he weren't, he would crush them both.

After he'd gone to Lotte in the hospital, the nurse, charmed by his office or his face or both, had let him wander about as he might. Wander he did, right to the nursery window, where he didn't recognize his own daughter out of the sea of babies. When the nurse had pointed her out, what had he done? Stared and shrugged. Nothing primal rose in him the way it had when William told him about the birth. Only vague curiosity that he might see Lotte's chin or hands or something, that was all that held him longer than a moment.

Henry had gone home and cried after that. Lotte had told him that the baby was beautiful, that she looked like him, but he didn't see any of it, and the faint scent of Lotte's hair still clung to his clothes. Before the birth, he'd worried that his love for Lotte might pale next to his love for the child, but he wasn't even a good enough father to love his child for any other reason than because he was supposed to.

Still, though. It was only right that he baptize her and offer up the suffering that watching Albert Walheim's sister sponsor her would cause. Maybe he wasn't such a devoted father—his punishment, perhaps—but the baby deserved a good family. Once Henry got her away from Albert Walheim and his man friend, Clara, David, Anna, and the rest would adore her and put him to shame.

Henry knelt upon the cold floor and offered four half-prayers before giving up and kneeling in silence. Voices sounded in the vestibule, and it was time. Lotte's reaction would likely give them away, and he wished William had had time to at least telephone them with the last-minute change.

A deep breath did nothing to steady his hand, which trembled on the leather-bound book. He strode down the corridor with measured steps and greeted the small group with a smile.

"Good afternoon," he said. "Father Kestner regrets that he's not able to be here. An emergency summoned him elsewhere." He ushered them back out to the church door and avoided Lotte's eyes. The child was secure, snoozing in her aunt's arms, pink and peaceful as any other baby.

"What do you ask of the Church of God?" he said to Cynthie, and when she answered back,

"Faith," her voice was nasal, grating as Barbara Morris's.

Henry cleared his throat before proceeding, still determined against looking at Lotte, and cringed at Cynthie's 'eternal life.' He finished off the Latin, bent forward, and his breath sighed over the baby's face. Seven little wisps of hair danced on her forehead. The second time, her eyes fluttered, and he wondered at how delicate the eyelashes were. Third time, her mouth stretched out of its pursed little rosebud and was wide like Clara's, like Helen's, like his own.

When at last his hand touched her face, his breath caught. Her skin was at once the most fragile and the most substantial thing he'd ever felt. He lingered at her breast, her heart beating against the rapid pulse in his thumb. Although he stared into the lines of his book, he could finally say it all from memory. His anger vanished, likewise his sadness at Albert's presence. Suddenly, waiting was the best thing they could have done, for if everything was public now, he'd be deprived of this, of the feel of Daisy's soft head beneath his hand as he pleaded for the safety of her soul.

Henry led them indoors to the baptistery, although he wanted to take Daisy in his arms the way he had taken up the long-ago practice baby. He wondered if she would feel the same way, warm, elastic, and alien. *The War of the Worlds*, the diamonds-on-glass shriek, the heat, John Markwell, the itch of his sweaty collar, their smirking professor so like William, it all came rushing back, and with it, the same impulse to run to the hill overlooking the river, to stare out at the world. Only this time, he would not be alone. He hadn't really baptized the Martian Child, and his family had been fifty miles away. Now, his family was beside him: Lotte's eyes intense when he met them and Daisy still peaceful in her aunt's grasp.

He cleared his throat and continued, "*Exorcizo te, omnis spiritus immunde...*" and then touched a finger to his tongue, which he usually did not. Caressing one seashell ear, the other, the pert nose, he spoke with unusual care, for he had baptized dozens of children, spoken the *ephphetha* every time. Of course, those were not his children, and he had not felt then that his own soul was being opened, his own senses awakened.

When he anointed their child, he saw a tear escape from Lotte's eye and tremble on the very edge of its black lash. She was thinking, he knew, of their stolen few moments in the hospital, the smell of oil still on his hands. However sweet it was to think of Lotte, Henry didn't like to be reminded of the hospital, for there, he was an idiot who thought seeing Daisy would be some type of instant magic, rather than this long, glorious sunrise that shimmered on the horizon and spilled color across the shadowy baptistery.

Shrugging out of his violet stole, he took up the white one, his self-pity flying away with the old. As he asked Cynthie and Lou the final questions, he knew his voice was husky, but was confident no one would know why, save for Lotte. In passing, he wished that she, not Cynthie, could hold Daisy, but he knew neither of them could bear that and keep their countenance. His hand was already trembling on the little silver vessel.

Just as the first time, he found the Latin tucked against his cheek, a sweet red Easter jellybean, and steadied his breath.

"Elizabeth Margaret, *ego te baptizo in nomine Patris.*"

A quick splash, and her wisps of hair fluffed into tiny ringlets.

"*Et Filii.*"

Her eyes blinked. Just once.

"*Et Spiritus Sancti.*"

Daisy squawked three times and fell silent. The water flowed through Henry's fingers, and he was reborn.

After Daisy was well and truly baptized, Lotte was too raw and sad for the little party she'd promised Lou and Cynthie, but she said nothing to dissuade them before they drove away. Albert shut her in their car, climbed inside, and she prayed he'd leave her alone. Instead, he began to chortle as hard as she'd ever seen him and dropped his head on the steering wheel, shoulders shaking.

Daisy was impatient, tugging at her blouse, so she unbuttoned, settled her in, and finally asked,

"What on earth is so funny?"

Albert wiped his eyes because he was actually crying with laughter and raised a brow at her. "Aw, come on, doll. You being so sly and all."

Panic shot through her, and she nearly jolted Daisy away from her breast. "Sly? What on earth?"

"The priest, Lotte." Another snicker. "The goddamned priest. I thought you went to Mass every day to get holier than thou or something. Come to find out you're going there to get— Well." He leaned back in his seat, shook his head, and started the engine. "To get something else, anyway. You're something else yourself. Never would've thought it."

"Albert, if you're insinuating that Father Henry and I are somehow immorally… Are doing—"

"Now, now." He held up a hand. "I'm not insinuating a thing. I'm saying it plain out. Father Henry's a father, all right. A guy doesn't look at just any kid like that. I've only seen that look on one other guy lately, and that's Lou. Look, doll, I'm not here to judge you. Glass houses and all that. It's just funny. Sister Lotte Klopstock and the priest." He sighed then, evidently remembering his manners and James. "I'm not wrong, am I?"

"No," she said and hated that her voice broke. "No, you're not wrong. But you don't understand. Henry and I love—"

"Now," he said. "I think we both know I understand pretty damn well. What I want to know is, what're you going to do about it? Is he quitting the priesthood or what?"

"It's not so simple to leave," she said. "It's not like quitting your job at the factory. There are rules. The Holy Father has to allow it. And I think Henry's afraid of hurting Father Kestner. And there's the scandal to consider, of course."

"Well, good." Albert's voice was hard. "That's no job to be quitting anyway. And you. You know what would happen if you ran off with Father Henry."

"Yes," she said, a little distracted by Daisy's tug on her collar. "I met that Father Markwell last year after he left Holy Trinity; he went to seminary with Henry. It was dreadful for him, and it would be dreadful for us. I know."

"Yeah, dreadful," Albert said and slammed the brake so hard Daisy's mouth jerked away from Lotte, who yelped with pain. Neither the sight of his wife's breast nor the child's cries appeared to make any impression on him. "You and Father Henry won't get the worst of any scandal. Sure, Barbara Morris will gossip. Father Kestner will cry a river until he finds somebody new. You know who'll get the worst? Me. James. That's who."

"And what if I don't care about you and James?" Fury blinded her while she shushed the baby and laid a brief hand over her throbbing wound. "What has either of you ever done to make me give up my happiness for you? Don't you think I'd rather Henry and I raise our own baby—his baby? Why should he and Daisy and I be miserable because you're an unrepentant sinner?"

"Glass houses, doll." Albert's voice was quiet now, almost soothing. "Glass houses. Now come on. Let's have our party with Lou and Cynthie, and you can take the baby to see Father Henry all you want. Like I said before, see him all you want. But keep it under wraps."

"For now," she said. "For now, we will." For, of course, she would. Lotte hated that she cared about Albert and even cared about James, no matter what she said in anger. More than that, she hated that Lou and Cynthie were waiting for them when Henry was sitting at home without them. She could see in his face and hear in his voice as he drew closer and closer to Daisy. While Lotte had fallen in love with Daisy the moment they brought her into the room, Henry's love had unfolded over the course of the ceremony until she had no idea how he'd been able to send them off. Daisy was a month old, and she hadn't been to Henry's house once. Why was Lotte plagued with Cynthie and Lou today?

"Hey, honey, there's my little goddaughter." Cynthie reached out her arms and grabbed for Daisy. "What took you two so long?"

"We were just talking." Lotte summoned a smile, squeezed Cynthie's arm, and led her into the kitchen. "Would you like some lemonade?"

"Sure. Can I help at all? Need me to give her a bottle?"

"No, thank you," Lotte said. "I'm not giving her bottles much."

"You'll get an infection." Cynthie was all disapproval and confusion. "Least, that's what my doctor says. We're not cows, Lotte. He says there's no way we can keep up with a hungry little one."

"It's fine. She just ate, and I've kept up with her well enough so far." With one fluid movement, Lotte poured the lemonade and grabbed Daisy away from her supposed aunt. "Really, I wouldn't worry."

"What're you two doing for your anniversary this summer? Can't believe it's going on five years already." Cynthie tipped the vodka into her lemonade and carried a tray out to the men. "If you wanna go away, Lou and I'll watch Daisy."

"I doubt we'll go away," Lotte said. "But thank you."

"Maybe a nice dinner one night and dancing," Albert said. "Nothing too fancy."

"Well, you oughta do something fancy, shouldn't he, Lotte? A new bracelet, anyway." Cynthie slugged her drink, and her cheeks flushed. Lotte hated more and more that this woman was to be Daisy's spiritual guide and pined for the mysterious Clara.

"I'm sure whatever Albert decides will be lovely," she said. Although her mother had never felt more like it, it was Daisy who began to cry. The wail was relentless, a harsh, high siren's shriek that refused to be quelled. Her belly was full, her linen clean, her skin neither hot nor cold.

After Cynthie had made everything worse, she and Lou departed with kisses and empathy. When his sister and brother-in-law were safely down the street and around the corner, Albert clicked his lighter and breathed a heavy sigh along with a lungful of smoke, the tension melting from his bones.

"She's a good kid so far, doll. She got rid of Cynthie real quick. Remind me to get her a bike when she's old enough."

Lotte wanted to smile, but the baby's face was red and angry, her lips back in an animal snarl. She tried patting Daisy's back again to no avail.

"You think maybe the baptism didn't take?"

"Oh, shut up," she said. Why should she be patient and obedient with him, anyhow?

"Why don't you take her outside for a walk, doll? It's a nice enough day." Albert grabbed for his hat and let the cigarette dangle from his lip. "Thought I'd go for a walk myself."

"You're going to James now?"

"I'm going for a walk." He winked and tossed the crocheted baby blanket across the room. "Maybe you ought to do the same."

He was telling her to go to Henry, she realized, just as he went to James. And not just for today, either, but all the time. Albert would be with James all the time, and she with Henry. Before, they had lived together separately, and now they would live separately together.

"It is a nice day," she said. "Perhaps you're right."

"I am right." With one shove, he sent the carriage reeling toward her. "See you around, doll." Albert nodded once, a twinkle in his eye—no doubt leftover amusement that she and Henry would be together—and went out.

She couldn't take the carriage, of course; it was bound to cause attention. The only thing to do was carry Daisy and hope Henry had something to improvise for a crib. If a manger was good enough for

Our Lord, she reasoned, a decent-sized basket ought to be plenty for Daisy. The screams were still going strong, but she couldn't leave just yet. How odd would it look to leave the house for a stroll five minutes after her husband? Lotte reached for Cynthie's glass and polished off the last of her spiked lemonade. After a moment, Henry's hand trembling against his white stole came into her mind, and she knew she couldn't delay any more, neighbors be damned.

The walk to Henry's, once so familiar, seemed longer than it used to, even though Daisy had quieted down in the sweet spring sunshine. A baby was a lot to carry all those blocks, and she felt like everyone was staring out their windows at them. And that everyone knew exactly where she was going and why.

Lotte forgot Father Kestner and her worries about barging in on them. She flung wide the door, shut it, and stood for a brief second in the foyer. Henry sprang from the couch, enveloped them both, and she let her own tears fall at last.

"I knew you'd come back," Henry said. "I prayed all afternoon you would. It's been almost unbearable without you. William's still gone; Mr. Holz died." He crossed himself and muttered a quick *requiem aeternam*. "Lotte, please, may I?"

He stared at Daisy with such unabashed longing that it nearly shattered Lotte's heart.

"Please," she said and held out her arms. "I want her to know you."

Henry was cautious, his hands clammy when he took Daisy in his grasp, and so clumsy with nerves, he nearly dropped her. "I'm sorry."

"Go on now," she said. "Don't be shy; you're her father. You've got more right to hold her than anybody else, and heaven knows, everybody else tries to snatch her up."

"Let them try," Henry said and steadied. "Do you remember me, Daisy?"

"Are you this awkward with your nieces and nephews?" Lotte asked. "From what I've heard, you seem completely natural with them, Uncle Father Henry."

"Aw, come on, I've finally gotten them to stop with that."

Henry relaxed despite himself. "Who're you calling awkward? None of them are mine." But Daisy was his, and he seemed to remember it. With a gentle, low swoop, he lifted her into the air, kissed each of her cheeks, and settled her head onto his shoulder. "Come here, Lotte."

She went and buried her face in his other shoulder. Something like contentment, which she had never known, but presumed she would if she saw it, washed over her. She was, in that moment, safe, absolutely so. More important than that, Daisy was safe, Henry was safe, and they were together alone.

"So," Henry said and led them to the sofa. "So."

"So." Lotte smiled, bit her lip, and offered her finger for Daisy to squeeze. "I should tell you something. Albert knows."

"How?" He shifted, straightened. "Did he insist on the truth?"

"No, he figured it out this afternoon. His sister, Cynthie, the godmother, has a little boy, and you looked at Daisy the same way her husband looks at Charlie. That's what he said anyway."

"Huh. So, what else did he say?"

"He laughed 'til he cried, but I think he couldn't help but be scandalized. No matter how much he carries on with James, he was raised in the Faith as much as you or I. He said the priesthood is 'no job to be quitting,' but mostly because he's worried about himself and James. He needs a wife more than ever with all that's been happening, the arrests and the names in the paper. It's always worse during Eastertide, he says."

"And what did you say?" Henry was all quiet calm, ever the patient counselor. Daisy dozed in the bend of his elbow, and Donizetti hummed on the radio.

"I said I wouldn't give up my happiness for them, but we'd stay discreet for now."

"A wise compromise." The smell of Sunday incense dusted his hair, and the breeze teased it out. "The idea of getting them lobotomized doesn't sit particularly well with me, either, but we'll think of something. In the meantime, how long can you stay?"

"As long as you'll have me," she said.

"Forever, then. Fair enough. In that case, we ought to get some dinner."

"I'll fix us something if you'll take Daisy. And if you'll come talk to me. I feel like it's been years since I've been here."

"Of course I'll talk to you." He grabbed her hand, kissed her, and released her to rummage through his cabinets, to try and scrounge up a meal with leftovers from Clara and Barbara Morris. "It doesn't feel like years; it feels like decades. Centuries, even."

Lotte pulled out plates, pots, steamed slices of ham, warmed day-old bread, and opened a can of creamed corn. Yes, she had learned to cook for Albert, but that was simply for sustenance, since her parents' cook was a thing of her past. Cooking for Henry was that, too, but also a meditative act, one borne of love and vocation. Her small life of prayers, watercolors, and opera on the radio would be enough, full even, with Henry and Daisy in it.

"I'm sorry it isn't much," she said.

"Why on earth are you sorry about that? It's my paltry leftovers, after all. You've done much better than I could with them." He took a bite, sipped from a can of Schlitz, and settled back into his chair. "Did you hear William's adding a third Mass on Sundays?"

"Is he? It's been so crowded, I'm hardly surprised." The ham wasn't bad, but the bread was. She sighed, unbuttoned her dress, and reached for Daisy. "Who's going to say it, then?"

"We'll trade off, I suppose." He mussed up his curls in the back. "It's good of him to offer it, although he's adding back the extra penance, too. I'd swear he's trying to keep my hours too full to spend much time here."

"Do you think he suspects anything?"

"William always suspects something. I doubt he assumes outright, or he'd have called me out on it. I wondered this morning when he asked me to baptize Daisy, but Mr. Holz did pass on, so I suppose he was telling the truth." Henry shrugged and polished off his meal. "May the souls of all the faithful departed, through the mercy of God, rest in peace."

"Amen," Lotte murmured. When Daisy was through with her dinner, Lotte gathered up the plates and took them to the sink.

Much later, after Compline and Matins, when Daisy was fed and sound asleep, Lotte woke to find the bed empty. A breeze fluttered in from the window, the smell of lilacs with it. The hour was too early for Lauds; the moon wasn't even halfway to the horizon line. Daisy was silent; Henry was silent. Dragging the quilt from the bed, Lotte wrapped it around her shoulders and crept past Daisy's empty basket.

The door fell open without a sound, and she tiptoed into the living room. Henry stood in a slant of moonlight, his chest bare and a pair of grey sweats hanging from his waist. She was ten feet away and the light was low, but she saw the rise and fall of his breath and Daisy's, the gooseflesh on his forearms. The baby was burrowed in his arms, save for a stray foot that hung over his elbow.

Lotte watched them in silence. Henry cupped the bare foot in his hand, bent his head, and kissed the smooth, pink instep.

CHAPTER EIGHTEEN

Certain sounds were a given throughout Henry's week. The choir sang at High Mass on Sundays. The schola chanted more often than that. Sanctus bells, muttering servers, the clink of the thurible, all part of the fabric of his weekdays and his Sundays.

Always, however, without fail, was the bawling, shrieking cacophony of wailing babies. Here at St. Jerome's, in Cincinnati, and even—he'd swear to it, although it might be revisionist history—at the Athenaeum. Without exception, while he prayed the Canon, an ill-timed wail threatened his *igitur* or his *supplices te*. He gathered William was immune to all unromantic noise or simply entered another plane of existence during Mass, but after five years as an ordained priest, Henry was still caught unawares.

Adding to this now, although his back was turned and his head was down and she was halfway back in the nave, his ears could pick Daisy's cries out of the fussing of fifty other infants. And so, he would pray the Canon, but he would also wonder what the matter was. Was she sick? Was she hungry? Did she want him? Recognize him? Or worse, did she want Albert? He was recently obsessed with the idea that Daisy might think Lotte's husband was her father or prefer Albert to him. When he finally turned around, the temptation to glance over grew worse and worse.

"Henry," William said after one such Mass, when Henry was

181

on his way out of the sacristy and wondering how long it might be until he could steal away again.

"Hello, Father."

"Yes, hello. Listen, Henry, do you have a moment?" William's arms were always stiff, his shoulders back as though he was up for uniform inspection.

"Of course I do. Anything wrong?"

Rather than respond, William led Henry to his own office and settled into the chair behind Henry's desk. "You've been distracted once again."

"A lot on my mind, I guess." Henry shrugged, but he was wary. Had his eyes slipped to Daisy after the Canon one too many times?

"Such as?"

None of your damned business, he thought, but said,

"Family things. Nothing's really the matter. I'm sorry, Father. I'll do better."

"You needn't apologize," William said. "It occurred to me that neither of us has gone away in the past entire year. I'd be more than willing to allow you to go first. A month's retreat would surely do you some good. Get away from it all. Take in an opera. Enjoy yourself for a change."

"A month?" The horrified tone wouldn't be quelled. He cleared his throat. "That seems like an awfully long time." But maybe he could bring Lotte and Daisy somewhere? No, William would notice they were gone. "I don't think I could be away for a month."

"Why ever not, Henry?"

"Don't want to leave you in the lurch," he said. "There's too much here for one person to handle for a month. Listen, Father, I'm fine. No need to go away. If you feel the need, though, you should go." Perhaps William would leave, and they'd both breathe a little easier for a few weeks.

"Perhaps I shall." He sounded a bit surprised at his own willingness. "But when I return, I'll have to insist you go somewhere, too. You're distracted and irreverent sometimes, but you do have a young man's zeal. If you allow it to rage, my boy, it will burn itself out. And then you'll be of no use to anyone, least of all able to help the parishioners as you desire."

'My boy' again. Honestly. It irritated him just then that William might be right. He could use a vacation, but he'd not leave his wife and child behind. He wasn't sure when it had begun, perhaps when he'd turned around and seen Lotte watching him press his lips to Daisy's tiny foot, but he'd grown accustomed to thinking of her as his wife. The thought of her was tender enough to make him smile despite William's scrutiny.

"Yes, you're probably right. I will go away. I'd just rather not do it right now. Maybe in the fall, before Embertide." He could always manufacture an excuse then. "Are you planning to leave after Pentecost?"

"After the Octave," he said. "We shall see. Although, as you said, it's too much for one person anymore. Well, anyhow. Do take care to be more attentive to your duties."

"I will, Father." He should be attentive, but did William have any idea how difficult it was to listen to one's own unhappy child during a solemn service? Of course not. "Shall we say Terce?"

William nodded, accepted it as the olive branch it was, and back to the sanctuary they went.

Afterwards, Henry went out to the street, and there was a man in a night robe, walking backwards and singing "All Glory, Laud, and Honor" along with the church bells. Usually, they sounded a siren when somebody escaped from the nuthouse, but he hadn't heard anything. He hugged the handrail for a moment and waited.

To whom the lips of children
Made sweet Hosannas ring.

Of course, walking backwards and all, the man stumbled and fell on a rock. Henry hurried forward and offered a hand up. The man's grip was firm, but his expression was dazed, not dangerous.

"You all right there?" Henry asked.

"You're wearing a dress," the man said.

Henry couldn't help it. He chuckled, and it seemed to break the man's daze because he started laughing, too. You could call the nuthouse, and they'd come—everybody had seen the wagons. But it was a nice day, and the man was probably harmless, so Henry said,

"Why don't we take a little stroll?"

With a small nod, the man loped backwards beside Henry as he cut through the neighborhood back towards Wayne Avenue. *All glory, laud, and honor to thee, Redeemer King* looped through his head, and the lilac breeze tickled his curls. He'd be late for Penance, and there was no good way he could explain to William that he'd returned a lunatic to the asylum on a whim.

"What's your name?"

"I'm Father Henry," he said. "What's yours?"

"Winston Churchill."

"Ah." Figured, didn't it? "Nice to meet you, Mr. Churchill."

Winston stumbled backwards and fell again, this time in some poor woman's immaculately kept flowerbed. Henry plucked one of the crushed daisies and secreted it away for later. Although he offered a hand, Winston leapt to his feet unaided and continued backwards. They were only halfway to Dayton State.

"You stole a daisy," Winston said.

"Yes, I suppose I did." A thought shimmered before him then, beside Winston's plain, pale face. There were things he could talk about with a crazy man that he couldn't say to anyone else. "I have a little girl named Daisy. It's for her and her mother. Well, for her mother, really. Daisy's only a baby yet." He smiled and settled into his stride. Winston turned around and kept pace beside him. "She's the prettiest little girl in Dayton, and I'm not just saying it because I'm a proud papa. Takes after her mother."

Winston pulled another flower from the pocket of his robe and handed it to him without a word. He spun, crossed Clarence Street backwards, and started to hum, which soon became a full-throated song.

Daisy, Daisy,
Give me your answer, do!
I'm half crazy,
All for the love of you!

Henry wanted to smirk—Winston was clearly a bit more than half crazy—but he kept it back.

It won't be a stylish marriage,

I can't afford a carriage.

The spring sunshine skipped and shimmered across the sidewalk on Wayne. Everything heightened—the smell of gasoline, of lilacs, the clatter of the number six trolley. Immaculate, St. Mary's, and St. Jerome's all chimed eleven o'clock in polyphony. A shout rose from the guard shack beside the hospital wall, and a couple of real, live men in white ran out, grabbed Winston by the arms, and tossed a straitjacket over him.

"You should've called us, Father," one of them said. "This guy's off his rocker; he could've really gone nuts."

Peaceful, singing Winston began to scream and flail, but he sounded to Henry more frightened than insane.

"Is that really necessary?" Henry asked, following the men through the gate and over the path. "He wasn't hurting anybody, just wandered off."

The orderly raised an eyebrow that took in the guards and gates, the siren, and the walls. "You think you just wander off from here?"

"What's wrong with him?"

"Schizophrenic. Sees things that aren't there, hears things, thinks he's Winston Churchill. That kind of thing." He reached forward and shoved Winston along. Winston snapped and growled like a wild dog. "Listen, Father, thanks for bringing him back, but call us next time."

"Sure." Henry continued after them, the men panting now, and Winston whimpering. On the wide main steps, the orderly turned and said,

"You're free to go, you know, Father. No need to be coming in here."

"It's all right," he said and continued behind him. Although he had no particular desire to step beyond the threshold, some strange compulsion drove him to put foot in front of foot, the same compulsion that had driven him to walk Winston back. No one wanted to go inside. The building loomed over the neighborhood like a silent, domed specter, and nobody in his right mind would get within ten feet.

Everyone feared the place, but when he'd been in for a couple of sick calls last year, it hadn't seemed so bad. Cold, yes. Full of crazy people, of course. But none so terrible. It seemed like the kind of place that would give Albert Walheim a few pills or a stern talking-to, not electrocute him or turn his brain into a—what had Lotte said?—a mashed-up beet.

The orderlies were consumed with Winston, who had begun kicking and had to be carried. Henry heard his screams as they dragged him off, with other screams mixed in, too. A woman huddled in fetal position on the floor to his left and rocked, her ragged gown open at the back. He blushed and averted his eyes, but not before he saw the lumps of her spine marching up toward her neck. Another woman staggered up to him, grabbed his sleeve, and tried to lead him down one of the corridors. As gently as he could, he prized her hands away, and they were crisscrossed with scars, big purple blooms, rich indigo and violet patterns intricate enough for a cope or a tapestry.

"Bless me, Father; bless me, Father; bless me, Father," she said over and over, until Henry laid a hand on her head and muttered a quick prayer for her, for all of them. Visiting the sick was a work of mercy, and he had always done it. Or at least, he'd thought he had, and hadn't known the sick were sanitized in deference to his office. His spine prickled, and he felt almost indecent, conscious of some unnamable sin. When Lotte had gone to the jail, she'd complained of it, had wanted to shower, although she'd touched nothing. Henry made a cross upon the woman's forehead with his thumb, nodded to her, and walked backwards toward the door, just like Winston, unwilling to expose his back and be caught unawares. The air was all oppressively sinister. It felt like Halloween night with Clara or his buddies, telling ghost stories until it seemed the air was oozing with evil and the next thump would be Satan himself.

Outside, he marched across the grounds, past the guard shack, fairly ran across Wayne Avenue to the neighborhood, and only drew breath when he'd rounded onto Edgar and the place was behind him. Penance was at eleven. No way he'd make it back before eleven-thirty. He continued up Edgar, and both hoped and didn't hope to meet Lotte in the street. Naturally, he'd take any chance to see her, but he felt somehow unclean with the woman's scrawny back burned into his mind and the grease of the other woman's hair still on his hand. Where were the nurses who had greeted him with tapers and led him to the sick? The orderlies who had let patients lean on their arms, rather than dragging them? No doubt they were busy turning a dozen brains into mashed-up beets.

When he passed Lotte's house, he strained for a glimpse of her and of Daisy, but didn't stop. He laid the two crumpled flowers at the base of Lotte's plaster Blessed Virgin and carried on toward St. Jerome's.

"I'm sorry to bother you, Mrs. Walheim." The woman at the door was of middle height, middle weight, and average features. And she knew Lotte's name. "But may I come in?" A car door slammed; a man came up the front walk and joined them.

"I'm sorry." Lotte spoke from behind the screen door as Daisy began to squawk and fuss behind her. "But what's this regarding? Have we met? I apologize if we have. I can't remember a thing since the baby."

"We know that's not your husband's baby," the woman said.

Lotte paled, and her vision swam. Her stomach clenched, but she didn't show it. Just like at the jail, she remembered her mother griping at the maids and bickering with the gardeners who'd planted her roses on the wrong side of the house.

"Of all the insulting things. Of course, she's my husband's child. How dare you come to my home and speak to me that way?" For now, she thought of Henry as her husband, and they called each other such during their stolen hours of family life.

"She's not either. Now, may we come in?" The woman pursed her lips. "I'm Mrs. Emily Mills, and this is my husband, Robert."

"You're James's parents?" Lotte stepped back and let them pass. They were planning to pass regardless. "Is James all right? Why would you say such an awful thing to me? My husband and your son are friends. You don't think...?" She tried to fight a snicker. "You don't think James is the father, do you? I assure you, he's nothing of the kind. He's just a friend of the family. There's no call to insult both of our morals."

"Young lady," Mr. Mills said. "You know as well as I do that James couldn't any more father somebody's kid than fly. He's queer as a maypole, and we all know it."

"All right," Lotte said. She picked up Daisy and squeezed her to protect them both. "What's this about?"

Mr. and Mrs. Mills brushed past them and took a seat on the sofa like they owned the place. "This is about your husband corrupting our son."

"From what I've heard," Lotte said and sat opposite them. "It was the other way around."

"Your pervert husband turned our James," Mr. Mills said. "Looks like his time in the nuthouse didn't do him much good after all."

On that, they were agreed, but Lotte wouldn't admit to it. "I don't think anyone can be 'turned.' I think they're just like that. Certainly, no one's had any luck turning them back. Why don't you let James be? He's not hurting anyone."

"He's hurting us," Mrs. Mills said. "And he's hurting you, too. You're a good Catholic, Mrs. Walheim. You must know he's hurting Our Lord, too. And damning himself to hell."

"I know it's sinful," she said. Daisy moaned and flailed and squirmed like an octopus in her arms. "But we ought to pray for them and do penance, not have their brains ripped out. Please, the baby's hungry. Will you just go?"

"Fine." Mr. and Mrs. Mills stood as one, and the wife continued, "But we're more than likely sending James off for the cure, and you should do the same with Albert."

"I never said my husband wasn't cured," Lotte said. "He doesn't need to go anywhere, and neither does your James."

Mr. Mills crept closer, glowered at her, and poked a finger in her face. "Now you listen here, you snooty little—"

"And what's this all about?" The front door thudded and

slammed. Albert thundered in and jerked Mr. Mills back by the collar. "You stay the hell away from my wife, Mills. Why'd you let this jerk in here, doll? Nothing but a load of damned trouble. Go on now, leave her alone."

Lotte trembled against the wall, her fingers numb, but managed to feed Daisy as Albert watched his lover's parents drive off. Mr. and Mrs. Mills would never start a rumor; her secret made James out to be a queer, and they had no idea that Henry was the father.

"Good riddance. Why did you let those two in, doll? They just butt right in or what?" Albert grabbed her free elbow and led her back to the couch.

"Basically, yes. They said they know Daisy isn't yours. I swore to them she is. They want me to commit you; they said—"

"They're putting James in the nuthouse?" Albert sounded more defeated than alarmed. "Yeah, not news to me. I've been telling him to move or at least get married, but he doesn't want to leave town, and he's dead set against getting hitched. Always has been."

"He doesn't want to leave you behind," Lotte said. "I can understand that. And being married this way is hard on both of us; of course, he doesn't want the same. But to go on as he is? His parents will get him... His brain..."

"I know, doll." Albert's head dropped between his knees just briefly, but long enough for Lotte to see how heavy the weight on his shoulders was to bear. She felt almost guilty, but she was the one who'd brought a child into the house. That was more than anyone else had done to further his lie. It was hard to even pinpoint what she felt guilty about. "I know. Thanks for sticking up for me with them. I know they're a rough crowd. They'd commit me themselves if they could."

"That I don't doubt," she said. "And you're welcome."

"Yeah, so." Albert rubbed the back of his neck. "How're things with Father Henry?"

"Excuse me?"

"Just asking."

"Fine, I suppose." She raised Daisy over her shoulder and patted her back. "Father Kestner keeps him busy, though. There are probably too many people for just the two of them. And Father

Kestner wants him to say an extra Mass and add extra Penance."

"You think he knows?"

"No. Can you imagine Father Kestner allowing it to go on if he did? He'd never sweep something like this under the rug."

"Huh, well." Albert's mouth stretched into a yawn. "You're probably right there. Can't say I envy you that, doll. Worrying about Father Kestner sounds worse than worrying about James's parents. Hell, I'm an atheist, and one look from him gets me halfway to the confessional."

"In that case," Lotte said. "What would it take to get you the rest of the way?"

"Jesus H. Christ himself in our sitting room." With one languid hand, Albert drew out a Marlboro, flicked his lighter, and pulled an ashtray from the side table. "Forget it, doll."

Lotte rolled her eyes. "Remind me why exactly I was sticking up for you. I'm going out tonight; are you?"

"Probably. We found another spot to replace the Wayne, finally. Probably better that way. Usually, when everybody talks about going to Wayne Avenue, they're meaning the nuthouse, not the queer bar. Never sat right, seeing as how that's where most of us from the queer bar end up."

"I'll pray for James," she said. "And so will Henry."

Albert snorted. "You do that. Will Father Henry be praying for the conversion of the lowly sinners before or after tumbling my wife into bed?"

Before she realized what she was doing, Lotte reached out her hand and slapped Albert's cheek. He was pale, and her palm and fingers left a red outline.

"Don't make me hate you," she said. "Things are difficult enough for both of us as it is."

"Fair enough." Albert stubbed out his cigarette and reached for his hat. He hadn't flinched or even blinked despite the lingering mark on his face. "Sorry you had to bother with James's parents. Never thought they'd come find you."

CHAPTER NINETEEN

I s slapping Albert a mortal sin?" Lotte asked, after the prayer was said and the plates cleared away.

"What's this?" Henry was far more absorbed in Daisy than he was in Albert and mortal sin. "Nah, he probably deserved it. Did you mean to?"

"Not really."

"Then no." A soft bit of skin like velvet or lamb's wool beckoned beneath Daisy's chin. How had he never noticed it before now? It whispered against his lips, and he kissed it over and over. Her hand passed over his cheek, and he kissed that, too. "Why'd you do it?"

"Do what?" Lotte started; she'd been in a daze, staring at the two of them.

"Slap Albert."

When she pried Daisy out of his hands, it left him cold and reeling. Lotte yawned, slid onto the sofa, and patted the space next to her. "He said some pretty awful things about you. I was angry."

"Hm. People who live in glass houses. What did he say?" Henry hated being curious, but he wondered what stones a homosexual atheist might be throwing his way now that Albert knew the truth of Daisy's parentage.

"For heaven's sake. Fine. He wondered if you'd be praying for the sinners' conversion before or after tumbling his wife into bed,"

Lotte said. "His wife, indeed. That's what made me angriest. I'm only his wife for appearances. He's never, er, tumbled me into bed himself, has he?"

That line of conversation didn't bear following or repeating or picturing in any sort of detail. Since Henry had been the one to bring it up, he was going to presume the question was rhetorical and drop the line dead in the water. Tumbling Lotte into bed was a suggestion with merit.

Henry drew Lotte against him and kissed her temple, which smelled of lavender. "I don't think I told you this yet. You're even more beautiful now than before Daisy came along. Wouldn't have thought you could possibly get any prettier."

She blushed. "Oh, Henry, stop."

"I mean it." He'd ignored his desire for her these past weeks, but found it far harder to abstain from one person in particular than to abstain from all women in the abstract. "I've missed you, you know." Said low in her ear.

Her head turned a fraction of an inch, her lips met his, and he found his ardor no less bright than before Daisy. Lotte's face was a little fuller, her eyes softer, and she was the mother of his child.

Daisy squealed. It broke the spell. He remembered Clara saying something about this sort of thing happening after Helen was born, and she didn't know where Mom and Dad had found the time to produce the seven of them. She'd been tipsy when she'd said it, but she had a point. With a rueful look, he scooped Daisy up and said,

"All right, I think it's bedtime."

"For whom?" Under Lotte's sly, sideways glance, he blushed to match her—he would never outgrow that—and tweaked the end of her hair.

"For all of us. Come on, let's put her down." He watched as Lotte soothed and fussed, fed and changed, although he might have been saying his offices. He'd let a few of them go here and there. It wasn't always practical with the baby, and he did plenty else besides.

At last, Daisy was snug and snoozing in her basket beside them, and the radio was humming "Amami, Alfredo" at its lowest volume. Lavender, lemon, bitter incense swirled together, their breathing grew ragged, and Lotte nearly shattered him with a brief, whispered,

"Be gentle, Henry."

He nodded, kissed her, and buried his face in the hollow of her collarbone. Every color on earth mixed behind his eyes when he closed them, the deep ochre of the church's masonry, the fern of the altar stone, jeweled reds, blues, golds, Lotte's auburn hair. Gentleness might well kill him tonight, but gentle he was.

Afterwards, she lay against him and breathed so quietly and evenly, he thought she'd fallen asleep. With a tug at the braid spilling across his chest, he said in a murmur,

"*The beams of our houses are of cedar, our rafters of cypress trees.*"

Lotte propped her head on her hand. "Was it you who left the daisies by my statue? Why didn't you stop in?"

"I did leave them," he said. "But I was late getting back, and besides, I've never been inside your house."

"You could. Heaven knows James has. And his parents. They came to see me the other day. They want to send him up Wayne Avenue and Albert, too."

"Hence the slap, I take it? No, I imagine it's easier for James to come and go from your house unremarked upon than it would be for me. It's difficult enough to get you in and out of here unnoticed."

"True." She yawned. "What brought you out into the neighborhood?"

"Oh." Did he want to sully her with all that? "Nothing much."

"Nothing much, indeed. What was it?" In the darkness, he could see her peering at him.

"I went over to Dayton State on an errand. Long story." He shuddered, and she felt it, tightened her grip on his shoulder. "It wasn't like before, Lotte. It wasn't like those sick calls. It was awful."

"I've heard," she said without much irony. "I'm sorry you had to go there."

I didn't have to, he wanted to say, but she was nodding off, and he was tired himself. There'd be time for all that later. For now, he tucked his knees behind hers and drifted into sleep.

Too early, much too early, he woke. At first, he thought his well-trained mind was ready for Lauds, but when the first haze burned off, he caught the dull purr of the telephone. Lotte had been up to feed Daisy, and her body now smelled of sweet milk and of them together.

The telephone rang again, and he buried his face deeper into Lotte's hair. His hand passed over a warm bundle of flannel—Daisy, glutted and snoozing beside her mother. Irritation threaded through his thoughts and knotted there. Just once, he would like an unbroken sleep, to be like any other father, needed urgently by only his wife and their baby. Responsible only for leading their nightly rosary, no bounding out of bed every three or six hours, no one's soul in peril at the most inconvenient hour of the night.

The ringing had died off, but started up again, seemingly louder and more grating than before. How many times would it ring before they'd give up? Would they give up? Did he truly want them to? Someone was probably dying, in need of Viaticum and his final blessings. With a deep groan, although quiet enough not to wake the others, he swung his feet from the bed and padded out to the kitchen.

"Hello?" His voice sounded thick and raspy even to his own ears.

"I'm so sorry to wake you, Father Henry. This is Dot Dailey. Listen, Tom's dad's in a bad way. We're thinking this is..." Her voice ended on a squeak.

"I'm sorry to hear it," he said. "What's the address?"

"1204 Carlisle."

"I'll be there as soon as I can," he said. "Do you have everything prepared?"

"Yeah, erm, yes, Father. We're out of lemons, though."

"It's all right; I'll bring one." He set the phone down, went to the crisper for a lemon, and set it among his oils. After yawning and rubbing his eyes with two fists, he groped in the dark for his cassock, which he hoped was buttoned right, found a stole, his surplice, and his shoes. Bending over in the dark, he kissed Daisy, then Lotte, and nudged her slightly. "Lotte."

"Hm?" She reached back and patted his empty space on the bed. "What's wrong?"

"Extreme Unction," he said against her ear. "I'll be back

194

before morning. Don't leave before I get home."

He kissed them both again, sustenance for his journey into the cool night, into another somber house that smelled of imminent death. No lights glowed in anyone's windows. A quick flash behind William's shades before Henry went into the church told him that his mentor was just finished with Lauds. Too bad the Daileys hadn't gone for him, although William deserved a night off more than anyone.

Henry rounded the corner, walked a couple of blocks beneath the streetlamps, and pushed open the gate at 1204 Carlisle. Dot greeted him with a taper and led him through the dark house, which was dotted with women in bathrobes and handkerchiefs folded over their hair, men in shirtsleeves. When he recited the Asperges, water flicked against his face, and a lone feather molted from his aspergillum. The water made him think of Daisy's soft head beneath his hand at her baptism. He drew nearer to Mr. Dailey and dismissed everyone else with one glance.

The door closed, and Mr. Dailey began his confession on a bare vapor of a whisper. Henry hardly understood him. Something about having an affair? Or was it that he didn't care? Despite the garbled words, he heard true contrition underlying the tone. Young though Henry might have been, he could tell when a voice was rote and monotonous and when the throat thickened, even the tiniest bit, with real sorrow. The weight of sorrow and contrition settled into his own breast, even as he muttered the absolution. To think he had nearly denied Mr. Dailey the grace of a happy death due to his own sloth. Denying someone the last sacraments was a mortal sin in itself, far worse than laziness.

He pinged the little bell, for Mr. Dailey hadn't much time, certainly not enough for Henry to dwell on the sin of sloth. Everyone trooped back in, but he didn't take his eyes off the dying man until the Host was secure on his papery tongue. Henry was perfectly sober and correct throughout and went through each prayer at a reverent pace.

So devout was Henry that when he finished and left the Daileys to their grief, the sun was peeking through the horizon line, and the clouds were tinged with rose pink. He could guess at the time, but wasn't sure he wanted to know, not when the Masses started at seven-thirty. Despite the many people he'd prepared for the journey to the next world, especially lately, it seemed he was sadder, and his soul felt heavier now than before. His wickedness made him ashamed—the spiteful thoughts for his own comfort, the idea that some poor man's death was inconvenient while his whole family grieved for him, and he could barely eke out a proper confession without his voice faltering.

When he got home, the first bell of the day struck six. He'd been gone for over two hours, and there was no hope of coffee until at least eight o'clock. A cry pierced the air as soon as he crossed the threshold. So much for finding his girls just as he'd left them.

"Oh, Henry." Lotte ran to him and rubbed the stubble on his face. "My goodness, I was worried. You were gone for so long. Daisy's a little feverish. I need to take her over to the doctor's this morning."

"What do you mean, feverish?" He reached for the baby and pressed his lips against her forehead, the way his mother used to do. "You don't think she's got the measles?"

"Doubt it. Cynthie's little Charlie gets fevers all the time. Babies just get them. But I'll take her in once they open."

Henry yawned, which shifted his shoulder into Daisy's gut. She coughed, and before he knew it, vomit was splattered halfway down his back. "Aw, now—"

"Just take it off. I'll wash it." Perhaps Lotte was as tired as he, but he could tell she wanted very badly to laugh. She took Daisy back into the crook of her elbow and held out her arm for the stained clothes. "You ought to shower before you go."

"I'm late, Lotte," he said, a little peevish. "This'll just have to do."

"But you look terrible. Father Kestner will—"

"I spent the better part of my night watching a man die," he said, more than a little peevish now and fully snapping at her. "That's excuse enough. William won't suspect anything just because I'm dog tired." Lotte winced, and he regretted his tone. "I'm sorry the baby's sick, sweetheart. Telephone when you're done at the doctor's." He kissed Lotte's forehead, but was wary of Daisy. Before he closed the door, he turned and caught a glimpse of the two of them, poor Lotte draped with his laundry, but waving the baby's hand.

Turning up the sidewalk, he rubbed at both eyes with the heels of his hands. The smell of sour milk was distinct and radiating from him. No one was at the church quite yet, so he staggered into the sacristy without bothering to hide his exhaustion.

"You might wish to reconsider the thought of a vacation." William raised a brow at him when he turned around. "You don't look well."

"I'm fine," he said. "Long unction last night. Mr. Dailey, *requiescat in pace*."

"I see. May God bless him and keep him." William's nose wrinkled, but he, of course, said nothing about Henry's apparent stench. "Well, I'll leave you to vesting."

Henry nodded, but as soon as William had gone, he sank into a chair, folded his arms on top of the linen chest, and drifted into sleep. Soundless, bright dreams washed over him—Rio or Venice, a beach, his feet wet up to the ankles as Lotte dandled Daisy in the surf.

"I'm not waking him up. You wake him up."

"No way. I'm not getting my chops busted."

"Aw, c'mon, Ralphie, Father Henry's not gonna bust your chops. D'you think he's sick? Should we get Father Kestner?"

"Your funeral." The bolder of the two altar boys darted his hand out like a fish and gave Henry's arm a tap so light it would never have actually woken him.

Henry snapped his head to full attention, a bad idea as it made him dizzy. "Good morning, boys. Is everything ready?" If he didn't refer to being caught napping, these kids sure as hell wouldn't.

"Yes, Father." The boys had both leapt back when he'd raised his head. "We're all done."

"Thank you." He squinted at the faded rubric, which he'd resigned himself to never memorizing.

"Say, Father, you're not sick, are you?"

"No, Ralphie, I'm not sick. But thank you for your concern." Henry wondered then if either boy was discerning a vocation and what he might say to them if they were. They would either never realize what they'd given up or would realize it when it was too messy and dangerous to stop.

197

The bell clanged; the three of them went out. The *Introibo*, the *Judica me*, Henry could ramble through those by rote when inwardly, he was as clumsy and ill-disposed as John Markwell ever was. He even slipped up—the boys exchanged sidewise glances—but his sluggish brain would only focus on Daisy. Was it measles? Mumps? Worse, maybe polio? Lotte said babies got sick all the time, but kids got awful diseases plenty. Ned's little boy had almost died from lockjaw back when Henry was in seminary. One of the few times Ned had ever telephoned. They'd all prayed for him, and he'd pulled through, *Deo gratias*. But Lotte, she was all by herself.

Still dizzy during the Agnus Dei, he managed to steady himself for the rest, but afterwards, dismissed the servers and went about his tasks with minimal effort. Everything was done correctly, if not particularly well.

"Henry," William said. "Go home. Why don't you call your sister and get her to nurse you back to health?"

"I'm not sick," he said.

"Go on. I'll call her myself."

"Very well, Father." Why was he fighting the chance to return to bed? "But don't bother Clara." On the conviction that she'd somehow just know, he'd avoided Clara since the baby was born. If she came into his house, she'd figure it out, although they were careful not to leave any of Daisy's things in plain sight. Of all people, he wouldn't mind Clara knowing, but his family all admired him to distraction, and well. It was messy and dangerous.

He sighed and threw himself down on the bed. If anything else bad happened today, he'd be the one sent up Wayne Avenue. The verses he'd quoted to John Markwell, speak of the devil, came whirling back into his head, and so did the distinct sense that he'd bitten off more than he could chew. What man in the world could cope with the demands of a few hundred parishioners, of William, of the offices of the priesthood, of his parents and siblings, of a wife, and of a sick child? One of those things alone was plenty for anyone. Living out two vocations might well kill him within six months, but the alternatives still made him uneasy. Everyone's crushing disappointment, his own crushing despair, or being crushed himself. He'd have laughed if he weren't on the brink of sleep.

When he woke, his stubble was longer, his cassock wrinkled, and his stench worse. And even better, Clara was staring at him from the doorway. Raising his head, which throbbed like hell, he tried to smile at her, but felt unaccountably awkward.

"Father Kestner called me," she said, awkward, too. "Even though you won't come over to my house anymore, I thought I'd be the bigger man, er, woman and make sure you're still alive."

"Still alive," he said. "I told him not to bother you. I'm not really sick, just had a long night."

"I guess." Clara smiled and brought in a cup of tea. "You look like David and I used to look when the kids were babies. Listen, you should let this cool off. Take a shower, maybe."

"A master of subtlety as always," he said. "But you're probably right. I'm ashamed to think when my last one was. It's not that I don't want to see you all; we're just up to our ears in work. We really do need a third priest." Not that they'd ever get one. Where would he live? The archdiocese would never hear of a third house. Besides, the last thing he needed was two Williams to avoid.

"See, and I've been saying it all along. Listen, Henry, we understand." She embraced him, unwashed body and all. "If I didn't know better, I'd say you smelled like baby spit-up."

"Well, thanks a lot," he said. "But you're right. Parishioner's baby this morning. Not the finest moment for either of us, I'd say."

"And here I thought it was just us married folks who got the brunt of all that. I'll get it washed for you. If there's one thing I can get out of fabric, it's that." She held it up after he shrugged out of it. "But it's not even stained." Clara's cold fingers pinched either side of his fuzzy chin. "Will you be honest with me? We've seen you less and less ever since you came back. The kids miss you. We all miss you." Her pupils shrank and grew, widening into the deep brown of her irises. Wet and pink, her tongue darted out to lick the edges of her lips. She was already steeling herself. "Where have you been, Henry?"

He didn't move to shake her hand away, just let her stand close and probe his eyes with hers. All breath left both of them, the deep gulp of air before a wild cadenza.

"I have a daughter." The notes gathered, sped, swooped high and low, and trilled off. Clara's hand trembled against his face in shivering vibrato. His stomach pitched forward, righted itself, but when his tongue found the words, he felt nothing but relief. "Her name is Daisy. She was born on Easter. I spend most nights with her and her mother."

"The woman," Clara said. "The one you talked about. She's her mother, isn't she? She was sad and... Henry, my God." For the third time in their adult lives, Clara's cheeks were wet with tears. "My God. Why did you keep this for so long?"

"You were proud of me," he said. "All of you were. And now—"

"And now you're my brother. I told you before that I wouldn't care, and I don't. You were trying to tell me then, weren't you?" She wiped her sleeve across her face. "I'm so sorry."

"You've got no reason to be sorry," he said. "And I was trying. You're right. Listen, you've got to keep this quiet. I don't want Lotte hurt. I don't want anyone hurt."

"Lotte? Is that her name?" Through her tears, Clara looked eager, ready to run down to Edgar Avenue and embrace her. "You love her?"

"Clara, yes." He closed his eyes against a sudden headache. "I love her."

"Truly?"

"With everything I am."

"Oh, Henry." Her voice rose on a wail, and she launched herself at him. "What in the hell are you going to do? Leave and marry her, right? For God's sake, she has your baby."

"I fully intend to do right by them," he said. "But you remember what happened with John Markwell, that whole mess. And there are complications. Secrets I can't even tell you. It's not as easy as it sounds. There's William; there's her husband. We're biding our time, Clara, and it's going to kill me."

"I won't let it," Clara said. "You talk to me, you hear? I've never said it plain out, but I have six brothers and sisters, and I love you the best. Always have, always will. I told off that hussy, Evelyn

Finke, and I'll tell off Father Kestner and your Lotte's husband, too."

"You knew about Evelyn?"

"I know everything," she said. "Now go get a shower, and I'll fix you something for your lunch."

"Thanks." His eyes were still dry, and it surprised him that he hadn't cried a drop. He was lighter now. "I don't think I've ever said... You've always been..." With a sigh, he let it drop. Perhaps it hardly needed to be said. "I'll take chicken, if there's any left."

"Sure." A pause, then, "When will I meet them?"

"Soon," he said. "Very soon. I can at least promise you that."

CHAPTER TWENTY

Cynthie dandled little Charlie on the floor and rocked him side to side in time to the record scratching from the corner of the living room. Charlie's chubby foot kicked back and forth against the rug. Lotte wondered what *there ain't nobody here but us chickens* actually meant, and why the whole world was obsessed with using the vulgar *ain't*.

The record wore on in bright, brassy tempo. Cynthie's music, which was also Albert's music, usually annoyed Lotte to tears, but today, *ain't* aside, she didn't mind it so much. For once, she envied Cynthie, for she and Charlie were all carefree lightness, sprawled out and dancing.

"Y'know, I think maybe he'll walk early," Cynthie said. "Albert and me, Mom says we were both early walkers. Talkers, too. Well, I was a talker. Albert took his sweet time, I guess."

"Hard to believe, really," Lotte said in a murmur. "You know, I think you're right. Maybe he will. He seems like a smart little boy."

Cynthie preened, flicked her lighter, and took a drag from a cigarette. When she dropped ash, it was into a jade glass candy dish still full of cellophane-wrapped butterscotch buttons. The plastic hissed and gave off acrid smoke. "Oops, sorry, sweetie. Say, you really think so?"

"Sure," Lotte said. After five years of practice, she'd learned it was easier to keep the conversation all on Cynthie, on praising Cynthie, on the minutiae of Cynthie's life. When Cynthie got bored, she turned to girl talk, and her idea of girl talk was intrusive questions about romance and the bedroom. Lotte held her expression straight and added, "You and Lou are both smart, aren't you?"

"Lou is, sure. Not just any fella can be a tail gunner and live to tell the story." Cynthie said. "Never thought about myself that way. Used to get good grades at St. Mary's, but once I got to Stivers, it was all cheer squad and getting pinned by the fellas."

I bet high school was just the same for Albert, Lotte thought, but didn't say. It was uncharitable of her. Albert hadn't been on the cheer squad.

"I remember this one time, we were all maybe sixteen. Ricky Wright's folks went out of town to his cousin's wedding, and he sneaked us all in for a rummage through their liquor cabinet, and he stole a Glenn Miller record from Rike's…"

Lotte glazed over again. Listening to Cynthie wasn't unlike tuning the wireless. Glenn Miller record, keep turning the dial; aria, tune in. It did give her pause to think about the errant Ricky Wright, boozing and stealing back in 1938. Had he reformed himself? He'd be twenty-five like Cynthie now, and she still sounded breathless and delighted. Would little Charlie grow up and steal records from Rike's and whiskey from Lou's stores? Could he understand Cynthie even now? Surely not, but suppose he could.

"But anyway, long time ago. Bet you Julienne girls never got up to anything like that. Say, are you thinking you'll send Daisy there?"

"That's quite a long way off," Lotte said. "I think I'll get her through diapers before I worry about high school. Who knows what will happen between now and then?" In all likelihood, she and Cynthie would no longer be sisters-in-law. What would Cynthie say to everything once it was public? Would she miss her? Shun her? Keep in touch, even?

"Ain't that the truth? Charlie can take his time walking. Once he does, I'll hardly ever catch a break. When he's a little bigger, then we'll see about getting him a sister. I'd love a little girl or two. You're so lucky."

"Now, Charlie's a sweet boy." Lotte tucked Daisy between

two pillows and scooped up Charlie. Robust and doughy on tinned milk formula, he was like a heavy down pillow in her arms. Even a murmur like that, although she knew what Cynthie meant, made her cringe. A child who was unwanted because he was a boy or she was a girl, because her mother had almost died at her birth, because her parents could have no more, and because their one child was too backward and too shy for high society.

"Well, sure, I didn't mean that. We love the little stinker. I know Albert dotes on Daisy, although I was razzing him about not keeping a single photo in his wallet."

"How'd you see his wallet?"

"Borrowed it." Cheeky grin. "Lou's a fine dad as long as I handle all the mess. As much as I want Charlie to stay little, Lou's ready to get him hitting a ball and all that."

Perhaps she had a bit of time, but the idea of Daisy talking worried Lotte already. Henry had guessed it would take about a year to free themselves from entanglements, whenever that happened. Both of them were wary, but she might need to push, if only because the thought of Daisy calling out for Daddy and wanting Albert was more than she could stand. She hated watching them together, for Albert was affectionate enough with her, and Daisy would sometimes coo. When Henry spoke or sang or chanted, Daisy folded into him like churned butter. Lotte liked to imagine their child could understand what he was to them.

"Maybe I better get home. This was a nice idea, though." Cynthie stubbed out her cigarette into the candies, rose from the floor, arched her back, and grabbed up little Charlie. "Why don't you come over to my place next time? You can see the new Frigidaire."

"Sure," Lotte said. "I'd like that. Give Lou my best."

"Sure thing, sweetie. Give my brother a big smack on the cheek from me."

Lotte tried not to visibly shudder, but the idea of asking Cynthie if Albert needed another literal smack on the cheek made her smile enough to nod her guest out the door. For a moment, she stood behind the door, the wood grains blurring into a foamy haze. What reason on earth did she have to be melancholy? A visit from her sister-in-law, some chatter, and listening to a record.

Perhaps she was low because Henry was out tonight celebrating his mother's birthday, or perhaps because the idea of Ricky Wright sinning, Cynthie sinning, influencing Charlie's morals, made her worry for Daisy's sake. Who knew what babies remembered? Maybe she'd think everyone's mother snuck away to the church at night and slept beside the priest. Or worse, she'd think all priests were dishonest and unfaithful to their promises. But was Henry dishonest and unfaithful? How could she explain all this to a child when she didn't understand it herself?

The door swung open. Lotte leapt clean out of her skin and yelped.

"Sorry, doll, didn't mean to scare you. How was your visit with Cynthie?"

"Fine." Lotte fought to steady her heartbeat and went to sit beside Daisy. "How was your day?"

"Same old. Got the problems with the lines worked out, but only half the lye shipment. Calling it a draw." He hung his hat and jacket, reached for a cigarette, and mixed a drink. "You all right? Cynthie being a pest?"

"No, she was perfectly nice."

"You sure it was Cynthie?" Albert chuckled and tugged his tie loose. "Look, it was nice of you to invite her over, doll. She's got all these big ideas about the kids being friends. You seeing Father Henry tonight?"

"I can't. He has to go to his parents'. Are you going to James?"

"No." Albert slugged the last of his sidecar, slammed his glass down, and poured another.

"I take it you're angry with him?"

"What, you and Father Henry never snap your caps at each other?"

"Not really." Did Henry snapping at her over not having time to shower count? Considering he'd been awake for over half the night, she was willing to be gracious. "Not seriously."

"Guess you're both too saintly. Or it hasn't been long enough. James and me, we've had plenty of bust-ups in seventeen years. He'll get over it." Even as he said it, Albert leaned forward in the lamplight, and his profile looked years older. "It'll be a couple of days before I head back over there, though."

"What happened? If you don't mind me prying." Lotte shifted Daisy into her lap and against her breast.

"Nah, it's all right. I told him his parents came around to see you the other week, right before Daisy got sick, and maybe we should be careful. Stay at home more. He should think about running with a beard, even. I says to him, 'So don't get married, just make 'em think you're going to.' There's girls who used to go to the Wayne. Dykes, you know? They'd do it in a heartbeat."

"He wouldn't do it, I suppose?"

"You know how James is, doll. Reckless as hell." Albert half-laughed. "In high school, that first time in the stairwell. Right before the bell rang, anyone could have seen us. Neither of us even knew I was queer. Could've had him expelled and worse."

"You didn't, of course."

"Found out I was queer real quick, didn't I? Kissed the son of a bitch back, and now I'm in this mess." His voice was soft, fond, rosy pink clouds at sunset fringed with gold. "I'd have found out sooner or later anyhow, and I got off easy that time at the nuthouse."

"Easy?" Albert's sleeves were pushed back just enough to show his scars. "They shocked you. And Henry was just there; he said it was awful. I guess they used to trick him during sick calls by shutting everyone away, but this time, he saw them."

"I kept my brain, didn't I?" His eyes twitched down the scars for a half second. "Look, this icepick thing is catching on big. Moody housewives, naughty kids, queers, even a bad headache. Sometimes it works, I guess, or why would they keep at it? The first time I was in, like I said before, it was harder to do. Now it's ten minutes and you've got a new personality, no memories, you're dead, whatever. I'm just trying to keep him, both of us, from all that."

"I know," she said. "You told me that already."

"He won't listen, Lotte, just sits there with his arms crossed. Damn idiot." He snorted. "I even says, 'You know, they say—'" And here, Albert colored up like a schoolgirl. He cleared his throat. "They say, *when I was a child, I spoke as a child, I understood as a child, I thought as a child. But when I became a man, I put away the things of a child.* And so—"

"Wait." Lotte wriggled to accommodate Daisy and held up a hand. "You quoted the Bible? To James?"

"Guess you're rubbing off on me after all," he said, color still high. "It was pretty meatball of me, I guess."

"I wouldn't say that." She was a little impressed, despite herself. "I'm guessing he thought so, though?"

"Yeah, he kicked me out. Said having a nagging beard was making me a stick in the mud, so I had to punch him, seeing as you're my wife and all."

"What chivalry." Men, even those who were lovers together, still solved their differences by hauling off and hitting each other. "Although I might not appreciate an avowed atheist quoting Bible verses at me either. You're right, though, he'll come around. He always has before. Do you want some supper? I've got pork chops I can fry up."

"Sure." Relief made Albert overly enthusiastic. "Sounds great, doll. I can watch the baby if you want."

"No." She was too sharp, but he ignored it. "I don't want her confusing you and Henry. Why should she get attached to you? You're not her father. Just leave it; I'll get supper."

"Are you going to leave, then?" He pressed both his palms together like he was in line for Communion. "The Pope's letting Father Henry off the hook?"

"Eventually, yes." Why bother pretending otherwise? Lotte set Daisy in her cradle. "She'll talk in less than a year. She'll grow up and notice things. Am I going to sneak to Henry's house with an eight-year-old child? A teenager? Talk about corrupting somebody's morals. Daisy will ask things someday, and if we don't make it right, she'll think it's fine to lie and sin. Or she'll disdain her own parents."

"Better she thinks it's fine to let somebody get the icepick." Albert took Daisy out of the cradle, but Lotte didn't argue this time. "And what're you going to tell her if you get married, anyhow? Unless she turns out dumb as a rock, she'll know you weren't married when she was born and her daddy was a fine, upstanding member of the holy priesthood."

"Why are you always so hateful about Henry? I know you worry about me leaving, but that's not to do with his character. He's a fine man. A good priest, too, despite all this."

"Just weird, is all. I'm an atheist now, but we were all raised Catholic as the Pope. Never thought about the priest having a girlfriend on the side. Rubs me the wrong way. Just imagine what Barbara Morris is going to say." He cleared his throat yet again and shifted Daisy onto his knee. "Besides, it seems like he's doing a number on you, doll. Says he wants to marry you, got you practically shacked up with him, took your— Was your first, right?" The crimson was back in his cheeks. "And now you've got a baby, and he's letting it drag on and on."

"It's partly dragging on for you, you know," Lotte said. "There's so much you don't understand about it; stop judging Henry. You and your set are so jaded that you don't understand when a decent man comes along. Talk about doing a number on somebody."

"All right, I'm sorry. Just sore because of James. Pork chops are fine, doll."

Later, Lotte, on the barest edge of sleep, caught the violin wail of Daisy whimpering, although she oughtn't have been hungry just then. She hoped the baby wasn't sick again. Taking her to get a shot had been dreadful and tiring for both of them. Again, the note sounded, thin and shivering, but when she went to the bassinette, Daisy was peaceful, arms outstretched, chest rising and falling in rhythm. Her rosebud mouth opened, blew out a bubble, which popped and dribbled down her cheek. Lotte wiped it with the hem of her dressing gown and heard a gasp, quickly muffled. Not Daisy, then. Albert.

She was tempted to let him mewl alone about how James had yelled at him, how his feelings were hurt. Heaven knew, she'd cried herself to sleep more times than she cared to count. Had Albert ever come in to comfort her? No, and she was glad of it. They'd never been in her bedroom together or in his.

The pathetic whine sounded again. Why, why hadn't she gone to Henry's tonight? She could have gone late, anything not to hear this. Probably a year ago, she could have ignored it, but her maternal heart was wavering. Loving Daisy, loving Henry had made her more tender all around.

Lotte tightened the sash on her dressing gown, kissed Daisy, and went out. Albert's door was slightly ajar. She pushed it with the flat of one hand and stood there in the dark, waiting. Another gasp and the rustle of blankets as he turned over onto the pillow.

"Albert? What's the matter?" She didn't leave the threshold, but her eyes adjusted to the moonlight streaming in, and she could see him rub his eyes with one fist and sit up.

"Lotte? What...?"

"I heard crying and thought you were Daisy." She crept a little closer. "What's the matter?"

"Wasn't crying. Probably the wind. Go back to bed, doll." He flopped back and dragged the blankets over his face.

"It was you," she said and ignored the tug of humiliation that her tender impulses had wrought. Maybe Albert loved men just like a woman, but he was undeniably male when it came to mush and crying. "I won't tell anyone. Is it about James?"

"Lotte." Although he sounded exasperated, when she reached the chair beside his bed, she could see that he was trembling. "Go away."

"Only when you've told me what's wrong," she said, wondering why on earth she cared. Why not go away, go to sleep, get up for Mass, and come home after Albert was already off to the factory, so both of them could pretend this had never happened?

"Are you this much of a pill to Father Henry?"

"No," she said. "But Henry's not this insolent to me." She pursed her lips and let the irritation subside. "Will you tell me?"

"Aw, fine." He rolled over to face her, but kept his eyes downcast. "It was just a dream anyhow. James and I were... He was here with... Anyhow, we're both here, naked as the days we were born—you asked for this, doll—and in walk his parents with knives.

His dad grabs my hair, acts like he's going to cut my throat 'til I scream for mercy, then he cuts off my Johnson instead. James's mom does the same to him. We're bleeding, yelling, all this, and his mom grabs the wires out of the lamp and shocks him senseless right here. Then she grabs an icepick from the table next to you and jams it up his nose. I try to stop her, but I'm still hurt, and I… I can't." A manful attempt to repress a sob, then: "I can't."

A tear worked its way down Lotte's cheek, and she grabbed his dry, pale hand. She hated that she could picture such things, that she knew about such things at all. "That's awful, Albert. I'm sorry."

"Just a dream." But his throat was thick. "Do you think they mean anything?"

"No," she said, although she had no idea. "You're just scared, is all. Why don't…? Tomorrow, why don't you make up with him?" Was counseling him to go back to James a mortal sin? Probably, but she hated to see him, usually so phlegmatic and detached, trembling in this wan heap. Of course, his soul was more important than his earthly happiness, but it wasn't clear to her anymore where earthly happiness stopped, or why things were wrong, or what was earthly and what was not. Even Henry no longer knew. "Or telephone him now. You'll wake him up, but at least you'll hear his voice."

Albert was quiet for so long, she thought he'd fallen asleep. "Nah, I'm not bothering him with his nonsense. Shouldn't've even bothered you. Thanks, though, doll."

"It's all right," Lotte said. "It's never easy to wake up or go to sleep like this. I used to back before I met Henry. Can you go on back to sleep now?"

"Think so," he said. "Can you maybe stay for a while?"

"Yes." She squeezed his hand and let it drop. The room was so bright with moonlight that she knew the hour wasn't very late. Any moment now, dozens would rise from their beds for Matins, and Henry would wake and think of her. Perhaps she should chant it for Albert, but she doubted he'd welcome falling asleep to the divine office. The air thickened like a wall, his open eyes etched in the semidarkness, and the magic lantern of his memory no doubt throwing nerves and patterns against them.

He and his lover castrated. James dead. Mrs. Mills, her expression blank and eerie, grabbing the wire out of the brown lamp beside her and sizzling it across her own son. Lotte shuddered and still wanted to fill the silence somehow. For whatever odd reason, she thought of a song they had sung in chorale at Julienne, back before she'd realized she couldn't sing.

Was once a pretty, tiny birdie flew where fruit in garden fair hung bright to view.

Albert smiled—she could sense it—but he didn't laugh. He rolled over and seemed to still.

If that a pretty, tiny bird I were I'd fly away and seek yon garden fair.

Overlaid in her mind were the words of Matins, now permanently painted in her mind whenever the moon looked like this and someone woke at this hour to keep vigil and sing. She'd grown accustomed to waking and feeding Daisy when Henry said his office, but already Daisy was bigger and didn't need her so much.

Limetwigs and treach'ry all its branches bore,
Ah, hapless birdie, thou wilt fly no more!

Albert's body relaxed; his fists unclenched. When he flipped his pillow over, the movement was heavy and clumsy. He snuffled into it and settled into deep, sighing breaths.

If that a pretty, tiny bird I were, I think of yonder garden I'd beware.

He was asleep, and she was singing to herself. His face in sleep was thoughtful and innocent, as though he'd never sinned mortally nor caused anyone years of heartache. She wasn't sure she'd miss him in her new life, but she would always wish him well.

If that a pretty, tiny bird were I, like him to yonder garden straight I'd fly, I'd fly, I'd fly

CHAPTER TWENTY-ONE

A nd little Stevie went straight into the cake. Of course, Helen got the switch since it was all her idea, and Stevie's only three." Henry smiled to think of it, although no one had gotten any cake, and Annie had cried a blue streak after she'd spent all day baking the thing.

"Stevie's your godson, right?" Lotte asked. "Sorry, it's quite the crowd to keep track of."

"Right, that's him, and he's been under Helen's thumb since the day he was born. I think David hopes Frankie'll straighten his brother out, and then they'll both team up and straighten their sister out. She's ruled unopposed for almost eleven years now." Henry chuckled and shifted Daisy, whose legs splayed out over his knee. She beat her fists against the top of his desk and smiled.

"Never a dull moment with them, I take it." Lotte leaned back in the chair opposite him and adjusted her hat brim. "Would they like me and Daisy, do you think?"

"Of course they would." He squeezed Daisy's chubby arms, clapped her hands together, and glanced over to meet Lotte's shy look. "Who wouldn't like you?"

"Probably anyone who wanted you to keep your vocation," she said in a low voice.

"Not necessarily." He took a breath and held her gaze. "Listen, I told Clara."

"You did?" Lotte's eyes widened, and her face lit with joy.

Someone, Albert, of course, had said things to her to make her doubt him. "Really?"

"Really."

"Was she angry with you? What did she say? Did she ask about Daisy? Why did you tell her?"

Pleased, he held up a hand. "All right, I'll spill. But not here. Let's suffice it to say she's happy. Or at least, she's not shocked and horrified, and she wants to meet you. Both of you. And there'll be no keeping her back; talk about ruling unopposed." He kissed the soft place on Daisy's head. "You know, I think when this one gets a little older, she could finally topple Helen's regime."

A sharp rap at the door, then William's face appeared around the doorframe. His eyes narrowed at Daisy in Henry's lap, at Lotte across from them.

"Good afternoon, Mrs. Walheim. Henry, I'm sorry to interrupt."

"It's perfectly all right, Father Kestner. We were nearly through." Lotte seemed to shrink and melt before William's stern countenance. Although Henry hated being thrown to the wolves, he handed back Daisy and watched Lotte bundle her into the carriage. "Thank you so much for your help, Father Henry. I'll continue to pray for you."

"Thank you," he said. "I suppose I'll see you at Mass tomorrow."

"Of course. Enjoy the rest of your day, Father. It was good to see you, Father Kestner." She almost curtsied or genuflected to William on her way out, and he could hear her rapid footsteps on the marble.

"May I?" Without waiting for a response, William entered, closed the door, and settled into Lotte's chair. "Such a nervous woman, Mrs. Walheim."

"She is a little shy," Henry said. He didn't quite like William's tone. "I guess that's why she and Mr. Walheim don't socialize much."

William harrumphed and leaned forward. "Henry, when I said you'd want to be careful with Mrs. Walheim, I did not mean for you to bond with her child."

"Oh, that." It cost him to dismiss Daisy. A clawing, choking clutch like jagged metal stabbed into his heart and throat, nearly as painful as what he'd squelched when he'd learned she was born. "Mrs. Walheim and I had an appointment. What else is she to do with the baby? You know I like kids."

"Yes, I know," William said. He sucked in his cheeks, which gave Henry the unfortunate image of a bloated goldfish in a cassock. When William spoke next, he actually blushed. "Henry, I do hate to pry into your life, but are you pining for that woman?"

"Father." He felt his own face grow hot and hoped William assumed the mere thought of pining for a woman was enough to embarrass him silly. "Do you honestly think I'd do something that lame-brained?"

"I don't think you would do anything untoward," William said. "But if my parents' story taught me anything, it's that the most innocent encounters can go awry if one is caught unawares. Mrs. Walheim is hurting, and you're the type to go charging in on a white horse. Most men are, when they're young. That's why I proposed that you go away. To regain your distance."

"I appreciate your concern," Henry said. "But I don't pine for her, Father. You have nothing to worry about." His heart twisted, for William suspected something. He had to if he'd actually suggested, out loud, that Henry might pine for someone. His mentor's eyes were grave, but William was easily swayed by the desire to believe he'd imagined the whole thing.

"So you keep saying." William rubbed his forehead with the palm of his hand and exhaled a long, goldfish breath. "Then why do I continue to do so? Henry, when you came to this parish, you were all afire to minister to their troubled souls. You've ministered only to one in particular, and she seems troubled still. Now you're troubled, too. You were sick; you're barely disposed to celebrate the sacraments; you wander about in a dream world."

"I'll judge the state of my soul, thank you." Henry cringed at his chilly tone, especially that he took it with William. "How would you know my disposition or dare question how I celebrate the sacraments? Perhaps you're older, but I've been an ordained priest for five years now. And you know very well that Mrs. Walheim is not the only person

I've counseled or confessed during my time here."

"I apologize, Henry. That was wrong of me to say." William's forthright humility startled him. "You're absolutely right that it isn't my place to question your conscience. It's only—" A man like William didn't talk of these things lightly nor accuse someone of grave sin and sacrilege without reason. He drew a shaky breath. "I see a good deal of greatness in you. It's well known you were one of the top men in your year at the Athenaeum. But like anyone else, you have faults. I make no secret of my own shortcomings, but I work at them prayerfully, and I don't think you do likewise."

"How would you know what I work at prayerfully?" Henry waffled between angry and chagrined and settled somewhere in the middle. "My prayer life is none of your business, Father, whether you've decided to mentor me or not. I do appreciate your guidance, but this is out of line. For God's sake, I let a parishioner's baby sit on my knee. I think accusing me of celebrating the sacraments in mortal sin is somewhat uncalled for."

"I never said—" William's brows drew together. "—a single word about you being in mortal sin. I merely said you seemed poorly disposed. A First Communicant could tell us the difference. If you are in mortal sin—"

"I'm not."

"I should hope so." William slumped down, and he seemed older somehow than his fifty-eight years. Within seconds, he was back on his feet. "Henry, I do hope you can forgive me for overstepping out of pastoral concern."

"Of course I can," Henry said and rose with him. It occurred to him that he should set the stage to ease William's shock when he did confess his life with Lotte. "Perhaps there's some truth to it anyhow. I've become very fond of Mrs. Walheim and her daughter. As a pastor, mind you. Maybe I'm pining for them and don't even realize it."

William clapped Henry on the shoulder. "I know it's not easy to watch them suffer, my boy. But we're not called to end their suffering for them. We're merely to help them bear it prayerfully and show them how to walk with Our Lord through their troubles. It's easier with some than others, I grant you. Even I've fallen prey to the temptation to know more or to overstep. I've just done it with you, after all." He offered a sympathetic sort of smile. "Shall we go to Vespers?"

"Yes," Henry said. "And, Father, I apologize if I've been errant in some way toward my duties here. I know that Mrs. Walheim isn't the only one in need."

"Now that you're aware, perhaps you'll work at it." William opened the door and led them out. "That's all I ask, Henry."

"What did Father Kestner say to you? I'm sorry I left. He always makes me awkward." Lotte lifted Daisy over her shoulder and burped her. "I always feel like I should curtsey to him like he's an earl or a baron or something."

"Nah, it was probably better. My heart almost stopped when he came in and saw me with Daisy." Henry's lips twisted, but his expression was mainly cheerful. "He accused me of pining for you."

"Imagine that." Lotte's lips twisted, too. She shifted Daisy to her hip before she kissed him. "I'd say you weren't pining at all, Mr. Werther."

"Mr. Werther?"

"That's what you'll be, isn't it? Sounds funny to me, too. Mr. and Mrs. Henry Werther?" A dam had burst inside Lotte when she'd found out he'd told Clara about them, and her anxiety about the future was all but gone. Like it or not, when Albert had ranted about Henry pulling one over on her, she'd listened, no matter how ridiculous it was. After all, there was always a reason the two of them couldn't be married, couldn't tell anyone they were together. Good reasons, sure, but Daisy was a good reason, too. "What will you do?"

"Teach," he said. "Philosophy or theology at U of D. If all else fails, I could go into business with Dad, Ned, and John. I'd rather teach Aquinas, though, than try and help manage the pie shop. Doubt I'll make as much money as Albert does at the factory, but—"

"Oh, do you think I care about that?" Lotte asked. "Albert's hardly a millionaire, first off. Besides, I, of all people, know how little money buys happiness. I'm not worried about that. I am worried about one thing, though."

"What's that?" Henry tugged at her arm and pulled them both into his lap. "I admit, I'm worried, too. William would take it —will take it—pretty hard when I tell him. He's a good priest, and he thinks I'm one, too."

"You are," Lotte said. She turned his head to face hers. "I feel badly, you know. Someday, Daisy will ask why we weren't married when she was born. I worry about influencing her morals, don't you?"

Henry closed his eyes and dropped his head back against the cushions. "All the time. I'm happy to be with you fully," he said. "But it doesn't erase the fact that I spent ten years studying for this vocation and five years actively living it. Almost half my life. But you never answered me. Are Daisy's morals what worry you?"

"Partly," Lotte said. "But it's also James and Albert. Albert's been having nightmares since Mr. and Mrs. Mills came to see us. The other night, I even sat with him."

Henry raised an eyebrow.

"I know, but you'd have held his hand, too, if you'd heard him. Honestly, Henry, I thought it was Daisy at first." Lotte could still hear the cries, abandoned and thinking no one would come. "I don't know why they don't just go away somewhere."

"Where?" Henry asked. "What they're doing isn't legal or moral anywhere. How long did you sit with him?"

"About an hour. I sang to him, and he fell asleep." She felt foolish confessing that, but Henry didn't laugh.

"I thought you said you couldn't sing."

"I can't, but how would he know? He likes all that Glenn Miller and Chesterfield trash. I felt silly, but I thought of how nice it is when you chant the offices and Daisy settles down."

"Maybe you'll sing for me sometime," he said. "What did you sing, anyway?"

"Brahms," she said. "'Pretty, Tiny Bird.' *Liebeslieder Walzer*."

"We used to sing those in seminary." Henry's eyes grew bright and fond. "A couple of us from my year formed a group. Really, we just wanted to get better at chanting the offices, but we started playing around with choral music, too. Silly, really, a group of seminarians singing about rosy maids locked in towers behind iron bars."

What, ten iron bars are a jest to me, as tho' they were glass they shall shatter'd be.

Daisy's eyes fluttered, and she squawked as though it was agreeable to her. Without speaking, Lotte handed her over and moved off Henry's lap to sit beside them.

"At least someone likes it," he said and watched the baby's fingers curl around one of his. "Our professor, Father Buff, heard us at it one evening. William's a lot like him, actually. We were out singing a madrigal, and the last line didn't sit so well with him." Henry took a deep breath and broke out into full-throated song. *"Say, dainty nymphs, and speak, shall we play Barley Break?"* He looked down, a little shyly. "Apparently, it was rather racy in Elizabethan times, back when Father Buff was probably born. Anyway, he said it was a near occasion of sin and made us sing Compline three times. That was the end of all that."

Henry's gaze drifted, and Lotte could see reflected in it a wide, grassy lawn, a hill, the orangey pink of a sunset. The river sparkled just beyond the rise, boats chugged past, and carriages and cars rattled on the streets. The sunset tinged everything warm and golden, molten; the air was warm, and the breeze light. Promise hovered everywhere – five or six men in new collars, freshly tonsured, young and on fire with the Faith, and singing meaningless songs just to pass the time. Life would have seemed simple then—a call, an answer. Each and every one of them absolutely convinced they were in the right vocation and that nothing would ever make them waver. She could almost hear it in honeyed male harmony, tenor, baritone, and bass layered with youth and giddiness.

Dreaming, by the world forgot, fleet the bright hour passes!

One look at Henry's face told her he heard it, too, and that he was elsewhere. Regret was scrawled across his expression, and she wondered whether he regretted the seminary or her. It didn't matter, she supposed. Both were irrevocable. Lotte closed her eyes and wove her fingers with his.

"I like the name Daisy," Clara said. "It's pretty. And no one'll get her confused with her cousin Maggie."

"She's really Elizabeth," Henry said. "Margaret's her middle name. Lotte liked Daisy, and I wanted to name her after Mom."

Clara squealed as quietly as she could and threw her arms around his neck. "Mom will love that, you know. You'll stay her favorite for sure now."

"You think?" Henry flattened his back. Clara detached herself from him. Amid the chaos after dinnertime, Clara had dragged him off, and they'd cloistered themselves in the stuffy room she'd shared with Anna growing up. A magazine cover splashed with Clark Gable was still tacked to the wall. "I don't know about all that. You know how they go on about their very own son being called to the priesthood. John Markwell's mom and dad cut him off completely."

"Maybe," she said. "But do you really see the old man doing that?"

"Guess not." Whatever his parents thought or didn't think, it frightened him more what William would say. Henry had it all meticulously planned out, a strict, inflexible rubric. At half past ten on a Thursday, he would go to William's office. Mass would be well over, no offices to say for a good while, no Legion of Mary ladies crowding the place, the sacristan off duty. Henry would clasp his hands, left over right, ask to sit, nod only once, and begin his speech. He could almost envision it written out with spidery serifs—instructions in red, *the penitent clasps his hands, left over right*; his carefully worded speech in black, "Father, there's something I must discuss with you. It's not easy for me to say."

Perhaps he ought to include the Latin text just to keep William from misinterpreting. Naturally, Latin gave him about a hundred different ways to simply say, 'Father, there is something I must discuss with you.' *Pater, est res de qua tecum loqui debeo* was too pastoral. This wasn't a conversation about repairing the roof leaks. *Pater, habeo quod tecum communicandum est* was almost too gentle. Practically an apology, and it would have William on the phone to the archbishop before Henry could say *communicandum*. It would have to be *Pater, adest quaestio de qua tecum tractandum est*. That would appeal to William's formality. He had thought long and hard about what would and would not hurt William, what explanation his mentor might accept that wouldn't dredge up a lecture about his father and being caught unaware.

"Aw, come on, Henry, you know he won't." Clara's eyes were anxious. She'd mistaken his silence and his Latin reverie for worry about their parents. "Look, we've all got kids; we're all married. There's not one of us who doesn't wonder how you do it. Yeah, you had a calling, or you thought you did, anyway, but you're human, right?"

"As far as I know." He tweaked a strand of her hair. "Brat."

"And yeah, you have us, but we both know nieces and nephews aren't like having your own kids, and there's plenty of stuff you don't want to share with anybody but your husband. Or your wife," Clara said. "Not even with me. I know it all anyway."

"Yeah, sure you do. How did you find out about Evelyn?"

"Tied her to the postbox by her braids."

"Very funny." Henry rolled his eyes. "She was nineteen. She didn't wear braids. Try again."

"Called her a cheap tramp and smacked her across the face." Clara scowled with remembered rage. "Found out she'd been bragging about it to Frances Engel, so I sorted her out fast."

"Hm. Well, good riddance and all that." He shook his head. "You won't have to worry about that kind of thing with Lotte."

"Oh, I know that," Clara said. "I love Lotte because you love her. Look, I saw you at ordination, remember? We all drove down, took forever? There's no way you'd be trying to leave if she weren't worth it. Hell, you'd never have been in all this mess in the first place."

"If I can get out of it," he said. "Listen, Clara, John Markwell lives outside the Faith now. He and Betty got married at the courthouse, rifle at his back, and now, from what Father Amberley's said, he's up in McCartyville hoeing corn and ushering at the Lutheran church every Sunday. Seems they're always glad to take the castoffs from us mean, old Catholics."

"Well, I don't see you turning Protestant."

"You're damn right you don't. And neither would Lotte. I don't take the Faith any less seriously, although I fell in love with Lotte while a priest. It would be easy enough to forget it and jump ship, but we can't." His expression, when he finally looked up, was bleak. "I'm responsible for their souls now, Lotte's and Daisy's, and I'm not leading them astray. William will try to send me away, and so will the archbishop. They'll want to hush it up, of course. But I can't think of a single thing that would make me leave them." He clenched his jaw. "After all, it's not just them I'd be leaving, it's you, too. The whole family. Who knows where I'd end up? With something like this, I bet they'd swap me out for someone in another diocese somewhere."

"You'll just have to say no," she said and flashed a crooked grin. "Or send me to the archbishop, and I'll have a word with him."

"As long as you don't slap him and call him a cheap tramp," he said, and the stone on his chest began to crumble. "I'd hate to see my own sister get excommunicated."

"Not as much as I'd hate to see you leave," she said. "Nobody missed you more than I did when you were gone."

"Do you ever wonder how come we're friends like this?" he asked.

"No. Do you ever wonder why you egghead priests overthink everything all the time?"

"Ha, ha," he said. "But come on. What about Anna? She's less than a year older than you. I'm two years younger and a boring twit of a boy."

"You are boring. And a twit." Clara chuckled. "Aw, I don't know, Henry. But think about Anna. She'd treat His Holiness himself like he was still in diapers. Honey this, sweetie that. She was too high and mighty for me by the time she was three. You're just easy, I guess."

"Easy, indeed. No doubt in a couple of days, William will agree with you." With a shake of the head, Henry stood and stretched. "Are you going to let me leave yet or you planning to grill me some more?"

"Nah," she said. "I'm sick of you grilling me. I'm going to team up with Lotte, just you wait. Say, how come none of us know her?

Seems like everybody in Dayton knows everybody else."

"I don't doubt it," he said. "And she's from Grafton Hill, went to Corpus. Only child. She started at Julienne the year you left. Her husband and his sister went to Stivers. Now mind your beeswax." She wouldn't, of course, and he didn't entirely mind. It'd be good for Lotte to have a sister and a friend who was neither shy nor prim nor proper.

"Yeah, yeah," She pulled him into a bear hug. "Look, I know you're worried about what people will think and all. Don't get bent out of shape. All we care about is that you're happy."

"I know," he said, and, "Thanks, Clara."

CHAPTER TWENTY-TWO

n the long, shuffling July twilight, the breeze was warm and steady, playing with the curtains in windows open just a hair. Outside, Henry heard distant echoes of children.

Allee, allee oxen free!

Milk, milk, lemonade...

Ready or not, here I come!

Barefoot and in summer linen, Lotte sat lengthwise on the couch and busied herself by flicking through the breviary and sounding out the Latin with her lips. He watched both of them with one look, Daisy fussing on a blanket spread in the middle of the room, her mother muttering *auxilium maneat* with a tip of the tongue and a click of the teeth.

The cops wailed past, the siren bleating loudly and oppressively into the room. Daisy drew the three breaths that always led to disaster.

"Aw, no." He crossed the room in four steps and picked her up. "Come on now, sweetheart."

Daisy let out an anticlimactic squawk and paused for five seconds to consider. The siren was indeed sufficiently traumatic, and she let out a high, piercing wail of her own. Her eyes screwed up. Her mouth stretched so wide he could see the back of her throat thrumming in angry vibrato as her face flushed red. Beaded tears trickled down her cheeks and soaked into his shirtfront.

"Oh, Daisy." Lotte's tone was weary when she laid aside the book and stretched out her arms. "Come here."

"It's all right," he said. "I've got her; go on with your reading."

Her eyes were troubled, but she nodded and picked up the breviary. *In adjutorium meum intende*, he thought he read on her lips and smirked. 'Come to my assistance,' indeed. Henry could handle this.

He hefted Daisy over his shoulder, upright in his arms, crosswise in his arms, and into his lap. She ignored him and sobbed on. She was dry, but he changed her anyway and put her in a new dress for good measure. Nothing. Her forehead was cool; she was fed. She probably just wanted Lotte, didn't she? Could she want Albert?

"Lotte," he said, like the useless man he was. "I'm sorry. Do you think—?"

"Give her here, Henry," she said, but her voice was gentle. "She's just in a mood. It happens sometimes. I doubt she'll quiet for either of us until she's good and ready. You do just fine with her. She doesn't want Albert."

"What're you, a mind reader? You're as bad as Clara. It'll be hell once the two of you team up. She's already threatening to."

"Really?" Lotte rocked Daisy to no effect. "Now that's an intriguing thought." She lowered her head and shushed and tried to soothe. "My poor baby, what's wrong?" The scream kicked up a notch instead of quieting. "Every time the cops go by, James and Albert skitter away like roaches. I think it's rubbing off on her. Honestly, Henry, the sooner she's away from all that, the better."

"I know," he said and took the thrashing baby back into his hands. "Is that what's eating you, Miss Daisy?"

"Why don't you try the pacifier again? She usually hates it, but when she's like this, sometimes—"

"Good evening, Henry. Mrs. Walheim."

Lotte was too distracted and surprised to hide her horror. Her mouth fell open, and her fingers tightened around Henry's arm. He imagined he looked quite the same way. Even the cars and children's voices outside fell oddly silent.

"Father Kestner," she said, voice faltering. "So sorry. Daisy and I were just leaving."

"Lotte." Henry kept his voice stern and his hand around her wrist. "You were not." So much for his plans, his speech, his carefully penitential rubric. William's face looked exactly as he'd imagined it would—as though he'd punched him. At once, his keen eyes took in Lotte's bare feet, Daisy's dark curls, and Henry's trousers and shirtsleeves. The comfortable fantasy that they were their own family, husband and wife, turned up dirty and tawdry under his mentor's gaze. They were nothing but mortal sinners and the baby evidence of their lust.

"But we were." Lotte's voice was at least an octave above usual. "You were very helpful as always, Father Henry, but the baby's fussy, and—"

"Do I look, Mrs. Walheim," William asked. "Like an inordinately stupid man to you?"

"No, Father." She drew back as though he'd bitten her.

"Then abandon the pretense, if you would."

"Lotte," Henry said again, this time gently, coaxing, although he didn't know where he found the strength for it. "Take the baby into the other room. I'll speak with Father Kestner."

"I'm not certain what you might have to speak with me about, Henry. It's clear enough to me." William crossed his arms over his chest and shook his head. "Will one of you see to that baby? It's enough to make one's ears bleed."

"She can't help it; she's just little." Lotte forgot her fear of him, snatched Daisy away from Henry, and clutched her to her chest.

"I certainly don't mean any disrespect toward your child, Mrs. Walheim," he said, reached in, and pried the infant from her. Mouth agape, Lotte stared at him as though he were a good-for-nothing kidnapper, but she had the sense to keep quiet. "Daisy, is it? You're certainly out of sorts this evening." He carried her away, toward the sofa, and sat, awkward, but well-intentioned.

Daisy, Daisy,
Give me your answer, do!
I'm half crazy,
All for the love of you!

Almost bodily, Lotte recoiled with confusion, but Henry was

transported back to the sidewalk, to somebody's crushed garden, to Winston singing and walking backwards beside him.

It won't be a stylish marriage.

I can't afford a carriage.

William's anger, Henry could bear, but this was close to making him weep. It hurt Lotte, too. She grabbed for his hand, and they stood without speaking while William sang. Henry wondered then about William's stern Jesuit father, his vulnerable mother.

Daisy was smart enough to fall silent or perhaps had finally worn out from the effort. With a shudder, she blinked at William through matted lashes and sighed. He smiled down at her, and Henry was struck with the half-crazy thought, *what if William has a child somewhere?* But William leveled a glance at them, fingers entwined, and he knew it wasn't so.

"Unless I'm missing the mark entirely, Henry," he said. "You have fathered this child with Mrs. Walheim."

"Yes, Father."

"You've been living as husband and wife without the benefit of marriage and while under holy orders."

"Yes, Father."

"You have indeed been celebrating the sacraments in mortal sin."

"I'm not certain, Father." He met eyes with Lotte. "I love Lotte and Daisy, and we—"

"Enough." He held up a hand and returned Daisy to Lotte's arms. "Mrs. Walheim, will you take Daisy to the other room? I imagine you'll have no trouble making yourself comfortable there."

"Enough indeed." Henry glowered at William. "You've known this woman longer than I have. She's not some cheap tramp, and you know it."

"I apologize, Mrs. Walheim," he said. "But Henry is right; he and I have things to discuss."

Lotte nodded once. "Apology accepted, Father." She threw a backward glance at Henry before pulling the bedroom door shut.

"Come," his mentor said. "I'm interested in the truth from you, if you're able to tell it."

"William." His mentor's eyebrows arched, but he let his Christian name pass without comment or correction. Henry sat beside him and buried his face in his hands. It was then that he realized they were trembling. His head was light, and in some ways, he felt like he was watching everything from above. Nothing of his speech remained in his mind, nor even anything of the actions that accompanied it. Which hand went over which? Which of his three Latin variations had been the least offensive? Would it even have mattered? He'd thought William might be hurt, but he couldn't imagine true hurt, the kind of hurt that sliced to the marrow. His world had become as rosy and bright as the swirling cope they brought out for Gaudete and Laetare Sundays. *Gaudete, iterum, gaudete...* He'd never felt more foolish than now. "William, I never meant to lie to you."

"I know," he said. "Truly, Henry, I blame myself."

Had he not predicted that exact phrase from William's lips back when this had all started?

"You shouldn't," he said. "I ought to have asked for a new assignment the moment I realized I was seeking her out. No, the moment I laid eyes on her. I knew, William."

"So did I," William said. "If we are both honest, so did I. When you came to St. Jerome's, all full of fire and love of neighbor, I should have sent you on or swapped you out for John Markwell."

"I know I'm not serious enough sometimes." Henry raised his head and looked at him. "You really wanted me gone?"

"That's the last thing I want, Henry, and that's why I should have done it." Even William's eyes were too luminous now. "You're a father to Daisy, and I shall never know what that's like. But upon meeting you—" He broke off, shook his head. "Anyone else, I would have pressed harder, ignored their explanations, come unannounced long before I heard a child crying here."

"But you didn't."

"I didn't." William closed his eyes for such a long moment that Henry wondered if he'd finally given up. "I suppose I've sinned mortally, too, for allowing it to go on. What did you mean, anyhow, when you said that you weren't certain of the state of your soul? If you've given her a child and continued on with her like this, it seems obvious enough."

"It does," he said. "But it's not a simple matter of lust. I know what that is. We truly love one another, William."

"I know you do, my boy." William's voice was soft, but stern, a cut piece of velvet over a silver chalice. "What might have been the honorable approach? Did you need to make love with Mrs. Walheim to know that you loved her?"

"Of course not." He knew what was coming, started to brace for it, but decided he deserved whatever he got.

"Once you realized it, why not seek to leave then? That might have been embarrassing, but this? What am I to tell the parishioners? That you and one of the faithful raised a baby right under my nose?" His mentor's hands began to tremble; his color rose. "Whatever hell they've put Father Amberley through, it'll be less than nothing by compare. And you sit there saying you've not sinned mortally? Whose idea was all this to begin with?"

Henry dug his fingernails into the flesh of his palms. The sweet simplicity of his world was crumbling to dust, and in its place, he had led Lotte astray and dishonored her with his concupiscence.

"Now wait just a—" Henry stopped to clear his throat before he said something truly regrettable. "Do you honestly believe, Father, that either of us would deliberately seduce the other? One of us under holy orders and the other, whom you've seen at Mass every day for over five years and who's too shy to stay for coffee hour on Sundays?"

"I see," he said. Henry wondered then whether William's father had seduced his mother or vice versa, and whether William even knew. "I see. You do realize that you've descended into relativism? If someone came to you in the confessional and told you they'd been doing what you did, would you absolve them if they denied it was even a mortal sin?"

"If they don't think they've sinned mortally," Henry asked. "Then why on earth are they confessing to me?"

"Answer the question, Henry." William's glower returned. "Would you absolve them or not? You're clearly planning to persist in this behavior."

"I'm not," he said and batted away William's tawdry picture.

"I wish to be laicized as soon as I can, and Lotte will have her marriage annulled."

"Annulled?" The keen eyes narrowed again. "No small feat. I've never met anyone who's succeeded, and I watched my father advise on canon law cases for decades. On what grounds?"

Henry opened his mouth and closed it with a snap. He'd become too good at keeping secrets, or perhaps he was right that Albert Walheim's secrets weren't his to confide, even to William.

"They are not validly married," Henry said. "I won't discuss the details, but any marriage tribunal with half a brain among them will grant it."

"Unconsummated?" He raised a brow at Henry's look. "Please, Henry. They spent over four childless years together, and you and she had Daisy in a matter of months. Perhaps she is in with a chance, then. Is that truly what you want?"

"Yes," he said. "When I baptized Daisy— Yes, that's what I want. Do you want to speak to Lotte?"

"What on earth could I say to her that would make her feel worse than she already does?" William pursed his lips before he stood. "Lecturing Mrs. Walheim would be rather like ripping the wings from a butterfly. No, I need to speak to the archbishop about transferring you."

"But I just told you I'm planning to be—"

"Despite our lovely chat," William said, "there is still the parish to think of and the impressionable minds of the faithful. Perhaps you glad-hand them, but I am concerned for their souls. You have no idea the breadth of scandal you would cause if this were known or the distrust of clergy that would ensue. Do not decide anything further tonight, aside from praying for an antidote to your selfishness."

Henry's throat swelled and choked him; he felt as though a cincture was tightening around his neck.

"And while you are in this limbo." Halfway to the door, William turned on one heel. "You will not celebrate the sacraments. Neither you nor Mrs. Walheim will partake of the Holy Eucharist, and you will not presume to counsel anyone, even outside the confessional. And the next time you or she sets foot in a confessional, it will be to unburden your consciences of this mess. Do I make myself clear?"

"Yes, Father." The loss of William's good favor, however expected, stung far worse than he could have imagined. For all his faults, Henry had never truly disappointed anyone. William was a good mentor, fair and honorable, and Henry might have done him proud.

"Henry." William had not turned back to the door. Intent on Henry's face, his eyes were sad, fatherly, almost kind. "You have made many mistakes here, indeed. But, my boy, you have an excellent heart."

"Thank you, Father." Henry's voice was a thick rasp, but it didn't matter anyhow because William was gone.

CHAPTER TWENTY-THREE

L otte thought she heard the door close, but couldn't be certain. After high school, when her father had found his way to the attic and discovered her circle of animals, that had been the first time she'd ever been caught in wrongdoing. The other children had always misbehaved at school. She had watched them get their backsides paddled and their knuckles cracked. When she saw that, she was never jealous of their friendships or sad that they ignored her. But without all that kind of thing, the squirming twist when horror broke open inside her was all the more raw once *Charlotte Maria Klopstock, why in God's name are these mangy creatures up here?* had cracked across the back of her skull.

"William's gone." The bedroom door creaked, and light tumbled in from the hallway. "Come on out."

"Do you want us to go?" Lotte looked up and squinted in the sudden brightness. She hadn't even thought of switching on a lamp.

"No." Henry's tone was horrified and emphatic and desperate all at once. "Do you want to go?"

"No." Lotte stood and went to him. "I never leave here because I want to." When she passed, she squeezed his hand, but continued to the kitchen and put on a pot of water. "Daisy's finally asleep. Henry, what's going to happen?"

"We'll have some tea and go to bed," he said. "In the morning, we'll get up, feed Daisy, and go to Mass. I'll telephone the archbishop.

You'll speak to Albert. It'll be all right, Lotte."

"Will it?" She knew she sounded breathless, that her look was imploring, but didn't care.

"Yes," he said, but paused. "Do you think...? Have you ever thought that I've led you astray? Or that we're in grave sin?"

"Never. Is that what Father Kestner was saying to you?" Of all the insulting things. She bristled at the set down Henry had had to endure while she sat in the dark behind a wall. "When I am in grave sin, I feel it. I helped Albert bail James out of jail, and there was that sense. You know it, don't you?"

"Sure. Like I said, I felt it with Evelyn, but never with you. I tried to tell him all that, but he's William. Accused me of relativism and barred me from the sacraments."

"Can he do that?" Although soon enough, he'd never celebrate them again, the loss of something so precious nearly made her cry. The kettle squealed; she filled two cups.

"Not exactly," he said. "Although he is in charge of the parish, and where else am I going to celebrate them? Or receive them? Lotte." His expression shuttered while his hand rattled the cup against its saucer.

"What? Oh God, he's sent you away, hasn't he?" She clasped her hands and pressed them to her heart. "What about Daisy?"

"No, he hasn't. He wants to, but he hasn't." The boiling kettle had made the room steamy and close. The evening breeze had stilled, as though it answered to Father Kestner, too. "He has exhorted us both to confess and—" Henry tugged at his hair the way he always did when he was agitated. "Listen, we can't receive the Blessed Sacrament until this is sorted, okay? William's orders."

"He's excommunicated us?" Her teacup shattered on the floor and splashed boiling tea across her calves. She barely noticed it. Nearly every morning since she was seven years old, and now nothing. "But you just said it would work out. Henry, what must we do?"

"And it will work out." He ignored the teacup, too, and she wondered how he could be so calm and inexorable. What else had Father Kestner said to him? "He said he was going to telephone the archbishop tonight, but I doubt he will. He's hoping I forget the whole thing, and if I do, it'll spare him an embarrassing call. I'll make the call myself tomorrow."

"Thank you." The flutter of panic in her chest subsided. She stooped and lifted the largest shard of crockery from the floor. Her feet were still bare, and they made her think of the broken bottle on the sidewalk, her soles sliced open, the burn of carpet against the wounds, and Albert's iced tea glass a few days later, his hands dabbing her cuts, his crooked grin. *Sure, I love him.*

"Come on, you don't need to do that." Just like Albert, Henry's hands fastened around her waist and lifted her above the linoleum. "Sorry I upset you. Believe me, it's making me nuts. William's making me choose between you and the sacraments."

"Should you...?" She hesitated. For all she was relieved and flattered and warmly, utterly grateful, it was unsettling. Given the choice between Lotte Walheim and the holy sacraments, should the answer truly be Lotte Walheim? "Should you choose me, then?"

"He asked me." Henry flopped down on the bed in the dark room. "What I would say to a man who confessed what we're doing. I didn't answer him. It's intrinsically wrong, yes, that we're not married. But have we descended into carnality? I shouldn't think so. I can't ignore—" He was growing restless and irritable, and he struck the soft mattress with a fist. "—the calling I felt to you from the very first. And what about Daisy? If we hadn't been together, what then? She'd never have been born."

He was completely absorbed and talking to himself, so she undressed as quietly as she could, looked in on the baby, and curled up beside him.

In the morning, after Mass, Lotte and Daisy waded through the throngs to the street. Henry had hidden in the back row, and she imagined he felt much the same as she did when it came time for Communion. Branded with sin, stared at, as though everyone knew, when really, people didn't go to the rail all the time. Maybe she'd eaten breakfast, maybe her attention had drifted, or she couldn't risk jostling Daisy. No matter what sensible motives she could have, she couldn't help feeling like the real reason was scrawled across her forehead. Would anyone notice that Henry hadn't gone up? He'd done that before, that time he'd skipped over the offices. Even if people noticed, not even Barbara Morris would dare say a word to him or to anyone.

Speaking of Barbara Morris, there she was, shepherding her brood toward the intersection. Lotte's glance swept up the street. If she hadn't been carrying Daisy, she might have considered trying to dart across in advance of the trolley. As it was, the thing rumbled past along with half a dozen cars in its wake.

"Good morning, Mrs. Walheim," said little Frances. "Can I see your baby?"

"May I," Lotte said. "And yes, of course you may." She stooped to where Frances could tug the blanket from Daisy's face and kiss her button nose.

"Hello, Lotte." Barbara Morris dragged one of her scowling sons the last few steps. "Frances, you be careful with that baby, now. Don't go getting germs all over her."

"Sorry, Ma." Frances straightened and wiped her mouth with her sleeve. "I'm not sick, though, honest."

"Barbara." Lotte nodded at her. "How nice to see you again."

"Yes." Barbara pinched her son's earlobe and finally set him free. "Will we be seeing you and Albert on Friday? It seems like it's been ages since you joined us."

"We may," Lotte said. "It's just hard to find somebody to watch the baby." Really, who knew what she'd be doing by Friday? Who even knew what would happen tonight? Everything was at once so uncertain, it nearly made her choke. Would Henry telephone the archbishop? Would Father Kestner? Were they on the telephone this very moment?

"Gram and Gramps don't watch her?" Barbara hid her gossip's gleam in a smooth, concerned mask. No matter how long Lotte lived among them, the people of Walnut Hills never stopped being curious about the august Klopstocks. Lotte gathered people thought she'd condescended to marry Albert on account of his good looks. The thought was funny enough to keep her polite.

"Sure, Albert's mom and dad do sometimes," she said. "But we don't like to trouble them. We'll certainly come if we can; thank you for asking." Miraculously, like the parting of the Red Sea, the remaining cars swept past, the street cleared, and Lotte scurried away toward freedom.

She wondered as she walked whether Barbara would be just as eager to invite her and Henry over for Friday night rosary. Probably, and just as now, not out of charity. Although everyone had stopped speaking to Father Markwell and his wife and had driven them out of town, she imagined that Mr. and Mrs. Henry Werther would be the most popular couple in Walnut Hills. What veiled comments would Barbara offer them; what sly looks would burn into the backs of their heads? What would be said to Daisy? She was an expert at bearing indifference, would be fine with being cut off altogether, but popularity of any kind would almost be too much for her. For Henry, too. He was outgoing, of course, but he'd never known anything except love and admiration. Jeers and jabs from the neighbors, his family, and Father Kestner would set him upside down.

The morning was already hot, the leaves clutching and curling in upon themselves in the sullen sun. Sunlight shimmered and broke upon the concrete, and one tired sparrow's chirp kept them company the last blocks home. Daisy squawked and fussed, her face pink, so Lotte unwound her blanket and slung it over her own shoulder. She probably looked dowdy that way, but she didn't care and kissed the spot on Daisy's forehead where Henry blessed her each morning.

When she reached the house, the front door was wide open, and fresh cigarette smoke lingered around the screen door. The windows, too, were open, Albert's hat still on the table, and his linen jacket tossed on the floor. She slipped Daisy into the cradle and poked her head around the corner.

"Albert? What are you still doing here? Are you sick?" But he was dressed and upright at the kitchen table, cigarette dangling from his lips and a half-empty rocks glass in front of him. "You're not at the factory. What's wrong?"

He took a long drag on the cigarette before stubbing it into an ashtray and polishing off the drink. When he finally looked at her, his gaze was so sharp and piercing that the hairs on her arms stood up.

"James is gone."

"Gone?" Her mouth fell open, and she began to shake. Just

because she'd never liked James didn't mean she wanted... "You mean with the—? The icepick?"

"No. Not yet, anyway." He rolled his head from side to side and popped the joints in his neck. "The brass got him again last night."

"Oh. Well, can't we bail him out again?" Mortal sin by counsel. Of course, she was already excommunicated, so what was one more?

"Nah. His parents found out about all that. And that other time. He and I were in the can for about half a second when somebody got us out. Never found out who."

Henry.

"But no," Albert said. "Some cop on the day shift goes to St. Mary's with Mr. and Mrs. Mills, found out what was going on at night, and he told 'em everything out of charity. Charity, sure. This damn city. Take a leak in the morning for Chrissakes, and half your relatives are talking about it by lunchtime."

"How did it happen? Was he out without you again?"

"Yeah. The new place we all go is over off Wyoming, not too far from St. Jerome's. I haven't really seen too much of him lately. You know we've been snapping our caps at each other over all this." The tiniest breeze ruffled at Lotte's kitchen curtain, and the air was like wet cotton. Albert lit another cigarette. "Don't know all the details. Heard them from one of the guys who got away. Anyway, the cops come screaming up—"

A siren, loud and wailing. Her with the breviary, Daisy on a blanket, Henry in his shirtsleeves. Everything simple, calm, and orderly until the siren frightened Daisy into shrieking loud enough to draw Father Kestner.

That tossed the dog that worried the cat
That chased the rat who ate the cheese.

She nearly laughed. After everything else, it was James who had made them get caught, get excommunicated. Like a drop in a puddle, sending ripples to each edge, each fragile event beat one upon the other until they had spilled over.

"You told him not to go out without you." Albert had finished his story, which ended the way all of them did: men and women dragged out of a secret bar and into cars and wagons, fighting, crying, running off, clasping hands before her front room window.

"Get your head out of the clouds. I just told you he wasn't going to take orders from me. Still thinks I'm a fuddy-duddy. Anyway, when there was a raid on the Wayne, old Marv used to shunt a couple of guys out the back, and he knew me and James pretty good. That's how we got away in that raid last year. But this new fella, Eddie, he's got a whole nother crowd. Doesn't care about James, I guess."

"I'm sorry that happened," she said. "Once he gets out, he could still go away, right? You could go together somewhere, pretend to be brothers. New York, maybe. Why not?"

A snicker snorted through his nose, and he stubbed out his cigarette. "What about you, doll? Going to go off and live with Father Henry at the rectory? Sure, nobody'll mind."

"Enough," she said. "Listen, Albert, Father Kestner knows. About Henry and me, that is. He came in last night, and now he knows." Lotte pressed her back to the wall and sank to the kitchen floor. "He wants to send Henry away, but he won't go. So go away with James. Henry will take care of Daisy and me."

"Can he send him away?" Albert asked. "If he doesn't want to go?"

"I don't think so," Lotte said. "Henry answers to the archbishop, really, not Father Kestner. So, he'll talk to him. We'll annul this."

"Annul?" Albert raised an eyebrow. "Friend of my old lady's, her fella beat her senseless every night, couldn't get an annulment to save her life. You sure, doll?"

"We'll tell the tribunal the truth. Henry said even Father Kestner thinks we have a chance."

"Father Kestner knows I'm a queer?" Albert's brows drew together. "Look, I haven't been flapping my jaws all over town that you've got a baby with the priest."

"He doesn't know," she said. "He probably figures, but we didn't say a word. Never will, unless the tribunal needs it. We don't want to hurt you or James, Albert. We don't."

"Yeah, I know." Albert stood and offered her a hand up. "I'll find him, make nice. See about getting him out of town before his parents swoop in with the icepick." He went into the foyer and crammed his hat onto his head. "Wait a minute. Didn't you say it'd take months to sort out all that churchy stuff with Father Henry? What'll you do 'til then?"

Damn him, he was right. Her mouth opened, closed. A sudden thought struck.

"One of his sisters can probably help. Clara. Henry's her favorite brother, and she wants to meet Daisy and me. Or we could stay with Henry's parents, maybe."

Albert nodded and shrugged on his linen jacket. "Good to hear. Wouldn't do for you to be alone. You know, you're a good wife, doll. Even to me. Father Henry's a lucky guy."

She felt herself blush and studied the tips of her shoes. "So is James."

Albert laughed, which finally reached his eyes, and went out. She closed the door and locked it. One visit from Mr. and Mrs. Mills had been enough; it wouldn't do to have them beating down the screen door.

After a while, she pulled Daisy from the cradle, settled her against her breast, and reached for the telephone with her free hand. With each whir of the rotary, she allowed herself a tiny shred more hope.

"Henry?"

"Lotte. Is everything all right?"

"I don't know," she said. For was it? What if Albert couldn't find James, or James argued about the need to flee Dayton? "James was arrested, but Albert's gone to find him. He thinks he's out of jail. They're going to run off together. Have you spoken to the archbishop yet?"

"Not yet," Henry said. "It's funny, but I was uneasy about all that. James and Albert getting sent up Wayne Avenue."

"So was I."

"But if they're leaving, I'll get everything sorted right away." She could almost hear the shake of his head in the rueful tone. "It's hell trapped in this house. William apparently thinks the mere sight of me will scandalize the faithful. Who, I might add, have no idea what we've done. I'll see to it. I love you, Lotte."

"I love you, too," she said. "And so does Daisy, don't you, sweetheart?"

"Give her a kiss from me," he said. "I'll see you both soon."

Henry set the telephone down and went to his desk for the leather-bound folio of telephone numbers. While he flipped and thumbed for Archbishop McNicholas's direct line, the door creaked, and William peered at him from the foyer.

"I've spoken to the archbishop," he said without preamble.

Henry's gut twisted, and the air seeped from his lungs. Why had he dawdled out of concern for Albert Walheim of all people? Surely he was the last person to warrant Henry's or anyone's tender sympathy. Whatever Archbishop McNicholas heard, it ought to have come from Henry himself.

"I was just about to call him, Father," Henry said. "I can deal with this well enough on my own."

"That I doubt." Without invitation, William settled himself on the same spot on the sofa where he'd been the night before. "There is a parish in Indianapolis. His Excellency has spoken to Archbishop Schulte directly. They're in need of a new curate, and one of the men recently ordained will come here to St. Jerome's." His voice remained calm, modulated, even cold. "You could take the evening train."

"The evening train tonight?" Before he knew what he was doing, Henry marched to the door and flung it wide. "Out of the question. We're through here, Father."

William didn't move, other than to raise an eyebrow.

"Go," Henry said, unable to believe his own daring. His hands shook, and his heart sped, but he knew he was right, and that steadied him. Parish in Indianapolis, indeed. Because he knew that he would never go, he was more outraged than worried. William was no longer his mentor. Henry could be rude to him. He couldn't remember in that moment how he'd ever admired the man who was sitting there on his sofa as distant and bloodless as the Arctic Circle.

"I know," William said, "what you are thinking. That I love nothing and no one, that water ice courses through my veins where blood should be."

"You're asking me to pack up my things right now, head to the train station, go further than I've ever been from home in my life, and abandon my daughter. And abandon the woman I love with no explanation."

"And Mrs. Walheim will recover from the shock. Her faith in God and the Church won't waver." William stood, crossed the room, and closed the door. "When a clergyman errs, Henry, it damages the laity's faith. They leave us, turn Protestant, or simply vanish. Either way, we both know what happens to their souls. *Extra ecclesiam nulla salus.*"

"Father, do you honestly—?"

"Perhaps you don't care if that rests on your shoulders," he said. "But I would have God strike me down before it rested on mine." William's color was high, his eyes bright and intense. When Henry glanced at his hand, still on the doorknob, the knuckles were white. Not ice, then. "If you marry Mrs. Walheim, you will lose souls from the Faith."

"I…" Henry sighed and mussed up his hair. He hated to think that anyone at St. Jerome's was so weak in the Faith that they'd turn Protestant if he did right by Lotte and their daughter. "Has this happened at Holy Trinity? I haven't heard anything about it."

"It hasn't been easy for Father Amberley." William didn't meet his eyes.

"No one has left, then."

"I don't mean," he said. "That the moment they hear of your departure, they'll flee in droves in the middle of Mass. Nothing so simplistic." William's silence and expression implied that their faith would start to split like the ground in a dry month, cracks forming and growing wider and wider, until finally rending apart.

Henry didn't buy it. William was passionate about something all right, and that was saving his own hide from everybody's questions.

"What do you think your Daisy will say if you marry her mother and raise her together?" William asked. "When she learns what happened? Will you have other children? Will you tell them?"

"I don't know." Irritation clawed at him. He shut his eyes against William's stare. "We'll cross that bridge when we come to it, I guess."

"As a child," William said. "And for my whole life long, I've adored no one more than my father. My mother, of course, I loved her. She was my mother. But she was always a very close second."

Henry lost his scowl and leaned back against the wall. When he tried, he found he could indeed picture William as a child: a pudgy boy with a serious expression, and wearing an ill-fitting romper suit while he curled up on his father's lap and held a tract for him. Whether the Kestners had been comfortable or poor, he didn't know, but his mind painted in a worn wing chair, an antique desk, shelves of heavy books. William's father Henry couldn't imagine, but his mind's eye decided upon a plumper, more old-fashioned version of William.

"I remember the day I found out about his former life with the Jesuits, quite by accident, too," William said after a pause. "I was eleven, serving almost daily, probably already discerning. But it shook my faith." He drew breath, paused again. "Badly." William's expression was bleak for just a moment, raw and open, before it shuttered. Well-practiced, Henry supposed.

"But you took Holy Orders," Henry said. "So you recovered it. I think the faithful are less fickle than you think. Everyone doubts, at times, but—"

"Most people are lukewarm," William said. "My household was devout as any, and I suspect yours was, too. We are priests; we've given our entire selves. We don't understand most of the laity, I'm afraid. They're not all like your Mrs. Walheim. Surely you've noticed in five years, in thirty-three years, how many are simply going through the motions. What would your departure do to someone showy and scrupulous like Mrs. Morris? Her salvation is just as necessary as Mrs. Walheim's."

"You think Barbara Morris will stop coming around just because I'm marrying Lotte?" Even as he said it, Henry allowed that

241

William had a point. The Morrises mightn't stop coming to Mass—appearances and all that—but any shred of real belief she had in the Church might leach away. This was a woman who confessed to Jell-O seconds. What might she think if she'd been confessing to an adulterer? He was tempted to say that Mrs. Morris's soul was her responsibility, but it wasn't so. The people were entrusted to him just as much as to William. But the fact remained. "We're only speculating on all of this, Father. Do you think any honorable man should abandon his family based upon what a few parishioners might or might not do?"

"I think," William said. "An honorable clergyman should do whatever is necessary to prevent the loss of souls."

His delicate emphasis on 'clergy' made Henry scowl. "It has happened to other men, William. The Church has lived through worse scandals in almost two thousand years."

"His Excellency agreed with me, by the way," William said. "He's rather anxious for you to depart. He didn't say it outright, but I think he wonders about the men of your class. First Father Markwell, now you. Certainly, he regrets ordaining Markwell, but you have stunned him."

Henry nodded, closed his eyes. "I'm not leaving, Father, but I wouldn't mind some time to think."

"Very well," he said. "But think quickly. The parishioners are asking after your whereabouts already."

"Of course." It could wait until James Mills and Albert Walheim were the ones safely on the evening train. "I'm sorry. That is, I'm sure your father—"

"Goodbye, Henry," he said. "Let me know when you're prepared to go."

Beneath her faded watercolors, Lotte paced the hallway with Daisy tucked against her hip. Albert had been gone one hour, five minutes, and...? She paused near the grandfather clock. Three seconds.

They'd bailed James out in no time before. James only went to a handful of places. What if Albert hadn't found him? Lotte shuddered.

Despite it all, she didn't hate James. Didn't much like him, but didn't hate him. What if he was in the hospital already? And what if they came up and grabbed Albert? Could they do that? She didn't think so. That was one of the reasons he'd married her, so his parents couldn't commit him as easily. The washer churned; she jumped a mile. The pressure cooker hissed; her neck snapped toward the door. She couldn't even breathe properly, and she was gripping Daisy too tightly, and what if James was gone? What would become of her and Henry?

Lotte reached for the radio dial and got Verdi of all unnecessary tortures. *Dammi tu forza, o cielo!* She crossed herself, but stopped. What prayer did one say, what saint did one invoke when hoping two homosexuals would find each other and run away into the sunset? With her free hand, she pinched her Miraculous Medal between her thumb and forefinger and traced the words *O Mary, conceived without sin, pray for us who have recourse to thee.* She buried her face in Daisy's curls.

Amami, Alfredo. The screen door did creak, finally, and the aria reached its crescendo. Lotte flew into the foyer. Her entire fate rested on what she saw in Albert's eyes. *Amami, quant'io amo.*

"Well?" Her face was hot, and she was out of breath.

His shoulders were slumped just the barest fraction. His jacket, wrinkled when he left, but well-tailored, hung loosely on him. He shook his head. *Addio.*

"Oh, Albert." Although her heart was jackhammering in her chest, it felt heavy. "I'm sorry." For the first time, she went to him and rested her head just beneath his chin. He gave her a hard squeeze and mussed Daisy's hair. "Is he…?"

"Dead? No." Albert stared straight ahead at the wallpaper and a bad landscape tacked above the hall table. "His parents have him up Wayne Avenue. I told him, Lotte. I told him. Be careful. Don't go out without me. You heard it, right? I told him."

"Yes, you did," she said and stepped back from his embrace. "Listen, there was nothing more you could have done."

"There was plenty I could do. We could've left the second I found out about you and Father Henry. I could've told him I'd give him the cold shoulder for good if he didn't find a broad." Albert lit a cigarette, and his hands were shaking so badly that the lighter clinked to the tile floor. "I thought it'd work itself out. It sure did, didn't it?"

"James was a grown man."

"James is a grown man. For Chrissakes, he's not dead." Albert's voice was a harsh snap, and he snorted smoke from his nose. "He's not dead."

"Fine. James is a grown man. He knew what he was getting into, and he knew how to stay safe, and he didn't do it." Lotte moved toward the kitchen to shut off the pressure cooker, and Albert followed close behind.

"Yeah, but I'm the one with sense. I was in the nuthouse; I know how to stay out. Now it's too late. They could be—" The cigarette dropped from his lips and into the sink. He beat against his closed eyes with the heels of his hands. "Right now, they could be—"

"Now," she said, and grabbed his wrist. "Does everybody who goes in there get the—? The icepick? Every single person?"

"Nah. Some only get shocked, or shot up with chemicals, or their privates hacked off. You're right, doll. Why worry?"

"You could still leave," she said.

"I don't—" When he looked up, teardrops shuddered against his eyelashes. "What, leave cold? There's Cynthie and Lou and Charlie. Mom and Dad, too. My job. And going someplace alone, without James? I don't know. And without you, doll, anybody could snatch me up and throw me in a cell next to him." He shook his head again and grabbed the smoldering cigarette. "You think Mr. and Mrs. Mills won't come looking for me the second our divorce goes through? 'Specially if we get annulled on account of an invalid marriage."

"What am I supposed to do?" Lotte's voice rose on a shriek that made all three of them jump. "Albert, I've had a baby with Henry. I won't let Daisy grow up not knowing him because you're too chicken to move all by yourself. You think Emily Mills is going to come looking for you in California?"

"I don't want to go to California."

"Don't be selfish."

"He's a priest." Albert's shout and the slap of his hand against the counter rattled the window. "God damn it, Lotte. You're every bit as selfish as I am."

"I'm not," she said quietly. "And I'll thank you not to shout our business so the neighbors can hear."

"Sorry, doll," he said, almost *sotto voce*. "You're right, you're not. It's something you could make right, you know? James and I, it'll never be."

She nodded. "I don't want you to be hurt, but I can't deny him Daisy or her him."

"I know." His voice was grim. He stubbed out the cigarette. The pressure cooker had made the kitchen smell of beans and ham. "Listen, doll, I've watched you go to Mass every day for five years and pray and fast and all that nonsense, and you still get the short end of the stick."

Their shouting had made Daisy cry, and Lotte shushed and soothed before replying. "So I take up my cross and follow. Religion isn't magic, Albert. I pray for happiness in the next life, not this one."

"And that's swell," he said. "But maybe, I don't know, maybe you ought to go to Father Henry. Whatever happens to me, it happens, right? And like I said, they'll at least throw me in a cell next to him."

"Oh." Elation fizzed in her breast, and so did fear. Albert was letting her off the hook, and it was more wonderful and more horrible than she'd ever dreamed. "Albert, you've just had a terrible sho— A terrible surprise. Maybe you should sleep on it for a night." Why was she trying to dissuade him? She and Daisy belonged with Henry, but she hated Albert's sad, defeated look. He would stay with her, if she wanted him to, or he would let himself get thrown in Dayton State. Only Henry had ever done anything heroic for her, and she was floored.

"Well, who knows, maybe I won't get tossed in. James…" Here, Albert swallowed hard and clenched his jaw. "He's gone. I'm not going to run around to the bars. You think your old man'll can me if you leave?"

"Oh, I hardly think so. You worked there well before we'd ever met. He doesn't employ you because he loves me. He does it partly for appearances, but mostly because you do a decent job. I don't think he cares whether I'm provided for or who I marry. He's not going to go giving Henry a job. When was the last time he even came to the factory?"

"True enough." With an awkward, curled fist, he bumped her on the chin in a gesture meant to be jocular. "Chin up, doll. Go take a walk. I'm going to bed."

It was three o'clock in the afternoon, but Lotte didn't argue. The shadows beneath his eyes were like rough bruises, and blond stubble bristled on his cheeks. She had to see Henry. Surely he'd have finished up with the archbishop by now. But when she went to the closet for her hat, the front door jumped with heavy-handed slams.

Albert burst into the hall. "Take her upstairs."

"Who's here?" She hugged Daisy against her chest, transfixed by the sight of the shadows on the other side of the door. A dart of worry pierced her, and she bit her lip. "Have they...? Will they try to take you?"

"Take her and stay up there." He didn't look at her and walked toward the door. "Now, Lotte."

She turned and fled, more concerned for Daisy and Albert, in that order, than for herself. She'd heard of people being dragged off to Wayne Avenue, and everyone in Walnut Hills had seen an escapee captured at least once, like the poor man Henry had found who'd thought he was Winston Churchill. He'd screamed and writhed— would Albert scream? Could they really take him without asking her? She was still his wife.

Lotte settled Daisy in her cradle and shut the bedroom door for good measure. With only a moment's hesitation, she slipped out of her shoes and crept just to the landing, out of sight.

"—with you." A woman's voice, hysterical and accusing. "Could have been a husband, a father, given us grandchildren." It wasn't Albert's mother, nor a police officer, nor an orderly from Dayton State. "And now he's nothing." No, it was Mrs. Mills.

"Nothing?" Albert's voice, trying to be phlegmatic, was inlaid with rage. "Who knows, maybe they'll cure him. Cured me, didn't they?"

"Hardly. You led him into— You turned him. And now—"

"Enough, Emily." James's father. "Look, Walheim. You had your fun spreading your perversion to our son. I don't care if you've got ten wives and a whole passel of kids. You're a pervert, and we're not resting 'til you're no longer a danger."

"Oh, yeah?" Albert, summoning up bravado from somewhere. "Is James cured now?"

A loud sniffle from Mrs. Mills. Lotte's fingers tightened around the banister.

"He's as good as dead, that's what he is."

Lotte couldn't stifle her gasp, but no one seemed to hear. All along, Albert had been right, and they'd taken James's brain, and now he was as good as dead.

"They did it right off when we had him put in," Mr. Mills said. "Takes ten minutes. They swore it worked on a couple of other fellows, but when he woke up…"

Tears prickled at Lotte's eyes, and she rested her forehead against the wall. How was Albert still standing? If it had been Henry, God alone only knew what she'd do. And what about Mr. and Mrs. Mills? When Daisy had gotten sick, she'd taken her to the doctor's for a shot they'd sworn would bring the fever down, and it had. But what if it hadn't? What if she'd come out of it a drooling invalid who did nothing but stare at the wall and hum Marv's tune about the green carnation?

"And now he'll never leave that place." Mrs. Mills again, raw and broken. So-called pervert or not, James was her son, and she loved him. "Never. Will he, Bob?"

"That's more than you deserve, Walheim." Mr. Mills' voice, drawing further away and closer to the door. "We'll see about telling the brass you're still a threat to the decent folks around here, how about that?"

Albert's shrug was almost audible. Probably didn't trust himself to speak much. "Lie to the cops all you want, Mills. Sorry about your boy."

The door clicked shut. Footsteps thudded across the foyer and halfway up the stairs. Albert reached the landing, and Lotte stood.

"Go away," he said.

"Albert, I'm so—"

"Go away. Take the baby."

She obeyed, and when she emerged from her room with Daisy, Albert's door was already shut tight, the space echoing with wails that reminded Lotte of a margin note beside the Kyrie, *the long cry of our wounded nature*, and the spiraling, shivering threads of song that wound their way from the choir loft to the sanctuary and back again. This time, she did cross herself before she descended the stairs and went out.

CHAPTER TWENTY-FOUR

The door swung open again. He considered finally using the locks, but Lotte and Daisy ran in, and he thought the better of it. Her eyes and Daisy's hair were wild, and it twisted his stomach with fear. He took the baby, kissed her, and smoothed her curls.

"Are they gone?" But of course, he knew the answer and tucked an arm around her. "Damn it."

"It was awful, Henry. They said the operation made him into an imbecile, and he'll never leave that place, and now Albert's in agony." She winced. "I'm glad you couldn't hear it."

"They?"

"James's parents."

"Ah." He tried to imagine Mr. and Mrs. Klopstock coming to him and telling him they'd had Lotte locked away, practically dead, for loving him. A wave of nausea swelled against his throat, and he choked it back. "Does Albert know you've come to me?"

"It was his idea." She pressed against him more tightly. "He said things, Henry. Disturbing things."

"You don't think he'd do anything drastic, do you?" If that happened to Lotte, Henry wouldn't do anything drastic, but only because it was a mortal sin and he'd end up in hell as a twisted tree, plucked by vultures and climbed by demons. What was the impediment for an atheist? Certainly not love of God or fear of hell. "Do you think

249

that's why he asked you to leave?"

"I don't think so," she said. "I wouldn't have left him alone there if it were. But when he's done crying, maybe he'll think of it then. Should I go back? Henry, what should I do?"

She sounded completely unmoored, which wasn't like her. He supposed, despite being Albert Walheim's wife for five years, nothing in her upbringing, nor in her watercolors, nor in her hours with the hiss of Verdi on the radio had prepared her for mashed-up beets and suicidal husbands and sharing a baby with the parish priest. Nothing in seminary or in backyard baseball had prepared him for it either.

"What all did he say, Lotte?" He took her hand and led her into the kitchen for a cup of tea.

"He doesn't care anymore what happens." Her voice was flat and dull, her eyes grave. "Even if they do take him, he says, at least he'll be there with James."

"It won't much matter if he doesn't know the wall from the grass." Henry filled the kettle and set it on the stove. "That's a kind of suicide right there, isn't it? What else?"

"He wants me to be with you and not suffer because we have a chance at being licit, and they never did."

"True," Henry said. "But…" His conversation with William snapped into focus, hit him like one swift punch. Barbara Morris. *Her salvation is just as necessary as Mrs. Walheim's.* He wasn't worried about that scrupulous woman. Albert Walheim's salvation was just as necessary as anyone else's. *You are mindful of the holiness of things, but you think too much of yourself: your tiredness, your needs, your inexplicable disgust of feet.* William had said that to him what seemed like a lifetime ago. *You told me when you arrived that you wanted to serve, so learn to serve.* "I am a priest, Lotte."

It had been done before. Men left; the world got over it. He could settle into a professorship, publish papers on the writings of Aquinas, sing baritone in the choir, and the scandal would fade. Something more interesting was bound to happen in a year or two. Perhaps in this other life, he would simply be so boring that no one would bother to gossip about him. It would be a comfortable life, a happy one. He thought about Lotte's laugh and her swelling belly, the eternal chatter of his family. Surely they would be in and out of his house as though it belonged to them, too.

But could he? With creeping unease, he allowed himself to discern the truth. His happy life, no matter how rich with love and laughter, would always curl around the edges like that faded sacristy rubric. He would be happy, but he would have failed. He was an ordained priest, and someday he would have to answer for even one soul lost from his flock. How could he stand before the Throne of Judgment and say he'd found something that suited him better?

"Henry," she said. "No."

"More than anything, I want to be with you," he said. "But I don't—"

"Don't do this, Henry." She shifted their daughter into her lap, and they both looked up at him with sad, imploring eyes. "Never mind me. How could you leave your child? I saw you baptize her. I know."

"I love both of you very much." He abandoned the kettle and knelt at her feet. "Please, Lotte, don't stop loving me."

"She won't remember you," Lotte said, voice hoarse with repressed tears. "She'll think Albert is her father."

"You won't tell her? Ever?" He thought of William and his Jesuit father, but this wasn't quite the same.

"I know what it is for a child to feel abandoned." Her tears finally fell. "To be chosen last. That will never happen to mine."

He hadn't expected that, and it cut him deeply. Henry wavered.

"Please," she said, noticing. "You deserve to know each other, and I want her to know your family, your parents, your sister, her cousins."

"I can't," he said. "Any life we build will be set on this foundation, and we will both be accountable. I've become your husband in a way, and I'm Daisy's father, and I'm responsible for your souls. If I change my mind, we will both have to give Our Lord an account of today, and then James and Albert will not be the only ones together in hell."

"You would sacrifice your life's happiness for Albert?" Lotte closed her eyes. "Have you ever even spoken to him? He has nothing but disdain for you, and he's an unrepentant sinner, besides."

"All the more reason," Henry said, and his throat grew tight, too. "I thought I was called to help you, Lotte, but it wasn't you. You don't need me."

"I do."

"You don't." He smiled through his tears. "I needed you. And it was Albert I was called to help. I used to worry that I wasn't truly called to this life, but I was, and I must live it."

New tears worked their way from the corners of Lotte's eyes, but he could tell she understood. He'd known she would, and it made him sadder in a way. Here was a woman who understood him perfectly, who had his child, who had opened his soul and his senses, and she knew why he had to flee from her.

"I know you do, Henry." She rose, set Daisy on the floor, and embraced him fiercely.

He inhaled, pressed his lips to her hair, her lips, her cheeks, and imprinted her upon his heart. So accustomed was he to being with Lotte, it was hard to grasp that he'd never embrace her, nor anyone, ever again. Her breath was probably cut off, her body crushed, but she didn't complain and held him more tightly.

When he finally released her, he stooped and scooped up Daisy in his arms. Just as with her mother, he tried to memorize her scent, the feel of her skin, the beat of her pulse beneath the cotton dress. He kissed her, rocked her, carried her into his room, and dipped his fingers into the font to give her one last blessing. The water dripped from his fingers, and when he spoke—*in nomine Patris et Filii et Spiritus Sancti*—he thought of his new life with her at her baptism and his new life without her now. He bent his head to whisper in her ear.

"Remember me, Daisy."

He handed her back to her mother, kissed them both, and left them. His fingers were still wet, and he crossed himself as he hurried down the sidewalk with his eyes fixed on the houses and the church in front of him. The bells started up with "All Glory, Laud, and Honor"; he thought of Winston and knew he'd done right.

When Henry climbed the stairs and moved through the vestibule, he tried not to think of her there with her tea towel or her plate of leftover restaurant cake. In the baptistery, he shut his eyes entirely.

"Father," he said when he reached William's office.

"Yes, Henry?" William stood and steepled his fingers together. "Was there something you needed?"

Henry hesitated. He could tell William off and go back to Lotte and Daisy, Albert Walheim be damned. One word, and he would acknowledge that he had sinned mortally for over a year and that he was leaving for good.

"A confessor," he said.

"Of course." William reached for his stole and led Henry to the confessional. His eyes, when they met Henry's briefly, were misted over, but unsurprised.

Henry cleared his throat and began.

"Bless me, Father, for I have sinned…"

Lotte stepped out of the confessional and shifted Daisy in her arms. She'd expected to feel light, loosened from the weight of mortal sin, and she did. But she couldn't shake the crushing sadness and the sense that life had finally swallowed her up. After all her heartache, here she was again, alone and desolate in an empty church, ready to run to the nearest office and weep.

Daisy squawked and cooed, and Lotte thought some more. Entirely alone, that wasn't quite right. She looked down at her daughter, kissed her, and knew that no matter what, she'd do everything exactly the same if she had the chance. If that made her contrition imperfect, she didn't much care, and it didn't much matter now, did it? Henry was gone. She hoped his parish in Indianapolis knew how blessed they were to have him.

Father Kestner was still in the confessional, probably waiting until the tap of her heels and the creak of the door crept through the thin walls. Lotte turned, genuflected, and blessed herself on her way out. The sky was bright azure, and she quickened her steps home. What if Henry was right, and Albert had done something drastic?

She didn't think he would, but he was weak, and James had been taken from him. He had nothing to sustain him without the poor man. Lotte wondered if he'd take another lover in time. She certainly never would. But what was Albert's life without James? His parents were just as bad as hers were, in a way, and there was only Cynthie who really cared. Solace through prayer was out of the question for an atheist.

When Lotte rounded Edgar Avenue, her heart began to beat faster and faster. Perhaps she was too late. Perhaps she would find him hanging from his bedroom ceiling, or maybe he'd shocked himself on the bare wire like in his dream. What would become of her then? Henry was gone. Would he come back for her? It was terrible and wicked to think it, but if Albert were dead, there'd be no reason to protect him.

"Albert?" The house was shut up and stuffy, dark, and quiet. No answer. "Albert?" Good God, she didn't want him dead. Maybe he'd gone walking, although his hat was still on the table, and where would he go? "We're back, we— Albert?" He had shut himself up in his bedroom earlier, but it was open now, the bed neatly made. With shaking hands, she laid Daisy in her cradle and hurried back downstairs. People left notes when they did this, didn't they? She hadn't seen a note.

"Albert, are you home?" Lotte skidded into the kitchen, and there he was, slumped back in a chair, cigarette smoldering in his hand. He wasn't moving. She took a breath, which ended on a whimper.

"Right here, doll." He squinted at her in the semidarkness. "Say, where's Father Henry? And Daisy?"

"Daisy's upstairs." Her knees were shaking so badly that she sank into the seat across from him. "Henry left."

"Left you?" Albert's blond brows shot up. "Left the baby?"

"He's going to a parish in Indiana. It's... Yes. He's left."

"I'm sorry," he said. "When I heard the door just now, I thought it was the cops."

"Don't worry anymore about them." The azure sky outside the window was starting to tinge with periwinkle. July was getting on, and they were losing light. It was almost time for supper. "Henry..."

"What about him?"

"He left because of you, Albert. He wanted you to… Hoped you'd have a chance at being redeemed now." She thought he'd laugh because she'd brought up God, but he didn't. "He was trying to save you from— From everything. He said he thought he was called by God to help me, but it was you all along."

"Me?" Albert stubbed out his cigarette. "Father Henry left town to save me from the cops and Dayton State?" His eyes lost their dreamy, lazy look; he straightened in his chair. "You mean that, doll?"

"Yes, Albert, he did." Lotte's throat tightened, and a tear worked its way down her cheek. "I always knew I'd spend the rest of my life with you." She bit her lip. "It just seems worse now somehow."

"That's what I thought, too, after James… After today," he said. "Will you visit Father Henry, though? Or send him photographs of the baby?"

"I don't think so," she said. "I don't even know where exactly he's gone. And we've both confessed."

"I saw him," Albert said. "When he baptized Daisy. So did you. He just left that behind?"

Lotte nodded.

Albert opened his mouth to say something, but instead dissolved in tears right in front of her. He crossed his forearms on the table, buried his head in them, and sobbed like one newly born.

Lotte didn't dare touch him, but slid a hankie across the table.

"I'm sorry, doll," he said, when he'd regained control. "I'm sorry."

Henry didn't resent him, but she was afraid she might.

"Maybe I said things about him that weren't too keen, but I know you—" He clenched his jaw. "Well, I know. Lotte?" Albert reached across the table and seized her hand. "Do you think you might forgive me sometime? You'd have been happy with Father Henry."

"I'm happy with Daisy," she said. Of course, she would always miss Henry, but found she couldn't hate Albert for it, just as he wouldn't have hated her for leaving. "I forgive you. But you have to promise me something."

"Anything. I won't go out to the bars ever again, I swear it.

Only went because of James anyhow." He closed his eyes briefly. "I won't bring home any more guys. It was only ever James."

"I'm glad of that," she said. "But no, that's not what I mean. I want you to be my friend. We'll never be husband and wife, not really, but I want you as my friend."

"Of course, doll," he said. "Of course."

CHAPTER TWENTY-FIVE

igh whistles sounded in eerie harmony, and billows of smoke rose around Henry and William as they made their way across the platform. Bells clanged somewhere; people surged around them. Aside from a few nods, no one paid either man any mind. Henry hurried over to the ticket counter, paid, and stood beside William on the gritty platform.

"Train leaves in twenty minutes," he said. "Thanks for coming down here, Father." Henry stared down at the leather suitcase that had been with him since he'd started at seminary. Its edges were worn and handles frayed, and he pulled a key from his pocket and turned the lock. "Watch over her for me, will you?"

"She does have a husband, you know. For what that's worth." William picked at his cuffs.

"Not Lotte," he said. "I've got someone else in mind for her. No, I mean Daisy. Watch over Daisy."

"Ah." He finally met Henry's eyes. "Of course I will." William cleared his throat, and his voice came out a bit hoarse. "I think you do right, Henry. It's what I've said all along. But it's also..." He cleared his throat again. "It's unimaginable. I should hope in twenty years that I have half your greatness in this vocation."

Henry bit the inside of his lips to keep from weeping in public. The train clanged up the tracks and squealed to a halt before them. In one hand, he hefted his suitcase, and with the other, he clasped his mentor's hand.

"May God bless you and keep you, William."

"And you, Henry." He bowed his head. "We'll meet again, *Deus vult*. In the meantime, I'll see that your Daisy is well."

With one last look at William, at the station, at Dayton, Henry climbed aboard the train, stored his luggage, and settled into a seat with a pad of paper and pen. He squeezed his eyes shut and kept them that way until a fuzzy, green aura formed, until they ached, until the train lurched forward, and the city was disappearing behind them. He blinked a couple of times, handed his ticket over to be punched, and at last put pen to paper.

Dear Clara, he wrote, *you're probably wondering why your rotten brother has gone off and left without stopping past for a big, boo-hooing scene...* Henry wrote and wrote and covered six pages, front and back. The pen was shaking in his hand by the end, his wrist going limp all on its own, his penmanship notably worse. *Lotte lives at 180 Edgar Avenue, so look her up when you get this. Keep an eye on her for me, and don't hate her husband for me leaving. I don't. I can't come back to Dayton for a while now...* Twenty years. His penance. *But I hope you can jump on a train sometime. I'm at Holy Innocents in Indianapolis. I'll send you the address. Kiss everyone and apologize that your favorite brother is such a jerk. See you soon, I hope. Love, Henry.*

After that, he closed his eyes and didn't wake until the conductor announced his stop and the brakes screeched. He yawned, stretched, and grabbed his suitcase from above his seat. The platform was dark, with a couple of lamps sprinkled here and there, and no trace of a crowd. Out of the handful of people, he picked out another priest, cassock billowing in the sticky breeze. The man hastened toward him when he disembarked and raised an inquiring brow.

"Father Werther?"

Father Werther. Like the start of a nursery rhyme.

"Yes, I'm Father Werther." He smiled at the other man, who returned it and led him across the platform, through the station, and into the street. He dropped the letter into the mailbox and offered one silent prayer.

When Lotte woke in the morning, it was sunny and still, just like the morning before, when she'd woken in Henry's house. Her narrow bed creaked, and she thought about getting a new one. Why had she done up her room like a nun's cell? Out of mawkish penance? Whatever the reason, it was time to have done with it.

Daisy bleated and fussed, so she scooped her up and brought her into bed to kiss the soft curls and turned up nose. She latched her onto her breast and closed her eyes. Lotte didn't think about Henry, but instead wondered what she might do and who she might be in this new life that no one else realized was new. She had a friend now, and maybe she would meet the mysterious Clara sometime, too. She didn't need him, Henry had said, and he was right—she didn't. She loved him desperately, probably would never stop, but she didn't need him.

The pipes creaked, and she heard water running, the toilet flushing. When Daisy finished, Lotte dressed her, set her down, and pulled on her own dress and stockings. The air in the hallway was steamy and smelled of Linden Soaps' best eucalyptus blend. Albert was already in the bathroom, shaving in trousers and shirtsleeves.

"Morning, doll," he said. He sounded nonchalant, but she was suddenly awkward. She shifted from foot to foot in the hallway. He splashed on some aftershave, and she washed the Pond's from her face. While Lotte pinned up her hair, he disappeared, *Deo gratias*, but reappeared in coat and tie with Daisy under one arm. Where would he be going now? It was far too early for him to be at the factory. Would he really be silly enough to visit James?

"Do you want to walk or take the Ford?" he asked.

"What?"

"To Mass," he said. "It's a long walk in the heat. We might as well drive." At once, his casualness seemed too studied and his hands too busy out of nervousness.

"Let's drive. I'll take Daisy," she said. She followed him

downstairs, where she smelled no bacon or eggs wafting from the kitchen, and picked up her missal from the side table.

"Grab mine, too, will you, doll?"

She held it out, and he grabbed it, smooth and just like new beside her worn, tattered one. He was embarrassed about going, and she didn't want to pry, but they were friends now, weren't they?

"You don't—" She paused; he shut the car door and climbed in the other side. "I'm always glad when you come along, but you don't have to just because...?" Because why? Did he think there were rumors about her and Henry? That she'd keel over at the thought of being there without him?

"I want to go," he said, not embarrassed now. And more softly: "I want to." He started the car and wound his way down Edgar, up Wyoming Street, toward the sound of church bells and the chatter of their neighbors. "I guess Barbara Morris invited us for Friday rosary again?"

"Saw her yesterday morning," Lotte said. "Should I tell her we'll go?"

"Sure," he said. "Been a while since I had decent lime Jell-O."

Lotte snorted, but blinked against sudden tears. She kept them back, and Albert parked along the street. They joined the stream of people on the stone steps, and Albert split away from them. When she saw where he was headed, she muttered a quick prayer and hurried toward her usual seat.

It was later than usual when Mass began, and Lotte was not the only one who shifted around in her seat to sneak a glance into the sacristy and even dared to look over her shoulder. Albert loped back toward her, pulled Daisy into his lap, the confessional opened and shut, and a little while later, the bell pinged. Father Kestner came once again into the sanctuary, and she could feel everyone's confusion radiating up into the coffered ceiling.

Although it was Thursday, he ascended the ambo after the Gospel, and Lotte's teeth began to chatter. Father Kestner looked tired and pinched.

"Two announcements today," he said. "Due to an emergency in another parish, Father Henry will no longer be here with us at St.

Jerome's." Some chatter rose, but he ignored it, of course. "And ladies wishing to join the Altar Society may contact Mrs. Morris."

And then, subtly, without any of the neighbors noticing, he cast his gaze over Albert and Daisy, met eyes with Lotte, and nodded just once.

ACKNOWLEDGEMENTS

This book's journey began in 2014—I started writing the manuscript after Easter and finished it in March 2015. After that, it sat in a drawer (ok, a digital drawer), while I pursued other projects, had a family, and career busyness took over. With such a long wait from start to finish, I'm especially grateful to be sharing this work with readers. Many thanks to Roxana Coumans, whose careful eye caught my most awkward typos; to Sarah Kil, whose cover design absolutely nailed the assignment; and to Sheldon James, for his patience and humor during the author photo session. Thank you so much to Fox and the Dove Press for supporting this story's journey and helping me dust it off ten years after writing it.

My biggest thanks of all goes to my husband, David, who supports my work even when I don't. And my parents deserve major credit for cheerleading this project (and all my other projects) as well.

And to you, my reader, thank you for making it this far. I can't wait for what's next.

SOURCES

Brahms, Johannes. *Liebeslieder-Walzer.* English translation by Natalia Macfarren; edited by H. Clough-Leighter. Boston: E.C. Schirmer Music Co., c. 1926. Public domain in the United States.

Dacre, Harry. *"Daisy Bell (Bicycle Built for Two)."* 1892. Public domain.

English College, Douai (trans.). *The Holy Bible: Douay-Rheims Version.* American Edition, 1899. Public domain.

ABOUT THE AUTHOR

Sara Thomas writes emotionally complex fiction with a vintage flair and a love for moral ambiguity. She has worked in the arts and culture sector, journalism, and digital marketing for more than 15 years. A former Fulbright finalist in Creative Writing, Sara studied Classical Languages at Duquesne University and earned her Master's degree in Art History and Museum Administration from the University of Cincinnati's College of Design, Architecture, Art, & Planning. Her work has appeared in magazines, anthologies, and lifestyle publications. She lives in Dayton, Ohio with her family.

ABOUT THE TYPEFACES

This book is set in **Garamond**, a timeless serif with a warmth and readability suited to long narratives. **Playfair Display** provides the headers with its high contrast and classical elegance, giving the page a refined rhythm. **Italiana** appears in subheads and chapter titles, lending a subtle flair that bridges the modern and the traditional.